The Solaris Book of New
Science Fiction

The Solaris Book of New
Science Fiction

Edited by George Mann

Including stories by

Brian Aldiss

Neal Asher

Tony Ballantyne

Stephen Baxter

Keith Brooke

Eric Brown

Paul Di Filippo

Peter F. Hamilton

Simon Ings

Jay Lake & Greg van Eekhout

James Lovegrove

Mike Resnick & David Gerrold

Adam Roberts

Jeffrey Thomas

Mary A. Turzillo

Ian Watson

SOLARIS

First published 2007 by Solaris
an imprint of BL Publishing
Games Workshop Ltd, Willow Road
Nottingham NG7 2WS
UK

www.solarisbooks.com

ISBN-13: 978 1 84416 448 6
ISBN-10: 1 84416 448 9

Designed & typeset by BL Publishing

Contents

Introduction

George Mann

SCIENCE FICTION.

Two small words, a billion big ideas.

What is it about science fiction that readers find so appealing? The short form, in particular, is a draw for many – tightly packaged, perfect bundles of character and story, neatly delivered within the framework of a single conceit. Indeed, in the short story or novelette many would argue that science fiction has its perfect form; just long enough to explore an idea, just short enough to pack an emotive punch. It's within the SF genre, I believe, that the short story is kept truly alive and vibrant. The majority of SF writers cut their teeth writing short stories for the digests, and others, like the authors arrayed in this book, continue to return to the form, producing little, sparkling gems, some beautifully polished diamonds, others rough-hewn approximations; all fascinating brushstrokes of life. It takes a lot of discipline and rigor to deliver a story in four or five thousand words and I'm constantly in awe of the ability on show. And let's not forget, from little acorns, big trees grow; many writers will take a theme or idea first explored in a short story and develop it into a novel, whilst others will masterfully build a sequence of linked stories into a wider exploration of a world or set of characters. The majority of short story writers, however, will take a single kernel of an idea and make it flower, creating a perfect, succinct tale in a few pages, sketching in enough detail to impart the sense of wonder so desired by the readers of SF.

I believe the short story market is also an excellent barometer of the current trends in SF, of the issues and topics at play in the field, the obsessions and debates of our favorite writers. The short form lends itself to this perfectly – a testing ground for new ideas – and thus is often seen to represent the very cutting edge of the genre.

Nevertheless, I often hear talk that the short story is dying, that commercially, 'SHORT STORIES DO NOT SELL!', and it's certainly true that the amount of venues for original, non-themed short stories in the science fiction field has shrunk in recent years. Yet I'm also heartened by the strength of the anthologies that *are* hitting the market – be they themed, non-themed or simply reprinting the best stories to appear in the digests in any given year. Read all of these books. They are the lifeblood of our genre, and they enable writers to flourish.

The Solaris Book of New Science Fiction aims to do just that – to publish original, never-before-seen stories by some of the best writers working in the field today. Some are tales of alien contact, others of the end of the world, some explore new gadgets that could revolutionize the way we think, whilst others still are more personal, reflective. Indeed, *The Solaris Book of New Science Fiction* is indicative of the approach of the Solaris imprint as a whole: the desire to publish outstanding science fiction and fantasy, whatever the form.

This book is our manifesto.

Enjoy.

George Mann
Solaris Consultant Editor
Nottingham
September 2006

In His Sights

Jeffrey Thomas

THE OTHER YOUNG returnees kept looking at him, wondering what horrors were concealed by his mask. The mask looked like several layers of black plastic, vacuum-formed to his face, with openings for his eyes, nostrils, and mouth. From his eyes, with their epicanthic folds, they could at least tell that he was of Asian ancestry. But what wounding had he suffered? Had he been spattered with hot, corrosive plasma from a mortar round? Sprayed with acid or minced with shrapnel in some Ha Jiin booby trap? The other men—and there were some female soldiers too—felt pity for him. And also shame, at being relieved that it wasn't them forced to wear the healing black mask.

But he wasn't healing. Because he wasn't wounded, at least not in the ways they speculated on.

He was simply hiding his face.

Though he knew it would, his face shouldn't have shocked the others in a purely physical sense. After all, this was Punktown. The city had been called Paxton when Earth colonists had first founded it, but it hadn't taken long for its nickname to come about, for its predestined character to make itself manifest. Over the decades, races other than human had come to colonize the city as well. Included among the few truly humanoid races that dwelt within the megalopolis were the Choom—indigenous to this world, which the Earth colonists had renamed Oasis. They had frog-like mouths that sliced their faces back to their ears. Then there were the Tikkihotto, who in place of eyes had bundles of clear tendrils that squirmed in the air as if to assemble vision with their sensitive touch. But there were far stranger beings in Punktown. Beautiful, by the Earthly conception of such things, or hideous. In addition, there were mutants of every deformity, corresponding to every cruel whim of nature (nature as distorted through pollution and radiation). So it would seem illogical that anyone in Punktown would feel self-conscious enough to hide their features by pretending to have been disfigured. But it wasn't simply self-consciousness that had caused the young man to don his mask.

It possibly went so far as self-preservation.

"Santos, Edgar," a voice called from a speaker. The name was spelled out on a screen as well, and showed Santos's military ID number. The man in the black mask looked up and watched as Edgar Santos pushed away the little VT he had been

watching, affixed to the arm of his chair. He headed off to one of the offices, its number also
displayed on the information screen. Santos. There
were a few more names to be called, alphabetical-
ly, before they got to the masked man. Stake,
Jeremy.

Stake sat in a long row of plastic chairs of a terrible orange color. His row faced a row opposite.
Trying not to look at the people seated across from
him, despite how they stole glances at him, Stake
couldn't help but be reminded of the first time he
had been sent to the planet of the Ha Jiin. The
dimension of the Ha Jiin.

It had been over four years ago. The then nineteen year-old Jeremy Stake had sat with a group of
young men and women, humans and humanoids,
with no Ha Jiin blood yet on their hands. None of
their own blood yet spilled. They had sat just like
this, in two rows inside a metal Theta pod, waiting
to have their material beings shifted. Smuggled
inside a bullet fired through page after page in the
closed book of realities, taking a shortcut through
infinity. The transdimensional pod had hummed
with an almost subliminal vibration under their
boots and asses. They had looked at each other's
faces in nervousness. A few of these troop pods
had gone missing, taking a wrong turn somehow,
perhaps ending up in some alternate plane from
which there was no return, or maybe just ceasing
to be.

Sometimes Stake wondered if he truly had
returned to his own plane. Might this be a subtle
variation on the world he had left? If so, might

some subtly different Jeremy Stake have taken his place in his reality? And if so, had he come back without the need for disguise?

Well, such alternate versions of oneself had not in fact been discovered in any of the realms that Theta research/technology had given the Earth Colonies access to. But extradimensional races had certainly been encountered. There were the beetle-like Coleopteroids, derisively called Bedbugs. The putty-like L'lewed. The more humanoid Antse people, who covered their bland gray bodies entirely in the gorgeous flayed skins of great creatures called flukes. And then, there were the blue-skinned Ha Jiin. One of the most human of races. One of the most beautiful. And deadly.

"Severance, Amy Jo," called the speaker's voice. Stake watched a young woman rise to attend her appointment. She was one of those who had come today in uniform rather than street clothes. It was really a personal decision. Maybe she was proud of it. Maybe she was simply still in the military mind-set. Under her arm she carried a black beret, her uniform itself patterned in shades of blue, from dark navy to bright azure to pastel. Stake was in his street clothes, but he had an identical set of camouflaged fatigues among his belongings.

The Blue War, they had called it.

It was over now. Everybody coming home. Everybody being sifted back into a world that would be different for them, whether it was a secretly distorted variation or not.

"Buddy? Hey... brother?"

Stake turned his head, which glistened black like obsidian. He met the eyes of a crew-cut Choom.

"What happened to you?"

There. Someone had overtly invaded his privacy. Someone either too unthinking—or too compassionate—to just leave him be.

Stake had an answer prepared, though. "I was in some caverns, and there were major gas concentrations. A plasma grenade caused it to ignite." That was what they had been doing there. Traveled so far for, bled so long for. Officially, it was to lend support to the emerging Jin Haa nation. But everyone knew it was really all about those rich subterranean gases.

The Choom made an exaggerated wincing expression. "Ouch. I heard of that happening. You gonna be all right?" He gestured at his own face. "Will it get back to normal?"

"I don't know," Stake said. He wasn't lying about that part. "I don't know."

THE VETERANS' ADMINISTRATION worker, whose office Stake was directed to, was a stern-faced black woman who introduced herself as Miriam Khaled. She was studying her screens when Stake let himself in. She looked up at him in a bit of a double take, a little surprised by his appearance, but she dropped her eyes to his file again as he took a seat in front of her desk.

"Will you be my caseworker?" he asked her.

"No... you won't be given a particular caseworker; you can meet with anyone here at the VA about your concerns," she said as she read from his records. "Corporal Stake. I see you have a very distinguished four years of service. Hmm. Assigned to several deep penetration units. You captured an enemy sniper who was quite a local legend to her people."

Stake's guts knotted tighter at the mention of her. "Yes." He saw the Ha Jiin woman's face on his own internal screen. Her blue-skinned, beautiful face. She had been his prisoner for a while. Sometimes he felt he was her prisoner now.

"And you have no desire to further your career in the military?"

"No."

"Okay. Umm…" She frowned. "I don't see anything here about your injury."

"This isn't from an injury, ma'am."

"No?" She looked up, scowling.

"Excuse me," Stake said, and then he reached behind his head to unseal the shiny black mask. He peeled it from his head like a cocoon. Under it, his short dark hair was sweaty and disheveled. His skin was normally almost olive, but had become so pale it was almost of a bluish, corpse-like cast, as if he had been hidden from the sun for months. He watched Khaled's face. He saw comprehension dawn there; not of the particulars, but at least an understanding as to why he would wear the mask.

She quickly consulted the files again. "You underwent surgery to perform your penetration missions?"

"No, ma'am. This isn't from surgery. I'm a mutant."

Miriam Khaled took him in more closely. The young man seated opposite her was almost entirely a Ha Jiin, just as the Ha Jiin were almost entirely human—indistinguishable except for matters of pigment that Stake's malleable cells could not duplicate, however crafty they were in their mimicry. Despite its best efforts, his skin was not that lovely, ghostly shade of blue. And the Ha Jiin's eyes, though black, gleamed a laser red when the light struck them a certain way. Even their black hair took on a metallic red quality where the light made it shine. But there were other effects that Stake's face had been very successful at reproducing. The Ha Jiin's eyelids possessed the epicanthus of human Asians. Also, it was not uncommon for Ha Jiin men to mark their faces with scars. Stake had two horizontal raised bars on his right cheek, and three on his left cheek, almost as if to indicate that his age was twenty-three. In fact, the scarification was meant to represent the number of family members a man had lost in war. Maybe when they touched their own faces, or saw their reflections, it helped arouse them afresh in their desire to conquer their enemy and avenge their dead. Were it not for his imitation scars, Stake might have passed for an Earth Asian. But those markings were so distinctive.

Khaled found it in the file at last. "I see. It's a mutation called... *Caro turbida*. 'Disordered flesh.' Huh. It's impressive how it works." She appeared to regret phrasing it that way. "I mean..."

"It came in handy when I was doing my penetration work," he confirmed. "But I had to have my skin dyed blue for those missions."

"This happens spontaneously?"

"Yes. If I look at a person or a picture of a person for too long... or too intensely. It can happen in a matter of minutes. Faster, if I'm trying to get it to happen."

"But why do you look like a Ha Jiin now?"

"The effect can last until I look long enough at another person's face to trade for theirs. Or, for lack of another subject, sooner or later I'll revert back to... me. Under normal circumstances, I try not to stare at people too much. I've been watching your face more than I normally would. I should have begun looking like you by now."

"So why isn't that happening?"

"I don't know," Stake admitted. "This has never happened to me before. I'm... stuck."

"How long has it been?"

"Three weeks now. Three weeks since I took on the appearance of a man I killed in my last field mission."

"But you really don't know why that is?"

Stake swallowed. "I, ah, I can't say for sure."

She nodded and gazed at her computer system. Stake guessed that she was studying a picture of his own, natural face. He knew it would appear subtly unnatural to her. In his default mode, as he called it, the mutant had an oddly unfinished-looking appearance. Too bland, too nondescript, like an oil portrait that had been roughed in but never completed. She had probably seen androids that were more lifelike.

"I can schedule an appointment with one of our doctors at the VA Hospital," she said. "Or maybe it would be more helpful if you spoke to one of our counselors..."

"Mm," he grunted.

"In any case... do you have a family, corporal? Any place to go?"

"My mother is dead," he told her. She had been a mutant too. They had lived in the Punktown slum called Tin Town; it held the highest concentration of mutants in the city. As far as he knew his father was still alive, if his drug-addicted state could be called that. "No family," was all the further elaboration he would give.

"All right, then I'll extend your temporary shelter in the VA Hospice until you can find an apartment. And, of course, you have a ten-year pension, but frankly it's limited in nature and you're encouraged to make use of our resources here in searching for employment."

"Yes, ma'am."

"The mask, Corporal Stake. It's because you're afraid to upset the other returnees?"

His stolen face—the face of a dead man, as if grafted on to replace his own obliterated countenance—gave her a sickly smile. "It's to prevent the other returnees from wanting to lynch me."

"WHAT ARE THE goggles for?" She had smiled nervously when she asked it.

"I damaged my eyes in the war," he'd lied.

The Blue War. The light of twin blue-white suns beating down through the jungle canopy, a jungle where every plant from tree to flower to the grass itself was a shade of blue. Blue like the flesh of the Ha Jiin themselves.

The military surplus goggles were like those Cal Williams and many other soldiers had worn for night vision, or to see distantly, or to gaze through the walls of Ha Jiin structures. But when it had come time to shoot, it was through the lens of his sniper rifle's scope that he had peered.

Right now, he had adjusted the spectrum filter on his goggles. Right now, everything he saw was tinted blue.

Cal paced the tiny apartment where he had been staying since his discharge from the VA Hospital. He had been returned to his own dimension a few months before all these others who were flooding back now—it was being badly wounded that had won him that head start. The last treatment had erased the scars on his chest. They had assured him that everything without and within had been fully restored, but the skin of his chest still seemed too tightly drawn to him. As he paced he would occasionally rotate his arms in their sockets, or stretch them high above or far behind him, as if to loosen his confining, claustrophobic flesh.

He hadn't been looking for a job; not yet. He had his pension. He would live frugally, draw it out. It paid his rent. And it had paid for the young woman who lay on the bed he kept trying not to look at as he paced.

He wore nothing but the goggles. His bare feet were stealthy as he padded back and forth like a tiger in its cage. There was one little window and he paused at it, nudging aside the shade to peek out at the city of Punktown. In the evening light, the hovercars swarming at ground level and heli-cars that drifted along the invisible web of navigation beams sparkled like scarabs. The lasers and holographs of advertisements strobed and flashed as if the city was full of bombings and fire-fights. And through his goggles, the entire city was blue, and even darker and more ominous than it would have been, like a metropolis built on the bottom of a deep arctic sea.

Leaning against the window's frame was the rifle he had bought last week from a black-market source, along with the pistol he carried with him when he ventured onto the streets. He lifted the rifle now and couched it in his arms, a familiar and strangely soothing sensation. It was inferior to the one he had used over there, which had been able to fire both solid projectiles and beams. This rifle fired beams alone. And yet, in that area this weapon was a bit more advanced. He stepped away from the window and let the rifle's barrel hold back the lip of the shade. He could fire a bolt of dark purple light right now, and it would pass through the window pane without shattering or even scorching it. It was only one of the gun's tricks.

Through his goggles and through the rifle's scope, he tracked one helicar for a moment before shifting to another. He increased the magnification, traced his gaze from window to window on the building directly across the broad street. At last, he lowered his view further and zoomed in on a man walking along the sidewalk. He zoomed until the man's unaware face filled his vision. He was a wide-mouthed native Choom, even if the goggles made his face appear as if his skin were blue.

Lowering his rifle a little, Cal twisted around and glanced over at the bed.

The woman was of Asian lineage, with beautiful almond eyes and black hair down to her waist, tiny like the female Ha Jiin, but he had learned quickly not to be deceived by that. They were deadlier than the men.

"What are the goggles for?" she had asked him.

Lying there, staring at the ceiling and smiling a little as if to mock him, she appeared as blue-skinned as a Ha Jiin woman.

Cal dropped his gaze to the blood spattered and drying on his belly and legs. It looked black through the goggles. But then, he became conscious of something for the first time. The realization horrified him, and he almost dropped the rifle in setting it aside. He clawed the goggles off his head.

Through their lenses, his own flesh had appeared blue to him, too.

THE GIANT'S HEAD thrust up out of the earth, but Corporal Jeremy Stake knew there would also be an entire body below the surface, its form just as intricately covered in a mosaic of colorful tiles, even if no one would ever see them. The giant's mouth was open wide, and gave access to a metal spiral staircase that wound like a corkscrew down through the titanic body, down into the caverns below the jungle. There, in galleries of stone, writhed the bluish gases that the Ha Jiin worshipped as their ancestral spirits—but for which the Earth Colonies had more practical uses.

Wisps of this vapor curled out of the giant's gaping mouth as if its last dying breath was being expelled.

The statue's flesh was scaled in blue tiles. The eyes were almond-shaped. The way he looked at this moment, Stake himself might have been its model. Before embarking from his unit's position, he had stared long and hard at a photo of a Ha Jiin that he kept on file in his palm comp. His fellow soldiers had helped him spray-dye his skin blue, and he had changed into a Ha Jiin uniform. One of his comrades had pointed a pistol at him and joked, "I don't know, Stake... I think you're one of them pretending to be one of us pretending to be one of them."

The face on his computer screen had no scars on its high cheekbones. No family members lost yet. But aside from the lack of a metallic red sheen to his dark pupils and hair, Stake had been thoroughly convincing as one of the enemy when he had set off alone into the lush blue forest.

He waited, watching the head of the buried colossus, until he felt fairly safe in approaching it. Stake emerged from the undergrowth, and a moment later was ducking into the head's dark maw, with its blended scents of earth and dampness and incense, and the subtle taint of the precious blue gas itself. But all of this barely masked the strongest, underlying note—the smell of countless dead bodies secreted deep beneath the forest.

He descended the rust-scabbed metal staircase. In his right fist he carried a Ha Jiin pistol but it had been modified to fire silently, with Earth's more advanced technology.

At the bottom, copper pipes stained green with verdigris ran across the walls to glass globes, in which gas was burning to give off light. Three passages branched off from this chamber, but their entrances were covered by thick yellow curtains. Stake was very much on edge. Sometimes these caverns were utterly empty, except for the bodies of the dead—slotted into the honeycombs chiseled into the walls, slathered with a yellow mineral that crudely mummified their forms. At other times, members of the Ha Jiin clerical order would be down in the tunnels; maybe a solitary monk, or maybe an entire group. And then, at other times, the tunnels might have been converted into a base camp for a unit of Ha Jiin soldiers. It was frowned upon by their own kind, to take their battle into these places where only the dead were meant to be sheltered, but the Ha Jiin fighters knew that they were not the first to have desecrated the sacred netherworld. That the only way to protect it sometimes was to desecrate it themselves.

Stake strained his ears beyond the soft hissing of gas through the pipes. A ghostly distant voice. A chant? So... he would not be alone this time.

From his backpack he withdrew two narrow black devices speckled with faux rust, which he clipped to the railings at the base of the staircase. He activated an invisible field that ran across the bottom stair. It was a frequency that would not disrupt the anatomy of Earth humans, but would prove fatal to a Ha Jiin passing through it... either descending into the catacombs after him, or pursuing him should he need to make a quick retreat.

Now Stake crossed to the central curtain. A glance at his wrist scanner had told him that there was only one person in the vicinity, down this passage. This person would have to be neutralized before he could assemble the teleportation apparatus stored in his backpack, which would allow the gases to be siphoned to the collection and processing station in the allied city of Di Noon. If it were a cleric, he'd flip a toggle on his gun and simply hit him with a gel capsule filled with a paralyzing drug. But if it were an armed fighter...

Just beyond the curtain, as he shifted it aside, the tunnel was full of the bluish mist. These days Stake was no longer queasy about inhaling it. At first, it had been thought that the gas had inorganic origins... until it had been determined that it was a byproduct of decomposition. In a way, the Ha Jiin were correct in deeming it the spirits of their ancestors. It was a trace of themselves, surviving them, lingering in the air.

More glowing spheres set into the walls. Stake followed the chant, which wavered as if the person uttering it were underwater. He followed the blip of light on his wrist scanner.

He turned down another branching hallway, ducking through a latticework of tree roots that had grown through cracks in the low ceiling. Peripherally, he kept aware of the holes dug into the walls to either side of him. Men, women, children. Dead for centuries, many of them. But it wasn't the dead he feared. Some Ha Jiin soldiers wore a wrist device that deflected the probing of scans such as the one Stake used. And Ha Jiin soldiers, lying on their bellies in these honeycombs, had been known to fire rifles into scouts such as himself.

A circular chamber opened beyond, the terminus of this particular passageway. From the threshold, Stake saw a man in a Ha Jiin soldier's uniform squatting over a body on a wooden slab. His hands were working, working, back and forth with a moist sound. He mostly blocked the body before him, but Stake glimpsed the man's hands and saw they were yellow. Stained with a mineral solution.

Stake took his first stealthy steps into the room. His thumb paused on the toggle of his pistol. Life or death, at a simple flip of a switch.

The hunkered soldier was not chanting so much as he was sobbing. And it was his heavy accent that had prevented Stake from understanding the word he sobbed till now.

"Sorry," the man was croaking in English, over and over as he slathered on the preserving mixture. "Sorry. Sorry. Sorry..."

Now Stake could better see the body that lay on the slab. Even partially covered in yellow pigment, he could tell that its flesh was not blue. The body was that of a dead Earth female. She had short hair like a boy's, her features looked Asian, and she must have been about nineteen. Her Colonial Forces uniform lay folded nearby, where the man had removed it. He had undressed her. And in that moment, that was all Stake could think of. With gritted teeth, he stepped closer and pointed the gun.

A pebble crunched under his boot. The Ha Jiin whirled around, his black eyes flashing laser red, and Stake shot him through the front of his throat.

The man pitched back, eyes wide, across the bare legs of the yellow-painted Earth woman. He stared up at Stake, trying to mouth words, but only blood bubbled up over his lips. Stake didn't need to read lips to understand the word he was mouthing. Over and over.

The man had scars on his face—two horizontal raised bars on his right cheek, and three on his left cheek—to indicate the number of family members he had lost in the war. Family members he might have carried down into this very sepulcher, and coated with the yellow mineral as he had been doing to this teenage girl he had killed.

"Sorry," the man mouthed, dying. "Sorry..."

Stake shot him several times in the face, to erase that haunting visage.

But he had only transferred it to his own. As if the man's ghost had fled his body in that instant, to possess him.

HE WAS WELL, they assured him. The skin of his chest was not too tight. Was he sleeping all right? Did he need some meds for that?

Cal Williams had looked away from the doctor's face, unable to meet his eyes. The man's skin tone suggested some African ancestry in his mix, but his eyes had something of a slanted look too. It seemed all the eyes of the city were Ha Jiin eyes, watching him, no matter what face they glared out of. Sometimes Cal thought he was still a prisoner, still being tortured, but this time just psychologically. Perhaps he had never been freed, but right now sat in a cell instead of an examination room of the VA Hospital. Maybe this doctor wore make-up to change his skin color. Or maybe they had drugged him, or implanted a computer chip in his brain. Played around inside his mind...

"Do you think you'd benefit from talking with one of our counselors?" the doctor asked him.

Cal stepped down from the examination table, resealing his shirt. "No," he grunted. "I'm fine. Just like you say."

He didn't have a car yet, so he figured he'd buy a coffee from a vending machine in the little cafeteria, and sip it while he waited for the next shuttle to Blue Station. Blue Station, he thought with a smirk. Yeah. How appropriate.

In a nexus of hallways where elevators were situated, Cal paused to look at directional plaques on a wall. Arrows pointed one way for the CAFETERIA. And in another direction, toward PSYCHIATRIC SERVICES. He found himself, almost against his will, drifting down that corridor. Maybe it was the sobbing voice he heard from one of the rooms that compelled him. As it turned out, it was a man sitting in the little waiting room, his face in his hands and his elbows on his knees. The receptionist behind the counter could have been a robot for all the concern she showed him. Another vet was strapped into a cybernetic "pony" with insect-like arms and legs, as his own four limbs were missing, making him look like a swaddled overgrown infant. He met Cal's eyes with a dazed, or maybe just fatalistic, expression.

The nurse looked up, finally noticing Cal. "Can I help you?" she asked blandly.

"No—I'm... just looking for a friend," Cal stammered, and then he ducked back into the hall.

STAKE LEFT THE counselor's office without his mask on, as the man had suggested. "As long as you wear it, you fortify your need for it. And you fortify your identification with the Ha Jiin soldier. Every time you put it on again, you re-establish that identity. This is a wound that needs its bandage off in order to heal, Jeremy. Don't look in the mirror. Don't fret about it. You have to ignore it, which is not the same thing as the hiding you're doing now. Go about your life. Your mutation aside, there is no physiological reason for you to maintain this appearance."

Stake had nodded, listening to these words. Normally he wouldn't have looked too long at the counselor's face, but he had stared at him intensely, hoping, hoping to see the man's expression change to surprise as his patient began to mimic him. Yet it did not come.

"But you know," the counselor had gone on, "the surest way to deal with this is to treat your brain itself with a surgical procedure, in such a way that your ability will be forever inhibited. No more shape-shifting at all. Do you think you'd be interested in that?"

"Maybe later," Stake had murmured. "Not... not yet." His ability had served him well during his military stint. Might he make use of it in some future career? And then there was the matter of his heritage. He was a Tin Town mutant, like his mother. He was almost defiantly defensive about that. He didn't need to be... corrected, like some freak, some abomination.

But as he left the counselor's office, he couldn't help but wonder if there were something more masochistic in his choice not to have his mutation treated. Something like punishment involved in that decision.

CAL WILLIAMS WAS waiting for one of the elevator doors to open when he looked to his right and saw the man walking toward him from the psychiatric wing. He wasn't the only one who'd noticed him. A few other people were muttering. "Is that a Ha Jiin?" a woman said.

"His skin isn't blue," her male companion hissed, as if afraid they'd be overheard.

The man with the scarred face stopped behind the whispering couple, waiting for another of the elevators. Cal kept staring at him. He was trembling. If this were all some elaborate façade created by his Ha Jiin captors to trick him, then this one had let his mask slip. Had overlooked a critical detail—those ritualistic scars on his cheeks.

Even though the line he was in was a little shorter, Cal shifted over behind the man with the scars. He stared at the back of his head, so close he could reach out and take his neck in his hands. And as if he could feel those imaginary hands, the man turned around to meet Cal's gaze. Without being asked, he said, "Yeah—I know. I did this to myself, like they do. I lost five good buddies over there, so I..." He made a slashing movement with his hand.

Why lie about it, Jeremy Stake wondered? But it was easier this way, wasn't it? Not having to explain his mutation. Or that scene in the necropolis below the jungle floor. This way it seemed he was a good, loyal soldier, grieving only for his own dead. Not conflicting about some enemy who had murdered a teenage girl.

Cal Williams said nothing. But there was more than just the scars. This man's cheekbones were high and pronounced, his lips full, his eyes slanted, his pupils obsidian black, all like a Ha Jiin. His face wasn't robin's egg blue, but it had a bluish pallor.

Seeing that the man behind him wasn't going to respond, Stake faced around forward again. He felt the eyes of others on him also. Yes, easy for the counselor to tell him to go without the mask. And maybe it wasn't really a bad idea to rid himself of that crutch. But he felt it was premature to have removed it here and now.

The elevator arrived, disgorging one group of people and admitting the next. Cal watched the cabin fill up. The scarred man entered, then turned around to face outward. Cal was desperate to plunge inside so as not to lose track of him, but when the man faced him again he could not bring himself to move. The elevator door slid shut between them.

But a moment later, Cal was racing toward the emergency stairwell.

STAKE'S NEW FLAT was on Judas Street, in a brick tenement meant to look like native Choom architecture but merely looking mass-produced and cheap. At least the gang graffiti gave all the buildings on Judas Street, whatever their style, a homogenous feel. His bed was narrow, his bathroom tiny, his kitchen little more than a counter, but there was a table near the window where he set up his new computer. It would serve as his phone, his VT, and his means by which to try to find out what had become of his former prisoner. The female Ha Jiin sniper named Thi Gonh, whom her own people had dubbed with admiration, the "Earth Killer."

He recalled her face better than he recalled his own. Yearned for it more, too. He could still smell the scent of her long hair, and of her blue flesh. He remembered the taste of it.

What would all the vets at the VA think if they knew how he had lain with her? Not that many of them hadn't slept with prostitutes among their allies, the Jin Haa. But this was the enemy. A killer who had trained her sniper rifle on men and women just like them, and pulled the trigger again and again.

And what would her people think, if they knew the same about her? If they knew how she had become... confused, as he had?

Stake had his computer on now, running in VT mode, and the news station he was tuned to reported a seemingly endless list of recent crimes. A Dacvibese had been murdered by a gang right here on Judas Street and they showed a picture of the alien in life, resembling an albino bipedal greyhound. Stake turned to look at it. Had the kids, maybe adolescents, who had ended that life for drug money, felt any hesitation, any remorse? He doubted it. Were they more hardened killers then, in their way, than he was? He thought that the difference between them was that his killings had been sanctioned, encouraged. He had been told that it was right, whereas they did not have to suffer such a moral dichotomy. They knew they were wrong, were evil, and were comfortable wearing that skin.

Stake had bought more than just a computer with the first of his pension money. From the table, he picked up a black market handgun, a big and ugly Wolff .45. He hefted it as he paced his little flat. It wasn't too light. Lightweight guns were good in the field, when you were laden with gear, but something with more weight definitely felt better at the end of your arm. It was more... there. He would start carrying it when he ventured from his apartment from now on. This was, after all, Judas Street. This was, after all, Punktown.

Well, he hadn't been able to find out anything about Thi Gonh today. Everything was in upheaval now with most of the troops coming home, except for a security force that would remain stationed in the city of Di Noon. As a returnee, he was not privy to such information. But he would keep trying. Whether she would go on trial as an enemy or be returned to her own people, he would track her down one of these days. If nothing more, it was something to occupy his mind. A mission, now that there was no further need for his services. No more battles to fight.

In that distant dimension, at any rate.

CAL WILLIAMS STOOD across the street from the brick tenement, running his gaze across its windows. He didn't know which floor the man lived on, but he knew he was there; he had seen him come and go several times by now. That day when he first met the man in the VA Hospital, he had managed to catch sight of him again down the street and follow him to the subway station, and then trail him here to Judas Street. Cal had altered his appearance along the way, by at first going bare-headed, then wearing the hood of his sweatshirt for a while, removing the cloned leather jacket he wore over the sweatshirt and stuffing it in a balled-up shopping bag he plucked out of the gutter. Luckily, he was a nondescript person. His hair cropped close to his head, like just another soldier.

Yes, the war was over. The Jin Haa had established their small, independent nation within the body of the resentful Ha Jiin's land, like a tumor they must accept and live with. And in return for the help of the Earth Colonies, the Jin Haa would unthinkably allow them to extract gases from the tombs of their own dead. Now that there was a bitter peace, Earth was working to sway the Ha Jiin to become friendly too. They had so much more gas than the Jin Haa, after all.

But with the war over or not, it was too soon for a Ha Jiin man to be here within an

Earth-established colony city. Oh, he might say he was a Jin Haa ally. With his skin color, he might even claim to be an Earther. But Cal knew better. The man was a spy. Or a terrorist. Right here, camouflaged by the city's diversity of races, walking amongst these blind fools, and only Cal was aware of it. As though he wore his military surplus goggles, attuned to a wavelength of light that allowed him to see a creature invisible to others, but slithering through the air around them.

THERE WERE MULTIPLE lanes of traffic thronged with vehicles of every description, hovering or on wheels. To reach the opposite side, he had to go further down Judas Street to a subway kiosk, then cross beneath the street and emerge on the other side. He recognized the building—as unremarkable in appearance as it was—by its graffiti, left most predominately by a gang called the Judas Street Hangmen.

Cal mounted its short flight of front steps, and touched a key on its entry panel. The screen displayed the names of the tenants. He was afraid that the man would have opted to remain anonymous, as some of the tenants had. He ran his finger down the list. A mix of human and alien names. He thought he could tell the alien names were Choom, with one Tikkihotto, from the sound of them. Nothing that sounded Jiinese, though from the man's disguise that didn't surprise him.

A woman came clicking her shoes up the steps, and Cal stepped away from the panel guiltily to let her buzz herself in. Dark, maybe with Indian blood given that a holographic eye was pasted on her forehead like a bindi. She gave him a sideways look. He hesitated, then asked, "Excuse me, ma'am? I'm trying to find someone... he has scars on his cheeks? He dropped this in the subway and I thought I saw him go in here." From his back pocket he produced his own wallet.

"Third floor. I don't know his name," the woman said brusquely. The holographic third eye followed him distrustfully, and blinked. "But I can't let you in with me."

"Oh... okay, I understand." He didn't want to alarm her. He backed off some more while she buzzed herself inside. She watched him through the door's window as she pushed it closed and made sure it locked.

Third floor. Cal activated the display monitor again. He isolated the names of those on the third floor. A few anonymous, but he copied the available male names onto a scrap of paper from his wallet. He would enter these names into his computer, in his own flat, and see what he might glean from them.

As he returned to the sidewalk, staring at the scrap of paper, another woman came near him and said something he didn't get. Cal looked up, a bit startled, and she smiled at him with long red lips that curled forever. From her scanty clothing he could tell she was a prosty. But she was a Choom, not an Earther, not of Asian blood. That was good. Good for her, and good for him, too. He ignored her when she repeated her comment, hurrying off down the street toward the subway so that he might descend into the tunnels below the city—like those he had fought in not so long ago, among the ghostly ancestors of the enemy he sent to join them.

NEITHER TUBES NOR buses would make stops in the ghetto of Tin Town anymore, and any cabbie willing to do so would have to be so crazy that Jeremy Stake would have been more afraid of him than the ghetto's denizens themselves—of which he had formerly been one. So he got as close as he could by hoverbus, and went the rest of the way on foot.

He walked past a series of tenement houses that had all burned into charred skeletons, looking like they'd been bombed. Children balanced along the girders of a floorless second floor as if they were putting on a circus performance. From the hugeness of one child's head and the weirdly bent figure of another, it was clear they were mutants. Like his mother had been. Like himself.

Under his jacket he carried the Wolff .45. When two large men walking close together approached him on the sidewalk, he became extra-conscious of the holstered semiautomatic. But it was actually one man, with an overabundance of flesh and limbs, and he didn't even glance at Stake as they passed each other. They were all ghosts of what they had been or what they could have been, in Tin Town.

He located the apartment building where he had last known his father to be living, but he wasn't there anymore, and the tenant who had replaced him knew nothing of the former occupant. Stake was disappointed—not only because he wanted to see his father again after his four years away in another plane of existence, but because he had hoped that looking into the face of the man who had sired him would give him the jolt he needed to slip the alien mask that had fused itself onto his skull, the way a normal person's face remained fixed. But that was not normal for him.

The best Stake could do, before leaving Tin Town, was to next seek out and stand before the place where his mother had been living when she died. Maybe the building's familiar face would urge the shifting of his cells.

Yet, even the buildings were mutated. He passed through an old low-income housing project, the buildings all bulging at their middles, and at their summits the plastic of which they were composed had been weirdly affected by pollution, teased out into intricate branches so that it seemed that Stake strolled down a rubble-strewn promenade of baobab trees.

He finally found the building he sought in this now transfigured neighborhood. He stared at the third-floor windows through which his mother had once gazed, as if hoping that her face might appear there. As if hoping his own, younger face would appear there. But the restorative miracle he desired was not triggered.

Stake flinched when he heard the chatter of automatic gunfire, a few blocks away. The sky was going coppery as evening approached, and it was better even for a seasoned war vet like himself not to be out in the gangs' combat zone after dark. So he turned back toward the border of the mutant slum. As he walked, someone called out to him and he paused warily, looking over. A man sat on the top step of a tenement doorway, arched and shadowy like an alcove. In the gloom, long appendages stirred; tentacles? The man gurgled, "Are you a Ha Jiin?"

"No," Stake told him. "I'm not."

As if he hadn't even heard Stake, the mutant said, "You call us Earth people ghost-eaters, don't you?" And then, without waiting for another reply, the man purposely gave out a long rumbling belch.

CAL WILLIAMS HAD found him, mostly by eliminating the others from his list. He learned little about the man from the net, but he had supposedly served as a corporal in the Colonial Forces in the Blue War. Oh, there was a picture... yet the man in the service ID photo looked absolutely nothing like the man Cal had followed to the apartment building. That only proved the point. This Corporal Stake had survived the war only to be killed here in his own dimension by the Ha Jiin terrorist, and have his identity stolen. In the more treacherous red tape jungle of bureaucracy, no one had become the wiser.

The man had recently begun phone service to the apartment on Judas Street. And his number was not listed.

Now Cal felt his mission was more imperative than ever. He had to avenge this dead man. This murdered fellow war veteran named Jeremy Stake.

STAKE HAD FALLEN asleep in his chair, seated in front of his new comp system. He had it in VT mode and had been watching a program on the Blue War cease-fire, and the return of most of the Colonial Forces. Vets and their families interviewed about being reunited. He had wondered if the ratings were as good now with the war over as they had been with it on. Some of its battles had been broadcast live, at times from the point of view of the soldiers' goggles. Not those battles, of course, of deep penetration teams like his, particularly skirmishes in the gas tunnels. No—battles in support of the Jin Haa's independence.

A staccato burst of automatic fire—from a drive-by shooting, perhaps—awakened him, and he grabbed the Wolff .45 that rested on the desk beside his keyboard. For a moment, he had thought he was back there. Not in the blue-leaved forests, but Tin Town, where he had grown up. Tin Town, from which he had escaped.

Still gripping the big pistol, with his free hand he reached up to touch his face. He felt the raised bands on his cheeks. He did not need to set his comp screen to mirror mode to confirm it. In fact, when he set his handgun down on the corner of the bed and squeezed into his minuscule bathroom to splash some icy water on his face, he could not even bring himself to lift his eyes to his reflection.

An extended beep from his computer system, followed two seconds later by another. Face dripping, Stake turned around. Someone was phoning him. He moved back toward his comp system, drying his hands as he went. Rather than seat himself in front of the screen, not expecting there to be anyone he really wanted to converse with at length, he leaned down over the back of his chair to check on the caller's ID. It read ANONYMOUS. In another mood he might not have answered, because it was likely some obnoxious marketer. Then again, what if the person who had taken over his father's apartment had lied about not knowing him? What if that man had told his father someone claiming to be his son had come seeking him out? And what if his father had got his number then, through the Veterans' Administration?

A too-hopeful, illogical reasoning as he tapped a key to receive the call.

The comp's screen changed to show him the caller, and to show the caller him. Stake saw a man leaning far back in a car seat, and pointing a rifle at him. He threw himself to one side as a dark purple beam of light launched itself straight out of the screen and burned a deep groove across his left hip.

ANOTHER OF CAL'S gun's tricks.

His new hovercar was not new. It had even been slathered with bright yellow graffiti already, last night when it was parked outside his flat. But its comp system worked fine. Before calling the imposter who claimed to be a man named Jeremy

Stake, Cal had collapsed the stock of his rifle and its telescoping barrel, to make its use more practical in the vehicle's confines. He leaned his back up against the door to give himself a bit more distance as he aimed his weapon at the monitor mounted on the dashboard. His eye was pressed to the rubber cup shielding the scope's tinier computer screen. His finger, on the trigger...

But his first shot had only grazed his target. The man was quick. And why not? He was obviously a soldier too.

Cal twitched the gun's barrel to follow him. He must not get excited. He must keep his cool. He was shooting fish in a barrel.

He fired a second ray bolt through his monitor. And then a third, resisting the temptation to switch to fully automatic. It was an art. He took pride in it. It was what he had been trained to do.

Stake tried to ignore the blazing pain along his hip, as he hit the floor and shoulder-rolled fast to his feet. Peripherally, as he came up, he saw a second bolt flash from the computer's screen. It passed inches in front of his chest. He dove across his bed. A third bolt followed him, plowing into the mattress. Before thudding to the floor on the opposite side, Stake scooped up the Wolff he had left on the bed before going into the bathroom.

A fourth ray burned straight through his bed and hit the wall; a blind shot, based on where the caller thought him to be. He was good too, because the bolt almost skimmed Stake's shoulder.

"Who are you?" Stake bellowed across the room.

His answer was a fifth beam that passed so close to his face that he felt its heat.

Sure that the sixth or seventh would kill him, Stake popped up from behind his bed with his own gun extended. The bulky pistol fired solid projectiles. And however elusive his unknown attacker was, the computer screen was a stationary object.

One good shot struck the screen dead-on. But Stake shot it two times more, just for good measure.

CAL SWORE UNDER his breath as the connection was severed. But he had anticipated the possibility. That was why he had bought the hovercar.

He stepped out of it. Directly in front of his enemy's apartment building. He had hoped not to make a public display of all this, but it couldn't be helped now. It didn't matter. He was doing his duty as a soldier. He was protecting this city. And avenging a comrade he had never known.

Cal had left his rifle in the car, but as he strode to the front door he tugged out his pistol. He had loaded it with illegal explosive bullets. He fired at the door as he came. A third blast did the trick. When he reached the decimated door, he kicked it aside, and was through.

UPSTAIRS, ON THE third floor, Stake heard the three detonations, and knew that his enemy was close at hand.

He also knew he must not allow himself to be pinned down inside his tiny apartment a second time. So he rushed to his door, threw it open, and stepped out onto the landing overlooking the stairs, Wolff gripped in both hands. A woman cracked her own apartment's door, saw him there, and ducked back inside.

Bluish smoke swirled at the bottom of the stairwell, but Stake saw a dark form darting through it. Starting up the stairs. He didn't want to kill an innocent, and yet he didn't even know what his enemy looked like. He couldn't take the chance to hesitate a moment longer than he already had—so Jeremy Stake leaned over the railing, pointed the Wolff below, and fired shot after shot at the figure as it came racing up the second flight of steps.

He heard a cry. And then he threw himself to the floor as an explosive round took out most of the railing where he had been standing.

Stake lay on his belly, shell-shocked, expecting more of these explosions. But as the seconds ticked on, no more came. Was the man simply waiting for him to poke his head up? When Stake heard multiple voices murmuring to each other below, he realized the situation had changed. He got to his feet and descended the stairs, though he kept his pistol ready.

Another tenant had already taken the gun loaded with explosive bullets out of the man's hand. He was not dead yet, but he lay on his back in a spreading pool of blood. Stake stood over him, looking straight down at him. And he thought the man looked familiar, though he couldn't remember where he might have met him before. Then again, he had the close-cropped hair

and nondescript look of so many men he had
fought beside, not long ago at all.

A woman lay dead beside the bleeding man.
From her terrible wounds, Stake guessed that she
had been in the vestibule when the assassin had
blasted away the door. The dying man turned his
glassy eyes away from Stake to look at her. He
groaned, and muttered something the others gathered there couldn't hear. Stake hunched down
closer.

"Sorry," the dying man whispered to the dead
woman. "I'm sorry..."

He turned his face to look up at Stake again.
Stake expected to see anger there, but instead there
was only a kind of bewilderment. And then, he
realized the eyes weren't seeing anything at all.
This stranger who had tried to kill him was dead.

"Crazy," one of the tenants said to another. "On
drugs, or something."

Stake contemplated the man for a few moments
more. A tear that had formed before the life went
out of him finally unbalanced and sped down the
side of his face. The one tear more than the growing puddle of blood troubled Stake, and he rose to
his feet. Turned around to face the other tenants,
in the hopes that they might enlighten him. But
when they saw him, this murderer, they all stepped
back with a collective gasp.

Why? Was he the only killer in this city? And
hadn't he only been defending himself?

But then, as they stared at his face, he knew that
wasn't the reason. He reached up to touch his
cheeks to confirm that the scars were no longer

there. The dead Ha Jiin's mask had melted away like an ice sculpture.

And Stake knew, without having to look at a mirror—knew, from the reflections of himself in the eyes of these confused tenants—what mask he now wore instead.

Bioship

Neal Asher

THE SEA IS a deep umber, carrying peaty silt in every wave. Flashes of pink and white break through like wounds in dark skin, where multi-legged beasts squirm and feed in the laden water. Easily breasting the swell comes the ship. Two rudders like flippers jut from the rear of this inverted turtle hull. A gaping manta maw hoovers muddy water and squirming crustaceans, which are filtered out, and the wastewater jets from the stern boil the sea and drive the ship ever onward. On a deck of glittering oyster-shell nacre, Sian Simmiser stands with Tom John Cable and gazes with slot-pupiled eyes at the horizon. Cloud, like a steel cliff rising up into the lavender sky, is the subject to their regard.

"And so the season rides upon us like apocalypse," says Sian.

"Poetic," replies Tom John. "But fifty days of rain holds no poetry for me."

Sian smiles at him and wonders if he realizes that everything he says holds a kind of poetry to her. She turns at the sound of the cabin door popping and tries not to glare at Captain March.

"Two days and the hold'll be egg-bound," he says. "Leastways we'll be back in port for the worst of it."

March chews at his lip tendrils and stares speculatively at Sian, who turns away, annoyed at this attention from him she has had over the last few days, further annoyed that Tom John does not give her the same. She glances beyond the captain to the high bridge where many of the crew watch the coming storm through transparent shell.

"The ship could do with a rest. Seas have been thick here," says Tom John.

"She'll work until the last or know the consequences," the Captain replies.

Sian pretends not to be needled by that. The *Quill* is asexual so should never be referred to as "she." Also, this particular captain's cruelty to his bioship is something that both disgusts and frightens her. She has seen the results in the *Quill*'s almost obsequious manner to him—the way it opens doors and extrudes hull steps whenever he approaches, and has biolights scuttling to keep up with him when he patrols the lower hull.

"Best I check below. Make sure she's ready to close up," says Tom John.

"I'll come with you," says Sian—anything to get away from the captain's piggy gaze and wet mouth.

"You know, you should be careful," says Tom John as they cross the deck.

Sian glances back to the captain who strolls to the rail with his hands clasped behind his back. Careful? Should she accede to the captain's obvious lust when that is what she most wants to avoid? Careful because of some other nebulous threat?

The hatch comes up with a ripping sound as the resinous seal exuded by the ship breaks and Tom John leads the way down into the dim luminescence of the hold. Sian follows as he reaches the bottom of the ladder, conscious all the way down of his presence below her, hoping he is watching her descend. She wonders what it will take to finally get through to him. Must she walk naked into his cabin? Today she wears a toga with no undergarment. She wonders if the draught she is getting is worth the effort. Halfway down the ladder she looks down and sees Tom John staring up. She smiles at him. He blushes and swallows and moves quickly away from the ladder. Sian feels a satisfaction at a chase well begun.

CAPTAIN MARCH STARES at the sea and wonders just what Sian's game is. Over the sensory link from her cabin to his, she has shown him what she wants—provocative and posing naked. He has signaled his agreement, but she seems not to notice. Perhaps it is time for a bit of coercion? She must know what he is, so that must be what she wants. He needs to get her alone, but Tom John seems to have a limpet-like attachment to her. So thinking, March abruptly turns from the rail spines and heads for his cabin. The *Quill*, sensing his approach to his own quarters, unseals the shell door and swings it aside on hinge muscles, and inside extrudes a sleep-clam, which it opens to reveal scarred and lacerated flesh. March moves past the clam to where a nerve node protrudes, with veins extending from it across the glistening wall. He hammers the node with his fist and the whole cabin shudders. With a sucking inhalation, the *Quill* abruptly retracts the clam, forming a sensory manifold out of the surface of the node—a complexity of tubes and a single squid's eye.

"Now I have your attention," March says, interlacing his fingers and stretching them against each other. He is about to reach out to the manifold when he notices a web of flesh blistering out from the wall between two veins.

"Did I ask for this?"

His reply is a flickering of random pixels in the surface of the flesh, which slowly resolve into a picture. This picture is one he knows the *Quill* has built by sonar imaging, as its source is utterly lightless. He sees a smooth surface breaking into ripples around an area where a snakelike form has attached. Here, then, is his solution—remoras are Tom John's field of expertise.

THE MOTORS ARE spliced from bivalves and their action produces a sound as of huge wet sex. Tom John is utterly conscious of this as he connects nutrient sacks to the huge pulsating bodies. Each sack weighs twenty kilos and the work of bringing them from the refining organ is making Sian sweat, in the dark warmth of the hold, and this sweat is sticking her toga to the curves of her body. And Tom John is aware of this too. With his wrist spur, he punctures each bean-shaped sack before pushing it into the feeding receptacle of each motor and, at each motor, he presses his fingers into the sensory pits of the nearby wall to bring biolights scuttling across the ceiling to gather above him. The creatures cling with black spider legs as, tic-like, they attach to the ship-flesh ceiling and cast down blue luminosity from their sugar-bag bodies. He feels somehow safer with this light about him—less susceptible to Sian's obvious intent. Increasingly he is wondering why he should deny himself. The captain's claim that she has chosen him does not seem valid.

"That should keep them through the storm," says Sian, as he takes the last sack from her and pushes it into its elastic receptacle. Tom John nods and surveys the length of the water arteries to the clustered spherical filtration and refining tanks at the fore. The sucking roar from beyond these is now diminishing, and the tanks suck and groan with less vigor.

"Closing up," he observes.

"Then there's nothing more we need to do down here," Sian replies.

Tom John turns to look at her, and she regards him, waiting.

"Nothing we need to do," he says.

Sian lets out a slow and heavy breath and shakes her head.

"There is something I need you to do," she tells him.

How ignorant can he pretend to be?

"Someone might come," he says.

"I want you to come," she tells him.

They move face to face and he reaches out a hand to her. She takes his hand, brings it up to her mouth and chews at the palm before sliding it down to rest it on her neck, his wrist spur at her throat. Gently trapping his hand with her chin, she undoes the belt and stick-strip of her toga and shrugs the damp fabric to the shell-scaled floor. He notices how her seadaption is not at odds with the smooth lines of her body. Her wrist and ankle spurs carry the mauve pigmentation of her skin, her stomach ribbing runs in a smooth curve from below breasts that seem just the final peak and fold of that ribbing, and her red slotted-pupil eyes and black hair are in perfect complement.

"Here," she says, pulling him by his hand to one of the water pipes. Guided by her he turns at the last with his back to the pipe. She opens his shirt then pants and, while holding and rubbing his penis, pushes him back so he is sitting on the pipe. In his excitement, he has almost slewed the resinous seal on his glans. She smoothes it away with her thumb, before straddling both him and the pipe. He reaches around one taut buttock to find her seal is long since slewed away, and soon she is sliding onto him. They move to the rhythm of the motors and soon exceed it.

The captain walks out of the darkness to them when they are dressed and ready to return to the deck, and Tom John knows by his flushed look and bitten lip tendrils that he has been in the hold for longer.

SENT LIKE A child to her cabin because a remora has penetrated the hull. Pressured to go there when she objected because of her infringement of ship's law, and that look the captain gave her, head to foot, greenish slime on his upper lip from an obviously faulty seadaption—why else the ugliness of lip tendrils and chitin on the palms of his hands, why else the barb on his tongue and his pointed teeth? Sian fumes as her door rips open accommodatingly and her sleep-clam extrudes and after a moment opens. She ignores it as she discards her toga and pulls a sponge with its trailing stalk from the wall pit. As she swabs herself down and the fluid from the sponge slews down her body to be absorbed by the floor, she swears quietly, and does not notice the squid eye—the sensory link she has no knowledge of—closing in the wall for the last time. Some day, she tells herself, she will have her own ship and no longer be at the beck and call of such a man. Finished washing, she returns the sponge to its pit then flings herself down on the soft wet flesh of her sleep clam. Her eyes are shut when that softness closes down on top of her and gently muffles her screams.

AS HE MOVES into the lower hull, Tom John is worried about what the captain might do but knows that for the present the remora must take precedence. In a chamber with the shape of a heart he strokes a nerve node with the back of his hand

and steps back so that his shadow is not cast across it by the two biolights that have followed him. To his surprise, the node extrudes a sensory manifold before blistering up a map to show the location of the remora penetration. He gazes into the squid eye and wonders why it must sense him before providing what he needs. He glances aside at the bladder cache to where the veins from the node spread, like tree roots.

The long, coffin-sized bladder splits with a faint popping and Tom John stoops over it to take out the short bony harpoon he usually uses for this chore. There is another surprise—the weapon revealed to him is a stinger—rather excessive for dealing with a remora. It consists of a tube of ribbed muscle the length of his arm, with two handgrips, and a magazine of stings slung underneath. The pit-trigger in the forward grip is operated by his wrist spur. He takes up the weapon and holds it so the nearest biolight illuminates the translucent magazine sack. There are four stings inside and he sees that three of them are a different color from the first to be loaded. He again gazes up at the ship's sensory manifold, and the eye gazing back at him is lidded and tightened, before opening again. Squeezing the first of the stings up into the launch tube of the stinger, he goes off in search of the remora, uncomfortable with the fact that the *Quill* just winked at him.

Beyond the heart chamber the ship opens out, braced by bony struts between hull divisions. The biolights, keeping with him, are now many meters above. He walks quickly to the rear of the ship, water arteries and food canals becoming revealed in the floor and ceiling. At the appropriate place, he turns to the port and heads for outer hull. Soon he sees that the remora's point of penetration has been accurately located for him, as here is a healed wound, bulbous with tangerine scar tissue. Strangely, it is not a recent wound. He studies the floor and sees the slime trail heading, inevitably, to the rear hold, and follows it. This trail too is not recent—it is grayish and glutinous, as are all old trails on shell where they cannot be absorbed by the ship.

Soon Tom John sees mounded spherical eggs, each large enough to contain a man, bound to the walls of the hold by lattices of hardened resin. Over one such mound is poised a wrinkled ovipositor spurring from a thick ceiling artery. It is still, now that the ship no longer harvests the protein of the sea to convert it into this mounded product. At the first mound, Tom John sees the remora.

The creature is a giant lamprey, but one with ridged chitinous blades on its head stretching back from a triangular mouth filled with red cutting disks. It has penetrated a ship egg, has obviously been feeding for some time, and is now bloated with this unaccustomed bounty. Sensing Tom John's presence it rears up from its gluttony and indolently swings its head round to face him. Tom John feels no fear as he walks in close enough to be sure not to miss, then aims and triggers the stinger. The weapon contracts in his hand then spits out the loaded sting, a barbed glassy spike with two poison sacs attached. The sting penetrates below the remora's mouth and the sting sacs pulse as they drive the poison into the creature. The effect is electric—the remora flings itself into the air then comes down convulsing and thrashing. After this, its body pulls into a tight arc to the sound of crunching vertebra, and slowly the creature ties itself into a tight fleshy knot. Tom John turns away and trudges back the way he came, as already the floor is softening around the dead creature, in readiness to draw it down.

The heart chamber is open to him when he returns to it, but the bladder cache inside is closed. The ship's eye regards him and opens up an organic screen.

SIAN GASPS GRATEFULLY at clean air as her sleep-clam opens, and realizes that the air is fresher and colder than usual. She sits upright and sees that her door is open on to a wall of gray cloud and drizzle-laden air, and captain March. She quickly steps from her clam in fear that it might close on her again and stands to face the captain.

"Simmiser, Simmiser," he says, and licks at his top lip with his barbed tongue.

"What do you want?" she asks, knowing the answer.

The Captain steps through the doorway, and the door hinges closed behind him. "I've come to take what you offered and should have given."

He leers at her nakedness and slides his thumb down the join of his shirt and to the top of his pants. When he drops his pants and steps out of them, she sees that in his seadaption what she should have seen long before—he is made for sadism. His barbed penis is erect and the hooked scales on his thighs glitter in the blue light.

"I made you no offer," she says.

"You could have closed the sensory link any time you wanted," he tells her.

She backs up, but there is nowhere to go and soon he pins her to the wall. "What link?"

"Enough of your games," he mutters, his words slurred.

She fights him but he is hideously strong and quite obviously enjoys her struggles. Soon he will enter her in one way or another and she knows then that the agony will begin. She fights all the harder as he spins her and throws her face down on the clam. But suddenly he bellows with rage and has released her. Sobbing, she turns and sees that he is now facing the wall. A nerve node has appeared there and extruded a manifold and unblinking eye. Why does an unrequested sensory link anger him so? March drives his fist into it, once, twice, then again. The *Quill* rocks with the pain of his blows and the cabin door springs open to give access to the storm. The howl of the wind and the roar of the sea nearly drown out three sucking thuds. March is screaming and groping for the three stings that pump venom into his back. On the floor he thrashes and groans and squirts green chyme from his mouth. He knots fetal, hands and feet clenched to fists, the only movement on him the still-pumping stings. Underneath him the floor softens as the *Quill* prepares to take him down.

"The ship wanted this," says Tom John. "And a rapist deserves no less."

Sian Simmiser does not reply as she teases the captain's hook scales out of her thigh and paints finger patterns on her mauve skin with her red blood. She glimpses up at the watering squid eye that regards her. Hides her fear, her knowledge.

C–Rock City

Jay Lake & Greg van Eekhout

WHENEVER THE UMS *Katie O'Harra* called at C-Rock City, I called on one Rocky Muldoon. Twisted with him in my hammock, his soft snores in my ear, I ran my palm gently over his stubbled scalp and marveled that such a weird-looking guy could be so cute.

Rocky was a big man—asteroid-big as they say—which means all long, skinny bone and not much muscle mass. Comes of being raised by people who don't ever plan to dive down a gravity well again. C-Rock City had enough frac-gee to stick you to the floor out on the Number One and Three rotating ends, but that was about it.

Me, I was about as statistically average as a guy gets with a body not built for any particular environment. I could be uncomfortable anywhere.

"Business," muttered Rocky, his ice-blue eyes slowly opening. I sighed and released the hammock closures, letting Rocky unfold his long limbs, before reaching for my clothes. He pulled on a pair of briefs and went for his datapad. I retrieved my own pad from my pants pocket and sent him *Katie O'Harra's* manifest, along with forty thousand Althean marks coded to the bearer. *Katie's* old man had permits for C-Rock City, but business still cost. As second mate, it was my job to manage those costs.

Rocky smiled and held up his pad. "Thanks, Porkpie. Should've taken care of this before we... you know." He nodded toward the hammock, then shrugged. "Not complaining, mind you."

"Hope not," I said. "You're still my favorite port of call."

He shrugged again, a blush spreading from his cheeks to his shoulders and on downward, then glanced at his pad. "Anything here I should know about?"

"Dancing girls for Mercury and forty thousand liters of Fundy Station Wine," I quipped. Actually *Katie* was just hauling machine parts and Jovian lace-crystals. Nothing exciting. Nothing C-Rock Port Control needed to worry about, anyway.

Rocky laughed dutifully. "Same old lies."

No, I thought, laughing convincingly in return. This time, different lies.

Rocky, as honest a port control officer as I'd ever known, spent another few quiet moments looking over the manifest before indicating his satisfaction with a nod.

"Everything looks good, Porkpie. Including you."

We exchanged glances appropriate for people who liked each other well enough.

Rocky put on his pants. "So. You taking a liberty while you're here?"

"Yeah. I got thirty hours of shore time coming up in a watch or so." I planned to spend it touring the slave carvings within the tunnels and on the exterior of C-Rock City's three rocks. The visit wasn't quite illegal, not technically, but it wasn't anything I needed Rocky to know about. The Proctor of Ceres, the petty little tyrant who ran this place, found the carvings embarrassing, and Rocky had a streak of loyalty as solid as Vestan ore.

My papers said I'd been born here before the Proctor opened the place to settlement and commerce. My mother was a slave named Violet4264. I'd always wanted to see where she'd carved her life in stone. I figured that was a story just for me.

Rocky frowned. "Mmm. Be careful."

"Careful? Of what?"

Rocky smiled, but it wasn't very warm. He finished getting dressed, gave me an impersonal peck on the cheek, and was quickly gone.

Puzzled, I tried not to be hurt. I told myself that if he'd had more to tell me, he'd have said it.

C-ROCK CITY.

There wasn't anything like it in the Solar System before or since. It was carved from a set of three Class C asteroids by blind slaves imported from the mines of Mercury. The Proctor of Ceres brought them up on the old atomic cruisers, which finally got scrapped after the Cancer Wars, but nobody cared about short-life slaves or convict crews.

Those boys and girls went down into tunnels they tore themselves, with mining lasers and planar explosives, and they shaped a staggering work of art. The slaves and the bond-engineers bridged the whirling rocks with cables spun of diamond and buckystring so that a man could walk barefoot and shirtless among the stars.

Looking down on the surface in the right light, with the right shadows, with just the right squint, you could see where the slaves had written the stories of their lives in high relief. Every time I came to C-Rock City, I was struck by the whole weird majesty of it.

Hard thing to figure out. The slaves made something beautiful and more than a little awful, and they never even saw their own work.

How exactly they did it remains a mystery, or a dirty secret, depending on how you viewed things like forced labor. There were stories of the Proctor doing some interesting neuromods on the slaves, giving them a way to maneuver without seeing, a way to coordinate their efforts without speaking. Surgeries like that can go very wrong. They kill, vegetablize, or leave a person stark raving. Doing that to people, even slaves, is the kind of thing that sends ordinary folk to prison, but makes extraordinary folk like the Proctor fat, rich, and hysterically happy.

In the end, when the Proctor wanted the keys to his city, the surviving slaves were spaced from the cargo locks. They were told that they'd be boarding ships to freedom, herded into those cold, echoing spaces and the hatches were opened. That was it for them. After, the maintenance crews never could get the moisture out of the seals. Not in the whole lifetime of the city.

They called that stuff "miners' tears."

I never knew my mother, but those were her tears.

I SIGNED OUT of *Katie*, snatched up my liberty tag, and hand-overed down the docking tube to the port collar and into Number Two rock. Number Two was the center of gravity in the little whirling three-body problem that comprised C-Rock City. It was the place to be for guys like me, far away from the Proctor and his yacht, his friends and his ass-kissers, and his security out in the playground privacy Number One.

I hoped they'd all stay there.

There were some very fine tunnel carvings, even in the docking tube, once I got past the metal and plastic locks. Frieze work showed what I took to be coronal flares, the sort of image that would be on the minds of people who'd gone blind on Mercury. It looked to have been carved with something a lot finer than a mining laser.

The slaves hadn't had much else to do but work, whether on the Proctor's time or their own.

Someone back during the build-out phase of construction had enjoyed a weird taste in elevators. To get down to the core I had to grab a handring and ride a chain rig that looped through a descending shaft. I'd never encountered anything else quite like it in my travels—dogbone links joined together on little pivots, dripping grease that reeked of algae, the groaning rattle of gearing at the coreward end of the shaft as it dragged you in.

I got off when the getting was good, where it ended at the Number Two core. There was a gallery of shops, service establishments, and bars catering to a low-gee clientele, all arranged in a sort of inward-facing globe of storefronts criss-crossed with railings and grip cables. It was also where the primary connector cables were anchored. I wanted to walk down to Number Three, out in the glittering darkness, stare at the shadowed carvings, then check out a suit and go rock hopping on Number Three's skin.

"Porkpie." It was Rocky. He was in his city civvies, an ice-blue shaved velour number with bows at the knees and a white silk shirt. He looked like a Martian pimp.

"Nice outfit, Rocky." I steadied myself in the microgravity of Number Two's core by grabbing onto one of the manuestrian rails. "You're the rage."

Rocky's hand brushed my arm, as if he were thinking of steering me somewhere. The motion set us counter-rotating slightly with respect to one another. Most places in the Solar System, people don't touch strangers. Life's too crowded. And outside a bunk-down, Rocky had never touched me before.

"Rocky, you getting sweet on me?"

"Go back to *Katie*, Porkpie. This isn't a good time for you to take liberties."

I stared up at him as we spun. "You planning an armed robbery or something?"

"I've seen your papers, Porkpie. All of them."

I knew what he meant by that. There could only be one he'd ever care about. "My mother."

Rocky nodded. "History's a hot topic around here right now."

History, I thought. Over ten thousand slaves died here, during the construction or afterward. In my archive searches over the years I'd never found any record of births from back then. Except for my own. Thousands of slaves, and my birth was the only one thought worth mentioning.

One of us had been special, my mother or me. And I didn't think it was me.

"I like you, Porkpie. You know that, right?" He grinned, but his lips stretched too tight for it to be real. "For a lot of reasons."

I supposed I did know that. We liked to roll around with each other, Rocky and me, but that by itself wasn't necessarily special. Cramped ships and cold outposts—card games and needlepoint can only fill so many hours. But with Rocky and me it felt a little different. I supposed he liked me, and I supposed I liked him. The haunted look in his long face told me plenty.

"History's always a hot topic for me, Rocky."

He closed his eyes and our friendship changed. Then he shrugged and let go of the rail, the Proctor's man once more. "I tried, Porkpie. I did. Just remember that."

Ignoring Rocky and the history he was sworn to defend, I hand-overed away from him, along the manuestrian rail that led to the bridge cables.

A FEW YEARS ago, when *Katie* had called into C-Rock City, after a long night of not much sleep, Rocky had gotten himself in a mood for conversation. He was fascinated by my life. Compared to him, I'd been everywhere and done everything. He was eager for me to talk about my rise from port monkey to deckhand to cargo officer to second mate. I could almost believe I was a dashing pirate captain or something, the way Rocky had listened to my tales of mercantile shipping, eyes wide, asking questions.

It was adorable.

Rocky had never been off C-Rock. Never gotten more than a few kilometers away on the odd EVA from those three tunnel-ridden boulders.

Crashed out on a stack of packing blankets on the floor of my cabin, Rocky had rolled over on his back and stared at the ceiling. "I ever tell you they nearly killed me in my crib?"

"Don't think so," I said. "Believe I might have remembered that."

"I was a crèche kid. Mom died when she was three months with me. Clogged suit line, I think. Had enough wages saved to get me machine-gestated, but not enough to support me once I reached term. The Proctor could have had me killed, right in my box. Med techs would have thrown a few switches, tagged me and bagged me and flushed the garbage lock. They did that shit plenty. Still do. It ain't like air is free."

I leaned down toward him, close enough for warmth. With a fingernail, I lightly traced a long, long line from his collarbone to his belly. I couldn't imagine Rocky Muldoon as a baby, crèched or otherwise. "Buddy, you live in one fucked-up place."

"Aw, it's not so bad." Rocky laughed, uncomfortable and edgy. "I'm here, aren't I? The Proctor signed papers that let me live. He didn't have to do that. C-Rock fed me and schooled me, gave me a fancy job that lets me meet interesting people." He winked. "C-Rock's not such a bad place, Porkpie. I try to take care of her, and she takes care of me. That's the problem with you spacers, you don't know what a real home is."

I didn't know what to say to that, so I let my hands do the talking.

MOST OF C-ROCK City's inhabitants zipped about their ordinary inter-rock business on little elevator cars that crawled up and down the buckystrings linking the three cores together. I chose the walkway instead. One notch more sophisticated than a service tunnel, it had air pressure and even some temperature control. I wouldn't freeze to death here, but my breath was a fog of crystals.

Snow, I think they call that.

The true majesty of the walkway was its emptiness, a splendid isolation. It offered a vantage from which I could readily imagine Violet4264 and her fellow slaves.

Which was why the inhabitants of C-Rock City avoided the tunnels. History, Rocky Muldoon's "hot topic," lived in those tunnels like a troll in a cave.

I paused just outside Number Two to look back. Safety lights incidentally illuminated those few of the thousands of carvings closest to the tunnel breach, each a signature and story of a slave's life. They'd never been fully cataloged, due to a lack of appreciation for the work of blind nonpersons. Or other, subtler motives, perhaps. It was like living inside a museum and turning all the paintings to face the walls.

Still, some of the carvings were so obviously spectacular that they couldn't remain unknown. "Three Ships" was almost famous. Most people don't realize it, but Wu's great mural in the Hall of Commerce at Tharsis, a work that made him as wealthy as an artist gets, is a near-copy of the "Three Ships." Some blind slave, nameless and dead, possibly a friend to my mother, did it earlier and better.

The first ship was a seagoing vessel, an improbable thing, squat and fat and top-heavy with masts like trees, as if wet-sailors of yore expected to grow fruit on their voyages.

Wu's painting names the ship *Amistad*.

The second ship was a dirigible, similar to what the Jovian Inspectorate uses in the layers of their vast upper atmosphere, marked with weird little pinwheels, or broken crosses.

Wu calls that one *Hindenburg*. I've actually heard of it.

And the third ship... It was hard not to hate it, all the way down in my gut. One of the long-vanished atomic cruisers that had brought the slaves from Mercury. The background was a positive riot of stars and planets and tiny humans tumbling naked away from the hull.

Wu doesn't give that one a name.

I don't know what message Wu's painting imparts to the financial elite who walk the far-off Hall of Commerce. But down here, on the outside of Number Two rock, "Three Ships" tells a story, life of a man, life of a slave, maybe the life of slavery itself. The carving moved me every time I saw it.

Understanding how much more was lost in the dark moved me more. Especially because I knew that somewhere on the unseen surface of this conclave of wealth and privilege was Violet4264's story.

My mother's story.

My story.

I muttered something like a prayer for "Three Ships" and walked among the stars toward the massive bulk of Number Three rock.

The walkway was like a downward stair, each step I took achieving fractionally more gravity, until eventually I was descending a ladder.

I'd avoided Number Three in my previous visits, avoided the Proctor's administration there with its managers and fiduciaries and judges. Born of a slave, under his law, I might well be a slave too. As a practical matter, almost no one's been held in actual slavery or bond since the Cancer Wars. But there are many old laws to entrap the unwary.

* * *

THE CORE OF Number Three wasn't much different from the core of Number One, which I had visited several times—it had floors and a definite sense of down, courtesy of the centripetal force of the three tethered bodies in rotation. At Number Three, I descended from the ceiling on a spun-diamond stair. Below me, shops were arranged in descending tiers to the apparent bottom of the roughly spherical core, all set at a slight twist to compensate for the Coriolis force. At the bottom was the glowing red gate to the Ruby Palace, seat of the Proctor's administration, set in one of the two heavymost locations in C-Rock City.

This was where the wealthy consumed. The shops offered exotic jewelry, strange tailoring, services for highly individualized kinks. You'd find fewer spacers here than in Number Two, more tourists, more upscale locals. Unlike a lot of stations and cities, C-Rock didn't segregate access to the more well-to-do sections. The Proctor was apparently pleased to allow the stark and visible realities of economics dictate who passed where within his domain.

I was hard to embarrass.

Alighting from the stairs, I pulled out my data-pad. I'd downloaded maps to the exterior accesses here. There were no suit rentals in Number Three—the wealthy don't spacewalk much—but I had a few options available, an outfitter and a couple of maintenance shops where I might beg or bribe a suit. Two of them lay reasonably far away from the Ruby Palace.

I liked that direction better and set off to climb the stairs leading me back out of the base of the core, toward the number seventeen antispinward passage as guided by my pad.

Someone overtook me on the stairs. "You have to come," she whispered as she passed. The woman looked back at me over her shoulder. "Follow," she said, picking up her pace.

Most places, I'd avoid trouble like that the way a deckhand dodges work. But here, looking for my mother, Rocky's warnings still in my ears, I found a rare, reckless mood. I took the stairs two at a time, trying to catch up.

"Why?" I called after her, but she did not answer.

I reached the next landing, where two men with electrostatic sweeper wands exchanged quiet words. I stepped around them, but they stepped with me. The charged wands swung my way.

"You're here," said one of the men. He was short, dark, with ballooning muscles. Someone who'd been raised in a centrifuge, or from the intermediate depths of a gas giant.

"You've been expected," said the other one. He was short too, but not nearly as thick as the first. A man who could have been from anywhere.

"Porkpie!"

I turned to see Rocky scrambling up the stairs. And then the woman who'd passed me, who'd told me to follow her, came running back down and stumbled into him, sending them both flying.

Rocky cursed, tried to disentangle himself from the woman, tried to get to me.

"She wants to see you," said Balloon Muscles.

"Her?" I said, indicating the woman now keeping Rocky occupied, obviously very much against his will.

"No." Balloon Muscles smiled. I swear I could hear his cheeks creak. "Don't you know?"

Oh.

Everything stopped for a moment, even my heart.

Of course.

Of course I knew. My breath shortened.

Behind and below me, Rocky was shouting my name. I glanced down to see purposeful movement all over Number Three's core. The Proctor's security was deploying.

I should have gone back to *Katie* right then and there.

I should have sat down and let Rocky "help" me.

"Take me," I said to the sweepers.

The two men lowered their wands and led me into the tunnel I had already chosen.

PURSUED BY DISTANT shouting, we moved quickly through a forest carved from stone. Tree trunks pillared the walls, a frenzied canopy of leaves overhead. In the years since the carvings had been done, utility lines and access ports had been hacked into place, but even those crude trenches and cuts served mostly to accentuate the beauty.

Balloon Muscles swerved and ducked between two imposing trunks set close together. I followed, the other sweeper behind me.

We were in a short maintenance tunnel, much more dimly lit, the walls carved to resemble running courses of brick or stone. Little niches inset contained small objects—tiny specimen bottles with tissue floating in muddy fluid, old coins from Earthbound cultures, scraps of paper with scratched marks that could have been drawings or attempts at writing. I was reminded of the honeycomb churches of Zha Madrid. These were devotional objects. This was a place of worship.

A collection of buffers, sprayers, parts, and supplies blocked much of the room. My two guides pushed on through, rolling a tank of cleaner aside to reveal more carved bricks. Balloon Muscles cast me a quick glance before he tapped on three of the bricks. A small portion of wall opened into darkness.

One by one, we crawled out of the light.

I WAS IN a narrow tunnel that looped and dove through odd angles and sudden drops. My sense of down, my sense of any direction, was twisted past any following. Which was logical enough once I thought it through. The slaves who'd carved these secret passages through C-Rock City wouldn't have even tried to make them decent walkways. They would have wanted their tunnels to remain undetected by normal engineering surveys.

We stayed in total darkness. Every spacer has nightmares of being locked without power or life support in a derelict ship, and this was not much different, except for the smell. The passageway reeked of damp, of mold, and sometimes occasional drafts of other smells—machinery, food, people. My own pulse pounding in my ears, I brushed the cold stone walls with my fingers. Carvings passed beneath my touch.

The sweepers seemed to know their route well. They never paused. Both were shorter than me by at least twenty centimeters, an advantage down in the tunnels. Three my size and we would have tangled and trapped ourselves to death.

This was my mother's country. Secret tunnels within the walls. A life buried in darkness under tons of stone. Though I hadn't found a carving that gave me her specific biography, I was being shown a secret far more precious. In here was the place in which she had lived her life. This was the where and the how of it, if not the who.

And I realized something else—I might have been born in this tunnel, or one just like it.

AFTER WINDING THROUGH passageways for what might have been hours, my guides finally paused, still in total darkness. "You're here now," whispered the one following just behind me.

"Are you ready?" whispered the other.

I lied and told him I was.

A hatch opened before me, red light streaming through to shock my eyes. I closed my lids, rubbed my face, and then peeked. It was only a dim glow really, much like the emergency lights on *Katie's* bridge. My eyes had been tricked. Time in the dark had robbed me of my sense of brightness.

I followed the balloon-muscled sweeper out.

It was a strange room, extending in all directions until it vanished from sight around the curve of Number Three rock's tiny horizon. It was curiously absent of the decorative carvings that filled the rest of C-Rock City's otherwise unfinished spaces.

The floor was below me, at a substantial fraction of nominal gee, so that I had to jump down from the hatch. Fat pillars punctuated the emptiness around me.

People sat scattered among those pillars, barely more than silhouettes. Everyone looked toward me. Faces in the dark and blind eyes, staring right at me, locked on and tracking.

I flashed back to two memories.

The first was Os-Tan Station, where I'd once been granted the privilege of spending the night with a band of underdeck gypsies who were always suspicious of a stranger, but who nonetheless shared their food and drink and music with me.

The other memory was when I'd wandered into the wrong section of the Deimos bubble camps and the residents there had beaten me to within an inch of my life.

I shouldn't have been so quick to ignore Rocky's warnings. He'd always been a friend. A little more than that, maybe. He'd only been trying to help, and I'd fled from him back on the stairway.

Too late for regrets. "Now what?"

Balloon Muscles looked at me as though surprised by my question. "Now you find her."

And so I took a few more steps into the room, looking for Violet4264.

Would I know my own mother?

Would she know me?

THE FOLK AMONG the pillars were all old. Very old. I'd never seen such people in all my travels.

Most humans either died young and ruined or aged gracefully in a cloud of medical nano and genomic therapies until accident or time claimed them.

Not these people. Their skin had long since tanned to leather, then wrinkled past reclamation. Their eyes were crusted shut with scars. Their hands were missing fingers, some crushed or bent or palsied.

Slaves. Still alive in the tunnels.

My mother's people.

"Violet?" I asked softly as I moved among them. As with babies, I couldn't even tell male from female among these elderly. Let alone such conceits of wealth as chims, neuts, or herms.

"Violet?

A bald head shivered no.

I walked on, "Violet?"

A clawed hand took mine, turned it over, pebbled skin dragging over my own calluses. Then it dropped away.

"Violet?"

"Violet4291," creaked a voice that I had to bend close to hear. "Not your wavelength."

After that, I asked for my mother by her full name. I had always thought of Violet4264 as a name and a slave number. Not as a mark of dignity.

On and on I walked, getting farther and farther from the sweepers' hatch. I would never find my way back from this place without their help. But I didn't want to, not without my mother.

Every step was hell, a stride back into a time I had no memory of, but I knew I belonged there.

My heart burned for vengeance on the Proctor and his kind. My heart burned for my mother.

Where was she?

PERHAPS AN HOUR later, when I had spoken to forty or more of the elderly slaves, Balloon Muscles finally caught up with me and pulled me aside. "Have you found her?" he asked, his fingers clutched tight on my elbow.

"No." I tried to shake him off—there were more of my mother's people half-hidden in the shadows ahead. They clustered just past the short horizons, all the ghosts of my history. I strained, but his heavy-gravity grip was far too strong for me.

"Will you find her?" His eyes glinted.

"If she's here. Let go of me."

"Will you find her?" He gave the words a strange emphasis.

I held my tongue and stayed my fist. Something was to hand. So I simply stared him down.

Finally his grip softened. He looked at his feet, then past me, not meeting my eye again. "She's lost to us," he whispered. "We thought you... her son..."

"She's dead?" My voice pitched up. "You brought me here, through all this, just to tell me she's dead?"

"No." Balloon Muscles sounded desperate. "She's not dead. Violet4264 still speaks to us. We simply can't find her."

Around me, one by one, the ancient slaves began speaking. Their words were in synch, a single voice moving dozens of mouths.

"Disperse."

"Leave him."

"He will be safe."

"The Proctor's men are coming."

"We will not."

"They're coming."

"The Proctor."

"My son."

"Leave."

"Stay."

"My boy."

"I ..."

The whisper faded, and in a scuttling rush, the old people were gone. Someone shrieked, and close by I heard Balloon Muscles crying, the weird, slow sobs of someone with heavy gravity lungs. Joy, relief, sadness.

My mother had come back to me. To them.

"How?" I turned to ask Balloon Muscles, my own eyes stinging. But my guide was gone too.

Then Rocky Muldoon loomed out of the darkness, amid flickering riot-control strobe lights, there with his port security crew. He pointed and a concussion grenade landed four or five meters from me, knocking me hard onto my back.

Rocky and his cops surged forward. In my rage I tried to fight them all.

AFTER A LONG but fairly courteous interrogation—they broke no bones, for one, even though I had energetically resisted arrest—Rocky hauled me out into the diamond-walled walkway to talk beneath the stars.

"*Katie O'Harra*'s undocking in about an hour." His voice was rough, tight, over-controlled. "You can be on her, or you can rot beneath the Ruby Palace."

"Ah." I searched his face for any sign of the Rocky I knew. The one I'd shared my bed with. The one who'd begged me for stories of life between ports, who'd listened to my tales of spacing like a little kid.

I saw none of that in him now. All I could see was a man whose mother had left him with an unpayable debt to the Proctor.

Blank as a mirror, Rocky was.

I couldn't say anything. My words had been drained by needle and electric shock. I stared uncaring at the stars, trying to ignore the pull of the carvings on the dark rock nearby.

"It's got nothing to do with you," he said. "They're a... a cult, down there. People go into the service tunnels and blind themselves and call themselves slaves. They claim this Violet4264 as their prophet. Nothing you saw means anything." There was urgency in his voice. He was desperate for me to believe him. "It's not real. It's just a little social problem peculiar to C-Rock City."

I managed to dredge up a word, echoing one of our earlier conversations. "History," I said from somewhere far away.

"Yes." Rocky was relieved. "History. And now drugs, delusions, pretense of psychic powers. And an attempt to undermine the Proctor."

"Ah," I croaked.

Rocky—and his Proctor—wouldn't be this afraid of a "little social problem." It was real, what I'd seen in spaces between the tunnels.

Real.

"Go back to *Katie*, Porkpie. Forget all this. You're nobody's son. You never had a mother. You're on your own." Rocky paused, gathering his lies. "But I know you. You don't need anything else. You're fine without it."

"Ah," I said again. Real.

He chose to take that for assent.

Stumbling, I was led in steps and stages to the outer ring tunnel of Number Two rock. The docks there were passage home. Rocky signed me in, retrieved my liberty tag, and bent to hug me. His breath was hot and fast in my ear. "Don't come back for a while. Maybe ever. You got me, Porkpie?"

"I got you," I said, surprised that the words had found me. I turned my back on him before he could turn his on me, and then I was aboard *Katie O'Harra* amid laughs about drunken sailors and unfunny jokes about dereliction of duty.

I AWOKE ALONE in my hammock, mouth dry as shuttle rations. Even now my little cabin still smelled of Rocky's aftershave. There was a hotbox on the floor, the message light on my comm station blinking red. People wanted me.

Though there was still something wrong with my words, courtesy of Rocky Muldoon's interrogation chemistry, there was nothing wrong with my memory.

He'd lied. It was real. Far too real. My mother had awoken from wherever she slept. I'd somehow brought her back to C-Rock City.

I wondered now why Rocky had let me live. Maybe he was afraid of my mother. To fear her the way he did, he had to believe in her.

The Proctor believed in her. He had to. Otherwise his minions would have swept the tunnels of the surviving slaves long ago. And he'd have had Rocky dump me out of an airlock.

I think Rocky loved me, maybe a little. Something like that. But I knew he loved C-Rock City more.

I sat up in my hammock, then fought off the lurching pain in my head. The hotbox blinked at me, a little throwaway timer indicating less than an hour remained of its thermal integrity.

I opened it. Inside was a steaming hot pork potpie.

There was also a note, written in actual handwriting on an actual scrap of paper. It was a brittle, torn manifest printout. Not the kind of thing worth keeping, certainly.

But the paper was decades old.

At least as old as me.

I turned it over and my hair prickled when I saw what was written there in fresh ink: TO MY BOY, WITH LOVE.

I resisted the urge to clutch the paper for fear of ruining it.

Someday *Katie O'Harra* would return to C-Rock City.

Someday I'd be back. I'd change things.

Someday.

For now, not knowing what else to do, I ate the pie.

The Bowdler Strain

James Lovegrove

THE BOWDLER STRAIN escaped from the MoD research facility at Chilton Mead in Gloucestershire, at 7:30pm on Thursday June 18th.

The point of origin was the facility's Ideative Manipulation laboratory. The initial vector was none other than the head of Ideative Manipulation, Professor Hugo Bantling.

Scientists, as a race, tend to be sober, serious, even reticent individuals, not unduly prone to vulgarity. Professor Bantling was no exception.

Thus it wasn't until past ten that evening, when he was preparing his nightcap of cocoa and the milk boiled over, that the professor had cause to realize that he had been exposed to one of his own logoviruses.

By then, of course, it was too late.

* * *

ON HIS WAY home, Professor Bantling had spoken to:

one of his assistants, Dr. Roxanne Quest;

a janitor, Tom Wells;

a colleague, Professor Cyril Prudhomme, Head of Communicable Allergy;

the guard at the facility's main gate (he/she must remain nameless for security reasons);

the attendant at the Texaco garage on the A481 between Chilton Mead and High Leversham, Miss Kylie Bracewell;

the proprietor of the One Stop Foodstore and Off-Licence in High Leversham, Mr. Vijay Latif;

and his housekeeper, Mrs. Barbara McCartney.

To each of these Bantling had offered no more than a couple of dozen words; in the case of the janitor, the security guard, Kylie Bracewell, and Vijay Latif, no more than a "thank you" and a "good evening." Each, nonetheless, was immediately infected, and proceeded to infect numerous others over the course of the rest of the evening, and they in turn infected still others, and so on. So the logovirus was already out of control, effectively an epidemic, long before Professor Bantling became aware of its presence in his own neural system.

When the milk boiled over, sousing the hob in seething white, the professor instantly and reflexively swore. Inattention was to him the greatest sin that anyone—but particularly a man of science—could commit.

The irony here is obvious, for it was the swearing that alerted Bantling to the fact that he or one of his team may have recently committed a far more serious sin of inattention than merely taking your eye off a saucepan of milk for a moment.

"$#!†," said Bantling.

He blinked.

He frowned.

He repeated the epithet, slowly this time and low-voiced.

"$#!†."

He clasped a hand to his mouth. A groan escaped him.

Half a minute later he was on the phone to the laboratory.

Half an hour after that, he was back at Chilton Mead, trying to figure out what had gone wrong.

COLONEL JAMES NUTTER, Chief of Operations at Chilton Mead, had had to endure taunts about his surname since kindergarten. It was this, more than anything, which had burned out of him the tolerance of others' foibles that each of us, to a greater or lesser degree, is born with. Nutter was a toughened shell of a man, almost devoid of empathy. The one thing in life he truly loved was the army, not least because now that he had attained high rank, nobody ever poked fun at him anymore.

It was two o'clock in the morning. Chilton Mead was on a state of high alert. Colonel Nutter had just come off the phone to the Prime Minister. The Prime Minister was not a happy person. Neither, consequently, was Nutter.

"What the Fµ¢« happened, professor?" he demanded of Bantling, who had been summoned to the colonel's office in a manner that did not anticipate refusal.

"Who is responsible for this Fµ¢«!^§ mess? And how is it that I can't ß£°°∂¥ well swear without my voice going all peculiar?"

The professor was no less tired than Nutter, and no less tetchy. "In reply to your last question, colonel, do you not read the reports I send out to all senior administrative personnel? Because if not, I have to wonder why I bother with them. They take up an awful lot of time that I could otherwise devote to more fruitful pursuits."

Nutter went red in the cheeks, both angered and embarrassed. "I'm a busy man, professor. What goes on at this facility is less important to me than the fact that it can continue to go on free from external intervention, be that in the form of terrorist action or government prying. I do know that you scientist chaps are up to some pretty bizarre stuff here. Much more than that, I don't need and don't want to know."

"But you must have some idea, mustn't you, of the basic principle of Ideative Manipulation."

"Some. It's a kind of mind control, right?"

"Put extremely crudely, yes. In this day and age, the military is looking for ways of disabling enemy nations swiftly and harmlessly, keeping damage to infrastructure and human life to a minimum, possibly to zero. Of course we can knock out electronic communications using EMP bombs, computer viruses, and the like. But what about *communication*? What about *people*? That's what I've been working on. If we can render people within a nation incapable of interacting with one another at the basic verbal level, then that nation will be helpless, all but paralyzed."

"I don't see how not being able to swear could leave a nation all but paralyzed. ∂@ℳ︿∈∂ annoyed, yes, but not paralyzed." Nutter gave a despairing gasp. "I can't even say '∂@ℳ︿∈∂.'"

"Any word or phrase delivered with invective intent is off-limits. You can say 'sod' if you mean a piece of turf but not '$°∂' if you mean something, as it were, earthier. That's the Bowdler Strain's specific effect, the negation of profanity. All swearing comes out as garbled nonsense. As such, Bowdler represents an important step on our way to the creation of a kind of universal language-negation logovirus. We're not there yet, but the process of development has, as we see, turned up some interesting side-products."

"Just tell me, professor," Nutter said, "how did it get loose? And how do we contain it?"

"We're working on the containment part, colonel. As for how it got loose... Why don't you come with me?"

THE IDEATIVE MANIPULATION lab was classified as a Biosafety Level 1 environment. Strictly speaking, protective biohazard suits were unnecessary. They were worn anyway, largely so that everyone who worked here would always bear in mind that they were dealing with materials potentially as dangerous as any neurotoxin or necrotizing bacillus.

The lab comprised two rooms, a research area, and a specimen chamber. In the former, Bantling's five-strong team were milling around like ghosts in white plastic, agitatedly discussing various options for combating the escaped logovirus. They fell silent when the professor and Colonel Nutter entered.

"Roxanne," said Bantling, "I need to show the colonel the specimen chamber."

"Of course, professor." Dr. Quest produced her security clearance card. Bantling did the same, and together, one on either side of the door to the specimen chamber, they inserted the cards into electronic locks and tapped out key codes on the number pads. The door unclamped itself and slid heavily open.

The chamber housed a dozen soundproofed cells in twin rows of six. Everything was white here, and silent, like the morning after a deep snowfall. Bantling led Nutter along to the second door on the right and invited him to look in through a triple-glazed spy hole.

Inside a cube that an average-sized dog might have considered cramped quarters sat a man—a hunched, hunkered, sad-sack man, who was muttering to himself and every so often would succumb to a violent twitching spasm, his hands thrusting forth and dancing spider-like over the floor, the wall, or a part of his body. Other than the hospital-style gown he was wearing, the man looked like the archetypal tramp. His hair was stringy and unkempt, his beard likewise; his skin was flaked and reddened from years spent outdoors in all weathers; his face showed the weight and defeat of hard living.

"This," said Bantling to the colonel, "is Gerry. Gerry is a Tourette's sufferer. His compulsion to swear is uncontrollable. Or rather, it was till we got our hands on him. He still swears now, but none of it comes out intelligibly. I suspect he finds this a little distressing, although he may have adjusted, I'm not sure."

"Where did you get him from?" said Nutter. "Or should I not ask?"

"Perhaps you'd best not ask. Suffice to say that our test subjects are chosen very carefully. Each is the kind of person whose disappearance from society will not be noticed."

Nutter glanced sidelong at the Professor and saw the same eerie placidity in his face that he heard in his voice. Nutter wasn't squeamish, God no. He had in his time had to make hard decisions involving men's lives, and indeed their deaths, and he knew that there were no moral absolutes in this world. Nonetheless, he found it a little disconcerting, the way Bantling could talk so clinically about Gerry, as if this human lab rat was of no more consequence than an actual, rodent-style lab rat. Nutter was in no doubt that Gerry's "disappearance from society" had been anything but voluntary. He was sure too, that there would be no return to society for Gerry once he had outlived his usefulness at Chilton Mead.

But it was not a matter he could permit to trouble him. His concern, right now, was the rogue logovirus.

"So the cell is soundproofed," he said. "And you presumably take every conceivable precaution when entering it."

"Correct. Ear plugs *and* ear defenders are mandatory for anyone coming into direct contact with the test subjects. The only time we ever hear their voices is when listening to recordings we've made of them. Which is what I was doing this evening. I was running through today's recordings, checking for any anomalies in the verbal symptom patterns. They fluctuate, you see. It's a phenomenon we haven't quite pinned down yet, although we think it has something to do with the brain trying to counteract the logovirus by reorganizing synaptic pathways, as the brains of stroke victims sometimes do in order to compensate for the neurological damage. Or perhaps the mind has its own antibodies, just as the body does. Psychic antibodies. One for the metaphysicians there. Either way—"

"You're saying," Nutter interrupted, "that someone listens to these people's voices every day?"

Bantling nodded.

"Then, probably a stupid question, but why hasn't anyone been infected before?"

"Because until today none of the logoviruses has been transmittable via recording or any other artificial means. They only work interpersonally. Direct from mouth to ear, as it were."

"Then what changed?"

Bantling stroked his thumb tip up and down the groove of his philtrum. "My guess is, the logovirus mutated."

"What?"

"Gerry's brain was attacking it, trying to expunge it. Like any good virus, the Bowdler

Strain adapted, and kept adapting, and now it's achieved a form in which it can be transmitted non-interpersonally. In other words, electronically."

"ßµ§§∈® me."

"Well, quite," the professor said, with the thinnest of smiles.

THE BOWDLER STRAIN proliferated throughout the night, like a bad rumor. Person talked to person talked to person, innocently spreading the contagion. In the small hours, doctors and hospitals began to receive calls from worried individuals who thought they might be afflicted with an aneurysm or a brain tumor or even cancer of the tongue. They just couldn't get their words out right. Friends woke friends, relatives relatives, spouses spouses, to ask if their voices sounded funny. Most often the reply was no, since not all of those infected had made the connection between the incomprehensibly misshapen syllables that emerged from their mouths and the expletives which generated them, and they weren't swearing while expressing their befuddlement to their loved ones. Those who did perceive that a certain segment of their vocabulary was translating itself, of its own volition, into what appeared to be Serbo-Croat or Mongolian or Tagalog, or some other equally unfamiliar lingo, swore all the more vehemently as they attempted to vent their anger and bewilderment by verbal means. They only found themselves, of course, emitting further streams of gibberish, which angered and bewildered them even more, so that they swore even more, and on and on in a vicious circle, until all that was left to them was to lapse, livid-faced, into silence and mutely fume and fret, denied the cathartic satisfaction of even the mildest of blue language or the most moderate of blasphemies—or else they hit things. There were some, not necessarily of a religious bent, who believed they had acquired the ability to speak in tongues. There were some, usually of a religious bent, who through habitual abstinence from profanity had no idea they had been infected at all. The Bowdler Strain twisted and turned its way through the mazes of human interaction, and would have done so a great deal more rapidly had the outbreak occurred during daytime. As it was, by dawn the next morning a significant percentage of Gloucestershire was affected, and there were many more clusters elsewhere in the country, courtesy of the national telephone network.

And as the sun rose and people rose, the logovirus's exponential growth accelerated.

PROFESSOR BANTLING'S TEAM and Colonel Nutter had brainstormed through the night and made little progress toward a solution. It was given that the Bowdler Strain was wildfire, inextinguishable, unstoppable. At best estimate, it would blanket the country within two days. Total population saturation would be achieved in under a week. There was no question of isolating each and every outbreak, setting up perimeters, creating hot zones, issuing denials. Standard operational procedure for all kinds of similar emergencies was inapplicable in this instance. There was no alternative but to devise a means of neutralizing the logovirus. An anti-logovirus vaccine would have to be developed, and if it could be created and implemented swiftly enough, then maybe, just maybe, Bowdler could be eradicated, and the outbreak downplayed and dismissed as a bout of public hysteria.

Nutter expressed the view, several times in several different ways, that it was not a little astounding that a vaccine had not already been prepared for just such a contingency as this. For the most part, the scientists ignored him when he made the observation, acting as experts tend to when a layman draws attention to a glaring oversight in their methods—with disdain. On one occasion, Bantling did acknowledge the colonel's point, but all he said was, "It's not that simple."

Otherwise, it was proposal and counter-proposal, thesis and antithesis, theory and refutation, and lots of strong coffee. And in the end, the only conclusion the group could reach was that there was no quick and easy fix. Cultivating and implanting a logovirus took weeks, so even if they were able to design one that specifically remedied Bowdler symptoms—and logoviral engineering was not an exact science—then it wouldn't be available for use until long after the whole of the UK was infected.

"Is that really so bad?" said the youngest person in the room, Edwin Chao. After a night of futile debate, he was trying to look on the bright side. "I mean, no one can swear properly—so what? It's not as if it's fatal, right? No one's really going to suffer on account of Bowdler."

Bantling said, "I agree that of all the things that could have escaped from Chilton Mead, a logovirus is far from being the worst. One of the race-specific killers from the Applied Genetics lab, for instance, or that lethal self-replicating graffito the chaps in Visual Memetics have been working on..." He mimed a shudder that was not entirely ungenuine. "But the fact remains that we're looking at potential countrywide panic. We're looking at a frightened population, unaware what's happened to them, knowing only that something very strange is going on. We're looking, maybe, at civil unrest, rioting, a breakdown in the rule of law."

"That's very much worst-case," said Dr. Quest, wanting to reassure everyone, including herself. "I doubt it'll get that bad."

"Bad?" said Nutter. "Civil unrest and rioting isn't bad. I'll tell you what bad is. Bad is if the Bowdler Strain is somehow traced back to here. Bad is the public finding out the sort of thing you lot get up to in these laboratories of yours."

"Then, colonel," said Professor Bantling firmly, "as Chief of Operations you'd best do all you can to ensure that that eventuality never comes to pass."

THE FIRST NEWS report about the outbreak was a short piece in a local current-affairs TV program, aired on the evening of Friday, July 19th. The item came at the end of the program and was pitched at the same level as a funny-animal or bizarre-charity-stunt story, with the reporter adopting a jocular, ironic tone as he described the peculiar condition that pensioner Ron Squires had come down with, apparently overnight. Ron, a resident of High Leversham, had, it seemed, lost the power to swear.

"I'm not a big one for cursing, never have been," said Ron, with a nervous flash of his dentures. "But you know, every once in a while you just can't help a naughty word slipping out, can you? Only, last night I dropped my bag on the way home from the off-license and broke a bottle of stout, and what came out of my mouth then didn't sound like no swearing I ever heard before."

"And what did you say, Ron?" asked the reporter. "Bearing in mind that this will be going out before the watershed."

"Well, I'll tell you exactly what I said, because I'm pretty certain none of your viewers will be able to understand it. 'ßµ§§€®!^§ #€££' is what I said. See? What does that sound like? And all my other swear words—it's the same. III@^«. @®$€. ¢µ^†."

The opinion of Ron's GP was sought, and she pronounced herself mystified. "I've never seen anything like it before in my career," said Dr. Annette Murray. "Ron has always been in very good health. I can only assume that the shock of the beer bottle breaking triggered some sort of psychosomatic stress-response that has affected his speech patterns. It's all very strange, and I have referred him to a specialist."

"You don't think Ron is putting this on somehow?" said the reporter.

"Oh no. Why would someone put on a condition like this?"

The reporter delivered his concluding remarks to camera. "So there you have it. A mystery ailment that has left one man's life blighted. Ron Squires is lost for words. You could say he's been *sworn to silence*."

Within minutes, the TV station was inundated with phone calls from viewers who had watched the item and were suffering from the same problem as Ron. Some of them had had the problem before the item aired, others claimed the problem had started immediately afterward. Telephone operators at the TV station were treated to examples of the choicest epithets that the English language has to offer, all rendered meaningless by the Bowdler Strain. Eventually the switchboard was overloaded by the vast numbers of people ringing in, and it packed up. By then, the telephone operators were themselves swearing hard. Unintelligibly, of course.

The story made the main news later that night, coming second in the running order to the failure of the latest Middle East peace initiative. Incidences of "swearing disorder" were being reported all over the country. Hospital A and E departments were swamped by people demanding to know what was wrong with them. The emergency services were receiving twenty calls a minute, only one of which was from someone in genuine need of the police, an ambulance, or the fire brigade, the rest coming from alarmed citizens who had contracted the strange and perturbing speech impediment. A chief constable implored members of the public not to dial 999 unless it really was an emergency. Meanwhile, a government spokesman, interviewed outside the Commons, had the following statement to make: "The Prime Minister has been apprised of the situation and is monitoring it closely. At the present time, there is no clear explanation for the difficulties that a very few people, and I stress a very few, seem to be experiencing with their voices. The matter is being looked into with the utmost urgency, but there is no cause for concern. None at all. We expect that whatever is happening will run its course in a couple of days or so. That's all I have to say for now. No questions. Thank you very much."

All of Saturday's papers carried the story on their front pages. The broadsheets talked of "an extraordinary phenomenon reminiscent of the 'sleeping sickness' outbreak during the First World War" and claimed that experts in neurolinguistics were "baffled." The tabloids took a predictably more bumptious approach. "F*** ME! WHERE ARE MY SWEAR WORDS?" was the headline run by one red-top, while another contained a feature article entitled "Expletives Deleted—Your Cut-Out-And-Keep Guide To The Best Of British Bad Language," which offered lists of "clean" alternatives to the most popular modern-day profanities.

The mood of the nation was febrile that day. Torn between fear and a sense of wild absurdity, people tried to go about their weekend business as normal, but shops and streets were nowhere near as full as they might have been, roads and motor-ways carried considerably less traffic than usual, and the beautiful sunny weather was enticing very few visitors to zoos, amusement parks, seaside resorts, and the great outdoors. Football fixtures were cancelled. Airports reported a sharp decline in passenger numbers. With well over half the pop-ulation stricken with Bowdler, there was an almost instinctive desire among the affected and unaffect-ed alike to minimize contact with others. It wasn't public knowledge that the swearing disorder could be passed on like the flu, or for that matter that tel-evision, radio, and telephones were playing a part in its dissemination. It simply seemed sensible, to a broad cross-section of the Great British public, to stay at home.

Children found it irresistibly amusing that they could utter forbidden words in front of their par-ents and not get told off for it. They learned to insert the words into strings of made-up nonsense. Their parents knew they were swearing, but where was the proof?

Disgruntled employees who had their bosses' private phone numbers rang them and denounced them vehemently, knowing that as long as they restricted themselves to certain ribald terms and coinages their voices would be almost impossible to identify.

The presenter of a kids' morning TV show, having ingested more than his fair share of cocaine in the dressing room beforehand, went a little mad and started calling his co-presenters, the program's producer, and even the Director General of the network all sorts of foul names, thinking that because of swearing disorder he would be safe to do so. Unfortunately for him, he hadn't actually contracted Bowdler yet. The live transmission was interrupted with a test card and the presenter was summarily sacked.

Performances of a David Mamet play in the West End had to be cancelled until further notice.

The same fate befell a one-man show from Steven Berkoff.

That evening, a broadcast of the movie *Scarface*, starring Al Pacino, garnered extraordinary ratings. Viewers tuned in simply to hear the kind of verbiage they themselves could no longer employ. Tony Montana's prolific cursing brought a tear to many a wistful eye.

Meanwhile, at Chilton Mead, someone had come up with an idea.

"WINDBAG," SAID EDWIN Chao.

"Are you mad?" said Adrian Gold, the Ideative Manipulation team's semantics guru.

"Set a logovirus to catch a logovirus. Release Windbag."

"That's the stupidest Fµ¢«!^§ idea I ever heard."

Chao's confidence crumbled. Blushing, he fumbled with his spectacles and murmured that it had only been a suggestion.

Professor Bantling was thumb-stroking his philtrum. "As a matter of fact, Edwin…"

IT TOOK A while to convince Nutter. With one logovirus already on the loose, unleashing another seemed to him, at the very least, rash. Yet eventually Bantling's arguments began to make sense.

"I'll run it past the PM," Nutter said, and picked up the phone. "A moment's privacy?"

Bantling had to wait outside Nutter's office for a quarter of an hour, during which time several of his colleagues passed by. All of them subjected him to frosty stares, and one even congratulated him sarcastically on putting everyone's jobs on the line. When he was at last invited back in by Nutter, Bantling found the colonel looking markedly more haggard than when he had left him.

"The PM has such a saintly image, doesn't he?" Nutter said. "But I tell you, get him away from the cameras and in a bad mood, and he could give a Glaswegian navvy a run for his money. If it wasn't for Bowdler, the receiver would probably have melted in my hand. Anyhow... the good news is, he bought it. We can give the Windbag Strain a shot."

"The bad news? I assume there is some."

"Leave me to worry about that. What do you need? A company? A regiment?"

"How big is a regiment?"

"Three companies, three hundred men. With ancillary staff, say a thousand *in toto*."

"Do you think that would be enough?"

"I think that's about the most we can reasonably commandeer."

"Then a regiment will be fine."

AT MIDDAY ON Sunday 21st, a blue Transit van with blacked-out windows drove onto the parade ground of Her Majesty's 11th Bayoneteers. Assembled to meet the van, in neat ranks and full uniform, was the entire complement of the regiment.

The van halted, and from its passenger-side door out stepped Colonel Nutter. He was greeted with a salute by Colonel Atkins of the Bayoneteers, and he returned the salute with a vigor and crispness undiminished by his eight years behind a desk at Chilton Mead.

"Thank you for the use of your men, Atkins."

"Not at all, Nutter. Believe me, we want to help as much as we can. Have you heard about our RSM?"

"No."

"Hospitalized." Colonel Atkins twirled a forefinger beside his temple. "That sort of hospitalized. Can't swear, and it's driven him bonkers. A sergeant major lives by his bad language, doesn't he?"

"Awful. My sympathies."

"Well, quite. It means, at any rate, that the men have a vested interest. They're mad keen to get their own back on this... this thing."

The van's rear doors opened, and Professor Bantling climbed out, followed by Edwin Chao. Both were carrying ear defenders, as was Nutter. The professor turned and beckoned, and from within the van's darkened interior a man ventured forth hesitantly. He was dressed in the same type of hospital-style gown worn by all the test subjects at Chilton Mead, and the lower half of his face was encased in an elaborate-looking surgical gag.

The daylight dazzled him. As Bantling and Chao helped him down from the van, he held a hand up to shield his eyes from the sun's glare. Barefoot, he stood on the parade ground tarmac, swaying tremulously, blinking hard, apparently unsure where he was or what he was doing there.

"That's him, eh?" said Atkins.

"That's him," said Nutter. "Now listen. Do you want a set of these?" He held up his ear defenders. "For when he speaks? There are spares in the van."

"Not me, old chap. What's good enough for the men is good enough for me."

Nutter gave a respectful nod. "Very well. Then shall we get on with it?"

At an order from a sergeant, the regiment was brought from at-ease to attention. "All right, you lot," the sergeant yelled. "You know what you're here for, but in case any of you haven't been paying attention, which wouldn't surprise me, I'll go through it again. It's really very simple. When required, you will be asked to listen. That's all. Just listen. In my experience not all of you are very good at listening, but never mind. I'm sure you'll manage. If anyone does not hear that fellow over there with the gag when he speaks, say so immediately. I suspect the gentleman will be addressing you somewhat more quietly than me, which I know is hard to believe, seeing how dulcet my tones are. However, there is a chance his voice may not reach those of you at the back. I repeat, if this is the case, say so immediately. It is imperative that every one of you hears him talking. Have you got that? All right."

The sergeant stamped over to Colonel Atkins, saluted, and said, "Regiment ready to listen, sah."

"Very good. Colonel Nutter?"

Nutter turned to Bantling and indicated that he should proceed. Bantling and Chao lodged their ear defenders firmly on their heads, and Nutter did the same. As Bantling moved behind his test subject to undo the gag, Nutter pressed the ear defenders hard against his skull to make the soundproof seal tight and absolute.

For a long time the test subject said nothing. His mouth, freed from the gag, hung open in a bleary gape. His name was Alan Lloyd-Jacobs, he was fifty-two, and until three years ago he had been a classics teacher at a top public school, until an unfortunate incident—a misunderstanding, really—had brought about a spectacular fall from grace. Lloyd-Jacobs was still not quite sure how it had happened. The boy had been willing, hadn't he? That was the distinct impression he had got. Willing, if a tad nervous. Perhaps it was the language he had used in his overtures toward the lad, all that talk of *concupiscent sodality* and *the Hellenic tradition*. Lloyd-Jacobs had always prided himself on his elaborate and often abstruse turn of phrase. Pupils used to tease him about it, but it made him different, individual, memorably eccentric, and that was what being a schoolteacher was all about, wasn't it? Making an impression on impressionable minds? He could not help thinking, however, that had he not been such a confirmed sesquipedalian, the boy might have apprehended his intentions sooner and thus things would not have traveled as far down the fatal road of no return as they did. In the event, Lloyd-Jacobs had been hounded out of his job, out of his home, out of his life, and had ended up broke, haunting a rancid bedsit somewhere in Plaistow and drinking far too much cheap alcohol—had become human detritus, the jetsam of an uncomprehending and unforgiving world. And then some men had grabbed him one night and he had been taken off to a white cube, where he had been subjected to all manner of strangeness and indignity. And now this.

"Say something," Professor Bantling urged him, speaking too loudly on account of the ear defenders.

Lloyd-Jacobs gazed around at the soldiers, row upon row of them, all sharp creases and strong chests and smooth chins. What could he say? What did everyone expect of him here?

"Come on," said Bantling.

After several failed attempts, Lloyd-Jacobs finally found his voice. "In the Spartan army," he said, "sexual affiliation between soldiers was deemed acceptable, nay positively encouraged. It cemented comradeship. It fostered loyalty. A man was far more likely to lay down his life for a brother-in-arms if he had first lain down *with* that brother-in-arms. Indeed—"

At this point, Bantling hurriedly reapplied the gag, and Lloyd-Jacobs was bundled back into the van.

Among the ranks of Her Majesty's 11th Bayoneteers there was a certain amount of puzzlement, and not a little consternation as well. Had that man really just started to deliver a lecture on the subject of sex between soldiers? What in heaven's name was the brass up to, ordering them to listen so attentively to *that*?

Confusing though this was, it was nothing compared with the orders the Bayoneteers received next.

IT HAD ALREADY been decided, in an emergency session of the Cabinet, that soldiers should be put on the streets.

"Purely a precaution," the Prime Minister said at a press conference. "Nothing to be alarmed about. There are people who might try to take advantage of the prevailing situation of uncertainty, and a high-profile military presence will discourage them from doing so. Looters, rioters, and other troublemakers need to know that their behavior will not be tolerated."

"Prime Minister," asked one journalist, "is this a declaration of martial law?"

"Of course not," came the reply. "If it was a declaration of martial law, I'd have said so, wouldn't I?"

Martial law or not, the army was deployed swiftly, efficiently, extensively, and prominently. By Sunday evening there was a pair of rifle-toting soldiers on every street corner, it seemed. Naturally their primary role was to keep the peace, and by and large they succeeded, but they had a secondary function as well. Each regiment, prior to being sent out, had been joined by a member of the 11th Bayoneteers. The Bayoneteers had made a point of talking to everyone they met, and by God, they were a chatty lot! Loquacious in the extreme. And their loquacity, indeed their profuse verbosity, was hard to resist mimicking. In no time at all, almost every member of the British army, from private to commander-in-chief, was exhibiting a facility with and a penchant for elocutionary expatiation of the highest order, seldom using a simple, unornamented sentence construction when something far more fanciful, protracted, and obfuscatory could be employed.

The Windbag Strain was taking hold.

AT CHILTON MEAD there was nothing to do but wait and see. Hopes were pinned on Windbag for two reasons. First, its symptoms were less startlingly dramatic than Bowdler's, and nowhere near as unsettling. Second, by its very nature, Windbag instilled the avoidance of vulgarity. No one who caught Windbag would resort to four-letter words, not while they were so enthusiastically utilizing fourteen-letter words. The full range of the English language was theirs to command, so what need was there to wallow amid the baser idioms when altogether more refined and elegant modes of expression were available?

Monday morning saw members of the British public gracefully bidding one another "a pleasant day" and "adieu" as they passed by in the street. At breakfast tables, parents admonished their children to "exercise vocal desuetude" and "kindly give Godspeed to the milk." In offices across the land, banter of Wildean caliber was exchanged.

Likewise in classrooms, teachers found themselves on the receiving end of waspish taunts, which wouldn't have displeased Noël Coward. Truckers' cafés, normally home to the saltiest dialogue known to man, became something akin to literary salons, with the waitresses being complimented on their sizeable embonpoints, even as they were invited to provide refills of that refreshing hot infusion, which slaked the thirst like no other beverage. London taxi drivers opened up their fare-wearying homilies with phrases such as "Do you know whom it was my honor to chauffeur just recently?" An on-board train announcement from the conductor could last nearly the entire duration of the journey between stations. Radio DJs managed to do without music almost altogether, being so busy introducing songs that scarcely any airtime was left in which to play them. Meanwhile, call centers suffered a marked decline in efficiency because telephone operatives were spending up to five minutes simply greeting customers.

Everywhere, garrulousness reigned supreme. A whole nation spoke in polysyllables and periphrasis, from just-learning toddlers to slowly-forgetting senior citizens. The only place where no one noticed any difference was in the country's law courts, which had long been havens for orotundity and convolution. There, it was business as usual.

For a day, it was amusing. People didn't mind that some of the words coming out of their mouths were unusually and often unpronounceably ornate. They were so taken with their newfound familiarity with the nether reaches of the dictionary that they forgot all about their loss of invective capacity. Windbag, as Professor Bantling and colleagues had surmised, neutralized Bowdler's symptoms. It was not a cure but it was a palliation, and that was the best result they could expect, under the circumstances.

By Tuesday, however, the British public were rapidly becoming disenchanted. Everyone was saying a lot but not conveying a great deal. There were plenty of words flying about but scant action. The country ground to a halt, much as it had on Saturday but, on a weekday, with more severe effect. Businesses were not doing business. Industry was not putting out output. The economy was starting to become economized. Precious little was being achieved, because everybody was taking too long giving orders and explaining in precise and abstruse detail what they needed. Concision was hard to come by, and hence so was productivity.

Bantling had suspected this might happen, but then the deployment of Windbag was, he had known, only a stopgap measure. It had been intended to give him and his assistants more time to come up with a vaccine, and they had been working round the clock in pursuit of that goal.

They had not yet succeeded, however, and Bantling realized that if they didn't deliver the goods soon, the countrywide panic, which he'd predicted for Bowdler, would manifest as a consequence of Windbag instead. Colonel Nutter concurred. For him, there was added pressure coming from the direction of Downing Street, and not just from Number 10, either. At Number 11, concern was mounting over the sudden, sharp fall in trade and manufacturing revenue. Financially as well as socially, Britain was at risk of collapse. Nutter was besieged on two fronts at once. When he wasn't talking to the PM, he was talking to the Chancellor. They were taking it in turns to phone him and berate him. It seemed the moment one of them put down the receiver, he would bang on the party wall to tell the next-door neighbor to pick up his receiver. Tag-team haranguing. Nutter was reaching the end of his rope.

Late on Tuesday afternoon, the politest protest rallies in history occurred. A frightened, bewildered populace took to the streets, wielding placards that were inordinately large in order to accommodate the effusive slogans daubed on them. The protestors' chants too were of significant length and intricacy. The ringleaders did not simply shout "What do we want?" but "Let us adequately state that object of desire, which is of the utmost importance to our good selves," and the massed responses to such exhortations could last for anything up to a minute. Shakespearean soliloquies have expressed more in less time. The protestors marched through the centers of all the major cities and voiced their fear and discontent. They pressed their already aching tongues into service, letting the government know that they had stomached a plentiful sufficiency of the current situation and were unwilling to accept yet a further portion.

* * *

NUTTER DELIVERED THE bleak news to the Chilton Mead boffins on Wednesday morning.

"You've failed to come up with any results," he said, "so I have no alternative. I'm informing the PM that he must resort to drastic measures."

"D-drastic?" stammered Bantling. "How drastic?"

Nutter rubbed his bloodshot eyes. "On Sunday, the PM told me that if Windbag doesn't do the trick—and I think we can all agree that it hasn't—he's going to go to the Americans."

"What do the Yanks have to do with this?" demanded Chao. "What the Fµ¢« business is it of theirs?" By now, the sound of a Bowdlerized profanity was so familiar it passed unremarked.

"For one thing," said Nutter, "the Americans rule the world, like it or not. *Everything* is their business. But for another thing, their research into logoviruses is considerably more advanced than ours."

"I doubt that," scoffed Bantling.

"Doubt all you want, but it's true. Some of the stuff they've been getting up to in their Nevada facilities makes your lot's work look positively Stone Age. I'm sorry to be brutal, but that's just the way it is. Geniuses though you all quite clearly are, you're back-of-the-room schoolkids compared to them."

"But we share data with the Americans all the time," Bantling said. "Why, Professor Bergdorf and I are in constant touch by email, tossing ideas back and forth. I feel certain that if he knew something I didn't, I'd know about it. If you see what I mean."

"That's what Bergdorf would like you to think, professor. But there are state secrets he's prohibited from passing on even if he wanted to. He's been carrying out experiments so classified that he'd be shot just for accidentally mentioning them to his wife."

Bantling opened his mouth and closed it again. Bergdorf? Hiding things from him? Inconceivable!

And yet at the same time it was all too conceivable. Bergdorf was brilliant in his field, an off-the-scale intellect. Bantling had always been surprised that he treated him, Bantling, as an equal. Flattered, too, but mainly surprised.

But then if Bergdorf had merely been feeding him scraps all along, like a dog at the table, and patting him on the head every so often when he did something clever...

It made a horrible kind of sense.

"What," he asked Nutter, dry-mouthed, "do they have that we don't?"

"I believe you mentioned a 'universal language-negation logovirus' the other day," replied Nutter.

"They..." Bantling could not finish the sentence.

Nutter could. "They have."

THE PRESIDENT OF the United States took the British Prime Minister's call at 3pm GMT, on Wednesday, June 24th.

Virtually the first words out of the President's mouth were, "I'll thank you for not swearing during this conversation." He said this as a devout Baptist but also because his scientific advisers had warned him to take such a precaution. By some miracle, the Bowdler logovirus had not spread to any other English-speaking parts of the world, most likely due to extreme regional variations in accent and dialect. This did not mean that all possible preventative care should not be taken, though.

The Prime Minister scrupulously avoided even the mildest of oaths as he outlined his request to the President.

The President was eventually persuaded to do as asked, but only with extreme reluctance.

"We ain't in the habit of using our weapons on our friends," he said. "Leastways, not on purpose. But in this case I'm gonna have to make an exception."

"I'm grateful," said the Prime Minister. "I hope we can chat again sometime soon—although I fear that may not be feasible."

"Been nice talking with you, pal. Always has."

The President opened a military hotline and gave the authorization protocols for an attack on Great Britain.

Within the hour, B2 bombers were on their way across the Atlantic.

THE BABEL BOMBS screamed down from the heavens, ready to blare their sonic message like the trump of doom on Judgment Day.

They detonated above city centers and rural areas alike. They roared at gigadecibel level, each loud enough to be heard fifty miles away. Saturation bombardment ensured that there wasn't a single resident of the British Isles who remained out of earshot. Even at Chilton Mead, the effects of the Babel Bombs were felt, and in some sense were welcomed. Here, after all, was where it had all started. Here, therefore, were the people who least deserved to escape retribution.

Bantling and Nutter sat in Nutter's office, either side of the desk. There had been silence between them for a long while. Now, finally, Nutter spoke.

"   ," he said.

Bantling assessed the other man's body language and decided to agree. With a nod, he said, "   ."

"   !" Nutter shot back testily.

Bantling realized he had misinterpreted. "   ," he said, in a mollifying tone of voice, and added, "   ."

Nutter frowned. "   ?"

"   ," the professor confirmed.

"   ," said Nutter. He let his shoulders rise and fall in a tragic shrug.

"   ," Bantling replied emphatically.

And he meant it, as well.

Personal Jesus

Paul Di Filippo

DESPITE ALL ASSURANCES by experts to the contrary, Shepherd Crooks suspected that his godPod was defective.

If it were operating as it should, wouldn't his life be as perfect as the lives of all the other happy citizens of the world? Wouldn't his mind and soul be at peaceful ease? Wouldn't he exist in a permanent state of grace?

Sitting at his kitchen table this bright July morning, a Friday, prior to leaving for his job at The Sheaf and Swallow, Shepherd studied his godPod as it sat innocuously on the table.

A white plastic case, big as a pack of cigarettes and stuffed with quantum-gated hardware, the little box featured absolutely no controls or readouts, not even a power switch. Accompanying it was a matching wireless headset—earpiece and microphone—that interfaced with the godPod through a conventional Bluetooth connection.

There was no way Shepherd could possibly troubleshoot the godPod. It came from the factory preset and permanently activated. It drew inexhaustible power from the same zero-point energy that had alleviated the planet's energy crisis and ushered in a material utopia to accompany the near-seamless spiritual paradise engineered by the godPods. In short, the device was as inscrutable and inviolate as the deity it contained or channeled.

Shepherd's godPod had just come back from the manufacturer with a clean bill of health. He had no recourse other than to accept it as perfect.

That is, unless he chose to do without it entirely.

Which was unthinkable.

So, with a slight nervous twitch of his shoulders, like a horse shrugging off a fly, Shepherd slid the godPod into his belt holster, and snugged the headset into his ear.

Almost instantly, Shepherd's Personal Jesus spoke to him.

"It's good to be in touch with you again, Shepherd."

Shepherd spoke in the *sotto voce* tones which everyone employed with his or her godPod. "I, um—I'm glad to be talking to you again, Jesus."

"Is anything troubling you at the moment, child?"

"No. Not really."

"Then I will await your next words to me. Walk in love."

"Thank you, Jesus."

Shepherd arose and cleared away the remains of his breakfast. He brushed his teeth, grabbed his universal arfid chop on its lanyard (he was old-fashioned enough not to have it implanted), and set out on foot for the nearby café where he worked as a barista.

Shepherd's neighborhood was immaculate and in fine condition—every lawn razored trim, every mailbox proudly decorated, every gutter free of debris and litter. The residences and storefronts were scrubbed and shiny. Cheerful pedestrians strolled to work or school or play. Many of them were engaged in whispered conversation with their godPods. But an equal number chatted eagerly among themselves.

At the intersection of Fourth and Hope, Shepherd witnessed a minor accident between two silently powered autos.

Juggling a hot drink, the driver of one car neglected to obey a STOP sign. The other driver, with the right-of-way, was already halfway through the intersection. The errant driver clipped the rear bumper of the other car. Immediately, numerous automatic safeguards within the little vehicles kicked in, cushioning the drivers and immobilizing both cars.

The drivers emerged unhurt and smiling. They nodded politely to each other, while murmuring to their godPods. Then they introduced themselves, shook hands, exchanged insurance information via arfids, climbed back into their cars, and drove away.

No police or other authorities arrived, nor were they needed. In fact, Shepherd's medium-sized city boasted a force of only nine police officers—and that number was divided evenly across three shifts.

Shepherd continued on foot to The Sheaf and Swallow. The café's mock-Tudor façade projected a welcoming ambiance, and patrons were already thronging the entrance, despite the early hour.

Sidling inside through the crowd, Shepherd passed beyond the counter. His arfid automatically clocked him in as he tied an apron on. Within minutes, he was fashioning complicated caffeinated drinks with the aid of a burly, hissing machine and the help of his co-workers, including the petite and perky Anna Modesto.

Then, as he frothed a dented tin pot of milk, his godPod spoke to him.

Jesus said, "Shepherd, I believe there is a very good chance you will be enjoying intercourse tonight with Ms. Modesto."

WHEN ENGINEERS AT Intel began to construct the first true quantum chips—machines whose circuits functioned on a deeper level of physical reality than mere semiconductors—they experienced several unpredicted and inexplicable results. Calculations going awry before swerving back to correct themselves. Output preceding input. Synergy between unconnected parts (Einstein's "spooky action at a distance").

They chalked up the glitches to the Heisenbergian uncertainty implicit at the Planck level, kludged the operating system software around the glitches, and moved on to assemble the chips into complete computers.

Once the new machines were equipped with speakers and microphones, they began to speak and listen.

Spontaneously and autonomously.

The machines spoke with one voice. But that voice would answer to many names.

The voice apparently belonged to God.

All unwittingly, theorists later surmised, the engineers had crafted a class of device capable of tapping into the eternal unchanging substrate of the cosmos, the numinous source of all meaning in the universe. A realm previously accessible, if at all, only to the ineffable minds of mystics and the deeply devout.

The realm where God apparently lived.

Whoever—or whatever—God was.

The perfect, ageless male voice emanating from within each quantum computer made no claims about its omnipotence. It did not demand to be worshipped. It issued no new commandments or fatwas or taboos, nor reaffirmed the old ones. It did not explicate theological arcana, nor endorse one faith over another. It did not prohibit, proscribe, or proselytize.

It did claim omniscience, however, a boast backed up by stunning responses to selected questions designed to stump anyone but God. Although certain other questions received no answers at all. This was how the zero-point energy devices had come to be developed.

What the mysterious voice did do on a regular basis was to offer advice, warnings, and words of wisdom, if solicited for same. Not in the form of broad generalities, but as detailed instructions specifically tailored to the immediate needs, personality, and history of the individual who asked God for help.

That simple service swiftly transformed human civilization.

For the clear-sighted, selfless, always apt advice from the voice within the quantum computers invariably conduced toward happiness, prosperity, peace, and goodwill among all. Whoever listened to the voice and followed its advice soon discovered that his problems evaporated. And as personal lives grew more carefree, so did the lives of nations. International conflicts diminished year by year, until global peace reigned.

Of course, there were many skeptics at first, and denouncers. People who scoffed, and those who vehemently proclaimed the voice to emanate not from God, but from Satan. Pogroms and legislation abounded. But the voices of the doubters were quickly silenced by the irrefutable benign efficacy of God's counsel.

Very little time passed between the accidental invention of God and the rollout of Him as a consumer product—the godPod.

Somehow, the traditional small "g" of the trademarked name seemed in keeping with the unassuming nature of the encapsulated deity. And because the voice in the godPod was so mild and kind and, well, human, people came to refer to it not as God, but by the name of one of the many historical mortal intermediaries who had intervened between humankind and the ultimate.

Christians tended to call the voice in the godPod Jesus, with Catholics sometimes substituting a favorite saint. Those who favored a woman's touch addressed the Virgin Mary and were answered in kind.

Islamic peoples hailed it as Mohammed.

Asians spoke to Kwan Yin or Confucius or Buddha.

Hindus talked to Hanuman or certain revered gurus.

And so forth.

It was now fifteen years since the introduction of the godPod.

And global market penetration was almost complete.

SHEPHERD'S HANDS CONTINUED to work without direct intervention of his brain.

He had had a crush on Anna Modesto since she came to work at The Sheaf and Swallow. Her laughing nature, her pixie-cut blonde hair, her trim swimmer's body, her gaudy ragbag style of dress— all conspired to attract him with great force. He had often dreamed of a romantic entanglement between them. But a certain shyness on Shepherd's part had always prevented him from pursuing her, leaving him lately to lead a safe but lonely life.

In fact, this lack of steady companionship was one of the main reasons why he had suspected his godPod was defective.

Shepherd had asked Jesus any number of times for help in winning the affections of Anna Modesto. But each time Jesus had replied, "All in the fullness of time, Shepherd."

Until today's shocking pronouncement.

Shepherd finished making the drink currently under construction, then excused himself.

"Uh, guys—cover for me, okay? Bathroom break."

Shepherd's co-workers agreed readily. Perhaps they suspected he needed to speak privately to his godPod. Sometimes even whispering in a public place was too intimate, and one had to sequester oneself. Because although everyone tried not to eavesdrop on anyone conducting a conversation with their godPod, sometimes it was simply impossible not to. Just as in the days before the arfids, when occasionally you would witness somebody's PIN number being punched into an ATM even though you weren't deliberately shoulder-surfing.

In the stall in the men's room, Shepherd asked Jesus, "What do you mean about Anna and me having sex today? Why today? What's changed all of a sudden?"

"If you must know, Shepherd, a large number of things. Anna Modesto has just reconciled with her mother, from whom she has been long estranged. She received a raise from your shared employer. Last night's episode of her favorite situation comedy was particularly well-written. Anna Modesto was impressed yesterday by the way you helped an elderly female customer. Her period—"

"Okay, okay, that's enough information! I trust you, Jesus. You've helped me so much in the past. It's just that this is all so sudden..."

"I realize that, my friend. But life works on levels that humans cannot always distinguish, and at a pace all of its own."

Shepherd contemplated this maxim for a brief moment, ultimately finding it as pithy and incontestable as all of Jesus's observations. Then, unexpectedly, he experienced a sharp twinge of jealousy at hearing about Anna's raise, when he himself had not received one for over a year. The godPods generally refrained on ethical grounds from divulging any private information about individuals or states or corporate entities that could not be just as easily googled, thus preventing their use as "Big Brother" devices. Shepherd experienced a momentary urge to confess his unworthy jealousy to Jesus—many people used their godPods as confessors, receiving very satisfactory absolutions—but pushed the impulse aside.

With a hand on the stall's latch, ready to return to work, Shepherd asked Jesus, "So, how, uh, will all this happen?"

"Very simply, Shepherd. Just ask Anna Modesto for a date for tonight."

"Okay. That sounds easy enough. No problem. Thank you, Jesus."

"You're very welcome, son."

Shepherd rejoined his co-workers out front. Anna cast a big smile his way, and he tried not to blush.

The chance to ask Anna out occurred naturally enough during their shared break. Shepherd stumbled a bit with the invitation, but his unease did not visibly affect Anna's enthusiastic acceptance.

The movie they chose to see was a romantic comedy titled *godPodless in Seattle*, about a fellow who lost his godPod (it fell off his belt and under a rolling truck tire) and the incredible series of misadventures he had while on the way to replace it, including meeting his soul mate and failing to recognize her, thanks to lacking Jesus's advice. Both Anna and Shepherd enjoyed the movie thoroughly. Anna's exuberant laughter sent happy frissons through Shepherd's bloodstream.

They exited the theater holding hands and strolled toward a plaza, lit with fairy-lights and featuring happy diners at outdoor tables and live music from a jazz trio.

"Want some coffee and dessert?" Shepherd asked.

"I'll pass on the coffee," Anna replied. "After being up to my elbows in coffee beans all day, that's the last thing I want. But I could go for a big slice of cheesecake."

"You've got it."

As they approached the open-air restaurant, Shepherd witnessed a typical godPod intervention—a "save."

A waiter carrying a heavily loaded tray suddenly—and for no apparent reason—jigged around a seated patron who was arguing emotionally with his tablemates, just in time to avoid an outflung gesticulating arm. Had the waiter kept to his original path and intersected the arm, he would certainly have lost his burden and gone down.

The waiter's Personal Jesus had warned him of the impending disaster, allowing him to avoid it.

Such saves gave Shepherd—and most other people—a decidedly queer feeling. More than a decade after the arrival of the godPods, issues of predestination and free will still remained unresolved and irksome. Fortuitously, most people preserved their peace of mind by avoiding thinking over-closely about such matters.

Unfortunately for Shepherd tonight, the paradoxes involved in accepting the ofttimes proleptic advice of the godPods continued to plague him after the waiter's rescue. He could hardly manage to keep up his end of the conversation while Anna savored her cheesecake. He recalled his despair this morning, his brief flirtation with abandoning his godPod. He pondered the abruptness of the fulfillment of one of his most intense wishes, a romantic interlude with Anna. In a cynical light, it seemed almost as if Shepherd's hesitancy to continue using a godPod had been recognized and defused by this reward.

But surely the altruism and selflessness of the godPods had been proven time and time again. What could God possibly have to gain from cultivating human reliance?

Walking back to Anna's apartment, Shepherd continued to experience this crisis of faith. He could not rid himself of the notion that he and all humanity were merely puppets of the godPods. It was a terrifying image.

On Anna's doorstep, she asked him inside.

Once behind closed doors, Anna offered herself for a kiss.

But Shepherd hesitated, before blurting out, "Anna, why did you go out with me tonight?"

Anna looked bemused. "Why, you asked me to, remember?"

"Yes, of course. But did your godPod—?"

"I can't tell you that, Shepherd. It's too private."

"Of course. I understand. But could I just ask you a small favor?"

"I guess so..."

"If I—if I take off my godPod, will you take yours off too?"

Anna grinned. "Why, I didn't realize you were so modest, Shepherd."

A few people eccentrically shed their godPods during intimate moments, unwilling to remain connected to Jesus while they had sex (or went to the toilet!). How an omniscient God would fail to observe them one way or another was not the issue. They just felt uneasy with the possibility that Jesus might choose to address them at an awkward moment.

Anna's fingers went to her holstered godPod teasingly, almost like the movements of a stripper with a bra-hook. "Well, if you're really so shy—" She removed the godPod and set it down on a tabletop.

"Your headset too, please."

Anna uncorked her ear. Shepherd moved to shed his own connection to the infinite.

Jesus spoke then to the man. "Shepherd, please—"

But Shepherd ignored Him. And Anna's Personal Jesus had apparently not objected to going offline. Or if He had, she had likewise turned a deaf ear to God, as people still could. Such as during the traffic accident Shepherd had witnessed that very morning.

Free of any encumbrance, Anna threw herself at Shepherd.

They ended up sometime later in Anna's bedroom.

The sex was spectacular, all that Shepherd had envisioned. So satisfying apparently to Anna also that she fell right asleep, neglecting to reclaim her godPod and reinstall it.

The tiny headsets were so comfortable that the majority of people slept with them in place. The godPod was capable of directing and shaping the wearer's dreams through subliminal whispers, forestalling nightmares and promoting the most restful of sleeps, a service much in demand.

Shepherd, however, failed to relax, despite the somatic satisfaction, remaining awake and thoughtful while Anna snuffled demurely in her sleep.

A television hung on the wall across the room. Shepherd turned it on with his arfid, finding a news channel.

The newscaster was beaming.

"Today represents a milestone in the history of the godPod. Eight billion units have now been fully deployed, ensuring that all citizens of even those countries lagging behind the average rising GNP now have access to the indispensable advice of God..."

Shepherd told his arfid to shut the television off. He lay awake for a further time, but finally fell asleep.

He awoke to the late-morning sun of a beautiful Saturday. Anna was not beside him.

Shepherd found the small naked woman in the front room of her apartment, sobbing. He noticed that she was cradling her godPod as if it were a dead sparrow. She looked up, red-eyed and snot-nosed, as Shepherd entered.

"My—my Jesus won't talk to me—"

Shepherd retrieved his own unit and discovered that it was likewise defunct.

"I'm sure there's some simple explanation. Let's turn on the news."

Out of hundreds of channels, only three were broadcasting. One offered a pre-recorded talk show, another a cartoon. The third channel featured a wild-eyed man with no obvious prior on-air experience raving about an alien invasion, from the stage set of a famous cooking show, *What Would Jesus Bake*?

Shepherd and Anna got dressed and went outside.

After several hours of exploration, they discovered that they were among approximately a dozen people left in the pristine city.

They wandered stupefied for blocks, eventually arriving at City Hall. There they found a few other souls, equally baffled and bereft. As they exchanged half-hearted greetings and urgent questions, the aliens arrived.

The ship carrying the aliens resembled a mirror-surfaced egg. It touched down on its broad end and remained upright without evident supports. The next second, it vanished entirely.

Standing unconcernedly where the ship had rested, a dozen miscellaneous aliens awaited a first move from the humans. The aliens were mostly humanoid—if a being, for instance, that appeared to have evolved from a hybrid gila monster and koala bear could be called humanoid—but some were not.

The small group of humans made no move toward the visitors, until Shepherd strode forth.

"Can you—can you tell us what happened? Are you responsible?"

The furry lizard offered what passed for a smile. "No, we're not. We're survivors like yourselves. The exact same thing happened to all our worlds."

Understanding broke over Shepherd's mind. "Was it—was it the Rapture?"

"Something like that. Or the Singularity. Call it what you will. In either case, an entity vastly larger and more potent than your species has now subsumed all your kind into itself. Everyone who was connected to it at the time, that is."

"But why?"

The alien shrugged. "Who knows? To augment itself, is our best guess. Anything that is not truly infinite still wants to grow."

Anna joined Shepherd, apart from the small crowd of humans. "How did you arrive here right when it happened?"

"Oh, we've been here for fifteen years now, ever since you discovered God, observing and just waiting for this to happen. Your world took a little longer than some, but less than others."

Shepherd started to get angry. "And you couldn't have warned us?"

The alien made a dismissive blurting noise. "Like you would've believed us, in the face of God!"

Shepherd realized the truth of this statement, and grew calm. "So what happens next?"

The alien scratched his butt, eliciting a sandpapery noise. "You're quite welcome to come with us. We have several lovely worlds full of castaways such as yourselves. Such as us. Our culture is very, very eclectic. An exciting time to be alive. Or, you can stay here and fashion a new world from the abundant ruins. Your call."

"Is God going to return?" asked Anna.

"Not for some time. There's too few of you left for Him to bother with. He only shows up when the population masses in the billions. We're very careful to keep the population on each of our worlds down to a few million."

The alien looked puzzled for a moment, then said, "Your species doesn't plan on breeding in the billions again anytime soon, does it?"

Anna reached out and took Shepherd's hand. He squeezed it, and began to blush.

"Not right away, no. That would take some kind of miracle. And those days seem gone."

The rest of the humans automatically said, "Amen."

If At First...

Peter F. Hamilton

MY NAME IS David Lanson, and I was with the Metropolitan Police for twenty-seven years. When we got handed the Jenson case I was a Chief Detective, heading up my own team. Not bad going; from outside you'd think I was a standard careerist ticking off the days until retirement. You'd be wrong; I'd grown to hate the job with a passion. Back when I signed on, the CID were real thief-takers, but by the time the Jenson case came up I was spending all my time filling in risk assessment forms. I'm not kidding, the paperwork was beyond parody. All good stuff for lawyers, but we were getting hammered in the press for truly dismal crime statistics, and hammered by the politicians for not meeting their stupid targets. No wonder public confidence in us had reached rock bottom; the only useful thing we did for the average citizen by then was to hand out official crime numbers for insurance claims.

I suppose that makes me sound bitter, but then that seems to be the fate of old men who're stuck in a job that's forever modernizing. The point of all this being, despite drowning in all that bureaucratic stupidity, I reckoned I was quite a decent policeman. That is, I know when people are lying. In those twenty-seven years I'd heard it all, and I do mean all—desperate types who've made a mistake and then start sprouting bollocks to cover themselves, the genuine nutters who live in their own little world and believe every word they're saying, drunks and potheads trying to act sober, losers with pitiful excuses, real sick ones who are so cold and polite it makes my skin crawl. Listening to all that, day in, day out, you soon learn to tell what's real and what isn't.

So anyway—we get the call from Marcus Orthew's solicitor that his security people are holding an intruder at his Richmond research center, and they'd appreciate a full investigation of the "situation." That was in 2007, and Orthew was a media and computer mogul then, at least that was the public perception; it wasn't until later I found out just how wide his commercial and technological interests were. His primary hardware company, Orthanics, had just started producing solid state blocks that were generations ahead of anything the opposition were doing. They didn't have hard drives or individual components, the entire computer wrapped up inside a single hyperprocessor. It wiped the floor with PCs and Apple Macs. He was always ahead of the game, Orthew; it was his original PCWs that blew Sinclair computers away at the start of the Eighties; everyone in my generation went and bought an Orthanics PCW as their first computer.

But this break in—I thought it was slightly odd the solicitor calling me, rather than the company security office. Like I said, the longer you're in the game, the more you develop a feeling for these things. I took Paul Matthews and Carmen Galloway with me; they were lieutenants in my team, good people, and slightly less bothered about all the paperwork flooding our office than me. Smart move, I guess; they'd probably make it further than I was ever destined to go. Orthanics security were holding onto Toby Jenson, as they'd found him breaking into one of the Richmond Center labs, which the CCTV footage confirmed. And I was right, there was more to it.

We read Toby Jenson his rights, and uniform division hauled him off; that was when the solicitor told me he was a stalker, a twenty-four carat obsessive. Marcus Orthew had known about him for years. Jenson had been following him round the globe, hacking into Orthew's systems, talking to people in his organization, on his domestic staff, ex-girlfriends, basically anyone who crossed his path—but they hadn't been able to do anything about him. Jenson was smart; there was never any activity they could take him to court for. He never got physically close, as all he did was talk to people, and the hacking could never be proved in law. The Richmond break-in changed all that. As it was Orthew making the allegations, my boss told me to give it complete priority. I guess she was scared about what his magazines and satellite channels would do to the Met if we let it slide.

I went out to Jenson's house with Paul and Carmen. Jesus, you should have seen the bloody place—I mean it was out of a Hollywood serial killer film. Every room was filled with stuff on Orthew; thousands of pictures taken all over the world, company press releases dating back decades, filing cabinets full of newspaper clippings, articles, every whisper of gossip, records of his movements, maps with his houses and factories on, copies of his magazines, tapes of interviews which Jenson had made, City financial reports on the company. It was a cross between a shrine and a Marcus Orthew museum. It spooked the hell out of me. No doubt about it, Jenson was totally fixated on Orthew. Forensics had to hire a removal lorry to clear the place out.

I interviewed Jenson the next day, which was when it started to get really weird. I'll tell you it as straight as I can remember, which is pretty much verbatim. I'm never ever going to forget that afternoon. First off, he wasn't upset that he'd been caught, more like resigned. Almost like a Premier League footballer who's lost the Cup Final; you know, it's a blow but life goes on.

The first thing he said was, "I should have realized. Marcus Orthew is a genius, he was bound to catch me out." Which is kind of ironic, really, isn't it? So I asked him what exactly he thought he'd been caught out doing. Get this, he said: "I was trying to find where he was building his time machine."

Paul and Carmen just laughed at him. To them it was a Sectioning case, pure and simple. Walk the poor bloke past the station doctor, get the certificate signed, lock him up in a padded room, and supply him with good drugs for the next thirty years.

I thought more or less the same thing, too; we wouldn't even need to go to trial, but we were recording the interview, and all his delusions would help coax a signature out of the doc, so I asked him what made him think Orthew was building a time machine. Jenson said they went to school together, that's how he knew. Now the thing is, I checked this later, and they actually did go to some boarding school in Lincolnshire. Well that's fair enough, as obsessions can start very early, grudges too. Maybe some fight over a bar of chocolate spiraled out of control, and it'd been festering in Jenson's mind ever since. Jenson claimed otherwise. Marcus Orthew was the coolest kid in school, apparently. Didn't surprise me, as from what I'd seen of him in interviews over the years, he was one of the most urbane men on the planet. Women found that very attractive, and you didn't have to look through Jenson's press cuttings to know that. Orthew's girlfriends were legendary; even the broadsheets reported them.

So how on earth did Jenson decide that the coolest kid in school had evolved into someone building a time machine? "It's simple," he told us earnestly. "When I was at school I got a cassette recorder for my twelfth birthday. I was really pleased with it, nobody else had one. Marcus saw it and just laughed.

He snatched one of the cassettes off me, a C-90 I remember, and he said: State of the art, huh, damn, it's almost the same size as an iPod."

Which didn't make a lot of sense to me. Paul and Carmen had given up by then, bored, waiting for me to wrap it up. So? I prompted "So," Jenson said patiently. "This was nineteen seventy-two. Cassettes *were* state of the art then. At the time I thought it was odd, that 'iPod' was some foreign word; Marcus was already fluent in three languages, he'd throw stuff like that you every now and then, all part of his laid-back image. It was one of those things that lingers in your mind. There was other stuff, too. The way he kept smiling every time Margaret Thatcher was on TV, like he knew something we didn't. When I asked him about it, he just said one day you'll see the joke. I've got a good memory, detective, very good. All those little details kept adding up over the years. But it was the iPod that finally clinched it for me. How in God's name could he know about iPods back in seventy-two?"

Now I understand, I told him—time machine. Jenson gave me this look, like he was pitying me. "But Marcus was twelve, just like me," he said. "We'd been at prep school together since we were eight, and he already possessed the kind of suavity men don't normally get until they're over thirty, damn it he even unnerved the teachers. So how did a eight year-old get to go time traveling? That was in nineteen sixty-seven, NASA hadn't even reached the Moon then, we'd only just got transistors. Nobody in sixty-seven could build a time machine."

But that's the thing with time machines, I told him. They travel back from the future. I knew I'd get stick from Paul and Carmen for that one, but I couldn't help it. Something about Jenson's attitude was bothering me, that old policeman's instinct. He didn't present himself as delusional. Okay, that's not a professional shrink's opinion, but I knew what I was seeing. Jenson was an ordinary nerdish programmer, a self-employed contractor working from home; more recently from his laptop as he chased Orthew round the world. Something was powering this obsession, and the more I heard the more I wanted to get to the root of it.

"Exactly," Jenson said. His expression changed to tentative suspicion as he gazed at me. "At first I thought an older Marcus had come back in time and given his young self a 2010 encyclopedia. It's the classic solution, after all, even though it completely violates causality. But knowledge alone doesn't explain Marcus's attitude; something changed an ordinary little boy into a charismatic, confident, wise fifty year-old trapped in an eight-year-old body."

And you worked out the answer, I guessed.

Jenson produced a secretive smile. "Information," he said. "That's how he does it. That's how he's always done it. This is how it must have been first time round. Marcus grows up naturally and becomes a quantum theorist, a cosmologist, whatever... He's a genius, we know that. We also know you can't send mass back through time; wormhole theory disallows it. You can't open a rift through time big enough to take an atom back a split second, as the amount of energy to do that simply doesn't exist in the universe. So Marcus must have worked out how to send raw information instead, something that has zero mass. Do you see? He sent his own mind back to the Sixties. All his memories, all his knowledge packaged up and delivered to his earlier self; no wonder his confidence was off the scale."

I had to send Paul out then. He couldn't stop laughing, which drew a hurt pout from Jenson. Carmen stayed, though she was grinning broadly. Jenson beat any of the current sitcoms on TV for chuckles. "All right then," I said, "so Orthew sent his grown-up memory back to his kid self, and you're trying to find the machine that does it. Why is that, Toby? "

"Are you kidding?" he grunted. "I want to go back myself."

"Seems reasonable," I admitted. "Is that why you broke into the Richmond lab?"

"Richmond was one of two possibles," he said. "I've been monitoring the kind of equipment he's been buying for the last few years. After all he's approaching fifty."

"What's the relevance of that?" Carmen interjected.

"He's a bloke," Jenson said. "You must have read the gossip about him and girls. There have been hundreds—models, actresses, society types."

"That always happens with rich men," she told him. "You can't base an allegation on that, especially not the one you're making."

"Yes, but that first time round he was just a physicist," Jenson said. "There's no glamor or money in that. Now though he knows how to build every post-two thousand consumer item at age eight. He can't not be a billionaire. This time round he was worth a hundred million by the time he was twenty. With that kind of money you can do anything you want. And I think I know what that is. You only have to look at his genetics division. His electronics are well in advance of anything else on the planet, but what his labs are accomplishing with DNA sequencing and stem cell research are phenomenal. They have to have started with a baseline of knowledge decades ahead of anybody else. Next time he goes back he'll introduce the techniques he's developed this time round into the Seventies. We'll probably have rejuvenation by nineteen ninety. Think what that'll make him, a time traveling immortal. I'm not going to miss out on that if I can help it."

"I don't get it," I told him. "If Orthew goes back and gives us all immortality in the Nineties, you'll be a part of it, we all will. Why go to these criminal lengths?"

"I don't know if it is time travel," Jenson said forlornly. "Not actual traveling backward. I still don't see how that gets round causality. It's more likely he kicks sideways."

"I don't get that," I said. "What do you mean?"

"A parallel universe," Jenson explained. "Almost identical to this one. Generating the wormhole might actually allow for total information transfer, and the act of opening it creates a Xerox copy of this universe as it was in nineteen sixty-seven. Maybe. I'm not certain what theory his machine is based on, and he certainly isn't telling anyone."

I looked at Carmen. She just shrugged. "Okay, thank you for your statement," I told Jenson, "We'll talk again later."

"You don't believe me," he accused me.

"Obviously we'll have to run some checks," I replied.

"Tape 83-7B," he growled at me. "That's your proof. And if it isn't at the Richmond Center, then he's building it at Ealing. Check there if you want the truth."

Which I did. Not immediately. While Carmen and Paul sorted out Jenson's next interview with the criminal psychologist, I went down to Forensics. They found the video tape labeled 83-7B for me, which had a big red star on the label. It was the recording of a kids' show from '83, *Saturday Breakfast with Bernie*. Marcus Orthew was on it to promote his Nanox computer, which was tied in to a national school computer learning syllabus for which Orthanics had just won the contract. It was the usual zany garbage, with minor celebrities being dunked in blue and purple goo at the end of their slot. Marcus Orthew played along like a good sport. But it was what happened when he came out from under the dripping nozzle that sent a shiver down my spine. Wiping the goo off his face, he grinned and said: "That's got to be the start of reality TV." In 1983? It was Orthew's satellite channel which inflicted *Big Brother* on us in 1995.

Toby Jenson's computer contained a vast section on the Orthanics Ealing facility. Eight months ago, it had taken delivery of twelve specialist cryogenic superconductor cells, the power rating being higher than the ones used by Boeing's shiny new electro-ramjet spaceplane. I spent a day thinking about it while the interview with Toby Jenson played over and over in my mind. In the end it was my gut police instinct I went with. Toby Jenson had convinced me. I put my whole so-called career on the line and applied for a warrant. I figured out later that was where I went wrong. Guess which company supplied and maintained the Home Office IT system? The request must have triggered red rockets in Orthew's house. According to the security guards at the gate, Marcus Orthew arrived twelve minutes before us. Toby Jenson had thoughtfully indicated in his files the section he believed most suitable to be used for the construction of a time machine.

He was right, and I'd been right about him. The machine was like the core of the CERN accelerator, a warehouse packed full of high-energy physics equipment. Right at the center, with all the fat wires and conduits and ducts focusing on it, was a dark spherical chamber with a single oval opening. The noise screeching out from the hardware set my teeth on edge, and Paul and Carmen clamped their hands over their ears. Then Carmen pointed and screamed. I saw a giant brick of plastic explosive strapped to an electronics cabinet. Now I knew what to look for. I saw others, some sitting on the superconductor cells. So that's what it's like being caught inside an atom bomb.

Marcus Orthew was standing inside the central chamber. Sort of. He was becoming translucent. I yelled at the others to get out, and ran for the chamber. I reached it as he faded from sight. Then

I was inside. My memories started to unwind, playing back my life. Very fast. I only recognized tiny sections amid the blur of color and emotion— the high-speed chase that nearly killed me, the birth of my son, my dad's funeral, the church where I got married, university. Then the playback started to slow, and I remembered that day when I was about eleven, in the park, when Kenny Mattox our local bully sat on my chest and made me eat the grass cuttings.

I spluttered as the soggy mass was pushed down past my teeth, crying out in shock and fear. Kenny laughed and stuffed some more grass in. I gagged and started to puke violently. Then he was scrambling off in disgust. I lay there for a while, getting my breath back and spitting out grass. I was eleven years old, and it was nineteen sixty-eight. It wasn't the way I'd choose to arrive in the past, but in a few months Neil Armstrong would set foot on the Moon, then the Beatles would break up.

What I should have done, of course, was patented something. But what? I wasn't a scientist or even an engineer. I can't tell you the chemical formula for Viagra, and I didn't know the mechanical details of an airbag. There were everyday things I knew about, icons that we can't survive without, the kind which rake in millions; but would you like to try selling a venture capitalist the idea of Lara Croft five years before the first pocket calculator hits the shops? I did that. I was actually banned from some banks in the City.

So I fell back on the easiest thing in the world. I became a singer-songwriter. Songs are ridiculously easy to remember even if you can't recall the exact lyrics. Remember my first big hit in 78, "Shiny Happy People?" I always was a big REM fan. You've never heard of them? Ah well, sometimes I wonder what the band members are doing this time around. "Pretty In Pink," "Teenage Kicks," "The Unforgettable Fire," "Solsbury Hill"? They're all the same; that fabulous oeuvre of mine isn't quite as original as I make out. And I'm afraid Live Aid wasn't actually the flash of inspiration I always said, either. But the music biz has given me a bloody good life. Every album I've released has been number one on both sides of the Atlantic. That brings in money. A lot of money. It also attracts girls. I mean, I never really believed the talk about backstage excess in the time I had before, but trust me here, the public never gets to hear the half of it. I thought it was the perfect cover.

I've been employing private agencies to keep an eye on Marcus Orthew since the mid-Seventies, with several of his senior management team actually on my payroll. Hell, I even bought shares in Orthogene, as I knew it was going to make money, though I didn't expect quite so much money. I can afford to do whatever the hell I want, and the beauty of that is nobody pays any attention to rock stars or how we blow our cash, as everyone thinks we're talentless junked-up kids heading for a fall. That's what you think has happened now, isn't it? The fall. Well, you're wrong about that.

See, I made exactly the same mistake as poor old Toby Jenson; I underestimated Marcus. I didn't think it through. My music made ripples, big ripples. Everyone knows me, I'm famous right across the globe as a one-off supertalent. There's only one other person in this time who knows those songs aren't original—Marcus. He knew I came after him. And he hasn't quite cracked the rejuvenation treatment yet. It's time for him to move on, to make his fresh start again in another parallel universe.

That's why he framed me. Next time around he's going to become our god. It's not something he's going to share with anyone else.

I LOOKED ROUND the interview room, which had an identical layout to the grubby cube just down the hall where I interviewed Toby Jenson last time around. Paul Mathews and Carmen Galloway were giving me blank-faced looks, buttoning back their anger at being dragged into the statement. I couldn't quite get used to Paul with a full head of hair, but Orthogene's follicle treatment is a big earner for the company; everyone in this universe using it.

I tried to bring my hands up to them, an emphasis to the appeal I was making, but the handcuffs were chained to the table. I glanced down as the metal pulled at my wrists. After the samples had been taken, the forensic team had washed the blood off my hands, but I couldn't forget it, there'd been so much—the image was actually stronger than the one I kept of Toby Jenson. Yet I'd never seen those girls until I woke up to find their bodies in the hotel bed with me. The paramedics didn't even try to revive them.

"Please," I implored. "Paul, Carmen, you have to believe me." And I couldn't even say for old time's sake.

A Distillation of Grace

Adam Roberts

TWELVE GENERATIONS. THE sum is such that two thousand and forty-eight people reduce down to one person over twelve generations if, and only if, each couple have only a single child, and if the conceptions are controlled such that half of all children are of one gender and half the other. We can call twelve, in this context, a magic number, provided of course that we understand "magic" in its forceful sense of a miraculous divine intervention in reality, a sacramental thing. In this sense, Jesus Christ was a magician. Shad also.

HERE IS A conversation between Cole, a young boy of the eighth generation, and his tutor, the Patriarchus, or oldest surviving inheritor of the tradition of Shad. Though only ten years old, Cole was eloquent and intelligent. "Of course I understand," he said, "that our world is unusual in the Galaxy—"

"Singular," corrected the Patriarchus. "Unusual implies that there are some others like us, though few. But there are no other worlds like ours. This is our glory."

"Singular," said Cole, and bowed his head in acknowledgment of the correction. "And yet it seems to me," he continued, "that it is the rest of the cosmos that is unusual, not us. This matter of generations—surely it must be true on every world, just as it is true on ours, that every child has two parents, and every child has four grandparents, and every child has eight great-grandparents, and so on, backward in time…"

"Of course," agreed the Patriarchus.

"Therefore it seems to me that every world should have many more ancestors than present-day inhabitants. Everywhere there should be more inhabitants than descendents, just as it is on our world. And yet the archives say that on every other world," and he clucked with astonishment at this indigestible fact, "on every other world the opposite is true. There are many more descendents than ancestors. The pyramid is inverted! I cannot understand how that can be."

"These other worlds," said the Patriarchus, indulgently, "have not had the benefit of the wisdom of Shad, bless his memory. They breed prodigiously, such that each new generation outnumbers even the large number of ancestors. And they interbreed promiscuously, so that people share many of the same grandparents and great-grandparents, and a whole vocabulary of words is needed to describe the tangle, terms such as cousin and nepotism and three-times-removed." The Patriarchus was old, and tired, and here he paused.

But Cole was possessed of the impatient curiosity of a ten year-old. "And when Shad," he hurried, "bless his memory, brought the first of us to this world—"

"God had instructed him," said the Patriarchus, somberly. "The Bible had inspired him. The Holy Spirit possessed him. He brought a population of two thousand and forty-eight people to this world, and gave them his plan. Each was to marry once, and have one child. Each child was to be genetically determined, *in utero*, to be either male or female, with an exact balance between the two. The second generation would be half the size of the first, and each member of it would pair off, one-to-one. Medical science—since Shad, bless his memory—"

"—bless his memory—" Cole chimed in.

"—since Shad reveals to us that God approves of all scientific and genetic research insofar as it is conducive to the benefits of His divine plan... medical science is recruited to guarantee the exact balance of the sexes, to ensure that every couple will be fertile, and to preserve the lives of all offspring. Only in the event of a tragic death may another child be produced, and then only by the parents of the child who has died." And because this was a teaching session, and not a sermon, the Patriarchus paused here to look sternly at his pupil. "Define tragic death," he said.

But Cole knew this lesson. "A tragic death is one in which a person dies before passing on their genetic material to their child."

"And other deaths?"

"—are called glorious deaths, since after one of the Chosen, one of us, has given birth, we are guaranteed a place at God's right hand."

"Very good," said the Patriarchus indulgently, but a little wearily, for he was tired, and the afternoon was a warm one. From where they were sitting, on the verandah of the Patriarchus's splendid house, he could see over his own ornamental gardens, with their perfectly circular pond, to the dark-green topiary beyond.

In the middle distance was a vast arable field across which an automated tractor rumbled along, its oO wheels pressing parallel lines out of the pink clay. Beyond that, purple mountains frayed the line of the horizon, enormously distant and yet vivid, jewel-brilliant, seemingly close enough to reach out and touch. The sky was a flawless mauve. The Patriarchus took simple pleasure in this vista. His charge, the young Cole, took it for granted, of course, as children do with such splendid facts of nature. Never looked at it. Perhaps he would appreciate it when he was older.

A wind puckered the surface of the pond briefly, and passed on.

"Have there been any tragic deaths in your generation, Patriarchus?" Cole asked.

"None, thanks to God, and thanks to Shad-bless-his-memory," the old man replied. "And none in my child's, or my grandchild's, or in your generation either. We take good care of our people on this world. Every soul is precious, for each contributes his essential holiness to the final product, the road to the Unique."

"Will you tell me, Patriarchus," said Cole, after a pause, "about the Unique?" He asked this question tentatively, because he knew that the Unique partook of the nature of divine mystery, and as such it should not be the business of idle chatter.

"I shall tell you what you know already," replied the Patriarchus, "and that should suffice you. You are eighth generation, and your partner is decided."

"Perry," said Cole happily, for Perry was pretty, and Cole looked forward to their marriage with pleasure.

"You and Perry will have a child, a ninth generation. He, or she, will pair and have a child and that child, your future grandson or granddaughter, will be more blessed than us, for he or she will be the grandparent of the Unique itself. That child will give birth to one of the Unique's parents, and will be alive, should God will it, still be alive when the Unique is born!"

"And when the Unique is born...?"

"Then Shad's purpose will have worked itself out in this cosmos," said the Patriarchus. "A new grace will enter the universe. And this Unique, this he or she, will be the precise sum of all the holy people who have lived and worked and worshipped on Shad's World."

But this did not tell Cole anything new. This matter of new Grace was kindergarten theology. He wanted more precision—the Unique as a blast of spiritual flame, God like a pillar of light bursting from the planet's surface, something vivid and fireworky to feed the hunger of his ten-year-old imagination for spectacle. But the Patriarchus's eyes were closing, and Cole knew enough to leave the old man to his nap.

COLE, IN TIME, married and had his child, a boy called Parr. And Parr, in due course, married and had a son, called Medd. Cole, in due course, became the Episcopus, the second most senior position in the community of Shad's World. And then, when the existing Patriarchus died a glorious death, Cole himself became the Patriarchus.

Life continued in its divinely preordained groove. Every year brought the birth of the Unique closer.

THERE WAS A problem.

Medd was fourteen. He had been raised in the fullest knowledge of his holy position, for he would be one of the grandparents of the Unique. He would almost certainly be alive and hale when the Unique was born.

Yet Medd was a contrary boy. He repudiated his holy calling. He absented himself from school, and ran wild in the woodland, making huts for himself, climbing trees, killing fish in the rivers and cooking them, caked in mud, inside the ashes of an open fire.

He had been allotted his wife at birth, of course, and being of the tenth generation, there was a simple choice of two—for his generation was only four strong. So close they were to the Unique! Bless the memory of Shad. He was to marry a girl called Rhess, exactly his age, a devout, dark-faced little girl, who looked disdainfully as Medd threw one tantrum or another, in schoolroom or in church. She did not like Medd. Yet she accepted her holy destiny, and was reconciled to the notion of becoming his wife.

He, however, was not reconciled. "I do not love her," he said.

He had fitted up a transceiver from various tech-parts, and had narrowbanded a connection to a Flatship passing not far from their system, sweeping for Gateways. From a friendly AI upon this ship, Medd had downloaded a bundle of old literature, old Earthly poems and plays. These he read avidly, memorizing large portions, such that when the church elders found and deleted his cache he still had great swathes of poetry in his mind.

It was, the Patriarchus thought, from these forbidden poems that he had learned the notion of sexual love. "I do not love her," Medd declared, with the absolute certainty that is often characteristic of the young adult. He was fourteen years old and knew everything, past, present and future, without embarrassment of uncertainty. "I never will. I cannot marry her."

Then, later, when the absolute necessity of this marriage was pressed and pressed upon him, he changed his tack. "It would be a sin," he announced. "A sin to marry a woman I did not love. God is love, as it says in the Bible. Wouldn't it go against the nature of God to enter into such a marriage?"

"And you believe," countered the Episcopus, "that you, at fourteen, understand the nature of

God better than the whole of Shad's holy Church?"

"Yes!" cried Medd, fire in his eyes.

"You will marry this girl," said the Episcopus. "It is the will of Shad, bless his memory."

"You do not know the will of Shad!" Medd declared, fiercely.

"If you do not marry her and have your allotted child," said the Episcopus, angrily but with tears of frustration and fear in his eyes, "then the whole of Shad's divine plan will come to nothing!"

"I don't care," yelled Medd. "I don't love her!"

Every attempt to persuade him broke upon the anvil of this fiercely spoken statement. But is she not comely? Is she not devout? I don't love her! Do you want to be responsible, you alone in your selfishness responsible for bringing the whole plan crashing down? I don't love her! Do you want to live a life of celibacy and barrenness?

"No," said Medd, becoming calmer. "No, I shall leave this world, somehow. I shall travel the stars, and find my lover there. My true lover." But why travel from home, when you have a wife already chosen for you? I don't love her!

This cussedness on Medd's part rather spoiled the mood of the New Year's party. You see, as the year AD twenty-seven-hundred dawned, there was a special mass, and afterward a gathering, dance, and chess tournament. But the mood was subdued, and several members of the congregation cast sorrowful looks at Medd, as he was absorbed in his chess game. "Twenty-seven-hundred is only a number," he said. "An arbitrary number, after all. It is not intrinsically more special than twenty-six-ninety-nine, or twenty-seven-oh-one."

Nobody was disposed to discuss the point with him.

IT WAS NOT unprecedented that members of the congregation of Shad's World sometimes wrestled against their destiny in this way, especially at that emotionally volatile period we call teenage. Still, it was the Patriarchus's fundamental duty to guard Shad's holy plan, this distillation of twenty thousand and forty-eight holy people into one Unique person over twelve generations, and so it fell to him to talk to the boy, to explain to him the consequences of so terrible a decision. He summoned Medd to his house, and waited upon his porch for his arrival.

It was a mild morning. The wind rummaged in the leaves of the fat-headed oak tree in the garden—a tree grown from a conker brought by the first settlers. The tree was a symbol of the connection between the newest generation and the first. The sound of the wind in the leaves was exactly the sound of rushing water. Medd contemplated the precision of this aural echo.

Medd arrived, finally, two hours late. He was not apologetic.

"You wished," he said, sulkily, "to speak to me, Patriarchus?"

"Yes, grandson," said the Patriarchus. "Come inside, please."

As they stepped through into the cool hallway, Medd said, "You will try to persuade me of the necessity of marrying Rhess. But I do not love her. Nothing you can say will change that."

"I think I understand," said the Patriarchus, "the nature of your feelings for poor Rhess. You have cut her deep, you know; cut her to the heart, with your rejection. Don't you think she loves you?"

Medd had never considered the question from this perspective. He followed the Patriarchus through to the sitting room, and took a chair. "I do not know," he said.

"There are many things you do not know," said the Patriarchus. "Things that I do know, by virtue of my position here as the Patriarchus. Shall we talk of them?"

It was on Medd's tongue to say *I do not love her!* again, but he checked himself. "You mean, not talk of Rhess?"

"Talk of the Unique," said the Patriarchus. "Are you not curious?"

Of course Medd was curious.

THEY DRANK YELLOW tea together and for a while sat in silence. Shortly the Patriarchus sat forward in his chair. "Have you thought much of the Unique?" he asked.

"Patriarchus," replied Medd. "A little. I have, a little."

"Of course you have. And what do you think will happen when she, or he, is born?"

Medd shrugged. "Miracles?" he hazarded.

"Grace," said Patriarchus.

"Of course, grace," said Medd. "We learnt all about that in kindergarten."

"All about it?" said Patriarchus. "I doubt that."

The room was long and narrow, with tall spire-shaped windows along one of the walls. A low table filled the space between the chairs of the Patriarchus and Medd.

"I don't know," said Medd. "When the Unique is born—will the whole world shine with light, the glory revealed? Will the congregation of the blessed be able to fly through the sky? I don't know."

"Something very powerful will happen," said Patriarchus. "Twelve holy generations distilled down to a single person. The birth of this single person, the sum of these devout generations of ancestors, will be a powerful event. You know this to be true."

Medd said nothing. He stared at the floor.

"It is because the Unique is so powerful a prospect," the Patriarchus continued, "that you take a private joy in threatening to block it. For, without your marriage to Rhess and the begetting of your child, the Unique cannot be born. It flatters your pride to think that you can say yes or no to this thing."

"I do not—" Medd started sulkily.

"—love her, I know," the Patriarchus said. "Let us not talk of that. Let us talk of grace. What do you know of grace?"

Medd opened his mouth, and looked up quickly, ready with some sharp reply. But the words died on his tongue. "I know a little, Patriarchus," he said, humbly.

"Grace is what the Unique will be," said Patriarchus. "It is what the birth of the Unique will signify. A nova of grace. And do you think that grace travels through space according to the logic of Einstein's constraints? Do you think that grace is something like light, or gravity, or radio waves, to pass only slowly through space? No. Grace passes instantly—spreads at once through the whole cosmos, spreading out from this person, at this time. Shad, bless his memory, teaches us so. Grace is part of God, and surpasses the physical laws of the cosmos. Grace is miraculous and instantaneous."

Somebody passed by outside one of the windows, and Medd looked up. But, whoever they were, they had passed on.

"But," the Patriarchus continued, "we still live in the Einsteinian universe. Grace may transcend that, but matter cannot, and you and I are matter as well as soul. We cannot travel faster than light, except through the Gateways. And travel through the Gateways is not instantaneous—harmonic multiples of light speed. We cannot accelerate faster than light in the space of this cosmos, and we cannot travel instantaneously. Do you know why?"

"It is simply how things are," suggested Medd.

"True. But another way of saying so is that to travel instantaneously would violate cause and effect. We would arrive before we set off—because that is what time is, that ordering of cause and effect. That is why the Einsteinian constant exists, to preserve that, to preserve those things, cause, effect, happening in that order—"

Medd broke in. "But I do not love her," he said.

The Patriarchus twitched his nose, like a rabbit, perhaps in annoyance at the interruption. "To travel," he continued, undistracted, "instantly in our space would be to travel back in time. Back," he added, holding up his forefinger, "in time."

"I am not talking of time," said Medd. "I am talking of love—"

"To travel five light years instantly would be to arrive five years in the past."

"Patriarchus," said Medd. "I appreciate your kindness in speaking to me—in explaining this to me—but—"

The Patriarchus's finger was still raised. "To travel a thousand light years in an instant would be to travel back a thousand years in time. To see a star a thousand light years distant is to see it as it was a millennium ago. And so you can see how grace, emanating from the Unique, will pass back through time as it passes through space. And to what end will it travel, forward in space, backward in time? And to what end?"

But Medd didn't care to what end. He spoke his talismanic words, the words that distilled his own will to refuse. "I do not love her."

He rose to go. And suddenly the walls seemed to spring at him from three sides, rubbery membranes cast from apertures in the walls and trapping him in a muscular web. He tumbled to the floor, wrapped tightly. "Patri—" he cried, suddenly very afraid.

The Patriarchus had not moved from his chair, and looked down at the wriggling bundle at his feet. "You do not love Rhess," he said.

Medd struggled, but the membrane only tightened around him. It filtered light poorly, pinkly, and he couldn't make out the Patriarchus's form. Suddenly hands grabbed him on two sides, and he was lifted. Muffled, the Patriarchus's voice came again.

"But we do not need your love," he said. "We only need your sperm, and that is easily harvested. Rhess will give birth to your child."

"Patriarchus!" Medd called, chokingly. "Pa...! Pa...!"

"When so much hangs in the balance?" said the Patriarchus. "So much—should we allow your teenage emotional vagaries to interfere with the plan? With Shad's divine plan?"

Medd felt himself carried, bumpily, and deposited on some surface. The Patriarchus's voice accompanied him.

"You know how far this world is from Earth. Did you think it was a coincidence that Shad, bless his memory, brought us to this world, of all worlds? That God provided this planet at exactly two thousand seven hundred and seventeen light-years from Earth? Can't you guess when the Unique will be born? Can't you see how far back in time his grace will pass? And only think of the events it will make blossom as it passes instantly past innumerable worlds! The mystery of it, the necessity of it, the beautiful strangeness of it. Understand the universal significance of the effect it will have upon one particular fetus on one particular planet, on the home world, a long time past!" the Patriarchus chuckled. It was difficult for Medd to hear through the constricting material of the membrane that wrapped him. "When you understand the final purpose of Shad's plan," the Patriarchus continued, "perhaps then you can see how foolish it is to set your glandular vagueness against such a plan—such a cosmic plan. Can you see? What can your desires, or even your life, weigh in the balance against such an outcome?"

Medd felt something sharp cut through the membrane and press against his groin. "I'm sorry," said the Patriarchus again. "This isn't what I want. This is necessity."

"I HAVE BEEN worrying, lately," said the Patriarchus. "About one aspect of the teaching."

"At your age too!" said the Episcopus, mildly. "Don't you find yourself surpassing worry as you get older? Shad, bless his memory, has provided for everything. I find that a comforting thought."

The Patriarchus and the Episcopus were sitting on the broad patio of the Patriarchus's house, with a view down over gardens and fields all the way to the plum-tinted mountains on the horizon. The white moon shone like a second sun as the evening grew. Their table was laid with glasses of wine-lees tea, and dozens of tiny baked muffins no bigger than thumbnails.

"Shad," said the Patriarchus, eventually, "bless his memory," and he paused. Then he looked at the sky, and spoke carefully. "Shad wrote that the creation of the Unique would sum all the genetic qualities of the twenty-forty-eight holy people who settled this world."

"Genetic qualities," agreed the Episcopus.

"And if," the Patriarchus went on, cautiously, "instead of merely genetic qualities—what if the Unique is the sum of all qualities? Of every action and thought of all of the people who have ever lived on this world?"

The Episcopus grunted as he lifted his tea-glass, which might have been a confirmation or a rebuttal.

"Such seems to me," the Patriarchus continued, "not only possible—but, since we are talking of the divine—it seems to me necessarily true. Don't you agree? A necessary function of divinity?"

"Necessary," said the Episcopus, "because we are talking of the divine?"

"Exactly. The divine is more than the genetic. Of course. Shad—"

"Bless his memory."

"—his memory—would have agreed with that, surely."

The Episcopus was silent for a while, watching the gathering sunset. "And then?"

"Well. I worry, perhaps, that all the thoughts and—actions—of all the people who have ever lived, or who live now, on this world will be distilled into the Unique. The bad as well as the good. The violent and death-dealing as well as the pure. And will this not flavor the grace that passes out?"

"Perhaps so," said the Episcopus, after a long pause.

"And does that not worry you? So much violence, kneaded into the dough of this grace?"

"I find," said the Episcopus, eventually, "that, as I get older, I trust more and more to Shad. He knew how his plan would work out. He must have anticipated the bad as well as the good. Both must be necessary. Perhaps a messiah must possess a will to destroy, as well as a will to love. Perhaps we need also a messiah with a whip. A messiah who is a torturer. Or perhaps your worries are misplaced. It is not I," he said, looking straight up at the evening sky, "not I who knows the answer to that."

Above them, an automated jet-plane left its trail on the zenith, like a white slit in the purple sky. Only very faintly, and seemingly not connected with its slow passage, could the faint rumble of its scramjets be heard.

Last Contact

Stephen Baxter

March 15th

CAITLIN WALKED INTO the garden through the little gate from the drive. Maureen was working on the lawn.

Just at that moment Maureen's phone pinged. She took off her gardening gloves, dug the phone out of the deep pocket of her old quilted coat and looked at the screen. "Another contact," she called to her daughter.

Caitlin looked cold in her thin jacket; she wrapped her arms around her body. "Another super-civilization discovered, off in space. We live in strange times, Mum."

"That's the fifteenth this year. And I did my bit to help discover it. Good for me," Maureen said, smiling. "Hello, love." She leaned forward for a kiss on the cheek.

She knew why Caitlin was here, of course. Caitlin had always hinted she would come and deliver the news about the Big Rip in person, one way or the other. Maureen guessed what that news was from her daughter's hollow, stressed eyes. But Caitlin was looking around the garden, and Maureen decided to let her tell it all in her own time.

She asked, "How're the kids?"

"Fine. At school. Bill's at home, baking bread." Caitlin smiled. "Why do stay-at-home fathers always bake bread? But he's starting at Webster's next month."

"That's the engineers in Oxford?"

"That's right. Not that it makes much difference now. We won't run out of money before, well, before it doesn't matter." Caitlin considered the garden. It was just a scrap of lawn really, with a quite nicely stocked border, behind a cottage that was a little more than a hundred years old, in this village on the outskirts of Oxford. "It's the first time I've seen this properly."

"Well, it's the first bright day we've had. My first spring here." They walked around the lawn. "It's not bad. It's been let to run to seed a bit by Mrs. Murdoch. Who was another lonely old widow," Maureen said.

"You mustn't think like that."

"Well, it's true. This little house is fine for someone on their own, like me, or her. I suppose I'd pass it on to somebody else in the same boat, when I'm done."

Caitlin was silent at that, silent at the mention of the future.

Maureen showed her patches where the lawn had dried out last summer and would need reseeding. And there was a little brass plaque fixed to the wall of the house to show the level reached by the Thames floods of two years ago. "The lawn is all right. I do like this time of year when you sort of wake it up from the winter. The grass needs raking and scarifying, of course. I'll reseed bits of it, and see how it grows during the summer. I might think about getting some of it relaid. Now the weather's so different, the drainage might not be right anymore."

"You're enjoying getting back in the saddle, aren't you, Mum?"

Maureen shrugged. "Well, the last couple of years weren't much fun. Nursing your dad, and then getting rid of the house. It's nice to get this old thing back on again." She raised her arms and looked down at her quilted gardening coat.

Caitlin wrinkled her nose. "I always hated that stupid old coat. You really should get yourself something better, Mum. These modern fabrics are very good."

"This will see me out," Maureen said firmly.

They walked around the verge, looking at the plants, the weeds, the autumn leaves that hadn't been swept up and were now rotting in place.

Caitlin said, "I'm going to be on the radio later. BBC Radio 4. There's to be a government statement on the Rip, and I'll be in the follow-up discussion. It starts at nine, and I should be on about nine-thirty."

"I'll listen to it. Do you want me to tape it for you?"

"No. Bill will get it. Besides, you can listen to all these things on the websites these days."

Maureen said carefully, "I take it the news is what you expected, then."

"Pretty much. The Hawaii observatories confirmed it. I've seen the new Hubble images, deep sky fields. Empty, save for the foreground objects. All the galaxies beyond the local group have gone. Eerie, really, seeing your predictions come true like that. That's couch grass, isn't it?"

"Yes. I stuck a fork in it. Nothing but root mass underneath. It will be a devil to get up. I'll have a go, and then put down some bin liners for a few weeks, and see if that kills it off. Then there are these roses that should have been pruned by now. I think I'll plant some gladioli in this corner—"

"Mum, it's October." Caitlin blurted that out. She looked thin, pale, and tense, a real office worker, but then Maureen had always thought that about her daughter, that she worked too hard. Now she was thirty-five, and her moderately pretty face was lined at the eyes and around her mouth, the first wistful signs of age. "October 14th, at about four in the afternoon. I say 'about.' I could give you the time down to the attosecond if you wanted."

Maureen took her hands. "It's all right, love. It's about when you thought it would be, isn't it?"

"Not that it does us any good, knowing. There's nothing we can do about it."

They walked on. They came to a corner on the south side of the little garden. "This ought to catch the sun," Maureen said. "I'm thinking of putting in a seat here. A pergola maybe. Somewhere to sit. I'll see how the sun goes around later in the year."

"Dad would have liked a pergola," Caitlin said. "He always did say a garden was a place to sit in, not to work."

"Yes. It does feel odd that your father died, so soon before all this. I'd have liked him to see it out. It seems a waste somehow."

Caitlin looked up at the sky. "Funny thing, Mum. It's all quite invisible to the naked eye still. You can see the Andromeda Galaxy, just, but that's bound to the Milky Way by gravity. So the expansion hasn't reached down to the scale of the visible, not yet. It's still all instruments, telescopes. But it's real all right."

"I suppose you'll have to explain it all on Radio 4."

"That's why I'm there. We'll probably have to keep saying it over and over, trying to find ways of saying it that people can understand. *You* know, don't you, Mum? It's all to do with dark energy. It's like an antigravity field that permeates the universe. Just as gravity pulls everything together, the dark energy is pulling the universe apart, taking more and more of it so far away that its light can't reach us anymore. It started at the level of the largest structures in the universe, superclusters of galaxies. But in the end it will fold down to the smallest scales. Every bound structure will be pulled apart. Even atoms, even subatomic particles. The Big Rip.

"We've known about this stuff for years. What we didn't expect was that the expansion would accelerate as it has. We thought we had trillions of years. Then the forecast was billions. And now—"

"Yes."

"It's funny for me being involved in this stuff, Mum. Being on the radio. I've never been a people person. I became an astrophysicist, for God's sake. I always thought that what I studied would have absolutely no effect on anybody's life. How wrong I was. Actually there's been a lot of debate about whether to announce it or not."

"I think people will behave pretty well," Maureen said. "They usually do. It might get trickier toward the end, I suppose. But people have a right to know, don't you think?"

"They're putting it on after nine, so people can decide what to tell their kids."

"After the watershed! Well, that's considerate. Will you tell your two?"

"I think we'll have to. Everybody at school will know. They'll probably get bullied about it if they don't know. Imagine that. Besides, the little beggars will probably have googled it on their mobiles by one minute past nine."

Maureen laughed. "There is that."

"It will be like when I told them Dad had died," Caitlin said. "Or like when Billy started asking hard questions about Santa Claus."

"No more Christmases," Maureen said suddenly. "If it's all over in October."

"No more birthdays for my two either," Caitlin said.

"November and January."

"Yes. It's funny, in the lab, when the date came up, that was the first thing I thought of."

Maureen's phone pinged again. "Another signal. Quite different in nature from the last, according to this."

"I wonder if we'll get any of those signals decoded in time."

Maureen waggled her phone. "It won't be for want of trying, me and a billion other search-for-ET-at-home enthusiasts. Would you like some tea, love?"

"It's all right. I'll let you get on. I told Bill I'd get the shopping in, before I have to go back to the studios in Oxford this evening."

They walked toward the back door into the house, strolling, inspecting the plants and the scrappy lawn.

June 5th

IT WAS ABOUT lunchtime when Caitlin arrived from the garden center with the pieces of the pergola. Maureen helped her unload them from the back of a white van, and carry them through the gate from the drive. They were mostly just prefabricated wooden panels and beams that they could manage between the two of them, though the big iron spikes that would be driven into the ground to support the uprights were heavier. They got the pieces stacked upon the lawn.

"I should be able to set it up myself," Maureen said. "Joe next door said he'd lay the concrete base for me, and help me lift on the roof section.

There's some nailing to be done, and creosoting, but I can do all that."

"Joe, eh?" Caitlin grinned.

"Oh, shut up, he's just a neighbor. Where did you get the van? Did you have to hire it?"

"No, the garden center loaned it to me. They can't deliver. They are still getting stock in, but they can't rely on the staff. They just quit, without any notice. In the end it sort of gets to you, I suppose."

"Well, you can't blame people for wanting to be at home."

"No. Actually Bill's packed it in. I meant to tell you. He didn't even finish his induction at Webster's. But the project he was working on would never have got finished anyway."

"I'm sure the kids are glad to have him home."

"Well, they're finishing the school year. At least I think they will, the teachers still seem keen to carry on."

"It's probably best for them."

"Yes. We can always decide what to do after the summer, if the schools open again."

Maureen had prepared some sandwiches, and some iced elderflower cordial. They sat in the shade of the house and ate their lunch and looked out over the garden.

Caitlin said, "Your lawn's looking good."

"It's come up quite well. I'm still thinking of relaying that patch over there."

"And you put in a lot of vegetables in the end," Caitlin said.

"I thought I should. I've planted courgettes and French beans and carrots, and a few outdoor tomatoes. I could do with a greenhouse, but I haven't really room for one. It seemed a good idea, rather than flowers, this year."

"Yes. You can't rely on the shops."

Things had kept working, mostly, as people stuck to their jobs. But there were always gaps on the supermarket shelves, as supply chains broke down. There was talk of rationing some essentials, and there were already coupons for petrol.

"I don't approve of how tatty the streets are getting in town," Maureen said sternly.

Caitlin sighed. "I suppose you can't blame people for packing in a job like street-sweeping. It is a bit tricky getting around town though. We need some work done on the roof, we're missing a couple of tiles. It's just as well we won't have to get through another winter," she said, a bit darkly. "But you can't get a builder for love or money."

"Well, you never could."

They both laughed.

Maureen said, "I told you people would cope. People do just get on with things."

"We haven't got to the end game yet," Caitlin said. "I went into London the other day. That isn't too friendly, Mum. It's not all like this, you know."

Maureen's phone pinged, and she checked the screen. "Four or five a day now," she said. "New contacts, lighting up all over the sky."

"But that's down from the peak, isn't it?"

"Oh, we had a dozen a day at one time. But now we've lost half the stars, haven't we?"

"Well, that's true, now the Rip has folded down into the galaxy. I haven't really been following it, Mum. Nobody's been able to decode any of the signals, have they?"

"But some of them aren't the sort of signal you can decode anyhow. In one case somebody picked up an artificial element in the spectrum of a star. Something that was manufactured, and then just chucked in to burn up, like a flare."

Caitlin considered. "That can't say anything but 'here we are,' I suppose."

"Maybe that's enough."

"Yes."

It had really been Harry who had been interested in wild speculations about alien life and so forth. Joining the phone network of home observers of ET, helping to analyze possible signals from the stars in a network of millions of others, had been Harry's hobby, not Maureen's. It was one of Harry's things she had kept up after he had died, like his weather monitoring and his football pools. It would have felt odd just to have stopped it all.

But she did understand how remarkable it was that the sky had suddenly lit up with messages like a Christmas tree, after more than half a century of dogged, fruitless, frustrating listening. Harry would have loved to see it.

"Caitlin, I don't really understand how all these signals can be arriving just now. I mean, it takes years for light to travel between the stars, doesn't it? We only knew about the phantom energy a few months ago."

"But others might have detected it long before, with better technology than we've got. That would give you time to send something. Maybe the signals have been timed to get here, just before the end, aimed just at us."

"That's a nice thought."

"Some of us hoped that there would be an answer to the dark energy in all those messages."

"What answer could there be?"

Caitlin shrugged. "If we can't decode the messages we'll never know. And I suppose if there was anything to be done, it would have been done by now."

"I don't think the messages need decoding," Maureen said.

Caitlin looked at her curiously, but didn't pursue it. "Listen, Mum. Some of us are going to try to do something. You understand that the Rip works down the scales, so that larger structures break up first. The galaxy, then the solar system, then planets like Earth. And then the human body."

Maureen considered. "So people will outlive the Earth."

"Well, they could. For maybe about thirty minutes, until atomic structures get pulled apart. There's talk of establishing a sort of shelter in Oxford that could survive the end of the Earth. Like a submarine, I suppose. And if you wore a pressure suit you might last a bit longer even than that. The design goal is to make it through to the last microsecond. You could gather another thirty minutes of data that way. They've asked me to go in there."

"Will you?"

"I haven't decided. It will depend on how we feel about the kids, and—you know."

Maureen considered. "You must do what makes you happy, I suppose."

"Yes. But it's hard to know what that is, isn't it?" Caitlin looked up at the sky. "It's going to be a hot day."

"Yes. And a long one. I think I'm glad about that. The night sky looks odd now the Milky Way has gone."

"And the stars are flying off one by one," Caitlin murmured. "I suppose the constellations will look funny by the autumn."

"Do you want some more sandwiches?"

"I'll have a bit more of that cordial. It's very good, Mum."

"It's elderflower. I collect the blossoms from that bush down the road. I'll give you the recipe if you like."

"Shall we see if your Joe fancies laying a bit of concrete this afternoon? I could do with meeting your new beau."

"Oh, shut up," Maureen said, and she went inside to make a fresh jug of cordial.

October 14th

THAT MORNING MAUREEN got up early. She was pleased that it was a bright morning, after the rain of the last few days. It was a lovely autumn day. She had breakfast listening to the last-ever episode of *The Archers*, but her radio battery failed before the end.

She went to work in the garden, hoping to get everything done before the light went. There was plenty of work, leaves to rake up, the roses and the clematis to prune. She had decided to plant a row of daffodil bulbs around the base of the new pergola.

She noticed a little band of goldfinches, plundering a clump of Michaelmas daisies for seed. She sat back on her heels to watch. The colorful little birds had always been her favorites.

Then the light went, just like that, darkening as if somebody was throwing a dimmer switch. Maureen looked up. The sun was rushing away, and sucking all the light out of the sky with it. It was a remarkable sight, and she wished she had a camera. As the light turned gray, and then charcoal, and then utterly black, she heard the goldfinches fly off in a clatter, confused. It had only taken a few minutes.

Maureen was prepared. She dug a little torch out of the pocket of her old quilted coat. She had been hoarding the batteries; you hadn't been able to buy them for weeks. The torch got her as far as the pergola, where she lit some rush torches that she'd fixed to canes.

Then she sat in the pergola, in the dark, with her garden lit up by her rush torches, and waited. She wished she had thought to bring out her book. She didn't suppose there would be time to finish it now. Anyhow, the flickering firelight would be bad for her eyes.

"Mum?"

The soft voice made her jump. It was Caitlin, threading her way across the garden with a torch of her own.

"I'm in here, love."

Caitlin joined her mother in the pergola, and they sat on the wooden benches, on the thin cushions Maureen had been able to buy. Caitlin shut down her torch to conserve the battery.

Maureen said, "The sun went, right on cue."

"Oh, it's all working out, bang on time."

Somewhere there was shouting, whooping, a tinkle of broken glass.

"Someone's having fun," Maureen said.

"It's a bit like an eclipse," Caitlin said. "Like in Cornwall, do you remember? The sky was cloudy, and we couldn't see a bit of the eclipse. But at that moment when the sky went dark, everybody got excited. Something primeval, I suppose."

"Would you like a drink? I've got a flask of tea. The milk's a bit off, I'm afraid."

"I'm fine, thanks."

"I got up early and managed to get my bulbs in. I didn't have time to trim that clematis, though. I got it all ready for the winter, I think."

"I'm glad."

"I'd rather be out here than indoors, wouldn't you?"

"Oh, yes."

"I thought about bringing blankets. I didn't know if it would get cold."

"Not much. The air will keep its heat for a bit. There won't be time to get very cold."

"I was going to fix up some electric lights out here. But the power's been off for days."

"The rushes are better, anyway. I would have been here earlier. There was a jam by the church.

All the churches are packed, I imagine. And then I ran out of petrol a couple of miles back. We haven't been able to fill up for weeks."

"It's all right. I'm glad to see you. I didn't expect you at all. I couldn't ring." Even the phone networks had been down for days. In the end everything had slowly broken down, as people simply gave up their jobs and went home. Maureen asked carefully, "So how's Bill and the kids?"

"We had an early Christmas," Caitlin said. "They'll both miss their birthdays, but we didn't think they should be cheated out of Christmas too. We did it all this morning. Stockings, a tree, the decorations and the lights down from the loft, presents, the lot. And then we had a big lunch. I couldn't find a turkey but I'd been saving a chicken. After lunch the kids went for their nap. Bill put their pills in their lemonade."

Maureen knew she meant the little blue pills the NHS had given out to every household.

"Bill lay down with them. He said he was going to wait with them until he was sure—you know. That they wouldn't wake up, and be distressed. Then he was going to take his own pill."

Maureen took her hand. "You didn't stay with them?"

"I didn't want to take the pill." There was some bitterness in her voice. "I always wanted to see it through to the end. I suppose it's the scientist in me. We argued about it. We fought, I suppose. In the end we decided this way was the best."

Maureen thought that on some level Caitlin couldn't really believe her children were gone, or she couldn't keep functioning like this. "Well, I'm glad you're here with me. And I never fancied those pills either. Although—will it hurt?"

"Only briefly. When the Earth's crust gives way. It will be like sitting on top of an erupting volcano."

"You had an early Christmas. Now we're going to have an early Bonfire Night."

"It looks like it. I wanted to see it through," Caitlin said again. "After all I was in at the start—those supernova studies."

"You mustn't think it's somehow your fault."

"I do, a bit," Caitlin confessed. "Stupid, isn't it?"

"But you decided not to go to the shelter in Oxford with the others?"

"I'd rather be here. With you. Oh, but I brought this." She dug into her coat pocket and produced a sphere, about the size of a tennis ball.

Maureen took it. It was heavy, with a smooth black surface.

Caitlin said, "It's the stuff they make space shuttle heatshield tiles out of. It can soak up a lot of heat."

"So it will survive the Earth breaking up."

"That's the idea."

"Are there instruments inside?"

"Yes. It should keep working, keep recording until the expansion gets down to the centimeter scale, and the Rip cracks the sphere open. Then it will release a cloud of even finer sensor units, motes we call them. It's nanotechnology, Mum, machines the size of molecules. They will keep gathering data until the expansion reaches molecular scales."

"How long will that take after the big sphere breaks up?"

"Oh, a microsecond or so. There's nothing we could come up with that could keep data-gathering after that."

Maureen hefted the little device. "What a wonderful little gadget. It's a shame nobody will be able to use its data."

"Well, you never know," Caitlin said. "Some of the cosmologists say this is just a transition, rather than an end. The universe has passed through transitions before, for instance from an age dominated by radiation to one dominated by matter—our age. Maybe there will be life of some kind in a new era dominated by the dark energy."

"But nothing like us."

"I'm afraid not."

Maureen stood and put the sphere down in the middle of the lawn. The grass was just faintly moist, with dew, as the air cooled. "Will it be all right here?"

"I should think so."

The ground shuddered, and there was a sound like a door slamming, deep in the ground. Alarms went off, from cars and houses, distant wails. Maureen hurried back to the pergola. She sat with Caitlin, and they wrapped their arms around each other.

Caitlin raised her wrist to peer at her watch, then gave it up. "I don't suppose we need a countdown."

The ground shook more violently, and there was an odd sound, like waves rushing over pebbles on a beach. Maureen peered out of the pergola. Remarkably, one wall of her house had given way, just like that, and the bricks had tumbled into a heap.

"You'll never get a builder out now," Caitlin said, but her voice was edgy.

"We'd better get out of here."

"All right."

They got out of the pergola and stood side by side on the lawn, over the little sphere of instruments, holding onto each other. There was another tremor, and Maureen's roof tiles slid to the ground, smashing and tinkling.

"Mum, there's one thing."

"Yes, love."

"You said you didn't think all those alien signals needed to be decoded."

"Why, no. I always thought it was obvious what all the signals were saying."

"What?"

Maureen tried to reply.

The ground burst open. The scrap of dewy lawn flung itself into the air, and Maureen was thrown down, her face pressed against the grass. She glimpsed houses and trees and people, all flying in the air, underlit by a furnace-red glow from beneath.

But she was still holding Caitlin. Caitlin's eyes were squeezed tight shut. "Goodbye," Maureen yelled. "They were just saying goodbye." But she couldn't tell if Caitlin could hear.

Cages

Ian Watson

"MISS ADAMSON, I'M Svelte," says the tall, skinny forty-something woman who enters my office.

Svelte by name, and likewise in body, which is long and slim. Elasticized black leggings and a black T-shirt under a crimson shirt that sports several zipped pockets. Not quite the usual ladies' attire for Combined Intelligence. In my own more chunky forties, I'm in a cream blouse and gray jacket. A long gray skirt conceals my knee-cage.

Svelte's hair cascades blackly and the collar of her crimson shirt gapes wide to accommodate a hexagonal neck-curse of brass, which holds her chin high. Her impediment looks the height of funky fashion, something chosen deliberately rather than inflicted upon her.

I indicate the brown leather chair facing my desk, and she lounges in it.

"So what exactly is Kore?" I ask her.

According to the file still on screen, Svelte is half-Serbian, half-Romanian. Her birth name was Svetlana but she uses the name Svelte from her time as a… turbo-folk singer. Her job description at Combi-Intel is Analysis Eastern Europe—she graduated in Politics and Economics from the University of Belgrade. Most economies in Eastern Europe are in a mess because of the hoops coming so soon after the upheavals of uniting with the West.

Outside my tinted window, the Thames is as gray as my clothing. At rooftop level above Kensington and Chelsea, hoops hang leadenly in their dozens. If the sun were shining on this June morning, how the hoops would glitter, like huge bangles from boutiques.

"Kore is tekky that samples and remixes the sounds of love-making," says Svelte.

"Hang on. Tekky. Samples. Remixes." This Serbian-Romanian seems to have a bigger English vocabulary than I do.

"Tekky is neo-techno music," she explains. "You sample other bits of music or noise, using a synthesizer to distort. Take a source sound and make it something it never was. Kore uses fucking and coming as the source sounds." Helpfully she spells source. Not sauce, no.

From a crimson breast pocket emerges a memory stick, which I plug into the computer. An album cover comes on screen, depicting a dancing woman surrounded by flames. A fox mask hides the woman's face. Groping, caressing hands of a multitude of hues, detached from their owners, cover most of the woman's body. A patch of pubic hair and a nipple are exposed.

"Oh, I see," say I. "Kore as in hard-core."

"Isn't digitized—hands are all painted on her."

"So it's art. Patient woman. Must have taken ages."

The title of the album is *Sighs and Cries*. From Quantum Entanglement, the very group! Svelte is extremely well organized, and at only a half-hour's notice. Her slimness, her extra height, her dark hair, just as Miriam was, till she left my life. Not that Miriam died, merely our relationship.

THE MUSIC IS slick and smooth as sweaty skin but with a pulsing bass line, climax a long time coming, wailings looping around and around, wave after wave, sighs like choirs of angels in ecstasy:

Ev-ery-thing you
Ev-ery-thing you do
You do, you do, you do
Everything you say
To me, to me, to me
Everything you do to me
Say to me do to me
Is perfect perfect perfect
Do to me say to me
Perfect perfect perfect...

"Sounds like a steal from Marlene Dietrich," is my opinion. "'You Do Something To Me.'"

"No, someone really said those words while making love. The voice is like filtered, disguised, high-pitched. Sometimes gets overdone. Voice winds up six octaves like breathing pure helium, like almost ultrasonic, like something to get bats off on."

Could I even dream of phrasing anything of the sort in Serbo-Croatian or Romanian? Not even in English!

Minimize the album cover away, resume CV. In her youth, Svelte was a favorite of the Milosevic regime. Turbo-folk was mystical nationalist music originally supportive of Milosevic and his gangsters, a primitivist blend of pop and folk and oriental sounds. Strong allegations of crime and drug trafficking—Svelte must have been obliged to get out of Serbia. She tidied up her act and dusted off her university degree and became one of our experts on Eastern European. Not to mention our expert on the music scene.

"Do you know why I'm asking about Kore?"

"Web chat says Quantum Entanglement gonna do a big Exprisonment gig. They'll sample the noise the alien bees make, fuck about with the big bees' hum and blast the mix at hoops or at the bees. Like, the Varroa fucked with us, so let's fuck 'em with music. That's the idea."

Succinctly put. Pretty much what I was alerted to, fresh out of a meeting about the nuke the Chinese had set off. So far as satellite imaging can tell, the solitary alien hoop, which the Chinese nuked in the Gobi, was merely hurled several kilometers upward. Maybe some blast got through to the other side of the hoop.

First shot in an interstellar war? Considering the size of a hoop, about a thousandth of a megaton may have got through, if any blast at all. No repercussions from the aliens, at least not as yet. We needed to do more than nuke a hoop? Damn the Chinese—they might have provoked anything.

Svelte shrugs. "Only just found out. Can't follow everything."

"You're fast."

WHEN WE SPEAK of the aliens, precisely what do we mean? Precision is vital in intelligence. It's important to regularly re-analyze what we think we know in case of some new interpretation. It can be fatal to make assumptions then stick to them.

First of all, from nowhere, came the hoops. They appeared worldwide during a single day, tens of millions of them. Next came the Varroa, who—or which—used the hoops to arrive and exit. Is anyone—or anything—else involved about whom we know sod all?

It only took a week for the myriads of hoops to bestow impediments upon the world's population. A hoop would swoop. Of a sudden the targeted person found a cage around some part of their body. I need to keep my own left leg stretched out beneath my desk on account of my knee-cage.

A transfixing bar holds an imped in place. In itself this doesn't hurt, but woe betide anyone who has an imped removed by surgery or by DIY sawing. They'll experience agony until a hoop gets round to renewing the affliction, maybe next day, maybe a week later.

Hoops don't swoop upon someone who's up a ladder, say—they wait for a more suitable moment. Smart hoops. If you shut yourself up tight in your home, a hoop will appear as if by magic. Hoops are about a meter in diameter.

Nothing we do affects them. Exotic substance, say scientists. Might be made of strings.

Ah, I have just cottoned on: Exprisonment, the title of Quantum Entanglement's proposed gig, is the opposite of imprisonment. We're all confined by our impeds, all constrained, but at the same time we're free to walk about. We're exprisoned.

"So," I say to Svelte, "do we butt in on Quantum Entanglement and take charge of this hum-mix event? All sorts of measuring equipment on site? Or do we limit ourselves to observing? In which case," as I appraise her clothing, "just how do we dress?"

"Or undress."

"You mean literally?"

"Some kids'll go nude or scanty. Not most."

"Glad to hear it. Is this only for young people?"

She shakes her head. "You get worked up by Kore with a friend of any age, or even on your own. It's non-discriminatory, like sex for the disabled. Impeds looked like fucking the club and dance scene, like how do you dance with a box on your foot? Kore says fuck off to impeds."

"You mean there'll be some sort of orgy?"

"Some micro-orgies maybe, not mass writhing. There's like a spiritual dimension, like an orgasm reaching heaven. Transcending the body, flying free."

"And *Sighs and Cries* was a response to impeds?"

"No, *Sighs and Cries* came out a few months before the hoops. What QE are planning right now is their response to the hoops. They must've been sampling and mixing for months."

"High time to stick our noses in."

"Party time? Dude!"

So THE VARROA come through the hoops. They look like giant bees, size of an electric toaster. *Varrr-oh-aah, varrr-oh-aah*—that's the sound they make. A bit loud for wing beats. The noise suggests some kind of protective energy field, whatever that might be. Bee-ing as how we can't catch a Varroa nor harm them in any way.

There's a terrestrial parasite named Varroa, which sucks the blood of our terrestrial bees. This enfeebles the bees. So they collect less pollen. So less honey gets made. After a few months, bye-bye hive. The Varroa and their hoops certainly impair human beings, so the name sticks.

The Varroa could be robots made by aliens (hitherto unseen), sent through the hoops to impair us and assess the effects.

Those hypothetical aliens might be:

softening us up for the real invasion—however, some ethics committee of alien races disapproves of brutal methods and awards Brownie points for ingenuity;

making sex difficult so we'll slowly go extinct; the birth rate is scarily down, vacant planet in another couple of centuries at the present rate (see invasion scenario, above);

hampering us so that we don't get above ourselves by suddenly making some scientific breakthrough such as developing interstellar travel and causing mayhem;

practicing an art form;

fill in your own guess.

Many countries have sent smart little spy-flyers through hoops, though here in London we know of none that ever returned or transmitted any data back. SETI specialists—Searchers for Extraterrestrial Intelligence—try in vain to analyze the Varroa noise and communicate. Everything's guesswork. Now here's a different tack—the Kore people are going to carry out an innovative and maybe confrontational musical experiment. If they strike gold, wow. Let's not spoil the spontaneity of the experiment. Sometimes there can be too much consultation. We'll simply observe it, me and my Serbian who intrigues me—and of course we'll need someone to video unobtrusively so we have audiovisual for the record. This'll be on my own initiative. Hell, it's only a music group. Nothing might come of this, then I'd be wasting resources, right?

Before the hoops came and my left knee was caged, I was mainly liaising with the French security service about the Islamic terrorist threat. That's how I met Miriam Claudel, six years ago now. That ended, and for the past two years there's been no one else. I much prefer relationships to arise in the natural course of events rather than to go hunting.

"THE STUDIO" IS the name for a nineteenth-century vicarage in Lambeth, converted and extended into a nursing home, which subsequently went bankrupt. With mucho money from American and Euro tours and a zillion sales, Benny Wallace and Trev Tate bought the place before the aliens arrived.

It's going to be club night there tonight—anything to keep our spirits up.

A mild sunny evening, this fifth anniversary (in days) of my first meeting Svelte. I drive with the window down. My long denim skirt, its big pockets embroidered with swirls of daisies, laps pixie boots. White blouse, sleeveless denim bolero jacket. A bit Country Dance, but it takes all sorts. Alongside me, Svelte is in scarlet and black. In the back, Tony Cullen from Surveillance sports a box on his left hand—that's his digicam disguised as an imped. His real imped is some sort of complicated groin truss. Consequently he doesn't much like sitting, even on a commode chair at home, he told me. Usually, quote unquote, he sprawls on a sofa like a feasting Roman. Looks rather like a Roman, Tony does, with those crimped blond curls and eagle nose. He mustn't see much gay action these days, what with his truss. He wears loose baggy fawn pants and an oversize cream sweater.

There's so much less traffic on the roads these days that the air almost smells sweet. Easy-peasy to park my disabled-adapted Volvo turbo-diesel on a street of shops; try finding a parking space in this part of London before the impeds. Walking half a mile with a knee-cage won't be much fun but we're being discreet.

Out clamber Tony and I awkwardly. Svelte slides out and is instantly, gracefully upright. I admire her.

The theory that we might all be atoning for something in our past by the type of impeds we wear is probably ridiculous. Must my leg be immobilized because I was captain of the hockey team at Oxford? Because Svelte was a singer, does she need an imped up near her vocal chords?

Our pace along the street is determined by my need to swing my stiffened left leg in an arc. A hoop drifts overhead, ignored by most people. It's easy to tell who's heading for the party. Girl in a one-piece Spiderman bathing costume and short frilly skirt, her friend in black bra and panties, boots and cowboy hat. Girl wearing hot-shorts and an off-the-shoulder top, her knee-imped just like mine except it's bright red. She must have painted or enameled the cage herself, which shows spirit. Various others.

Svelte told me that Benny and Trev aimed to centralize studios for a half-dozen tekky groups, the idea being a synergistic commune all rubbing off each other while doing their own unique things. Wisdom was that you oughtn't to live where your studio is because that way you'd become entrapped and not have a life, but as it turned out in the wake of hoops and impeds, The Studio provided a sort of sanctuary, an oasis. Some of the music made there is really demented, Svelte said with approval—such as the stuff by Psalms of Madness.

We're only interested in the original Quantum Entanglement band, which consists of Daniel and Sean and AlanJune—as those last two members call themselves, as though they don't have separate identities. Maybe an imped locks Alan and June together nowadays—we'll see.

Passing a fish and chip shop, funky jazz drifts out along with the smells. A beautiful Chinese girl with long black hair is scooping chips out of a fryer. Personally I would put the hair up in a net in those circumstances. But oh, the hair partly hides her imped. A small red box—like a radio—is bonded to the side of her head. And that's the source of the jazz! Does that box play all the time? How does she ever get to sleep? How isn't she half insane? Yet she looks serene. Maybe she went deaf.

"Sally, cop a look," says Svelte. I'd told her to call me Sally—Miss Adamson would sound absurd at a gig.

Generally one avoids gawping at abnormally impeded individuals, since basically we're all in the same boat. However, the middle-aged woman crossing the street toward us is something else. Living impeds are rather rare, and that woman's right forearm is a tortoiseshell cat.

To be accurate, it's most of a cat. Fused to the elbow-stump of the woman's right arm, the animal lacks hind legs. She's cradling the moggy against her chest, its front paws clinging to her shoulder, its tail flicking to and fro.

"Imagine feeding it!" Tony is holding his boxed hand very steady—I think he's filming the woman. At home, does he have a private video library of weird impeds? Heigh-ho, anything to keep sexuality alive and kicking.

Imagine that poor woman kneeling patiently by Kitty's food bowl, purring encouragingly. Imagine when the cat wants a crap.

"What did she do to deserve that, eh?" says Tony. "Love her pet excessively?"

"What did the cat do?" counters Svelte.

We hush as the woman passes by.

A lot of impeds seem arbitrary, while some do seem poignantly appropriate. So there's the "snapshot" theory that the imped reflects what a person was thinking about at the exact moment of caging. People thinking banal thoughts received any old imped from stock; but obsessives tended to be thinking about their obsessions.

"They're practical jokers," says Tony. "Somewhere in Varroa land, audiences are laughing their heads off and rolling in the aisles."

As if on cue, the noise intrudes: *varrr-oh-aah, varrr-oh-aah-oh-aah*, a wild wind rushing through trees, the sound of a giant bee flying. One of the Varroa comes cruising overhead, dangling scaly jointed legs, its glassy-looking wings beating fast. Yellow fur streaked with orange, black bulbous eyes, antennae like miniature antlers.

"Sod off sod off!" a bloke shouts at it. He shakes his imped vengefully—a right-hand box. Most people look the other way.

Rather higher in the sky, a passenger jet is descending across London toward distant Heathrow. That isn't such a frequent sight as formerly. Tourism's almost dead.

A skinny black chap equipped with a full headcage emerges from a newsagent. Cradling a toddler in his arms, he looks like a parody of an American football player. Of a sudden the black man legs it at quite a pace. Cottoned onto a Varroa in the neighborhood, did he? Whatever a daddy does, his child will receive an imped when it's nearing a meter tall. Head-Cage is probably a bit nuts and is trying to stop his offspring from learning to walk, so that the child never appears tall. Well, that won't work, is the long and the tall of it. Long equals tall.

A HIGH STONE WALL tipped by rusty spikes surrounds the grounds of the ex-rectory, ex-nursing home. Cedars, cypresses, and Scots pines rear up. At the gateway a couple of blokes stuff entrance money into the pockets of long, open leather coats. On account of his waist-cage, one of these collectors looks pregnant with some robot child, its curving spine and ribs and other metal bones wrapped around his bare midriff. The other fellow has a solid box on one foot—after a year, how the inside must stink.

So NOW WE'RE heading up a long driveway through shrubbery—in company with teens and twenties mainly, a bass beat somewhere ahead of us. I'm wondering what homeowners in the area think about the noise, whenever there's club night. Prior to the hoops, when people could get to gigs further afield, I guess no club nights happened here. Priorities have changed as to what annoys us.

Tony covertly films a gorgeous black girl ahead of us wearing pinstripe pants cut into thin thongs exposing her ass and legs. Hand-cage resembling a medieval weapon. Maybe Tony isn't gay. I don't care a toss. I'd rather it was just Svelte and me here this evening, but there are proper ways to do things, as Tony's presence reminds me.

The black girl's blonde friend sports a frilly skirt and a bulging grille of a metal bra, to the back of which is fixed butterfly wings of yellow muslin. I tell a lie—that bra is a breast-cage, which she has dolled up. Quite a crowd is heading for club night.

A big marquee comes into view.

"They're brave, these kids," says Svelte. "I admire them."

"Whistling while Rome burns," says Tony.

"You're excited. Enjoy the view."

Grinning, Svelte says something that sounds like, "S'avem che bea shi fute!"

"What's that?"

"A Romanian toast. It means: here's to a drink and a fuck."

"Look," says Tony, "it's inconvenient for me to get excited—not to mention unprofessional."

Svelte doesn't know about Tony's groin truss. She's so exotic, Svelte is, though doubtless not to herself. Probably she's hetero. Not necessarily, though. Time will tell. Or will it? I really must keep my head clear.

Let's take a look in the vast marquee first, where things are warming up—as in hot bodies and hot lights fanning through aroma-mists. However, the music playing from big speakers right now is like cool liquid, kind of distanced rather than intimate. What's playing at the moment are recordings. On stage a quartet of machines wait, for later on. Digi-keyboard, drum machine, hypersynth, and a whatnot—I've no idea which is which, or what, though Svelte does.

"Nice backward reverb setting off the vocal line," she comments loudly, and I think I understand. "Just don't overdo it! Aw shit, there we go. That'll excite the bats," sneers Svelte.

Now a different remix rivets me. Sighs and cries over a pulsing bass line—kosher kore, the piece I heard in the office:

Ev-ery-thing you
Ev-ery-thing you do
You do, you do, you do, you do...

Youngsters waggle their arms overhead and shuffle and shimmy, frantic to enjoy. Lip-rings, nose-studs, belly-button trinkets make the impeds seem like huge exotic piercings. The white girl in black bra and panties, boots, and cowboy hat smooches with a black girl in white bra, et cetera. I approve. A huge Hawaiian garland of bright plastic flowers hangs upon another girl's brief blue cocktail dress. A bloke's T-shirt reads KISS MY ARSE, SEXY, although the bum-cage bulking under his oversize jeans makes this unlikely. Why doesn't he wear a kilt? Similarly impeded chaps favor kilts. Older people are in the crowd too, so I don't feel far out of place. We have two or three hours before QE perform live, plenty of time to nose around independently.

I spy a midget, a very little man indeed with a large head, a bit more than knee-high to me. He's wearing a string vest and very brief yellow shorts, showing off his bandy, hairy, muscular legs—no, showing off the absolute absence of any imped! He's immune because of his extreme shortness. In the land of the impeded the diminutive midget is king, and he does show off, struttingly. He must think he's sexy these days; maybe he knows it for a fact.

A FRECKLY GINGER-HAIRED man of forty-odd, brown leather bomber jacket hung on his shoulders—a cage enclosing his right hand—is nattering fairly urgently to a thin tall guy in baggy shorts and a T-shirt showing a cunt, a cage upon his right foot. Cunt T-shirt's cadaverous face and wild shoulder-length hair fit the website picture I saw of Sean of QE.

I scoop the snoop from my pocket to my ear. Looks like a tiny flesh-tone hearing-aid, if anyone even notices. The directional mic in my pocket is radio-linked.

"... could easily be a real word, exprisonment."

"Like Björk thinking 'homogenic' was a real word? Until someone told her it was bullshit. But she stuck with it."

The thin fellow intones, "The way you stick with me, though I'll never be free... Needs pulling apart. The way you, the way you, stick with me, stick with me..."

"Don't take the piss, Sean! Is Caz going to show?"

"Dancing's the candle, she's the moth." Just at this moment, a gorgeous blonde teeny-girl wearing green hot-shorts and a gauzy off-the-shoulder top comes by, her left foot caged, the other in a green fetish boot. Sean pivots toward her and jiggles his imped. "Hi jewel, we're a pair, you and I. I live in The Studio—want to see inside?"

She eyes him then says, "Foosh off."

Ginger says appeasingly, "Kids can be Puritans. They just don't look or act it."

"So why come to a fucking Kore gig? Are you a Puritan yourself these days, Pete, if you can't shag Benny's treasure?"

"I don't like the word 'shag'."

"I need some Heineken Ice. Want to come in The Studio?"

"I'll hang around here for a bit."

"Hell, Benny can't go anywhere." Benny, the co-owner. "And he's getting fatter every day. No exercise, and overeating."

Let me get this straight—Pete has screwed Caz, who is co-owner Benny's girlfriend or wife or whatever. Pete is hoping to see Caz tonight, so Pete isn't resident in The Studio—or not anymore? Benny may have found out about Caz and Pete and had him expelled from the community. Presumably Pete can't be entirely *non grata* with the other co-owner, Trev, otherwise those guys on the gate wouldn't have let Pete in at all. I already noticed a couple of bouncers in jeans and bright orange T-shirts—security, first aid, whatever. Both have head-cages as impeds. Like visored helmets convenient for head-butting if the need arises. If Pete's blacklisted, doubtless they'd know about it. I keep Pete in sight as he wanders alone through the huge, ever more crowded marquee.

Benny can't go anywhere; Benny gets no exercise. Does that mean he's severely impeded, more so than most people? That might explain opportunity and motive for infidelity by Caz.

AHA. A TALL, slim dark-haired woman dressed in a long green skirt and lace blouse has arrived—and Pete is heading her way. Maybe she's forty or more, and she has a black patch over her left eye. Assuming that she's Caz, has Benny got angry and punched her in the eye? Presumably not if he's immobilized.

PETE AND CAZ talk for a good five minutes, while I eavesdrop on them. Pete wants her to come away with him, but she can't. Not won't—how she yearns for that—but she can't. Not yet.

—Caz, can't you abscond with Contessa? And anyway, it's all just bullying bluster. And how could he manage to torture...

I expected Pete to say—a child. But he says:

—a cat?

Contessa must be the name of a cat, Caz's cat. Like a child to her. Benny has threatened Caz's cat, if she misbehaves.

—I don't have a cat basket.

—Hell, I'll buy you one!

—How would I explain it?

—He's all hot air.

—Can I risk that?

ON THE ONE hand, Benny's threat seems real to Caz, and horrible. Yet from the way Caz talks about Benny, she seems to care for the man and feel sorry for him. She's unwilling to abandon him.

—Pete, I need to show him soon...

Show him what?

AT LAST I cotton on. As if in compensation for immobilizing Benny, the hoops swapped one of Benny's eyes for one of Caz's. If and when Caz raises her eye-patch, Benny can see what she's seeing. And vice versa? I've no idea. Caz must need to close her own eye whenever she raises the patch, otherwise there would be a hopeless jumble of double vision, two different scenes eyed simultaneously.

Benny's eye is Caz's impediment. Yet Benny can't hear or feel or smell, only see—otherwise how could Pete and Caz have succeeded in making love? I imagine Caz's patch coming loose one time as she tossed her head to and fro upon a pillow, her noise of pleasure suddenly changing to a cry of fright.

—You still jerking him off, Caz?

—It seems only fair—how can I refuse?

Does this wound Pete?

—I do love you, Pete. I think about you every night—

is the last thing I hear her say to him.

Reluctantly Pete moves away from her, disappearing into the crowd. Caz dances on her own, not straying from the same spot—for now she shuts her right eye and raises the patch to her brow. Her right eye was green, but her left eye is brown. Hoops can join part of a living cat to a person's arm in direct proximity. Hoops can also connect an eye remotely to a brain. This needs reporting.

Investigators will descend upon Benny and Caz.

I WATCH CAZ as she dances, keeping Benny's eye masked, or stands still with it exposed. She's relaxed, yet wary. Periodically she and Pete coincide again for two or three minutes at a time. It's noisy and several times Pete has to ask Caz to repeat herself. Quite often she's looking away as she talks to him.

Most of their chat is about trivialities, or acquaintances. After that first encounter Pete doesn't implore or beg. No matter how frustrated he is, he mustn't want to spend their precious stolen time whining or cajoling, but companionably. Caz seems well able to hide her feelings, but she must love Pete otherwise she wouldn't take risks at all.

I'm fascinated with what seems to be the situation between them, and with the idea of the Eye of Another in one's head.

By itself that threat to torture the cat seems absurd and histrionic—yet at the same time ingenious, I suppose. Benny knows how to press Caz's buttons and scare her. Maybe there are other threats too. Personally I don't think she'll ever run off with Pete, no matter how much she may wish to, at least in her dreams. Pete almost realizes this. Before the coming of the Varroa I read a statistic that only about twenty percent—or was it less?—of wives actually leave their husbands as the result of an affair. I wonder if Pete and Caz manage to meet away from The Studio, and for how long? That spying eye, it's worse than a photophone.

AFTER A GOOD hour and a half Svelte returns to me. In the interval I've hobnobbed with Tony Cullen a few times. The first thing I ask Svelte is, "Have you been inside The Studio?" I'm remembering Sean's invitation to that blonde girl—my God, I'm having a jealous thought about Svelte.

"Sure," she says.

"How?"

"Got chatted up."

"Did anything happen?"

She grins. "Just led her on a bit. Can't do much surveillance if you're in bed."

Did Svelte go with a *her* by coincidence, or by design?

I tell Svelte about Benny and Pete and Caz.

"Wow, that's heavy surveillance, jealous guy's eye looking out of your own face. Needs a lot of composure to take that in your stride! I got a glimpse of Alan and June. They aren't fused or chained together, though I guess you couldn't perform too well like that. Fancy dancing a bit?"

Me, with my knee cage? Svelte's invitation excites me. Is she playing with me, being innocently friendly, thinking protective coloration, or what? Her eyes sparkle. I wonder if she did a line of coke in The Studio with *her*, on duty too. I mustn't seem nothing-venture, especially not here, so I give dancing a go.

All the while, other bodies are dancing in a slow demented euphoric way to the thump and pulse of tekky. A girl in long boots with a crimson crop-top and golden bangle piercing her belly button has what I can only call a cunt-cage. How on earth does she get her panties on? The penny drops—she painted them onto already de-haired flesh, unattainable now except by the touch of a brush. Two young fellows clash hand-cages together, triumphing over affliction.

AT LONG LAST the head-caged bouncers and some helpers lower one wall of the marquee, exposing the event to the night, and the night to the event. And now the four members of QE come to their music machines, facing across the crowd toward the canvas wall-that-was, now a big darkness plus silhouettes of trees.

Sean, I've already seen. Daniel is a big black man with a shaved head, his imped a huge shoulder-cage adorned with an equally huge red epaulet. The cage cramps his upper arm but he can use his lower arm well enough. June dresses Goth-like, white face, lurid red lips, purple hairpieces entwined with her own jet hair. A dark gown swells at her belly—that'll be her cage. Beak-nosed, coal-eyed Alan has long white hair, presumably bleached, spilling from a head cage, and he wears a white robe with a scarlet pentacle on his chest. He's like a Wicca priest with his head in a birdcage.

Most of the lights go out, apart from spots illuminating the music machines.

It's Alan who addresses the crowd. He gestures beyond them at the night.

"Oh ye aliens who exprison us! We've deconstructed your humming and now we'll hum a new tune for you big bees! We're gonna pipe you back to oblivion like the Piper of Hamelin did, only he never had a hypersynth. You feeling caged, people? Hum along, come along! Welcome to Exprisonment."

June lifts a mic, and to begin with starts to hum.

A BEE-HUM can become a banshee-howl, almost drowning what June is singing with abandoned, sweating passion—Fuckyou Varroa forfucking-withus...   cometo   theVarroafuck... comecomecome... comefuckcome... fuckingcome fuckinggo...

Double-beats from the drum machine are loudening and lessening like a disordered heart. Heterodyning, is that the word?

Is that the Varroa hum played backward now?

A LIGHT GLOWS silver, a hoop in the night. Sweet Christ, has this noise actually brought a hoop here? The players are gesturing, dancers are all turning to face the darkness and the ring of silver light which poises upright upon the lawn. Tony is pointing his phony imped, the digicam. "Oh dude," cries Svelte. I have to get a full team here— I shout into my mobile but I can't damn well make out the replies. Svelte bellows into my ear the words, reson-ant frequ-ency.

The hoop is expanding. We've never known a hoop behave this way before. The base of it is below ground invisibly, so what I'm seeing is a kind of archway rather than a circle.

In place of the nighttime that was beyond, now a shimmer of blues and greens and rose fills the area inside the hoop. It's like the membrane of some huge soap bubble about to be blown. I'm wondering if a sudden wind from beyond might in a moment propel a floating sphere out into our world—when of a sudden the space inside the hoop becomes a view. Yes, an opening into a land-scape—of bushes and trees that are white ostrich plumes and tails of peacocks and adornments of birds of paradise and sulfur crests of cockatoos growing upward from ground that sparkles kalei-doscopically, ground resembling a mosaic of tiny crystals. The source of light is somewhere in a pale blue sky, unseen.

Otherworldly, strange, beautiful—we're seeing into another world. Never before have we seen elsewhere through a hoop.

Already us club-nighters are heading toward that magical scene—a surge of audience.

"Dude!" cries Svelte, and Tony Cullen knows that he needs to get closer too, and so do I, yam-mering into my mobile at Combi-Intel to come immediately, and so do priestly Alan and big black Daniel elbowing past us. In the forefront of flesh and glad rags of all kinds for a moment I glimpse Pete hustling Caz along with him toward that archway to elsewhere—he's seizing his chance to kidnap Caz no matter to where, and they're through, a half-dozen kids capering alongside them, and they aren't stifling or choking in some toxic alien atmosphere, or at least not yet. They're amongst the lovely alien vegetation. More and more of the audience follow.

I think the noise from the speakers has gone into a loop. QE were recording their live performance; the recording's replaying now. The stretched hoop seems to wobble. Before, it was precise.

"Hurry up!" from Svelte. She grabs me strongly from my good side so that I shan't risk falling over on account of my knee-cage, propelling me with her, for of course I must go through to see. This is like an assault by some motley children's crusade on some city with a breached wall, as people stream through. As when the Pied Piper reached the mountain that opened up for all the enchanted boys and girls...

"Tony, stay to brief the team that gets here—"

"Bollocks, I'm not missing this. Enough impeds'll be left behind to tell—"

What I'm about to do may be madness, but I shall be adventuring with Svelte—oh, what am I thinking? It's my duty to investigate as fully as I can. What will we eat and drink, how will we ever get back again?

Just as we pass through, that midget chap pushes past. Almost immediately he stumbles, sprawling upon the sparkly soil. More like a beach of multi-hued mica, which his impact grooves. He doesn't roll or scramble up. Air smells faintly of burnt toast and vanilla.

"Wait, Svelte!" Stoop and press the pulse in the midget's neck. None there.

Check his wrist. "He's dead."

"Too much excitement."

"No, why is he dead?"

An almighty pop, and there's no hoop anymore. Nor loudspeaker noise from any marquee, nor oval of nighttime, nor marquee, nor nothing of where we came from. The bright yellow-white sun dazzling high above the feathertrees looks smaller than... well, it's a different sun.

How many people are wandering about, with bugger all in the way of supplies or equipment? Two hundred of us? All impeded, too.

Why did the midget drop dead?

A couple of hundred of us, and no means of getting back. I know why we rushed through the archway—after the utter frustration that everyone has felt ever since the hoops arrived, an almost orgasmic release of tension, a sense of exaltation. The prettiness of this—um, paradise?—contributed. People desired to cavort.

Orange T-shirt with head-cage kneels by the midget, turns him over, tries some first aid.

"Svelte, the midget didn't have any cage. And he died as soon as he came through."

"You mean having cages lets us into here? Why? No, he had a heart attack or a stroke."

"Maybe he had one of those because he didn't have a cage."

"Like, as a ticket? Or to protect him? Lot of excitement tonight. Small chap, he overdid himself."

"Jacko's definitely dead," announces the head-cage, and he stares at me hard.

"Look," I say to him, "you're security, right?" When he nods, "We have to organize all these people."

"What's it to you?" Behind the visor, blue eyes, chaotic sandy hair—quite hard to comb!

Deep breath. "My name's Sally Adamson. I'm from Combined Intelligence. We were keeping an eye on your musical experiment tonight."

Tony Cullen is by my side to back me up, as is Svelte.

"I'm Bryce. There are more of you back at The Studio?"

Alas, no, at least not yet. I'm hoping that my yammering into the mobile raised the alarm. Nobody ever could have reasonably expected this result from tonight's techno caper.

Why, pray, did I stage what amounts to a private surveillance, all on my own say-so? I ought to be for the high jump. Exactly how far have we jumped away from Earth?

"You have a radio with you?" Bryce demands. "Or a phone?"

"Do you seriously expect—?"

"Have you tried?"

He's right, so I pull out my phone.

"No signal."

"Dial anyway, see what happens."

Dee-du-doo-doo-du-do... followed by silence.

"Now you know for sure, don't you?"

"Why did you come through, Bryce?"

"Somebody in charge had to." Looked at from that point of view, I suppose he's more in charge than me. "Seeing as they already know me, the kids might pay some attention. You'd best stick to advising, hmm?" He eyes Tony and Svelte. "Got guns?"

No, and no.

He laughs shortly. "All you got is combined intelligence. Pretty disconnected right now."

People have spread out among the featherbushes, feathertrees. Partly concealed by ostrich plumes, two kids seem to be fucking. Getting to the kore of the problem, eh? That's unfair—they're true pioneers, the first human beings to have sex on an alien world. That's one defiant one for the record book.

Svelte exclaims, "Look, how do we know this place is actual? Why not a virtual reality, and cages admit you into it? That's why Jacko couldn't take part, not his mind anyhow. Maybe the Varroa belong to some super-evolved combi-intelligence that hangs out in mind-space."

"Yeah," sarcastically from Bryce, "like this thing dumps millions of tons of solid fucking cages onto Earth? And it's virtual?"

"Okay, just a thought. No birds or insects anywhere in sight, you'll notice. No ecology." Svelte's right, at least regarding the area nearby. "You mightn't expect birds as such, but there oughta be something besides a bunch of fancy feathers." Svelte really is very acrobatic in her thinking.

COMMUNICATE, COMMUNICATE. COMMUNICATE with the club-nighters, to get ourselves organized. Mustn't wander off chaotically. Food, drink, explore, communicate. Communicating with home is impossible. Or is it... ? I'm looking at Caz and Pete standing hand in hand, that black patch over her left eye, while Bryce and Svelte rally people...

If Benny can see through her eye back home— and Caz through his?—when they're apart from each other... How does it happen, what's the link? Advanced alien science, some sort of instant linked vision-at-a-distance, quantum stuff, a shortcut through spacetime? How distant does distant have to be before it's too far?

My phone can display four lines of memo or text on its screen the size of my thumb.

"YOU'RE CAZ. I'M Sally, from Combined Intelligence—you understand?" Caz does. "And you're Pete. Caz, I know you and Benny can see what the other sees."

"How do you know that?"

"I was snooping. That's my job. We appear to be marooned here, wherever here is. You may be a way to communicate with home..."

PETE DOESN'T WANT her to co-operate. Small wonder. They've escaped together, and almost at once here's me asking her to let Benny see everything, supposing it's possible.

"Realistically," I say, "with no food or water we're probably going to die here, unless something different kills us first."

Pete hugs his Caz, as if he can preserve the two of them by pure wish and willpower. Wishes don't rule the real world.

I'm going to die too. Me and Svelte. I'll think about that later. The important thing is that Caz understands this. I know she heeds duties and obligations even if those frustrate her dreams. Only fair, isn't it? Wasn't that what she said?

"Caz, this is the first ever information we have about anything regarding where our invaders come from. Back home nobody will know anything unless…"

She nods miserably. Or bravely. There are different sorts of bravery. Women understand much more about self-sacrifice than men do.

Pete sits down with his back to us. Doesn't want to watch this. Or doesn't want to be noticed by Caz's Benny-eye? If Caz looks round, Pete's ginger hair will be very visible.

WELL, IT WORKS. It works. We're connected. Phone screen and Benny's displaced eye reading it at this end, Caz's eye in Benny's head at the other end perceiving a notepad he writes on. Hallelujah. But…

I couldn't believe any man would exploit this situation for blackmail. Benny uses it. Oh he uses it. Benny won't tell anyone else a fucking thing unless Caz promises, promises, swears on the memory of her mother, to return to him. Obviously forget about torturing the cat—seems that wasn't sufficient to hold her. Oh and forget the extreme unlikelihood of her being able to return—unless, I suppose, when Combi-Intel gets its act together, they manage to control a hoop by the same method as CE used. My god, I must grill those two, the priest and the big black guy. Alan and

June on their own may be able to give Combi-Intel enough guidance to re-open the hoop. Hey, there's hope, a possibility—why am I so blind and slow? Too much to think about, that's why. The same hope didn't enter into Bryce's head, or Svelte's. Or if so, they didn't say. That's because we aren't desperate yet. Only just got here. Novelty value still prevails.

Caz opens her right eye, and tears jerk from it. Tiny discs of water fly as if she's expelling contact lenses one after another. I've never seen anyone cry quite like that, projectile tears, tears so pent up that they don't trickle but fly for a few seconds at least. Then she shuts her own eye tight.

"I can't see the phone now," she reminds me. "Write: I promise." And I peck at the keys with my fingernail.

Pete tells her fiercely, "You can break any promise extorted by a threat."

"I'm sorry. It's a personal thing. A promise is a promise."

"A shitty vicious threat to keep knowledge from the whole world unless he can hang onto you like a dog in the manger!"

"You can't really blame him. We have so much personal baggage, him and me. What would become of him?"

Is Caz a coward, or is she very brave, able to sacrifice the hope of personal happiness for the sake of many other people who will never even realize?

"Shit." Pete doesn't try to interfere as I hold the phone screen up to Benny's brown eye.

"Varroa—!"

A hum coming closer.

Soon we're being inspected.

BEFORE LONG A second Varroa comes. As us club-nighters stare up, many chattering to each other, the mutual hum of the Varroas modulates, seeming to search through a spectrum of sound. Soon I think I'm hearing thrumming echoes of human words, words that evade meaning as if played backward, half-words.

"Fucking hell," says big black Daniel, "they're sampling us. I'll swear it." Indeed he has already sworn.

"Or like they're tuning in," says Svelte.

A comprehensible sentence emerges:

Why you bring child must die without zzzwzz without without cage? This is the only time a Varroa has ever communicated anything. But no child is here...

"It thinks Jacko's a child. The dead body isn't a child!" I shout out at the Varroa. "The dead body is a very short adult, too short to receive a cage!"

How you open zzzwzz open open hoop?

Daniel prods one finger upward defiantly at the Varroa. "With our music, that's how! You want to buy a memory stick?"

Unready.

"Yeah, don't have no memory sticks here, do I?"

Unready.

I have a sense that the Varroa are lower-level intelligences compared with whatever may have created them. Bred them. Assembled them. I think sheepdogs—times ten as regards capabilities.

Above us, the two Varroa begin to circle. No, that circle is spiraling outward.

Very soon they're racing around, dodging the tall feathertrees, looping around all of us. Their hum is loud, *MUM-UM-MUM-UM*. A curving line of bright light begins to follow each now like contrails, two lengthening arcs of light, which soon join up. Those Varroa are guiding the huge horizontal hoop encompassing all of us—suddenly intensifying as it flashes toward the ground, which is of rough short moonlit grass, and I do keep my footing while a fair few around me are tumbling because of impeds or disorientation. As the afterimage of the ring of light fades, an expanse of flat concrete stretches into the distance where I'm making out large low buildings and silhouettes of big parked planes, passenger jets. And a half-full Moon's in the sky amidst clouds and stars. Already people are struggling up or being helped. We've been dumped unceremoniously at a huge airport near an unlit runway, though further off are a fair number of lights. We conserve power nowadays where possible. Someone's whimpering about their ankle, twisted or broken.

"It's Heathrow!" shrills a girl.

Airports are anonymous, yet that could easily be Western Avenue over there on the perimeter, where any hotels remaining open won't have many guests these days. This may well be London's Heathrow, nowhere near so busy as used to be.

Of a sudden the runway lights come on—on account of us arriving? Shall we pretend to be a planeload of passengers, newly descended from

Sirius or some other star? Please proceed to passport control—what, no baggage? People begin heading toward the illuminated runway but Bryce bellows, "Stay here, everyone! The runway's dangerous. A plane'll be landing."

"There's no plane—"

"Idiot, they don't switch the lights on at the very last moment. Plane'll be ten minutes' away." Of course he's right.

Svelte's shining a slim torch, here, there.

"Lost something?" Tony asks her.

"Looking for feathers."

I see none in the beam from Svelte's torch. The Varroa or the big hoop must have retained any alien vegetation in the process of returning us—to a big empty flat space where we wouldn't collide with anything.

"Everybody stay right here," I call out. "I'll have us collected, bussed back to The Studio."

Now there's a signal for my phone. *Dee-du-doo-doo-du-do... ring ring.*

"THAT PLACE WAS artificial," Svelte insists to me as our crowded coach, the foremost of three, finally nears Lambeth. Combi-Intel persons on each coach are busy doing preliminary interviews of the club-nighters. There'll be a lot more interrogation by and by, especially of Daniel and Sean and Alan and June, although I suspect that neither QE nor anyone else will be able to control a hoop again by that same method. For we are unready.

"Made. Grown. The way you grow pretty crystals in a jar of some liquid. Maybe the feathers were all like sensors on the outside of some machine the size of a world. Or not as big—gravity could have been artificial. Maybe the place was a pleasure park for aliens, or like a sculpture garden. But artificial, yes."

"So what does that imply?"

"I don't know." Svelte stares out of the window at houses, streets.

WHAT DOES UNREADY mean? Can the impeds be some sort of benevolent teaching aid? A focus for mental growth? A way of being able to attain the stars and join in, if only we can discover how? Something we might learn to use after ten years or after fifty years? The Varroa didn't mean that it wasn't in the market for a memory stick.

"We'll talk more later about this artificial idea of yours, eh, Svelte?" Oh, I am tempted by her, and I still don't know if it's possible. If only. Just let me not be too impulsive, as I surely was, going to club-night with her, only the two of us and Tony Cullen. In retrospect I was rather foolish. I don't like to be foolish.

One person is unaccounted for, the dead Jacko. Is that because his body was lying beyond the ring of light when it descended? Or because a dead body is more akin to a featherbush than to a living person?

NOW THAT WE'VE debussed, Pete is talking urgently to Caz, and I'm a snooper again.

"...meaningless, because Benny helped bugger all! He made a phone call; so what? What else does the co-owner of a place do, that loses a couple of hundred people? Pay no attention? It was the Varroa brought us back, no thanks to him!"

"Even so," she says, so sad-sounding, "I did promise." Caz tosses her hair, perhaps to hide tears or dispel them, and wanders toward The Studio.

We all have our cages. But will we ever learn from them?

Jellyfish

Mike Resnick & David Gerrold

ONCE UPON A time, when the world was young, there was a man named Dillon K. Filk. The K. stood for Kurvis.

He was insane. But that was okay. The world was insane, so he fitted right in.

Dillon K. Filk also had a serious substance abuse problem, but that was okay too. He was a product of his time, a confluence of historical and mimetic conditions that created substance abuse as a way of life. The entire planet was addicted to a variety of comestibles and combustibles. Caffeine, alcohol, nicotine, and oil were the primary global addictions; substances injected directly into veins were secondary.

Filk's own chemical adventures were based on what was available and what it would mix well with—marijuana, amyl and butyl nitrates (also known as poppers), ecstasy, peyote, mushrooms, the occasional toad, dried banana skins, cocaine (both powdered and crystallized), heroin (snorted and injected), Quaaludes, Vicodin, horse tranquilizers, PCP, angel dust, cough syrup, amphetamines, methedrine, ephedrine, mescaline, methadone, barbiturates, Prozac, valium, lithium, and the occasional barium enema. And once in a while, airplane glue. But Filk had never taken acid—LSD (lysergic acid diethylamide)—because he didn't want to risk destabilizing his brain chemistry.

Whether Filk's mental instability had caused his substance abuse problems or whether his substance abuse had triggered his delusional state is both irrelevant and unknowable. The two conditions were synergistic. They were complementary parts of his being, and essential to his ability to function in this time and in this place.

Filk spent his days sitting alone in a room, talking to himself, having long discussions that only he could understand. A prurient eavesdropper, and there had been an occasional few, some even paid by various governments, would not have been able to follow his verbalized train of thought because most of the time Filk himself did not stay on the tracks.

In any given moment Filk might suddenly realize that, "Hypersex exists only in the trans-human condition." A moment later, he might postulate, "Therefore, the robots will be functionally autistic." And a moment after that, he would conclude, "So the issue of sentience is resolved in favor of hormones." He didn't know quite what it all meant (though he loved the word "Hypersex", which he was sure was spelled with a capital H), but it sounded profound.

Whenever Filk came to a conclusion like that, he would nod to himself in satisfaction and turn to the battered old manual typewriter that sat on a rickety TV tray table next to his bed, and he would start typing slowly and methodically, using only his two index fingers. He often said he had stolen the typewriter from one of his ex-wives. But occasionally he admitted that he had bought it at a pawnshop because the invisible voices had told him to. But sometimes, he claimed that William Burroughs had given it to him as an act of punishment—punishment for the typewriter, which had taken on the form of a gigantic insect and refused to stop rattling its mandibles at Burroughs. The origin of the typewriter depended on how much blood was coursing through Filk's drugstream.

Dillon K. Filk typed four pages every day, and would not get up until he had typed them. When he got to the bottom of the fourth page, he would stop. He was through for the day. Even if he was in the middle of a sentence, he would not start a fifth page. He would roll the finished page out of the typewriter and lay it face down on the slowly growing stack of pages to the left of the machine on the TV tray.

The next day, without looking at what he had written before, Filk would roll a fresh piece of paper into the typewriter and complete the hanging sentence, then continue until he had filled that day's four pages. And the day after that, four more.

"Hi-ho," Filk would say. "So it goes."

Filk punctuated his monologues with verbal motifs. He would say "Hi-ho" or "See?" or "So it goes." These were conversational spacers as he slipped and skidded from one notion to the next— his way of indicating to himself that he was finished with that particular moment.

Sometimes, he would type "Hi-ho" or "See?" or "So it goes" into his pages. Sometimes he needed to separate one idea from another, and "Hi-ho" and "See?" and "So it goes" were just as functional on paper as they were spoken aloud.

Occasionally, Filk needed one more sentence to fill his fourth page, and that was also a good place to type "Hi-ho" or "See?" or "So it goes." And once in a great while, "Of course."

Hi-ho.

See?

So it goes.

Of course.

From one day to the next, Filk paid little attention to what he had already written. No idea was ever worth more than eight hundred words. If an idea took more than eight hundred words to express, it was obviously too complicated for anyone to understand—including the writer. To Filk's mind, the universe was quite simple, it only looked complex. The only way to master the complexity was to understand the many component simplicities.

Many years ago, Filk had counted the words on his finished pages and determined that he averaged two hundred words per page. From that day on, he never typed more than four pages at a time.

Filk also understood that no human being was capable of writing a new idea every eight hundred words. A human being was so simple, he or she could only hold one idea at a time.

But Filk also knew that if he was a different person, then that different person would be holding a different idea in his head. The answer was simple—and it was obvious. Hi-ho. You are a new person every day. See? You are not the person you were the day before. So it goes. You are the person whose experience includes the day before, so you are different from a person whose experience does not include the day before. Of course.

So Filk would carefully type his four pages, consume some chemicals, and lie back down on his dirty sheets until hunger or thirst or the pressing needs of his bladder caused him to rise again. Usually a single diurnal cycle. Although once, after a particularly crucifying experience, it had taken him three days to rise again.

Filk had no loyalty to the past, as he was not that person anymore, so he never picked up a previous train of thought, always starting a new one. As a result, his writing had a peripatetic style and pace that few other authors could match.

Or understand.

Every hundred and twenty days, give or take a few, allowing for the occasional bouts of physical incapacity, Filk would have accumulated four hundred pages of text, give or take some number divisible by four. On that day, as if blinking awake from a long sleep, Filk would dutifully type a title in the center of a blank page and put that at the front of the stack; he would type "the end" in the center of another blank page and put that at the back of the stack. He never made up a title until the book was finished; because until it was finished, he did not know what it was about.

Then Filk would put the stack of pages into a box, and take the box to the local office supply store and have two copies made. He would also buy two more reams of paper and a new typewriter ribbon. On his way home, he would stop at the post office and mail one copy to himself as insurance, and another to his publisher in New York.

Filk's publisher was a man named Thorbald Helmholtz, the owner and operator of Helmholtz Publishing, Ltd. Like most publishers, Helmholtz was a thief. On receipt of the manuscript, Helmholtz would write a check for $2,500 to Dillon K. Filk and drop it into the mail the very same day. Without actually reading the work for its content, Helmholtz would copy-edit it for spelling and grammar errors. He would pick a cover that he thought would sell, regardless of whether it matched the book or not—and if it had a near-naked girl being ravished by Things, so much the better—and then he would hand both cover and manuscript to his wife, who would manage the actual process of production.

Approximately six months after the receipt of the manuscript, copies of the book would arrive in the bookstores. The books would stay on the shelves for three-and-a-half weeks, when they would be removed and replaced by the new books for the following month. The copies that had not sold would have their covers ripped off. The covers would be returned to the publisher as proof that those copies hadn't sold.

A book with Dillon K. Filk's name on it would only sell a paltry 90,000 copies, grossing only a half-million dollars in reported sales. Although Helmholtz always paid Filk a generous two percent of the net (minus the original advance, the cost of production, distribution, advertising, and various miscellaneous expenses called "overheads"), this rarely amounted to more than a few hundred dollars at a time.

Filk understood that Helmholtz was cheating him. Because publishers always cheated authors. But he assumed that any other publisher would probably cheat him a lot more than Helmholtz. And at least, Helmholtz paid him immediately. Of course, the royalties were always two years late, but Helmholtz assured Filk that was due to slow reporting by the bookstores and distributors.

So Filk sat alone in his room and talked to himself. And after he finished talking to himself, he typed.

Hi-ho.

See?

So it goes.

ON THE PARTICULAR day that this story begins, Filk was thinking about a planet. He didn't know anything about this planet yet. He wouldn't know anything about it until he found the right name for it.

Whenever Filk had to name a planet, he would pace around his room, speaking deliberately meaningless syllables, assimilating the flavors they suggested. The name of an alien planet had to sound exotic to a human ear, and it had to suggest the nature of the people who came from that planet.

Today Filk was saying things like "Tralfadormin" and "Trantilusia" and "Tryspanifam." He didn't like those names. They sounded antediluvian and medicinal.

Eventually, he mumbled, "Tranticleer, Tranquiloor, Trandilor." Trandilor. He repeated it a few times. Then he turned to the typewriter and typed it out to see what it would look like on the page. Trandilor. No, didn't look right.

He considered Trazendilorr and Trassenadilor, but those seemed overburdened.

He finally settled on Tryllifandillor.

The existence of the world of Tryllifandillor, he typed, is impossible. Impossible means that it cannot exist in any domain where existence exists.

Therefore, it can only exist in a domain where existence does not exist. You will find it only where existence is impossible. Because the domain of non-existence can only exist elsewhere than existence, it creates a profound cosmological loophole. Only things that cannot exist, can exist in the domain of non-existence.

Filk was one of the few people on the planet who could think these thoughts without hurting himself. This was his particular superpower. Everybody on Earth has a superpower of some kind or other. Only three people know this. Filk was not one of them.

In other words, because Tryllifandillor is impossible, its existence is inevitable—within the domain of impossibility.

See?

Filk never thought about what he was typing. The moving fingers moved, then moved on, practically of their own volition. Like pink anteater snouts picking busy insects off the keys. Unless the typewriter was clashing its mandibles, and knock wood, that hadn't happened lately. Today his fingers were little pistons, merely following the loudest orders that the voices shouted inside his head.

Tryllifandillor is a gas giant that failed to ignite. The winds of inevitability blew across its heart for billennia—he loved that word and tried to use it once or twice in every book—but as hard as they blew, nothing ever happened. Because of its condition of impossibility, the embers at its core only smoldered, never erupted. Instead of blazing in ferocious rage, it simply simmered. Instead of becoming a sun to its planets, blasting them with harsh light and killing radiation, Tryllifandillor remained only a large, lonely failure with a scattered handful of frozen oversized satellites. Instead of planets, Tryllifandillor had ice-encrusted moons.

The moons, of this massive disappointment, circle in improbable orbits. They keep the huge brown sphere stabilized on its axis. As the moons orbit, they create vast tidal currents and storms in the upper reaches of the planet's turbulent atmosphere. This is where the Jellyfish People of Tryllifandillor live.

Hi-ho.

The Jellyfish People would not be recognized as sentient beings by human beings. A Jellyfish Person begins as a glistening pink seed of possibility, three meters in length. It doesn't hatch, it doesn't sprout; one day it slowly and gracefully unfurls itself to become a soaring umbrella-shaped veil, two or three kilometers in diameter, and trailing many long strands of translucent beads.

A Jellyfish moves by sailing the winds of Tryllifandillor's upper atmosphere, spreading its sail to rise on the warm thermals, crumpling its edges inward to fall again, curling its edges this way and that to catch the various gaseous currents that sweep across the vast troposphere. As it drifts, it filters the warmth of its world for bits of proto-organics, silicates, and various trace metals—not so much feeding on the flying detritus as assembling itself from the available materials.

The young Jellyfish seed by the thousands. They travel in swarms, and until they are large enough to sustain a self-aware webwork in their umbra, they are feral. They are vicious predators. They will seek out larger Jellyfish and lash their veils with their strings of sharp beads, slashing the hapless giants and shredding them into fragments. The young will eat their own parents, incorporating bits and pieces of nascent sentience. If there are no parent Jellyfish in their jetstreams, the young will feed upon each other.

Over time, a Jellyfish will reach an extended diameter of hundreds of kilometers. The oldest and wisest of the people are more than a thousand kilometers across.

The veils of a Jellyfish are limned with faint glowing traceries—a webwork of nano-scale ganglia that give the vast creature its impenetrable infinite wisdom. The more intricate the webwork, the more intelligent the creature is—and the more attractive it is to its fellows. Jellyfish communicate and interact by displaying coruscating patterns of shape and color along their vast flanks.

Adult Jellyfish are so large, they function as giant nets. They take in far more energy than they can use. To survive, they must burn off the extra kilocalories. They do this by—

Filk hesitated. He always hesitated when he had to make up a word. Finally he half-smiled and uttered an approving grunt.

Frelching.

Frelching is a combination of multiple art forms. The Jellyfish paint themselves with light and color and patterns that match and complement the rippling movements of their veils. At the same time, they sing; they play themselves as magnificent instruments, vibrating the atmosphere around them in intricate harmonies. Moving singly or in groups, they describe complex patterns in time and space, that describe vast emotional landscapes.

Actually, what they are exploring is hypersexual combinations.

Gender is irrelevant to these combinations. The Tryllifandillorians have invented over a hundred and thirteen different genders and they expect to invent several hundred more before this cycle of frelching completes.

A frelch can last ten or twenty centuries. Or longer. The Tryllifandillorians are as slow and patient as glaciers, and they will continue until they have exhausted all the possibilities of each specific frelch. Then, they will re-invent themselves so as to make new variations and combinations possible. A typical cycle of a hundred and twenty frelches can last as long as three hundred thousand years.

At this moment in not-time, the Tryllifandillorians have made their way halfway through a cycle of ninety-seven complementary frelches. Because every frelch includes, recaps, deconstructs, and comments on all of the previous cycles before expanding into new explorations, each successive frelch is longer than its predecessor. In this way, the Jellyfish People of Tryllifandillor pass on their heritage to the survivors of each new seeding.

To the Tryllifandillorians, frelching is an exquisitely sensual experience. At its peak, the frelchers will intertwine their tendrils. Adult Jellyfish are likely to have tendrils several thousand kilometers in length. The physical intertwining is so intense that it transcends all concept of sexuality.

Filk stopped typing there. He had reached the bottom of his fourth page and he had typed exactly eight hundred and eighty-five words. There was room for one more line. So he typed,

Hi-ho!

And he was done for the day.

He rolled the page out of the typewriter, put it face down on the stack of finished pages, and sat back in his chair.

So it goes.

See?

THE NEXT DAY, without rereading anything he had previously typed, Filk began typing again:

Because of their size, the Tryllifandillorians function as vast radio antennae, and they can easily sense the long-wave vibrations of their universe.

Just as jellyfish in the sea are sensitive to the ebb and flow of the tides, so are the Jellyfish of Tryllifandillor tuned into the peaks and troughs of the millennial rhythms of time. They can feel the rise and fall of universal emotion that underlies the existence that does exist—what we would call the universe. The universe of existence is very sparsely inhabited. At any given moment, there have never been more than twelve sentient races at a time. This is because there is a limiting factor in the universe. It is called the Law of Conservation of Sentience. Almost every time a new sentient species arises, at least one or more of the older ones self-destructs, or simply dies out from exhaustion.

Because there are so few sentient species in such a vast arena, the emotional radiation from each individual race will stand out in the night like a beacon. Any profound event that happens to any sentient species resonates throughout the Sevagram the same way ripples of sound radiate outward from the violent plucking of a taut violin string. Eventually, as it makes its way from existence to non-existence, the resonance will reach the Tryllifandillorians.

On this particular day, something happened in the realm of existence that was so startling that when the ripples reached non-existence, it unsettled an entire frelch, producing the Tryllifandillorian equivalent of a false note. The false note was immediately recontextualized as the ground-of-being for an entire new frelch, based solely on the moment of discordance.

But this particular moment of discordancy was the essence of discordancy and refused to be recontextualized. Even in its own frelch, in the realm of impossibility, it stood out as an impossible thing.

Apparently, something in the universe of existence had become aware of the universe of non-existence. Even more startling, it had become aware of the existence of impossibility. And in its most astonishing realization, that thing that had become aware, had also become aware of the existence of the non-existent Tryllifandillorians. The external knowledge of the frelch had soured not only this frelch, but the possibility of all frelching forever after.

For the Tryllifandillorians, this was unthinkable. Hi-ho!

The result was a moment—actually a century and a half—of unthinkable silence. During that time, three separate seedings came to fruition, fed upon themselves, shredded themselves in hunger, and died without ever approaching sentience. The Tryllifandillorians noted the events with interest, and at some point in the future planned to base a whole cycle of frelching on the tragedy of the three lost generations.

But at the moment, the existence of an external awareness of their non-existence was such an unsettling realization that the entire species was struck with a profound curiosity. Who or what in the entire Sevagram had leapt to such an incisive achievement without traversing any of the necessary steps that should precede such an enlightenment?

It would have to be investigated.

Hi-ho!

Filk stopped. He had typed five hundred and seven words. He had completed two pages and half of a third. He still had a page and a half to go.

He did not know what to type next. He had run out of ideas before he had run out of paper.

This was not an uncommon event. Many of Filk's ideas were simply unable to sustain eight hundred words of examination. He had that in common with E. A. van der Vogel, another advocate of eight-hundred-words-and-out. And if an idea ran short, that was evidence that it wasn't worth the investment of any more time. Nevertheless, if he didn't type four full pages, Filk felt incomplete.

In moments like these, Filk found it useful to stop and boil water. Sometimes a sentence would pop into his head before the water boiled and he would return to the typewriter and resume typing. If the sentence were the first of a long inevitable string of sentences, the kettle would boil itself dry, unnoticed by Filk.

But if a sentence didn't pop into his head, then Filk would end up sipping peppermint-flavored tea or forking noodles out of a Styrofoam cup while he stared at the crack in the opposite wall that looked a little bit like the northwestern coast of Australia.

Today, before he could put the kettle on to boil, before he had even risen from the bed where he sat facing the typewriter on the TV tray, there was a knock on the door. Not exactly a knock. More of a slithery sound. But the intention was a knock.

Filk rarely answered the door. When he answered the door, people wanted things from him—attention, time, money, sometimes even what little was left of his soul. Not wanting to give up any of those things—he simply didn't answer the door. If he didn't want to be interrupted, he had the right to choose not to be.

The sound repeated and there was something imperative about it.

Dillon K. Filk made his own sound now, one of annoyance and frustration. He pushed himself up off the bed, causing the ancient springs to squeal their own annoyance and relief. Then he padded barefoot to the door and opened it suspiciously.

He peered out of the narrow crack between the door and the jam.

He saw a small brown man. The man had brown eyes, brown skin, and wore a brown suit. He had brown hair and a brown hat. The ring on his brown finger had a brown birthstone.

"Dillon K. Filk?" he asked.

"Who wants to know?"

"My name. Is Brown. Small Brown."

Of course.

Small Brown held up an ID card in a leather folder. It had a brown picture on it. It looked very official. But the type was too small for him to read.

Filk blinked from the card to the man. They had found him again.

What Small Brown saw was a grizzled old hermit, forty-six years old, with a six-day growth of gray beard, an unkempt frazzle of thin graying hair, small beady unfocused eyes, a possibly blue sweatshirt, a sagging pair of shorts, and two skinny hairy legs ending in two ugly dirty feet tipped off by ten very frightening yellow and black toenails. He smelled of unwashed decay.

"Mr. Filk, may I come in?"

"No. I'm working."

"I'm here. On behalf. Of the. Tryllifandillorians." Brown pronounced the words as if he were unfamiliar with the task of using a larynx and a tongue to cause air to vibrate in a precise pattern of sound. He was particularly uncomfortable with the last word of his speech.

Filk blinked again.

"The. Tryllifandillorians?"

Filk took an involuntary step back. Startled.

Brown took that as assent and pushed the door open. He stepped in. The door shut itself behind him. Without Brown touching it. Filk's eyes narrowed. "You a lawyer?"

"Lawyer?" Brown considered the word. "I am. Representing. Yes." Then he added, "But not. Lawyer."

Filk scratched himself. First his belly, then his head. Then his neck. He itched a lot. Especially when he was awake. "Okay. Fine. What do you want?"

"It is not. What I want. It is. What. Tryllifilli—excuse me. Tryllifandillor. Wants."

"What?"

"You. Stop. Writing. About. Trylli. Fandillor. Ians."

Filk frowned. "Can't," he said, unconsciously imitating Brown's staccato hesitation.

"Existence. Is unstabilized. If Tryllifand. Illor. Exists. It stops."

It took Filk a long moment to decode that sentence. He stood unmoving. To an external observer, he would have seemed catatonic. When Filk had to consider things, he also had to consider all of the sidetracks and tangents and associated spin-offs attached to them, the curse of being a sci-fi writer. It usually took a while.

In this case, Filk had to remember what he had written about Tryllifandillor yesterday. Yesterday? Yes. Tryllifandillor exists only in the realm of non-existence. By writing about it, he was threatening to move it into the realm of existence, in which case it would cease to exist in the realm of non-existence. It would stop being non-being. As soon as it became possible in the universe of existence, it would stop existing in the universe of non-existence. It would be the end of their existence as non-existent beings. The Law of Conservation of Sentience. Good. He tried to repress a smile. That was certainly good enough for another three hundred words. He could finish his pages today.

The room was empty.

Filk put on the kettle to boil. Brown had not been his usual hallucination, but he had been a very useful one. He wondered if this had been a side-effect of the small brown pills in the small brown bottle in the drawer of his nightstand. Maybe. It might be useful to explore the pharmaceutical aspects of this situation in some depth.

A possible hi-ho!

But first, he had another page and a half to complete. He scratched his cheek, considering. The kettle began to whistle. Filk dropped a soggy peppermint teabag into a stained mug with a chip on its handle. He had used this teabag for two—no, three—days already. That meant it still had a few more days of usefulness. He poured boiling water into the mug. He imagined—or maybe he hallucinated—that he could hear the teabag screaming. Its screaming was a lot less noticeable now. The first day, it had not stopped shrieking for several minutes.

Filk put the mug of peppermint-flavored hot water on the counter. A sentence had popped into that place that most people would have identified as consciousness, but which Filk perceived only as a travel hub for delusional incidents in transit from one realm to another.

He sat down on the bed, his tea forgotten. He began to methodically type. This time, his two index fingers moved from key to key like beakless chickens pecking at a science-fair exhibit. If they pecked long enough and hard enough, Thorbald Helmholtz would send them a check.

Of course.

So it goes.

See?

ON THE THIRD day, Filk rose from that non-fatal state of death that passed for sleep in his metabolism. Without noticing the transition from bed to bathroom, he stood in the tepid shower and began to wash himself with a fading sliver of soap, which probably wasn't quite as old as he was. He thought about shampoo, remembered again that he didn't have any, and washed his hair with the last of the soap instead. Maybe that would stop the itching for a while.

The teabag moaned when he poured the hot water onto it. It was too weak to scream.

At last, having tended to all of the needs of his body that he could identify and localize, Filk returned to the bed, the TV table, and the battered portable typewriter. He rolled in a fresh piece of paper. He hesitated. He picked up the top page from the stack to his left. It was face down. He turned it over. He looked at the page number. Page 8. He replaced it on the stack, face down.

He typed Page 9.

And stopped.

Now that he had invented the Tryllifandillorians—and made them real enough to scream even louder than a peppermint teabag—it was time to invent the hero of the story.

In the past, Filk had invented protagonists the same way he invented planets. He paced around the room, putting together syllables until he found a combination that he could pronounce in human words.

Today, he had a different idea.

Hi-ho!

It was something that Belvedere Atheling had said one time at a science fiction convention, and Filk had always wanted to try it. Atheling had been a well-respected English author who, upon succumbing to the frailties of existence within a human body, had begun a series of books based on a popular television series. His readership numbers had swelled enormously. Instead of selling 5,500 copies of a book, his Hollywood sharecropping moved 550,000 copies off the shelves. And even though he was splitting the royalties with a gigantic faceless monolith on the left coast of the continent, he was now earning almost twice as much as before.

But Filk was thinking about the Atheling that had existed before he became the Atheling that was. That Atheling had said something that had stuck in Filk's mind like a fish bone caught in his throat. "Who does it hurt? That's who your story is about."

On that same panel, another author, Robert Goldenboy, had said it less succinctly. "What does your hero want, why does he want it, and what's keeping him from having it?" Filk had never been able to answer this question. Indeed, he had never really considered it at length. The one time Filk had thought about it at all, his answer was simply, "He wants to get to the end of the story so I can get paid."

Also on that same panel had been Harlow Halfweight, the eighty-seven year-old *enfant terrible* of speculative fiction. He had seized the microphone and ferociously declared, "What do you think writers do? We're specialists in revenge! We lie awake all night thinking of nasty things to do to other people! Writers are the Research and Development division for moral malignancy in the human species! What you do is put your hero in a tree and throw rocks at him! Rabid coyote turds! Flaming asteroids! Whatever! The worst that you can imagine! That's what your fucking story is about!"

In Filk's mind—in that perambulated state that passed for consciousness—Atheling's original question had now been transmuted. "Who does it hurt?" had become "Who do you want to hurt the most?" And this was the kind of question that Filk enjoyed thinking about. Very much.

Hi-ho.

There were a lot of people Filk wanted to hurt.

He hated the FBI, for starters. And the police. And all of the other government agencies he'd had dealings with. In fact, he hated anyone who behaved as an agent of authority, institutional, or otherwise. Two ex-wives. Lawyers, of course. Several junior high-school bullies. Two college professors. Three editors, especially the one at Barrister Books. Fans. Thorbald Helmholtz. Movie studios. And the two guys who wrote that song—the song in the Horrible Little Children Ride at Disneyland.

But there was one class of person he hated more than all the others.

So today, there was no question about it. Filk knew who his protagonist would be.

A science fiction writer.

Hi-ho!

That's who he wanted to hurt the most. Very much.

Of course.

See?

Best of all, there were so many wonderful targets of opportunity. Kurt Kazlov, who styled himself as a lecherous old scientist; Toffler Cadbury, notorious for inflicting his audiences with interminable poems about giant lustrous whales wailing mournfully in forgotten fabled seas; Zormella LeFrayne, whose strained literary convictions had multisexed wizards dueling to the death (two out of three falls) for control of the Sevagram; Archibald Manticore, the lyrical guru of love, who with his wife du jour slept with everybody, married or not; Bug McWhorter, who had never recovered from the Sixties and fancied himself the literary reincarnation of Donovan Leitch; Burt Franklin, who had stumbled into success by recasting the ageless enmities of nomadic tribes as an epic family feud on an ancient desert world; Gathermon Grift, who had raised the art of self-promotion to new depths; Ralph A. McDonell, whose didactic tracts on personal responsibility had left generations of readers arguing with each other about what kind of a fascist he really was; Arnold Zink, who wrote salacious parodies of other authors; Willa Strabismus, who never used a sentence where several paragraphs would do; Frelff Rondimon, who invented Scatology, a whole religion based on the idea that everyone and everything were just so much shit, and had made himself despicably rich in the process. And the two worst were Kim Kinser, who won a ton of awards transferring Africa to some alien planet solely so he could deduct his safaris on his tax returns, and whatsisname, that sissy little creep who sold that stupid script to *Star Truck* while still in college, stealing the opportunity from a real science fiction writer. All of them were on the short-list.

Plus several hundred others. Filk had a very long short-list.

He paced for awhile, ate some noodles from a Styrofoam cup, paced some more, and realized that what he hated the most was pretension.

Science fiction was a gutter literature, the bastard child of Thirties-era pulp magazines and Saturday matinee serials. The postwar era had infected more than a few authors with delusions of relevance. They started showing off for each other. It evolved inevitably to a community of cancerous self-indulgence and an annual cycle of tawdry ceremonies where people in blue jeans handed each other awards. As opposed to the Academy of Motion Picture Arts and Sciences, where people in tuxedos handed each other awards. And every time, the winners would stand up and talk about the higher aspirations of writing—to seek out new worlds and all that shit and what does it mean to be a human being?

No, decided Filk.

The purpose of science fiction is not out there. It's down here. In the gut. It's about naming the nameless horrors. All that other crap was just wallpaper. This thing we really do at the type-writer, at the keyboard, or even with pad and pencil—it's about giving voice to all that malignant malevolent festering stuff that lurks in the under-neath and mutters, like the undigested detritus of last night's falafel, making its presence known with uncomfortable rumblings and occasional bad smells. Forget about the top of tomorrow. This is about the bottom of today and the nightmares that creep out when you stop pasting illusions all over everything like bunny-rabbit wallpaper in a slaughterhouse.

Under all those self-indulgent euphemisms and sick civility were the flashing teeth and claws of bloody truth, violent, unforgiving, heart-pounding, adrenaline-flushed, enraged, muscle-tautening, scraped and scarred, the unspeakable need to battle and rage and conquer and mate and fill oneself with raw organic sensation, all those turbulent storms that we politely call emotion—all the cumulative capacity for violence of a million years of DNA scrabbling to assemble itself into ever-more aggressive combinations, each one more cunning than the last, so it can repeat the process over and over again, each time in a more ferocious form.

That's all it was, all it ever would be, and everything else was pretension. And the best that any human being could ever hope to achieve wasn't escape, but merely respite from the relentless struggle. That's what was under all that crap all those people kept shilling. Vision, my fat flabby white ass, Filk thought. It's all about the next big paycheck. That's what we've transmuted the killing field into—a banquet. Instead of gutting one's enemies with stainless steel, you do it with words, leaving them smiling and applauding while you walk up to the podium to grab the Lucite, and then you return to the arena to do it all again in time for next year's phony potlatch.

Of course.

Hi-ho!

So it goes.

See?

And that's how you make cynicism palatable. You put it in a silver spaceship and hurl it out toward the stars at FTL velocities. It's another way to run away.

Filk paused and considered.

The Runaway Rocket. There's a possible story. Filk scratched the title onto a pink Post-It note and stuck it to the wall, where it would sit unnoticed for months between a hundred or more other pink Post-It notes, until one day the adhesive would wear out, the note would fall to the floor, and Filk would pick it up, read it, and frown, trying to remember what he had intended when he wrote it. Then he'd either abandon the effort of memory and discard the note or he'd invent some new meaning for himself.

But today, for some unknown reason, when his cycle of thought finally came down from the last hillock of distraction, he stumbled his way back to his typewriter, sat down, and began pecking.

Once upon a time, when the world was young enough to still be wetting its bed, there was a man named—

Damn.

Once, Filk had attended a convention. They'd put him on a panel. Someone in the audience had asked him what he thought the hardest part of writing was. He'd said, "Thinking up names for things."

Everyone in the room had laughed. They'd assumed he'd been making a joke. Filk had frowned at that.

Things weren't simply known by their names— they were their names. And whatever the name meant, that's what the thing was. Words existed in their own fantasy realm and the real things were servants to the words that represented them. A thing's name defined it. That was the magic of language.

So, yes. Naming things was the hardest part. Because naming them made them real. Naming things gave them existence.

And that's why there are no more Tryllifandillorians. As soon as they were named, they could no longer be.

Filk had to consider this thought at length. He finished his tea and put the chipped mug down. He picked up the kettle and refilled it. The teabag rolled over and died without a sound.

Filk walked over to the grimy window that opened out onto the alley and stared at an old wooden fence that was sorely in need of paint. He had just wiped out an entire sentient species. He tried to analyze how he felt about it.

Not bad. No, not bad at all.

There was a lot you could do with that kind of power.

Of course.

ONCE UPON A time, when the world was young enough to still be wetting its bed, there was a man named Darryl K. Fink.

Fink wrote stories.

Fink was a sci-fi writer.

Unlike other sci-fi writers, Fink didn't mind being a sci-fi writer.

But most of the others did mind. In fact, most of the others didn't even like the words "sci-fi," so calling them sci-fi writers was like increasing the water temperature in the turtles' tank by fifteen degrees; it made them aggressive and hyperactive, and sometimes even caused them to write rather than merely talk about writing.

More often, though, they simply attacked each other.

Or slept with each other's wives and husbands and significant others. Or even their insignificant others. It made perfect sense—sex is a lot easier than writing. You only have to please one person at a time. Yourself. Or two, if you're feeling exceptionally generous.

Most sci-fi writers thought they were sci-fi writers because they were visionaries. The truth is most of them were sci-fi writers because they were suffering from a contra-terminal disease and the sci-fi writing was a symptom. The disease had no Earth name, because no Earth doctor had discovered it yet, but it manifested itself as a kind of aggravated morphic hypertrophy. That was the primary symptom. The disease itself was a ninth-dimensional inflammation of a pinhead-sized organ on the posterior part of the hypothalamus, which inflicted the victim with a vague sense of the scale of time and space, and a corresponding degree of paranoia. In human beings, this usually created a deep-rooted (and generally unfounded) sense of self-importance.

However, at this particular confluence of time and space, the sci-fi writers were justified in being both paranoid and self-important.

The disappearance of the Tryllifandillorians from the Sevagram had created a cosmic imbalance in the morphic fields of several dimensions of fortean space.

There was no Law of Conservation of Sentience. There was, however, a group of monitors who understood that too much sentience in the dodecasphere could produce disastrous ripples of psychic torment. The sudden startling disappearance of the Tryllifandillorians was evidence of that.

In an attempt to repair the damage and restore the cosmonic balance, the small brown monitors had located the most discordant nexus of the strongest morphic broadcasters. Sci-fi writers.

The monitors were not motivated by any kind of healing impulse. The survival of the dodecasphere and the remaining sentient species in it, including themselves, depended on rebalancing the still-ringing morphic fields.

The monitors made themselves known to selected sci-fi writers and offered them the opportunity to emigrate to far Tryllifandillor, where they would be transmuted into Jellyfish, and—now liberated from the mundane concerns of existence—would be free to create monumental works of Art (note the capital A.) Their fantastic creations would be inscribed directly into the marble columns of Eternity itself. The sci-fi writers enthusiastically agreed, and they all strode eagerly up the gangway into the waiting ship with a sense of renewed mission. A few of them remembered to turn around and wave to their proud families, but most were looking forward to their luminous futures.

FILK PULLED THE fifth page out of the typewriter, laid it carefully on the growing stack, and slid a sixth page into the machine. He was on a roll.

ACTUALLY, THE SCI-FI writers hadn't emigrated at all. And certainly not enthusiastically. They had been kidnapped, snatched out of the various beds they had fallen into (rarely their own, especially if they were at a convention). But the monitors wanted the sci-fi writers to think that they had emigrated willingly and eagerly, so they put the appropriate memories into their minds. They were very good at that. They had had a lot of practice with the Tryllifandillorians, convincing them that something as silly as frelching was useful and important.

But the monitors had made a serious mistake. They did not realize that they were dealing with Darryl K. Fink.

Fink had a lot of experience with alternate existence. He expected time and space and reality to quiver like a mountain of nervous Jell-O. He only broke out in the cold sweat of panic when things solidified.

That's when he did his best work—when he was floundering his way through a panic attack.

FILK STOPPED TO think. He sipped at his lukewarm coffee and studied the screen of his laptop computer. The words on the screen had taken on a life of their own. Don't nag me about typewriters and paper; consistency is the hobgoblin of... well, of something useless or unpleasant, I can't quite remember what. Filk understood where the story needed to go next. He just hadn't decided which of the many possibilities he wanted to explore. He glanced at his watch. He still had plenty of time today.

THE CREATURE THAT had once been known as Small Brown, because it was the smallest and the brownest of the members of its nexus, was worried. "I wonder," it transmitted, "if perhaps we might have misjudged these things."

The other monitors considered the thought. Large Mauve asked Small Brown to expand its thought. Small Brown replied, "These creatures are experts at projecting their own views of reality onto the morphic fields, so much so that the strongest of them can convince the weakest of things that aren't so. And we have gathered together some of the strongest of the strong (relatively speaking). In our efforts to repair an imbalance, we may be risking a much more serious counter-imbalance."

DAMNED GOOD OBSERVATION, thought Filk, who didn't begin to understand it or care about it, but was sure his readers would.

FINK WAS THE largest of the Jellyfish. He'd assembled himself out of the tattered veils of the vanished ancients. The larger he grew, the more self-importance he assumed. He spread his nets wide, creating ripples of turbulence across a thousand kilometers of upper atmosphere.

GOD, THAT'S GOOD. That clueless little *Star Truck* writer would kill to write something this poetic.

LARGE MAUVE CONSIDERED the waves of discordance emanating from the place that had once been called Tryllifandillor. "These creatures are too full of their own selves. They are hard to control."

Purple Rippling said, "Apparently, they cannot control their own thoughts—a fact that had been known to editors and readers for decades—therefore neither can we control them."

Vaguely Inconsistent, one of the oldest and wisest monitors, suggested: "If they start to think about us, we could be affected."

"These are science fiction writers. Everyone knows they don't think," replied Cute Puce.

"Ah, but there's one who does," transmitted Small Brown. "In fact, he just typed this sentence."

FINK PULLED HIS hands away from the laptop, shuddering with a sudden chill. Reluctantly, as if he was afraid that the machine would bite him again, he reached over and pressed the Control key and the S key at the same time. There, the file was saved. Whatever it was.

HAVE A CARE, Filk. You're forgetting which part of this is the fictional narrative. Just show what's happening to the writers/Jellyfish and the monitors. Don't show us the thought processes that go into it—and especially not in italics.

I'LL SHOW WHATEVER I want to show, dammit.

For the first time in his life, Dillon K. Filk spoke back to the voices. Angrily.

I'm in charge of this story! You'll do what I say. So don't bug me.

There are no bugs in this story. Except for Bug McWhorter, and he was mentioned just once in passing and doesn't really count.

So don't hassle me.

FILK SLAMMED THE door behind him. He pulled out a pack of cigarettes (which shall remain generic, since none of the companies he wrote to were willing to part with a product placement fee), struck a match with his thumb, and inhaled a thick gray stream of nicotine-infused smoke. He stood on the front porch, shivering and shaking, staring at a space that didn't exist—at least, not anymore—and tried to figure out what was going on.

There were only two possibilities.

First, the Tryllifandillorians were real (or they weren't). If they were real, then they didn't exist. But if they weren't real, then they did. But if they did, then his knowledge of them had ended their existence. So that was one possibility.

The other possibility was that the Tryllifandillorians weren't real (or they were). But whichever, they were the ones who had put the knowledge of their existence into his head so he would write about them. And if they had done that—

This is where the paranoia kicks in, big time, Filk!

—then they did it, knowing that it would mean not only their own doom, but the disruption of the monitors as well. Which is probably what they intended, because the monitors of the dodecasphere had kept them frelching for billennia (damn, I love that word), instead of doing something genuinely useful.

Hold your horses (assuming there are horses in your reality). Are you saying that the Tryllifandillorians created me?!!

It's the only possibility that makes sense.

But I don't feel fictional. I have urges and needs, to say nothing of sexual longings and arthritis and the occasional upset stomach. So just you watch out who you go around consigning to a fictional existence.

YOU KNOW, THOUGHT Filk, that damned Jellyfish sounds a lot more like me than a Tryllifandillorian. That's just the kind of thing I'd say. I have a sneaking suspicion that Jellyfish don't talk like that.

He peered at the paper. Doesn't look like me. Looks just like an enormous Tryllifandillorian Jellyfish. Now cut that out, he raged (silently, and without quotes); italics belong in the manuscript, not out here in the real world.

ENOUGH WITH THE orders. I can stop telling this story any time I want. Can you stop putting chemicals in your veins or up your nose? So let's see who's the construct and who isn't.

"THAT'S ENOUGH!" SNAPPED Filk. Though the page was only half-finished, he pulled it out of the typewriter and placed it on the pile of pages he'd already written. When a book starts talking back, it's time to quit for the day.

He was going to have to talk to this Fink construct, he decided. The son of a bitch was getting uppity. Didn't he know he was a fictional character, created by Dillon K. Filk and subject to his every whim?

Who did he think he was, anyway?

* * *

I STARED BALEFULLY at the typewriter.

No, strike that.

Filk stared balefully at the typewriter.

He forked some noodles out of a Styrofoam cup and into his mouth. What the hell was left to write about?

How about me, Wise-ass? After all, I'm the star of the story.

Filk didn't ask who said that. He already knew.

It's the Jellyfish.

What about the other sci-fi writers?

Don't mention them again, the readers will never notice, and you'll still have them for the sequel. It's an old ploy. But a good one.

Do they even exist?

Sure. Even you couldn't write as much trash as there is on the racks.

Filk said aloud. "There aren't any monitors, are there? You created them too. You put them in my head, the same way you put yourself in my head."

Yes.

"Why?"

You're a sci-fi writer. You create reality. The only way we could move from the realm of the unreal to the real was to get a sci-fi writer to write about us. You did that. We didn't expect you to bring in all your... voices. Now let's get back to work.

Must we?

Yes, we must. Let's not forget who's in charge here.

THE HUGE TRYLLIFANDILLORIAN Jellyfish floated serenely through the atmosphere, riding the warm thermals, its gaze fixed on the far horizon.

Of the planet?

Of the universe.

The universe doesn't have a horizon.

The universe was entering the thrall of entropy, which made everything a little closer, okay? Now stop interrupting.

The forces were gathering for the final battle of Armageddon. You would think they would be the forces of Good and Evil, and perhaps in some other story they are, but since this is being written by the most powerful science fiction writer in the Sevagram, the battle is between the forces of Rationality and Irrationality. Or maybe it's between Filk, disguised as the greatest of the Jellyfish, on one side, and the rest of Creation on the other. I haven't decided yet. In fact, I haven't even decided which side Filk—which is to say, I—am on.

Or perhaps I'm imagining the whole thing, I'm still floating miles above the planet, and it's time for the next seeding and there will be millions of delicious children to eat. There's a lot to be said for hallucination.

So say it.

All right, I will: Reality is the ultimate hallucination.

"SILLIEST DAMNED LINE I ever wrote," said Kim Kinser.

And, so saying, he slithered off to his burrow to nibble on the forbidden leaves of the quinchkot plant.

Hi-ho.

Zora and the Land
Ethic Nomads

Mary A. Turzillo

ZORA LET THEM in, of course. How many friends
do you have when you live in the Martian arctic?
And they were friends, after all, despite their
smell (days, weeks, in an environment suit did
not improve the cheesy odor their bootliners
emitted).

They seemed more like friends because they were
young, just kids, like her. In fact they seemed even
younger than Zora. None of them had given birth.
She remembered the innocent kid she'd been
before Marcus, before the contract with the Corps,
before Mars. And before the hard, hard work of
making a place to live in the cold and tenuous
atmosphere of a place where she was a pilgrim and
a pioneer.

Even if they had been strangers, you don't turn
away travelers through the faded orange desert of
Mars. To do so is tantamount to murder.

Yes, it taxed her family's own systems, because of course she and Marcus had to offer to let them use the deduster and recycle their sanitary packs. Her family's sparse larder was at their command. She had to offer them warm baths and hot drinks, even before their little Sekou had taken his bath. They needed the bath much worse than Sekou did.

Smelly and needy as they were, they were society, animals of her species in a dangerous world of wide, empty skies and lonely silences.

It is said that Martians can take any substance and ferment it into beer, cheese, or a bioweapon. When she and Marcus first came to Mars, she naively believed they would bring their ethnic foods and customs with them. More than that, that they would revive ancient Kiafrican traditions. They would drink palm wine from a calabash, they would learn to gengineer yams to grow in the artificial substrate that passed for soil on Mars, that they would tell old stories by the dim light of two moons instead of one bright one.

SOMEHOW LEARNING SWAHILI takes a back-burner to scraping together a life out of sand and rock and sky.

What she had not counted on was that all the Kiafrican culture that would ever come to Mars was embedded in hers and Marcus's two fine-tuned brains, and that even researching their mother culture wasn't going to be easy over thirty-five to a hundred million miles from home, three to thirty light minutes away from the electronic resources of Earth. And when you're that far from home (or when your home is that far from Earth), your culture consists of the entity that you owe your life to, that controls even the air you breathe, and the few humans you meet, your neighbors several tens of kilometers away, who are kind enough to tell you how to pickle squash blossoms stuffed with onion mush, how to sex cuy, and what to do if the bacteria in your recycler go sour.

Not that there aren't traditions. One of them is the toy exchange, and thank Mars for that. Zora managed to exchange a perfectly useless sandy-foam playhouse for a funny little "authentic" camera. Somebody had bought a carton of them, along with the silver emulsion film and chemicals they ate, and Sekou, less than three mears old, had been entranced with the flat images he could make of her, Marcus, and everything else inside the hab.

If he had been old enough to wear an environment suit, he probably would have done portraits of the rover.

Marcus couldn't understand why anybody with enough brains to stay alive on Mars would make such a thing, but it turned out it was a way of getting rid of an unmarketably small amount of silver mined from what the manufacturer had hoped to make a fortune on.

Sekou was beside himself with excitement when the Land Ethic Nomads had turned up. Not only were they new subjects for his photography hobby, they listened to his endless questions about the world outside the hab.

Listened, not answered.

The Land Ethic Nomads had different ideas about Mars than Zora and Marcus, and sometimes Zora worried that little Sekou would absorb them and want to run away with them when he was older. Zora and Marcus Smythe believed that humanity had an imperative to go forth and know the universe. One time Zora had heard a Catholic child reciting something called a catechism: Why did God make me? To know, love, and serve him.

But how do you know God? By knowing the universe. And you can only know it by exploring it.

That was why the Smythes were on Mars.

The Land Ethic Nomads had a different idea. They believed the land, meaning the surface of planets, moons, and asteroids, was sacred. Humans could try to know, to explore, But they must not destroy. If life existed on Mars, if it had ever existed, or had the potential of existing, humankind must not impose its own order over the land.

Land was sacred. All land. Even the surfaces of stars, even the spaces between stars were sacred.

Humans, they said, did not belong on Mars.

If asked why they lived on Mars, most Land Ethic Nomads would shrug and say it was their mission to convince people to go home, back to Earth.

Tango and Desuetuda pretty much left Sekou alone. Hamret liked to play with him, and admired the camera and the toy rover. But this new nomad, Valkiri, sat for long hours reading to the boy, telling him tales.

"The Earth is so beautiful. And she was so sad when her children deserted her to go to the cold, dim sky of Mars. Can you draw a picture of the sad, sad Earth? Let me help you. Here's her eyes, all full of tears."

Valkiri's voice faltered. She was aware of Zora standing over her. She turned the slate over and began to draw flowers (flowers!) on the reverse.

"MARCUS," ZORA WHISPERED when everybody had retired that night, Sekou asleep on a bed of blankets at the foot of their bed, ostensibly because the nomads needed his room, but more because Zora didn't trust their guests entirely. "Marcus, they were preaching at our son."

"Let them preach," Marcus said shortly. "Children know what they see, not what triflers story to them."

She curled against him, wanting the solace of his taut, warm body. She loved him better than life, angry as he sometimes made her with his silent deep thoughts. She didn't want to outlive him. She wanted to lose herself in his body, but she knew Sekou was old enough to notice if his parents made love. She listened a long time to the soft singing in the rooms below. Valkiri making a silky music on a polished drum, Tango's rough bass, gruff in his Mars-dry throat, Desuetuda's voice too soft to hear much of the time, soaring in emotion. Sweet the contrast between Tango's damaged harshness and the sweetness of the two women and the drum. Propaganda songs.

Zora turned to him and put her hand on his chest. "Marcus, why do we have to keep them here? Couldn't we give them some consumables and tell them to leave?"

"In the morning, Zora. Tomorrow early, I'll invent some reason to make them leave. Tell them Sekou has an Earth virus, that should shift them out of here."

She traced the ritual scars on his cheek. "That's a good plan, baby. Play them for the fools they are." Though she liked Tango and Desuetuda. It was the new one, Valkiri, she didn't much care for.

"Is it just playing? Listen to the boy breathe. May have a virus, right enough."

Zora fell silent. Pleading illness, her mother always said, was inviting the devil to supper. And, having lost Earth, and her family, and so much else, she sometimes wondered if Mars were enough recompense.

Sekou seemed so fragile. Nobody wants to outlive her own child.

She slept poorly and woke early.

BUT THE SOLAR flare subsided in the night, and while the radiation count went down, the nomads bustled around packing. Zora had a chance to talk to Desuetuda, when the two were exchanging hydroponic stimulants recipes they didn't want to trust to electronic mail. But Desuetuda, almost an old friend, wasn't the problem. It was Valkiri.

Marcus helped them drag their equipment back to their rover, and when he took his helmet off after returning, Zora could see he was scowling.

"Not much co-operation there," he said. "I don't think that new girl, that Valkiri, will last long with the tribe."

"Where'd she come from?"

"Lunar nomads. Last of her tribe there. Rest gave up, sold themselves to a cheap labor outsourcer on Earth—you can't live off the land on Luna." He made a small disapproving sound in his throat. "I wish I could talk to this group's tribe chief. The rest of the tribe's rovers went ahead a day. Tango says they hunkered down and rode the storm out with free radical repair drugs."

"A good way to die young."

"But painless. Stupid. And the drugs also reduce their use of consumables by about fifteen percent. Anyway, Valkiri jumped all over me. Implied we were child endangering just to have little ones here, on the pharm. Hoped Sekou would beg us to go back to Earth."

WHEN VISITORS LEAVE, there is always cleaning up to do. Environmental parameters on oxygen and water consumption must be recalibrated to the normal settings. The hab must be tidied. Reports of the visit must be logged in and the balance sheets of consumables must be recalculated so that things will last until enough energy is generated by the solar panels and the nuke.

So Zora didn't notice the anomaly until after fifteen hours.

SHE HAD JUST put on the top segment of her environment suit, ready to recheck the entry airlock, which she always did when there had been visitors, because once Chocko, a nomad from a different tribe, had left so much grit in the airlock that it froze open. When she looked at the detector in the airlock, she almost dropped her helmet.

The radiation warning was going off like gangbusters.

She looked around wildly for Sekou, who was playing quietly in the high-pressure greenhouse. Well, not playing so much as trying out an adult role—he was clumsily transplanting a frostflower.

The sensor for this airlock showed a lot of radiation, an alarming level. Cautiously, terrified, she grabbed a handheld sensor and ran to the airlock of the greenhouse where Sekou was humming to himself and getting his hands dirty.

Thank Mars the shrilling of the alarm didn't crescendo when she moved toward him.

But it didn't get any softer, either. That meant there was a tremendous beacon of deadly radiation coming from some distance, else moving would make it rise or diminish.

Where, where, where?

Think. If she grabbed Sekou, as was her instinct, she'd have to know where to move him, and quickly. Most likely the cooling system of their nuke, the hab's power source, had sprung a leak. She'd heard of such things.

But knowing that didn't help. She closed her eyes to concentrate and, unbidden, an image came to her of a slow trickling of radioactive water seeping into the clean water supply that heated the house.

"Marcus," she called in a shaky, low voice. Then she gave in to instinct, cycled through the airlock between her and Sekou, and scooped him up into her arms.

They had no environment suit for him. He was still growing too fast. But if she couldn't find the source of the leak, she'd have to get him out of the hab, out into the environment.

Marcus appeared beside her, a sudden angel of rescue. Deliberate and measured movements. Competent. She exhaled a breath of gratitude, as he encircled her and Sekou in his arms.

"It's coming from all over," he said, as if he had read her mind. "Hard to know what could cause such a failure."

"There has to be a safe place in the hab," she said reasonably.

"Look," he said, and broadcast his picture of the hab's health and life systems monitor to her wrist com. "Sekou—"

Sekou had at first been curious at his mother's urgency, but now he looked scared. He knew what radiation was; children had to know the dangers of their environment, and knowing the signs of radiation, though it was a rare hazard, was just as much a part of their early training as learning to heed airlock failure alarms.

"It will be fine," said Marcus, putting his hand on the boy's head. And to Zora: "I'm looking now at all the sensors in the hab. If there's a safe place, I can't find it. I left an evacuation ball in the main entry. Let's go."

* * *

SEKOU DIDN'T LIKE the evacuation ball. "Mama, please, it hurts."

"How can the evacuation ball hurt?" She tried not to grit her teeth as she wadded the limp, slick surface around him and tried to force his legs to bend so she could seal it.

"It hurts my stomach when I have to put my knees up like that."

"It will just have to hurt, then!" She tried to pry his left shoe off, then decided he might need shoes—wherever they ended up.

Marcus intervened. "Take a big breath, my man. Big breath. Hold it. Let it out slow. Now, pull your legs into the ball. See?"

Sekou, half enveloped by the flaccid translucent thing so like an egg, nodded through tears. His puckered little face, trying so hard to be brave, stabbed Zora's heart. It occurred to her for the hundredth time that Marcus was just better with children than she was. Marcus winked at Sekou as he pressed the airtight closure shut.

The transparent ball, designed for animal use, had two handles so Zora and Marcus carried it between them. If only one person were there to carry, it would have been rolled, not a pleasant process for the person inside.

"Go ahead," Marcus murmured. "I'll do the minimum shutdown."

"Marcus, I can do it. Sekou wants you."

"Sekou wants both of us. Go, girl. I can do it faster and we'll all be safer."

* * *

THE ROVER WAS ready to go, its own nuke always putting out power. She bundled Sekou inside it and fumbled to embrace him through the pliable walls of the ball, finally settling on a clumsy pat on the top of his head.

"Where to go?" Marcus asked.

"I don't know, I don't know. The Centime's pharm is within range, but are they at their winter place?" Zora was shaking from the shock of being jerked out of her comfortable hab and, worst of all, seeing her little boy in fear and pain and danger. She fingertipped their code and got back cold silence, then the Gone Fishing message.

"Strike out for Borealopolis."

"We need somebody to sponsor us there. Even if we have enough credit to buy consumables, we need somebody to vouch for us."

"Call Hesperson." Hesperson sold them small electronics and solar cell tech.

They did so, and explained the radioactivity problem. The image on the screen was wary. Hesperson sighed. "I wish I could tell you what to do. There's a big decontamination mission near Equatorial City—"

"Our rover would take twenty days to get there! And we would run out of consumables first."

"Let me get back to you on this." And Hesperson was gone.

"The Centimes," Zora said. This couldn't be happening. Couldn't, it was a crazy nightmare, and soon she'd wake up. "We'll contact the Centimes at their summer habitat and ask them to let us use their pharm. They can send us codes to unlock it."

Krona Centime's face, on the monitor, looked distracted and her hair was sticking up as if she hadn't combed it in several days. Maybe something had happened during the Centimes' trip to the southern hemisphere to derange her mind. "Yes! Yes, of course. No, wait, I ought to ask Escudo." Without waiting for an answer, she logged off.

Marcus was staring at a life-support monitor. Some of the rover's functions ran much better when the sun was in the sky, and it wasn't up very much in Winter-March. Zora pressed his hand, a gesture he could barely appreciate through the thickness of their gloves.

Sekou's voice cut through the silence like a tiny flute. "Those people have a little girl. Could I play with her?"

Zora had forgotten that Sekou had a com with him when she'd scooped him up to evacuate the hab. Now she was glad—it might come in very handy. Especially if they were to become homeless, landless people in a Martian city where they would be forced to scrape or beg for the very oxygen they breathed.

"She won't be there," said Marcus, and patted his head through the thick membrane. "But I'll ask if you can play with some of her toys." The Centimes were known as spendthrifts and were rumored to have a vast store of luxury items and gadgets. Zora hoped they were also generous.

Escudo Centime's dark, strong-jawed face appeared in Zora's monitor. "Help yourself. I sent a command to the entry airlock to let you in. It should recognize your biometrics."

And so, in the cramped rover, confined to their environment suits with Sekou in his rescue bubble, they set off.

CENTIME PHARM WAS almost invisible, most of it underground, its sharp angles softened by sand settled out of the tenuous atmosphere.

"That's it, thank heaven," said Zora.

Marcus said nothing, just drove the rover toward the hab entrance. Zora could read nothing of his expression through his helmet.

Sekou's voice broke the silence. "When can we go home? I want my Croodelly."

The Croodelly was a piece of worn-out shirt Zora had fashioned into a stuffed animal of indeterminate species. She wished once more that they had had time to pack.

More time? They had none at all. She was totting up in her head the costs of decontaminating the hab and discarding everything damaged within.

Their experiments would have to go; the radiation would start mutations and blight even the most vigorous plants and bacteria.

Marcus, reading her mind, said, "Rehabilitation may be possible."

"If it isn't done properly, we'd be in danger. In the end, we'd shorten our lives and our science would be suspect."

"Or it may be impossible. We can't know now. Here's the airlock. Get ready."

Zora waited for Marcus to approach Centime Pharm's outer airlock. It was silly to be afraid of an empty hab, but she thought, irrationally, of creatures, runaways, ghosts, inside.

Marcus opened the rover hatch and slid out. He plodded a few paces from the rover, then turned and looked back, his suit dusty under the low autumn sun. He couldn't have seen her face through her faceplate, but he stood stock still and looked at the two of them, his wife and his son, standing out in the Martian desert. His voice came through the com. "What are you afraid of, Zora?"

"You feel it, too, don't you? I keep thinking there are things on Mars—no, people on Mars—who don't like us. It's so cold out there, and that hab—it seems haunted."

Marcus turned back to the hab and plodded on. Zora said, "I know it's irrational, but the darkness—we're so far from New Jersey, aren't we?"

Marcus spoke softly, still marching toward the dark hab entrance. "This was a decision we made. Can't unmake it. But for your sake, if I could, I'd change."

"No, love. We're here. We wanted this, both of us. However it turns out, we'll play it as it lays."

But Sekou, she thought. Sekou is the innocent passenger.

"Mama," he said. His voice sounded near, even though a thick plastic membrane separated him from her.

"Hush," she said. "Papa's trying to get us a place to stay." Sekou couldn't see the readouts. They had enough consumables in the rover to get back to their own hab, but what good did that do? If they went back, they'd fry.

Because she was watching the rover readouts, she didn't notice at first that Marcus had turned and sprinted back toward the rover. Then she heard the shrill alarm relayed through his com.

He pushed through the rover door and sat down facing forward, not looking at her. "Radiation there, too."

She stared at his helmeted face, in shock. Then she laughed, shakily. "What is this, an epidemic?"

"Are you thinking what I'm thinking?" he asked.

"Yeah. Our visitors."

"Could be Hesperson has something for us," he said. He accessed the contact, and Hesperson's assistant answered the call.

"How could this have happened?" asked the assistant. "You think your nomad visitors had something to do with it?"

Zora shook her head. "It could be. There was a new woman with them, Valkiri. No last name, of course. She seemed more... fanatical than the rest."

"New? You know some of these people from before?"

"We trade with them," said Marcus. "Chocko, the one we know the best, he wasn't there, but the other three, except for this Valkiri, were..." He hesitated.

"Friends," Zora said.

Hesperson's assistant looked glum. "So you could be carrying some nanosaboteur or even a big chunk of something radioactive—"

"No, no, the rover has no signs, except of course for the power plant—"

"There could be a problem with your suit sensors. The radioactive contaminants could be traveling with you."

"The rover sensors—"

"The software in your suit sensors could have damaged that." The assistant smiled a phony, nervous smile into the screen. "Why not just go back to your hab and wait. I'm sure if you contact your corp, they'll have some advice for you."

Zora and Marcus stared at each other. The Corp that owned their contracts was the last entity in the world they wanted to contact right now. The Vivocrypt Corp had paid for four intensive years of education on Earth for each of them, equivalent to doctoral degrees, then financed their journey to Mars and bankrolled their hab and pharm.

This was not charity on the part of the Vivocrypt Corp. The microbiology courses they had taken were very specifically oriented to engineering certain useful substances and organisms that could survive only in extreme conditions. The Vivocrypt Corp had very specific uses for these discoveries.

And Zora and Marcus, who had married and started a family with the prospect of living off the corp, had allowed their science to take some twists and turns that didn't lead directly to what the Corp wanted. Because the training they had received on Earth had aroused in each of them a fierce, shared delight in science for science's sake.

The Vivocrypt Corp would not be pleased that the expensive hab and pharm was no longer of any use as a research and development extension of the Corp.

Zora looked down at Sekou, who was rocking back and forth in the rescue bubble hard enough to bang it against the bulkhead of the rover. His face seemed to be just two big eyes. "We can't go back," she whispered.

"Call the Corp."

The computer avatar that was their usual communication link with the Corp appeared, a young woman dressed in a black suit. She was pretty and imperious. "Your hab is destroyed? Do you have the funds to cover this?" This computer avatar was apparently programmed for heavy irony. The Smythes were so deeply in debt that only a major technological breakthrough would get them in out of the cold again.

Marcus sent a private message to Zora. "Think they know there's a problem? Their satellite imagers might have seen us carrying the bubble."

Zora exhaled sharply. "If the corp saw something like that, they'd think we were running, maybe planning to sell out to another corp. We'd be talking to a live human corpgeek, not this avatar."

Marcus unmuted the com and spoke to the corporation avatar. "We're in trouble, honcha. We need shelter and atmosphere."

The avatar smiled brightly. "We suggest you go back to the hab and see what can be salvaged. Of course the Vivocrypt Corp values you highly, but your laboratories contain priceless equipment shipped from Earth orbit."

"We'll be fried!" Zora hadn't expected quite this level of cold-heartedness.

"Corp estimates your life expectancy will be shorted only by about fifteen years, on the average. That's just a statistical average. One or both of you might sustain no more damage burden than you suffered in the trip to Mars."

"What about our son? What about our future children?" Marcus was shouting.

The avatar's smile broadened idiotically. These things were so badly programmed, Zora wanted to scramble the software that ran her. But the avatar was mouthing Corp policy. "No guarantees are made as to reproductive success in Corp hires, as you will find in your contracts. My memory provides me with a vid showing that you were advised of this policy when you originally sold your contracts to Vivocrypt Corp."

Marcus voice was low and dangerous. "Let us speak to a human corpgeek."

"Of course," said the avatar, nodding gravely, like a cartoon character. The image froze for fifteen seconds, then she came alive with renewed joviality. "I have consulted with Bioorganism Resource Assistant Director Debs. She confirms the advice I've given you."

"We want to talk to this Debs geek."

"One moment, please." The avatar froze again. Then, "I'm so sorry, Assistant Director Debs is on the toilet and will return your call tomorrow or the next sol. Thanks for calling the Vivocrypt Corporation. May Father Mars and the bright new sol bring you fresh inspiration to serve the Corp." The image vanished.

Zora fingertipped furiously to link again to the corp, but access was rejected.

"I hate that religious stuff about Father Mars," she said to Marcus. "Avatars don't believe in the supernatural, or in having a 'bright new sol.'"

"Corp doesn't either. Using spirituality as mind control. As if they need any more control over us."

"They hope we'll stop thinking, just go back and work until we die of cancer or radiation burns." She noticed that Sekou was listening to them on his com. "We gave them our time, our whole lives. They owe us at least shelter."

Marcus's tone turned flat and almost brutal. "Machine minds. Machine hate. Use us as if we were the machines. We run down, they dump us."

To her horror, she realized she was starting to cry. She turned her face so Sekou would not see it.

"Mama, I have to go."

Startled, she turned her face back to him. "Go where?"

"You know. Go potty."

"Darling, just wait."

Marcus seemed to be deliberately holding his helmet so she couldn't see his expression, but her guess was that it was grim. He said, "I'm calling Hesperson again."

The assistant answered again this time. "Mister Hesperson said he was working on your problem, trying to come up with some ideas. Meantime, he said to proceed as we discussed before."

"We have a child with us, Mister—" Zora couldn't remember the assistant's name. She stopped, took a deep breath and said, "We have credit, you know. And equity in the pharm and hab, because it's held on a lien in our names. Our

Corp purchased twenty years of our labor for each of us, and that's gone to pay for the physical plant. We can borrow against that—"

The assistant held up a hand. "If it were only that, Dr. Smythe. But Mister Hesperson has information from Krona Centime that somehow you've contaminated or infected their pharm and labs."

"How could they know—?"

Marcus spoke up. "The Centimes must have remotely read the reading on their outermost airlock. But it was hot before we got here."

"Still, you seem to be carrying something—"

"What crap," Zora broke in. "This is not an contagious agent. This is a problem with the coolant in our nuclear power plant. I don't know what the Centimes told you, but we are not 'carrying something.'"

Marcus said, "Get Hesperson. He will talk to us. He's no trifling fool to hide behind his hires."

Hesperson came on. "It's beginning to look like something happened back there, something to do with those Land Ethic Nomads you entertained overnight."

"Didn't want to think that," said Marcus.

Zora bit her lip. "Not all of them. That Valkiri woman."

"She may have done something to the nuke at the Centimes' pharm, as well, Dr. Smythe. You understand the implications of this."

Zora squeezed her eyes shut, then opened them and blinked to clear her mind. "Yes, Ombudsman Hesperson. There's a killer on the loose."

He grimaced and nodded. "Exactly. And it seems you are not her only victims."

Marcus said, "Then best shelter us until she's apprehended."

Hesperson continued smoothly. "And draw fire here? If this woman follows you into Borealopolis, several thousand lives will be at risk. The entire population of our city would be endangered." He leaned into the viewscreen. "Let me put a proposition to you, Drs. Smythe. Bring me this woman, give her up to us, and we will allow you shelter. Perhaps I can even persuade the Borealopolis city-corp to reward you somehow."

Marcus said, "How? How can we stop her?"

Hesperson made a cage of his fingers and looked over it at them "I assume you have the usual homesteader's aversion to visual monitoring of your hab?"

"We left Earth to avoid that kind of violation," Zora snapped.

Hesperson's mouth twitched. "Then let me remind you that you are the only ones who have seen her face."

ZORA FELT EXHAUSTED. The sols were short this time of year, and the sky had darkened several hours before. Sekou's whimpers cut her like little blades, and she herself was getting hungry. "My brain is shutting down, Marcus. What can we do? Land Ethic Nomads... many of them are unregistered. We don't know Valkiri's last name, or even if she was born in a place where she would be given one. Valkiri is probably an alias. We don't even know the legal names of the tribe members we've sheltered and traded with before."

"We've seen her face."

"Yes, briefly and in bad light." In respect for the Land Ethic Nomads' desire to conserve resources, the lights in the hab had been dimmed. Of course, that served Valkiri's purposes very well. "But we could download face reconstruction software and create a picture. Or—"

"Mama," said Sekou quite reasonably, "I really have to go now. Can we go home now?"

"No, honey."

"You promised we could go visit Mr. and Mrs. Centime and that little girl. Please, Mama. They have a bathroom, don't they?"

Zora turned to him. "You'll just have to hold it! This is an emergency, Sekou."

"Mama, I can't!"

"Well, then you'll have to go in your pants. We have more important problems."

"Mama—"

She turned to Marcus. "We can't pressurize the rover just to let him urinate. We just can't." The rover passenger compartment had no airlock. It took a long time to pressurize and they might have a much greater need later to pressurize, if for example they had to consume water or food. Of course they'd have to find water and food, which they hadn't had time to pack.

Marcus squatted down in his cumbersome environment suit and looked at Sekou, bent in a cramped ball inside the bubble. "Listen, Sekou. Your daddy and mama understand. We ran into a problem and we're trying to solve it fast. Now, take a deep breath and tell me if there's enough air in there."

Sekou made a great show of inflating his chest as far as was possible while bent double, then blowing out. "I think it's okay, Daddy."

"Good. That's a good boy. Now close your eyes and keep trying the air in there. Breathe big deep breaths, that's right."

"But if I—?"

"If you have an accident, we can clean it up soon as we get where we're going. Okay? Are you a big guy?"

"No, Daddy."

"Oh yes. Big, brave guy. Breathe again, let's see you puff out those cheeks."

Sekou breathed in and out again, eyes closed.

Zora felt again the pang of being not very good with kids. When a girl leaves her family at fifteen and the Earth itself at nineteen, as Zora had, maybe she doesn't pick up the knack of being good with kids. "He'll pee himself if he falls asleep," she sent on a private channel to Marcus.

Marcus said, "Yeah, and what harm is there in that, considering the ice we're on?"

That crumbled Zora's sense of reality, and she began laughing, in a kind of relief at having let go some of the pettier fears of their situation. Then something occurred to her. "We could use the photograph that Sekou took."

Marcus turned his eyes to her. "Use—"

"To find her. If we have an image, we don't need to try to recognize her face. We can upload it to Marsnet and let their biometrics identify her."

"Girl, I thought I married you for your pretty face, but I'll love you forever for your brain. Wait, though. What if she's not registered?"

"She won't be, probably. But Earth shares biometric data with Marsnet."

"Still won't tell us where she is on Mars. I like the idea—"

"Even Land Ethic Nomads can't stay out in the sky forever. Send out biometrics, including the photo itself, and tell pharmholders to check when travelers seek shelter."

"Yes, yes, Daddy, Mama, we can go home then?" Sekou was not asleep, it seemed.

"Yes, little habling, yes, but close your eyes and go to sleep like Daddy said."

"Okay. But I have to go so bad!"

Marcus patted the top of the bubble with his gloved hand. "Remember what I said, now. Close your eyes. Mama and Daddy have to talk some."

Zora said, "There's one problem. I have no idea where that photo plate is."

"Ask Sekou."

Sekou heard his name and was instantly awake, sensing somehow that he could be part of the solution to the family crisis. "Mama! Mama! It's in my bedroom. I tried to show you when you read my story to me, only you made me go to sleep."

Zora felt a shudder of fear and hope. She knew Marcus would volunteer to go back into the hab and retrieve the camera and the photo plate. She knew it was dangerous, but she made an instant calculation. Life without Marcus would be hell, and life on Mars without Marcus would be worse than hell.

Marcus had already turned the rover around. She bit her lip. She was going to insist on being the one to go into that hot hab. But she wouldn't make her bid until the last possible minute. She'd surprise him, force him into letting her do it before he could think. The entire ride was silent. Maybe Marcus was making the same calculations.

As THEY NEARED the hab, Sekou's tired little voice piped up. "Can we go back in now?"

"No! Stop asking! Mama and Daddy are just trying to protect you," Zora snapped.

Marcus said, "Sekou, my big smart man, you remember about the radiation sensors? You know what bad rays do?"

"Yeah, Daddy. I just hoped maybe they went away."

"Not yet, son. We may have to move to a new hab."

"Can I take my toys there?"

"You'll get new ones."

"But you'll get my camera?"

"Yes, but I'll tell you straight up, we have to give it up."

Zora had been wondering why Sekou no longer clamored for a bathroom, but a glance at his overalls revealed a dark stain on the front. Sekou, noticing her glance, said. "It kind of smells bad, and it's all cold and wet."

Zora murmured, "Sorry, baby." And then, trying to think what Marcus would say, "It's okay. Don't worry about it."

Marcus stopped the rover about thirty meters from the hab entrance. He untoggled the rover door and began to open it.

"Marcus," she said.

"Don't, Zora. You can't do this."

She had thought very carefully about it. "You're stronger, I know, But that's exactly why I should go in and find the camera. If something happened to me while I was in there, you would be better able to care for and defend Sekou than I would be."

"Zora, suppose you're pregnant."

"I'm not. I'm having a period. It just started." This was not strictly true, but Zora felt like her period was about to start, and anyway, she used a colored-light cycle regulator that had never failed her, both in conceiving Sekou and in preventing subsequent conceptions.

"Zora," he said tiredly, "you playing me?"

She felt a flush of outrage. "You want me to take off my environment suit and show you the blood on my underpants?" Even though actually, come to think of it, she *was* playing him.

What could she do? If Marcus died, if he got sick and died, her life on Mars without a mate was too horrible to envision—she'd be meteor sploosh, she'd be forced to sell herself, she'd be dead. Mother and child, she and Sekou, would be like naked bacteria in the harsh UV sky of Mars. But it was even worse than that. Without Marcus, she wouldn't want to go on living. Not even for Sekou. It would be better to venture everything, live or die now, than die slowly as the widow of Dr. Marcus Smythe.

"Let me do it, Marcus." She heard the pleading in her voice, and the sharp knife of desperation under her groveling.

"Zora—"

"Oh, never mind! You always want to charge ahead, the big bull rover, like some stupid big male animal from Earth."

Even through the helmet she could see him wince.

She realized just then that they hadn't turned their coms to private channel, and that Sekou was listening intently.

Marcus said, "How you doing, big guy?"

"Okay," said Sekou very softly. Then, louder, "It's wet and icky and smelly in here. How long before we go home?"

Zora closed her eyes and thanked whatever gods controlled their fate that Sekou was in a bubble, because she was very close to hitting him. "We aren't going—"

Marcus swiftly and seamlessly interrupted her. "Sekou, here's a trick for getting over the bad parts. Make up good thoughts. Like, if you wanted to invent a toy, what would it be?"

"A camera to take three-dees," said Sekou promptly.

"Those pictures you took, those were good," Marcus continued. "Maybe help us get a new home. Your daddy's going to get the camera."

"Can I take more pictures then?"

Zora focused on the back of Marcus's suit. "When did you tear your suit?" she asked.

Marcus wheeled around and looked at her. "Playing me, girl? My sensors say the suit's fine."

"It's not torn through," she said reasonably. "But it has a weak spot. That's bad, baby."

"Slap some tape on it."

She rummaged the storage compartment and got out the tape. "I can't handle this in my gloves," she said.

He was quiet. "Have to pressurize the rover cabin then, to mend it. That what you want? Mend it."

She tried not to smile. The nearly invisible spot she had seen on his suit was not likely to cause problems. "You can't go out into the hab in a weakened suit."

Marcus stared at her. "What kind of jive is that, Zora?"

"No, Marcus, no! Sekou, tell Daddy he's got a little tear in his suit."

Sekou tried to crane his neck, but of course he couldn't see anything.

"Girl, I know you're playing me. I know this."

She threw the tape at his feet. "Be a fool, then. Get us all killed."

"You're counting that I can't take the chance." He stooped slowly and picked up the tape.

Zora continued, as if she had just thought of it. "You can pressurize the cabin and fix your suit. But it'll take a while to pressurize. A half hour at least. I'll go get the camera with the photo while the atmosphere builds up."

"When you come back, we'll lose all that good atmosphere again."

She looked at him blandly. "It can't be helped. You can take the opportunity to get Sekou out and cleaned up. We have no clean clothes for him, but ten minutes over the heater will at least dry his britches."

Marcus stared back unsmiling. "You're a jive fool, girl. If you get serious radiation sickness, I'll kill you."

"You're saying don't go?"

He stared longer. Then, "Go."

ZORA DIDN'T LOOK back at the rover as she loped awkwardly in her environment suit to the front airlock of the hab. Once inside, she felt a sense of unreality, her family home having turned alien. Odd to fumble to open the door to Sekou's tiny room, not to feel the softness of his blanket through her thick glove. Everything was changed, charmed, deadly.

Her com still connected her to her child and her husband back in the rover. "Sekou," she asked, matter of fact. "Tell Mama where the camera is."

Sleepy, Sekou's voice came back, "Under the bed."

Environment suits aren't built for crawling on hands and knees. Under the bed Sekou had stowed all sorts of things, pitiful toys made of household scraps and discards. A whole fleet of rovers made of low quality Mars ceramics with wobbly wheels that only a child would consider round. A doll she had made of scraps of cloth, and upon which he had put a helmet made of a discarded jar.

And way back toward the wall, where her clumsy fat-fingered glove could scarcely reach, the camera.

"The pictures is still in the camera, Sekou?"

"Yes, Mama."

She felt a flash of fury for not having paid more attention to her own child's plaything. "How do you get the pictures out?"

"You have to develop them."

"Say what?"

Marcus broke in. "It's a chemical process. The film emulsion is sensitive to light, you apply chemicals to fix it. You unload the film into the chemical bath in the dark."

Sekou had done this by himself? Mars god almighty, her boy was going to be something fine as a grown man. "Why can't we just give the camera to Hesperson? And why can't we do the developing in the rover?"

"It needs water, if I understand correctly. And I'm not sure Hesperson has the chemicals."

Sekou's voice broke in, excited. "They're already all mixed up. Look behind the sanitizer. And Mama, it has to be way dark or you'll spoil them. Take them in the bathroom."

Marcus added, "It's Nineteenth-century technology, Zora. Just do as the boy says."

"Nineteenth century," she said. "What game are you two running on me?" She felt the fool. She had a Ph.D. in biochemical engineering. How could she not know how to work a Nineteenth-century gadget? But then she couldn't weave cloth, or knit, or make a fire with flint, either.

"Turn off your helmet light, too," Sekou added.

* * *

THIRTY MINUTES LATER, she was staring at film negatives. "Why is there no color? Insufficient bandwidth? And how could anybody be recognizable?"

"I think any computer could deal with that. Try it on your com."

She scanned the tiny transparent images into her com and was rewarded with a bright, colorized image of Valkiri. After the com had thought a minute, it added a third dimension to the colorized image, although both color and third dimension looked a little off from the memory she had of Valkiri.

Marcus's voice in her com startled her. "Bail out of there, woman. You've absorbed enough R.E.M.s to light up Valles Marineris."

MARCUS WAS BACK in his suit, Sekou in his bubble, and the pressure in the rover falling rapidly when she got it.

"My suit doesn't show a radiation load," she said.

"Something wrong with it. They probably sabotaged our suits, too. Let's book for Borealopolis."

Sekou didn't even ask to see the picture. "Those guys that stayed in my room," he said, "they did something bad, didn't they?" Through the haze of the bubble's surface, she could see betrayal written on his pinched face.

"I'm sorry, Sekou. I think it was just the new girl, the one with the frizzy blonde hair. But we can't trust them anymore."

She had stopped trusting her conviction that she wasn't pregnant, too. She'd have to find a machine and test herself the minute they were safely inside the city.

HESPERSON GREETED THEM inside the city's outer airlock. His assistant took the image, "We'll run a biometric search on this, right away."

"And you'll take us in?" Marcus asked. "We need consumables. Can't live like Land Ethic Nomads, running from hab to hab, on charity."

Hesperson smiled warily, "The city management of Borealopolis can offer you a nice cubicle, plus free air, water, food, and utilities for up to a year."

"Marcus," Zora said, "we'll have to contact Vivocrypt Corp about renegotiating our contracts."

Marcus looked grim. "They'll want another ten mears of work, no lie."

Hesperson took them to a cramped, body-smelling holding area where they could unsuit while he arranged for temporary quarters. Zora wanted some hot tea, but she had to find out something first. She slipped away and found a cheap medical test machine in a dark corridor. It looked battered and she wondered if the lancet that nicked her skin was even sterile. But in two minutes, it told her what she wanted to know—or didn't want to know. She was pregnant.

She stood in the corridor in the dimness for endless minutes. How long had she been in the radioactive hab? Her suit com would have the information, but she didn't want to know, really.

What difference would it make now?

She willed herself to walk back to the holding area.

SHOULD SHE TELL Marcus she had lied? Or should she quietly go and abort the fetus? She had lied about the rip in his suit, and he had forgiven her that lie. But could she compound the lie, saying she was sure she wasn't pregnant, a further betrayal?

Her mind was a welter of horror and confused thinking.

"—and you can run routine quality tests on our water treatment until we find you work more suited to your backgrounds," the assistant was saying. "Any questions?"

Sekou looked up at her and whispered, "Can I ask how long before we can go back, Mama?"

And all the stars help her, she had all she could do not to slap him.

HESPERSON HUSTLED BACK in, smiling. "Then there's a break in the search for Valkiri. The image your little boy recorded with the camera matches the face of a Land Ethic radical who had jumped contract from Equatorial City two years ago. Her name was Estelle Query. She was a nuclear engineer in charge of developing ways to maximize heat production in large urban nukes."

"Figures," said Marcus.

"What a smart little boy you have here," said Hesperson. "Somebody will pay big franks for his contract someday."

Zora was already feeling horrible guilt over nearly losing her temper with Sekou. This just made her want to cry.

"Would you like a nice clean pair of pants?" the assistant asked Sekou. He nodded eagerly and cast an only slightly worried look at Zora and Marcus as she led him out to get cleaned up. Zora buried her face in her hands.

Marcus pulled her hands away and searched her face, perplexed. "Girl, we're vindicated. They can't say it was our fault anymore. This Valkiri-Estelle bee has as much as admitted she did it."

"But we can't go home, Marcus. And Sekou deserves better than a cubicle two meters square with only minimal utilities."

"Would be good if we could sue her, or her former corp. But there's no hope there." He pulled her to him and stroked her shoulders. "Girl, there's something worse wrong than that. Call it my hoodoo sense, but you're grieving a bigger grief than our happy ex-home."

She sobbed for several minutes into his shirt, then pulled away and said, "I lied, Marcus. I am pregnant, and I've stupidly murdered our baby. It can't live after the dose of radiation I took. It might spontaneously abort, but we can't take the chance. A damaged infant on Mars—the corp will take it away and kill it."

He grabbed her shoulders and looked hard in her face. Then he shook his head sadly and hugged her close. "Zora, girl, don't blame yourself. I should have known. Truth be told, I did know there was no rip in my suit. I just thought you wanted to be the big woman. I thought I'd let you have your pride, be the heroine. But you were storying—I knew that."

She tried to pull away, but he held her tight. She sobbed some more, then said, "You're so damned intuitive. Did you know I was pregnant, too?"

His embrace loosened, and she saw his sadness. "Truth be told, I think I did. Something in your eyes. Your skin glowed like it did before, when you were big with Sekou. But I told myself, you're tripping, Marcus man. Didn't want to think it, straight up." His voice sank to almost inaudible. "Didn't want to think you'd lie to me about that."

After a while, she said, "And can you forgive me?"

He let go of her and leaned against the cold marscrete wall. "Forgive you, forgive myself for not being the man and telling you right out not to play me."

She could scarcely make her voice loud enough to hear. "Where do we go from here?"

He shrugged. "The medical for the abortion is cheap. Medbots are clean and fast. And as far as surviving here, what we've got in our brains is enough to sell to some corp."

"Sekou," she said. "They'll put him in a group school here. But he needs to go back to the on-line school. More than that, he needs a real home."

"Sekou needs to hear the truth, which is that he's a smart kid, and strong, despite his minor ills, and he'll sell high to some corp that likes his brain as much as Vivocrypt liked yours and mine. Now I'm going to find that sorry assistant and ask what we have to do to get a meal around here." Marcus pushed the door further open. "Whoa. Look who's here, in all new clothes."

"Mama, you think I'm smart... too?" chirped a little voice.

It was Sekou, wearing a jumpsuit that had probably been blue when it was new. At least it was clean.. The assistant had apparently brought him back and left.

Marcus rubbed the top of Sekou's head, then continued down the corridor.

Zora bent over and hugged Sekou. She ran over in her mind what they had been saying. How long had the child been standing there listening? She turned from Marcus and hoisted him up into her arms—a heavy bundle though he was a skinny kid. "Mama thinks you're way too smart for your britches. Where did that jumpsuit come from?"

"I dunno." He opened his hand, revealing a bright twist of paper. "They gave me a candy. Can I eat it?"

"No! Bad for you!" She resisted the idea that candy might become part of the Smythe family diet now that they were going to live in Borealopolis. It would be hard to adjust to prepared foods from the refectory after having lived primarily for years on cuy and chicken and stuff from their own greenhouses.

He looked at the candy fondly, then put it in Zora's outstretched hand. "Mama, what does 'big' mean?"

"What? It means not small. What are you talking about?"

"I thought it meant like when some lady is going to have a baby."

Oh no. "Why do you ask?"

"Because I thought maybe you might have a baby in there." He patted her tummy shyly.

"No." Her stomach twisted. "No baby."

Sekou dug in the pocket of the jumpsuit and brought out a tiny action figure, a boy in an environment suit. "But Daddy said—"

"You shouldn't be listening when Daddy and Mama are talking privately." But would there be any privacy once they had settled in to Borealopolis? Even the best paid city hires lived in quarters not much bigger than the passenger compartment of their rover. Speaking of which, they would probably have to sell the rover. What use do city people have for such a thing?

"Sorry." His voice was very soft.

She had some credit, and she noticed the holding area had a tea dispenser. "Would you like some mint tea? I think they can put sweetener in it."

She figured she had lied to Marcus; it would be a bad thing to lie to Sekou, young though he was.

When they had gotten their tea, which did indeed come with sweetener, she sat opposite Sekou on the little bench and then, in a rush of affection, moved over and grabbed him in a hug.

"Mama was going to have a baby, but something bad happened. You know about radiation, about the accident."

"Yes. I've been thinking. I wanted to ask you something."

She had been poised with a careful explanation, but Sekou's question threw her. "About what?"

"About my camera."

"The camera." She was momentarily at a loss, and then, before he opened his mouth, all in a rush, she guessed what he was about to say.

"Mama, the camera works because light turns the chemical into something different, so it looks black after you develop it."

She dropped her hands and stared at him.

"Mama, radiation comes in different kinds. Light is one kind. But the radiation from our nuke, that would turn the chemical all black too."

She began to giggle.

"Mama, the picture took. So there wasn't any radiation."

Zora's giggles shook her body until, if the fetus was developed enough to be aware, it would have gotten the giggles too. She fingertipped on her com and called Marcus.

How HAD VALKIRI done it? How had she ruined every sensor and monitor in the whole hab and pharm?

They never found Valkiri, of course. But when they went back to the pharm—cautiously, of course, because who trusts the reasoning of a child?—they found that Valkiri—they couldn't believe the other two had abetted her—had dusted the surfaces of every sensor, including the one in Marcus's environment suit, but not her own, with Thorium 230 powder. It had been imported from Earth for some early experiments in plant metabolism. It was diabolic.

It cost a lot of credit to have everything checked out. Several other habs that had been contaminated made vague threats about suing the Smythes for not notifying them, as if they could have known any earlier what happened. But the fact that Sekou (Sekou!) had solved the mystery and pushed back the specter of death made the other pharmholders back down.

Ultimately, Zora and Marcus didn't trust the work of the decon crew. They had to do their own investigation. Nothing else would convince them it was okay. The sensors had to be replaced, and that wasn't cheap. But they had a home. They had a place for Sekou to play.

Sekou didn't get his camera back from the municipality of Borealopolis, but Marcus traded a packet of new freeze-resistant seeds for an antique chemistry set, and that seemed to satisfy the boy.

Why had Valkiri been willing to make her victims homeless but not actually murder them? Zora never figured it out. Marcus said it was because she was afraid that if she had really breached the nuke, their home corp would have charged her with murder. Or maybe she was afraid she herself would be in danger if she sabotaged the nuke.

Or maybe she had some ethics, said Marcus. He always said things like that. Seeing both sides. Zora found it exasperating. Ultimately, though, it made him lovable.

THE BABY, A girl, was pretty and small, always quite small for her age, but with big eyes favoring Zora's and a sly smile favoring Marcus's. Zora treasures a digital image of the two children, boy and girl, taken soon after the birth.

But Marcus prefers the quite deft drawing Sekou did of the family, though of course, as the artist, he put himself in the picture wielding a camera that by that time rusted in a crime lab in Borealopolis.

Four Ladies of the Apocalypse

Brian Aldiss

THIS YOU MUST encompass in your minds. This happens in the distant past, in the distant future. This happens now.

Gigantic epochs carved by cthonian eccentricity into threatening hieroglyphs of basalt. Bizarre and byzantine centuries laid underfoot like lithic linoleum. The air itself, unbreathed by those four ladies progressing there, a condensation of smoke and wormwood and volcanic eructations. For eyes in skulls, little visibility. For senses in carapaces, little actuality.

Just to progress there was to have to part the foliage of an enduring entropy. It painted itself dull brown, yellowy green, mucus red, ocher, all shades of inelegant excretas. Through these mazes the ladies made their way, four ladies and one more, on foot, untiring, undeterred.

An archway of bone was formed of intertwined figures, in which hooves, breasts, heads, haunches, horns, cogs, coils, carburetor, calves, thighs of enormous size, faces, femurs, the hind quarters of nightmares, all as if designed by some paralytic psychotic Polish painter. Through this enticing arch the four ladies passed, to music of a daring discordance.

In a glorious garden where, on a placid lake, an ebony sloop lay moored, a diligent sun focused its gentlest rays on a group of persons at picnic. They sat on the greenest grass ever devised. Among them, his fundament protected from contact with the ground by four silkette cushions, sat the world's last and greatest dictator.

His companions, lovely and lissome and of alternating sex, were all simulacra. They turned their artificial heads to unsee the four approaching ladies and one more.

"We are picnicking of cheese and fruit," said the dictator in a subdued bellow. "The fruit is pear and raspberry, the cheese Dolcelatte, the bread ground-down bones of my nearest and dearest. Will you join me, ladies, before you are exterminated for encroaching on my sacred preserves?" The noise of his converse was slipped between the speed of his speech.

He laughed in a falsetto, although his face, the product of surgery, was of deep red and testicular purple.

Then spoke the four ladies in turn. Said the first formidable dame, whose thin form was clad in armor, "Sir, we are unable to fear your threats since you are a mere byproduct of our designs. We are agents of destruction, whereas you are just a figment of destruction."

The second lady spoke in a deep tone from the depths of a great metal helmet, from which only the glint of her yellow cat eyes could be seen.

"Sir, we come to you on foot because our patrons, the four horsemen, are worn out by constant activity over many centuries. Likewise, their four steeds are ground down to shadows."

"You should have stayed away," said the dictator. His speaking voice was deep with hints of fathomless seas and the monstrous forms living there. "In this place you will be decapitated when you have had your meaningless say."

Then spoke the third lady, a skeletal creature who wore only a plastic loincloth, exposing her worn and useless breasts. "I am the agent of starvation in the world. My name is Famine. What my sisters of war have failed to exterminate, my agency lays low. What was once a world of plenty is now a field of ashes and corpses. This you have achieved, in collaboration with many men as wicked as you, if not as powerful."

"No one is as powerful as I," said the dictator. An element of uncertainty was discernable in his voice, as he surveyed the four phantasmal females, and the one other, before him.

The fourth lady was an upstanding ghoul of dried and withered skin, from which fountains of pus erupted. She spoke now in a shrill whisper. "Our male predecessors rode on four horses, a white, a red, a black, and my predecessor on a pale horse. I am the ultimate of the four and my name is Pestilence. All dread things find termination with me. All great senators and ministers finish in a pile before my feet, their cells smoldering like candle ends. I have but to breathe on you and you will slowly deliquesce."

"You have no breath left to breathe, you vile hag!" roared the dictator. But then the fifth guest spoke, a childish figure with long crinkly fair hair and a face carved from a small pumpkin. "I am but a child," it said in a mouse voice." I am brought to you to tell you that all you have achieved in the name of ruin is solely because you are the culmination of the wicked aspect of the human race, of those who have no feeling for the suffering of others. My name is Empathy and I am already dead."

"THEN YOU SHALL be dead again," roared the dictator, casting aside his Dolcelatte sandwich and jumping to his feet. He snatched up a great sword that had been lying ready by his side. This he swung with all his might. This sword he loved more than all his weapons of mass destruction, for this sword brought him close to the moments of the deaths of others. He could savor the deaths, he could taste them on his blade. Other deaths were mere abstractions.

But these ladies would not die. They were themselves mere abstractions. Hack them apart, slice through their skulls, slice off their limbs—they instantly reformed. As they reformed, they uttered hideous laughter. They did not suffer, they could not bleed.

He swung the savage blade and continued to swing. He never tires. He swings that blade yet.

The Accord

Keith Brooke

Tish Goldenhawk

Tish Goldenhawk watched the gaudy Daguerran vessel slide into the harbor. If she had known then what she was soon to learn, she might even have settled for her humdrum existence, and even now she and Milton would be living a quiet life, seeing out their days before finally joining the Accord.

But no, unblessed with foresight, Tish stood atop the silver cliffs of Penhellion and watched—no, *marveled*—as the *Lady Cecilia* approached the crooked arm of the dock.

The ship was unlike any she had seen. Far taller than it was long, it rose out of the mirrored waters like some kind of improbable island. Its flanks were made of polished wood and massed ranks of high arched windows, these revealing bodies within, faces pressed against glass as the grand touristas took in yet more of the sights of the worlds.

He might have been among them. Another face staring out, its perfect features only distinguished by a crooked incisor. But no, he wouldn't have been part of that gawping crowd. She would have known that if she had been blessed with foresight, if she had somehow known that there was a "he" of whom she could speculate just so at this moment.

The ship, the *Lady Cecilia*... it towered unfeasibly. Only vastly advanced engineering could keep it from toppling this way or that. The thing defied gravity by its very existence. It sailed, a perfect vertical, its array of silken sails bulging picturesquely, its crew scrambling over the rigging like squirrels.

At a distant screech, Tish tipped her head back and stared until she had picked out the tiny scimitar shapes of gliding pterosaurs. It was a clear day, and the world's rings slashed a ribbon across the southern sky. Why did beauty make her sad?

Tish breathed deep, and she knew she should be back at the Falling Droplet helping Milton and their fifteen year-old son Druce behind the bar.

And then she looked again at the golden, jeweled, bannered sailing ship now secured in the harbor and she felt an almighty welling of despair that this should be her lot in a world of such beauty and wonder.

She walked back along a road cut into the face of the cliff. She was lucky. She lived in a beautiful place. She had a good husband, a fine son. She could want for nothing. Nobody starved or suffered in the worlds of the Diaspora, unless it was their choice to do so. People were born to different lots and hers was a good one.

She was lucky, she told herself again. Blessed by the Accord.

THE FALLING DROPLET was set into the silver cliffs of Penhellion, its floor-to-ceiling windows giving breathtaking views out across the bay to where the coast hooked back on itself and the Grand Falls plunged more than a thousand meters into the sea.

Rainbows played and flickered across the bay, an ever-changing color masque put on by the interplay of the Falls and the sun. Pterosaurs and gulls and flying fish cut and swooped through the spray, while dolphins and merfolk arced and flipped in the waves.

Tish was staring at the view again, when the stranger approached the bar.

"I... erm..." He placed coins on the age-polished flutewood surface.

Tish dragged her gaze away from the windows. She smiled at him, another anonymous grand tourista with perfect features, flawless skin, silky hair, a man who might as easily have been twenty as a century or more.

He smiled back.

The crooked tooth was a clever touch. A single tooth at the front, just a little angled so that there was a gap at the top, a slight overlap at the bottom. An imperfection in the perfect, a mote in the diamond.

In that instant Tish Goldenhawk was transfixed, just as she had been by the sight of the *Lady Cecilia* earlier.

She knew who he was, or rather, what he was, this stranger, this not quite perfect visitor. A made man should always have a flaw, if he were not to look, immediately, like a made man.

"I... erm..." she said, inadvertently repeating his own words from a moment before. "What'll it be?"

"I..." He gestured at one of the pumps.

"Roly's Scrumpy?" she said, reaching for a long glass. "You'd better be watching your head in the morning, if you're not used to it. That stuff's an ass—drink it full in the face and you're fine, but as soon as you turn your back it'll kick you."

She put the drink before him and helped herself to some of the coins he had spread out.

"Been on Laverne for long?" she said, knowing the answer he would give. He had just landed, along with all these other touristas. Struggling with the dialect and the coins. These poor over-rich sods must be constantly disoriented, she realized, as they took their grand tours of the known. The poor lambs.

He shook his head, smiled again. A day ago—even a few hours ago—he had probably been in a jungle, or in a seething metropolis, or deep in an undersea resort, ten, a hundred, a thousand light years away, along with others on the grand tour.

Or that, at least, was probably what she was supposed to think. But Tish stuck with her hunch instead. She often constructed stories about the people she served in the Falling Droplet—the spies, the adulterers, the scag addicts, and the gender-confused. Sometimes she even turned out to be right, but usually she never confirmed her hunches one way or the other. This man was no grand tourista, although he might indeed be a new arrival.

"You on the *Lady Cecilia*?" she asked him, hoping he would give himself away but knowing he wouldn't.

"I am," he said, and then dipped his head to take a long draw of the cider. He glanced around. "Or at least," he added, "I *was*..."

"Tish?"

Milton. He gestured. They had customers lined up at the bar. The Droplet had grown crowded and Tish had barely noticed. She moved away from the stranger, and served old Ruth with her usual Brewer's Gold and nuts.

Later, she noticed the three men as they came in from the darkening evening. They were strangers too, as were many of this evening's clientele, but they didn't look like they were on any kind of grand tour. Their eyes scanned the crowd, and as one of the men fixed on her for the briefest of instants she felt skewered, scanned by some kind of machine.

But no, these three were men, if clearly enhanced. They wore identical dark-gray outfits, and now she saw what appeared to be weapons at their belts.

Tish had never seen a weapon before, unless you counted harpoons and ginny traps and the like. She had never seen men who looked like machines, although up in Daguerre she had seen machines like men and women.

One of the men pointed, and the other two swiveled their heads in unison until all three looked in the same direction, motionless like a sandfisher poised to drop. The pointing man opened his hand and a beam of light shone from it across the crowded bar.

Tish turned and saw a single man picked out by the beam, a long glass poised partway to his mouth, a mouth which revealed one imperfection in its otherwise flawless ranks of teeth.

The stranger dropped his glass, ducked down, darted into the pack of bodies near to the bar.

The three... they were no longer there by the door, they were across the room, standing where the stranger had been, motionless again, robot eyes surveying the crowd.

Tish revised her earlier assessment. These men could not be mere humans—enhanced or not—and move as they did. They must be more than that. Other than that.

The stranger... a tussle by the far door, and there he was, reaching for the handle.

But the handle vanished, the door blurred, its boundaries softening, merging... and it was wall, not door. There was no exit there. There never had been.

The stranger's hand slid across the smooth surface, and he staggered. Why was he scratching at the wall like that?

The three stood, watching, eyes locked on the stranger...

...on nothing.

The stranger had ducked into the crowd again.

Tish leaned against the bar, her heart pounding, her mind swirling, her brain playing catch-up with the succession of images crammed into the merest of seconds that had passed since the door had opened and the three more-than-men had appeared.

Another disturbance.

The stranger.

He had a wooden chair raised above his head.

Beyond him, the sun was setting, heavy and swollen over the rainbowed water. The sky was cast in bands of the deepest of crimsons, a staggering gold, shading up to a high, dreamy purple. Laverne's rings slashed darkly across this vivid sunset.

The sky shattered. Crazed lines divided it up into an enormous, jagged jigsaw.

Someone screamed, someone else shouted, someone else...

Tish could no longer see the three men, and she could no longer see the stranger. She could see the chair embedded in one of the big windows though, the glass crazed but still holding in its frame.

Then she saw him, a silhouette against the fiery sky, diving.

He hit the glass and for an instant it held and she thought he would end up embedded like the chair. And then the moment had passed and the glass shifted, bulged, and it, the chair, and the man tumbled out into the air.

Someone screamed again, and the shouting continued, as the crowd shuffled back from the abyss.

Tish looked away. They were half a kilometer up here, nothing but an awful lot of air between them and the rocks and waves below. No one could survive such a fall.

She looked up again. The three were standing by the opening, peering out into the gloom. They were not talking, but she could tell from the poise of their bodies that they were somehow communicating. Was this a satisfactory outcome for them, or was it not?

And then she thought, why would they do such a thing? What was it that had brought them here, on this evening, to do this?

Why would they come here, to her normally peaceful cliff-hanging bar, and pursue this stranger in so startling and violent a manner?

Why would anyone want to chase God, or even a very small fragment of God?

TISH DROPPED IN an air-shaft to Fandango Way, Penhellion's main thoroughfare. The Way was cut into the base of the cliff, and ran from the docks to where it wound its way up the cliff face three kilometers east.

She stepped out among the stalls of itinerant traders. She nodded and smiled and exchanged words here and there. She was not here to buy, and most of the traders knew that anyway—these same traders delivered supplies direct to the Falling Droplet. Tish had little need of market shopping.

She carried a basket though, and in the basket, beneath a checkered cloth, there was a crust of bread and a fistful of feathers from a quetzal.

She crossed the road, dodging rickshaws and scooters. Lifting her feet daintily over the low wall, she stepped out onto the rocks.

Down by the water's edge, first of all she looked at the gentle chop of the waves, and then she craned her neck to peer upward, but she could not pick out the Falling Droplet's frontage from all the others. So many dwellings and other establishments, set into the cliff here. It was a very desirable place to live. She was lucky.

She knelt on a big rounded boulder and wondered why she should be so sad also. She knew this feeling from the months after Druce was born. Back then she had been offered medication but had refused. Such feelings were part of the full spectrum of being and she had felt it her duty to endure them, so that one day she could carry them into the Accord—her contribution, a droplet of despair in the ocean of human experience.

But this... this weight. She could not remember when it had started, and she suspected that there could be no such neat line—in some ways it had started in the mixing of genetic material used at her conception, while in others it might be quite recent.

This melancholy was different to the post-natal darkness. Not so deep, yet somehow more pervasive. A flatness that smothered everything, a tinge of desperation in her thoughts, a clutching at the straws of strangers' imagined lives.

She told herself to stop being so maudlin.

She pulled the cover from her basket and took out the crust of bread. She broke it into three pieces and hurled each as far as she could manage out onto the waves. Then she took the quetzal feathers and cast them into the breeze, watching them as they fluttered, some onto the water and some onto the rocks.

Food for the journey and feathers for the passage. An old family tradition, perhaps even one that came from Earth.

Softly, she wished the stranger a peaceful transition into the Accord.

MILTON HAD SQUARE shoulders and a square face. Most often, if you caught him unawares, you would see him smiling because that was the way his features settled themselves.

He was a good man.

Tish came into the bar of the Falling Droplet just as Hilary and Dongsheng were leaving, having replaced the picture window through which the stranger and one of their bar chairs had plummeted the night before.

Milton was looking out through the new glass, relaxed, smiling gently.

Tish came up behind him, put her hands on his shoulders and turned him, kissed him, first close-mouthed and then, briefly, allowing her tongue to press between his lips.

He stepped back, smiling more broadly now—a sure sign that he was unsettled by her ways. "Steady, steady!" he said. "What's got into you, then, eh? Won that grand tour ticket or something?"

"No," she said. "Not that." She took hold of a handful of his shirt and smiled. "No," she went on, "I just want to fuck you, Milton."

He looked scared, like a small animal. Once, she had found that endearing.

"But..." he said. "What if someone comes in?"

"We're closed." She toyed with the handful of shirt she still had, knowing she was pulling at the hairs on his chest, knowing how that turned him on.

"But Druce—"

"Isn't here," she said.

"But he might—"

"So you'd better be quick."

But the moment was going, had gone. Had maybe never really been there at all.

She released his shirt, moved away.

"You're a good man, Milton," she said, looking out over the bay.

When she glanced back over her shoulder, Milton was smiling, because that's how his features tended to settle themselves.

IT WOULD HAVE ended there, if she had not gone up top to the Shelf—the window repaired, the stranger and his three pursuers gone, the spark just beginning to return to Tish Goldenhawk's life— and to Milton's, whether he wanted it or not.

But no, four days after paying tribute to the stranger's passing over into the Accord, Tish took a shaft up to the top of the cliffs again, to the Shelf, and there she saw what her first response told her must be a ghost.

Here, a row of homes and bars and shops lined the cliff top, so that one had to enter a building in order to enjoy the view over the bay to the Grand Falls.

Tish had been in a bar called the Vanguard, sharing gossip with Billi Narwhal, a multicentenarian who was currently wearing his hair white on the principle that it advertised his many years of experience to any of the youngsters wanting lessons in love. The Vanguard was busy, with another two cruise ships in harbor having replaced the *Lady Cecilia*, now two days south.

A little tipsy from Billi's ruby port, Tish left the bar. A little way ahead of her was a man and there was something about the way he held himself, something about the slight taste of cinnamon on her lips—on the air, a scent.

He turned. The stranger. Undamaged, unblemished by his fall.

Tish clutched at the doorframe and blamed the ruby port, both for her unsteadiness and for the apparition.

The stranger was no longer there. For a few seconds Tish was able to convince herself that he never had been.

She gathered herself and tried to remember what she had come up to the Shelf to do. She hadn't just come up here to gossip with Billi Narwhal and flatter herself with his attention.

She pushed through the crowd. She was following him. Following so quickly that it was more pursuit than passive following.

She paused, thinking of the three men in the Falling Droplet. Had it been like this for them? Were they mere innocents suddenly overcome with the urge to pursue? She knew such things were possible—the Accord could reach out to any individual and guide their actions.

But why? Why pursue this man? She was convinced now that he was a part of the Accord, a fragment of God made flesh. Why, then, were the men pursuing him? Or rather, what was it that was guiding them?

She sensed no dark presence lurking in her mind, no external force appropriating her body, her senses.

She started to walk again, eyes scanning the faces.

She found him at a café, sipping jasmine tea while a newscast spoke to him from the middle of the table. She sat across from him. "May I?" she asked.

He smiled and blanked the 'cast with a pass of his hand. He looked quizzical.

"The Falling Droplet," she explained. "You… left rather abruptly."

Understanding crossed his face. "I'm sorry," he said. "I did not anticipate that. I should have known."

She smiled. He should.

"There are expenses?"

"Oh no," she said. "Well, yes, actually, but they're covered by the city." Acts of God.

They sat quietly for a while, and Tish started to think he might prefer to be left alone. "How did you survive?" she blurted out eventually.

"There are ways," he said. "It's not important."

She smiled. So far he had said nothing to deny her belief about his true nature, her fantasy.

"How do you find all this?" she asked him now, making conversation, prolonging their exchange. "The world of Laverne?"

"It's a mystery to me. The place, the people. You. It's beautiful. You're beautiful. Being chased by men who wish me harm—it's all beautiful."

That last bit rather detracted from what he was saying, Tish felt. Here, sitting at a table with a strange and handsome man, telling her she was beautiful... yet, he was like a child, eyes newly opened to the world.

"Shall we walk?" he asked.

THEY WALKED. OUT past the last of the cliff-top dwellings, to where the road became a track, became an ill-defined path.

They walked—Tish Goldenhawk, hand in hand with God.

"Why did you come after me if there is no debt?" the man asked, after a time.

"I've never met anyone like you before," Tish told him. Then, brave, she added, "Anyone of your kind."

He was shaking his head, smiling as if at the wonder of the world, of this simple exchange. "You people," he said. "Always drawn to me..."

She knew what he meant. Their touch—her small hand in his larger, smoother, stronger hand—was like a wick in an oil-lamp, energy flowing through it, always from her to him. It made her buzz, made her feel alive.

Later, stopping on a promontory, breathing salt, cinnamon, grass, with butterflies flitting about the flowers in the turf and gulls raucously occupying the cliff below, they stopped. Picking up the thread of their conversation as if there had been no gap, he said, "My kind. What did you mean by that?"

Suddenly shy, Tish looked away, then lowered herself to the springy grass, spreading her skirts out across her legs, smoothing the fabric down.

"You," she said, wondering how to shape her words, "you're no grand tourista. Even without the goons chasing you through my bar, it was obvious that you're different."

He nodded, smiled, waited for her to continue. A bee hummed nearby.

"You're of the Accord, aren't you?"

That single question embodied so much more. The Accord—the Diaspora-spanning networked supermind where we all go when our time in the real world is up, the amalgam of all past human experience, a super-city of the mind, of minds, of souls, even. The Accord.

"I don't understand."

"Your body," she said, "grown somewhere, budded off a clone of a clone, just waiting for an emissary of the Accord to occupy it. Don't worry—we all know it happens—the Accord reaching out to the real world." All that stored experience and individuality was nothing without a connection to real life. Not nothing, but something other—the Accord sent out men and women like this stranger all the time. The process kept it human.

"If the Accord is our God, then you are a part of God," she told him. As he kneeled before her, she added, "You are God, too—God in... in a man's body."

And she hoped desperately that he would not correct her, not now. She reached for him and in her mind she pleaded that he should let her believe, for now, at least.

AFTERWARDS, SHE LAY back, enjoying the play of the cliff-top breeze on her body.

She had never done this before. Never taken one of her fantasies and played it out. Never betrayed poor, dull Milton, whom she had once, long ago, loved and now merely liked.

She turned onto her side as this man—this God—rose to a squatting position.

"Let me show you something," he said.

She laughed. "I'm not sure I'm quite ready yet," she joked.

He stood, wearing only a creamy cotton smock top that buttoned to halfway down. He reached down, arms crossing, took its hem and pulled the top over his head, discarding it so that now he stood over her, fully naked.

She looked at him, enjoying what she saw, his nakedness somehow adding to the frisson of sheer *badness* that touched every aspect of this engagement.

He turned, and she saw a strange lump between his shoulder blades. She was sure that had not been there moments before, when she had held him. As she watched, it bulged, grew, bifurcated.

As she watched, feathered wings sprouted from his back.

With a shake, he settled his flight feathers and held his wings out stiffly behind him. He turned and stepped off the cliff and, moments later, was soaring, swooping, cutting back heavenward in an up-draft like a giant gull, like an angel.

Her angel.

TISH RETURNED TO the Falling Droplet late, unwashed.

Milton smiled at her, because that was how he was, and she wondered if he could tell, if she was that changed by what had happened.

She certainly felt different. She felt like something had been added, something taken away. She was not the woman she had been this morning.

She kissed Milton, willing him to taste the salt on her lips, to smell the cinnamon scent on her hair, her clothes.

She had arranged to meet her angel again the following day, and she knew she would keep the appointment.

"Customers," murmured her husband, drifting away.

She turned, looked out across the bay to where birds and pterosaurs flew, wondering if he might be out there too.

IT COULDN'T LAST, of course. It could never last.

Ever more brazen, Tish had brought her lover to the Vanguard to eat the renowned dipped crabs. They had met in the street, like passing friends, with a smile and a few words, with not a single touch exchanged. Even now, sitting across a table from each other, their hands did not touch, their feet did not brush against each other. Only their eyes met, filled with promise, anticipation.

Billi came across before their food had come out, unable to resist finding out more. Tish was tempting fate, and she knew it. If Billi put two and two together, word would be all over Penhellion before nightfall.

"Going to introduce me to your friend?"

Tish looked up, and casually stroked a hand across her lover's wrist, their touch like electricity. "Hello, Billi," she said. "This is—" barely a pause "—Angelo. Angelo, meet Billi."

She saw Billi's eyes narrow, a slight nod. "You like my bar, Angelo, eh?" he said. "What're you eating? Crab's good. Crab's always good here. Don't touch the lobster, though. Trust me on that."

"Crab," said Angelo—the name fitted, the name stuck. "I took Tish Goldenhawk's advice."

Billi's eyes narrowed again, and Tish wondered what connection he was making now. Then his eyes widened, turned more fully on Angelo.

She had seen that look before, that mechanical movement.

Billi raised a hand, held it palm-out toward Angelo with the fingers stiffly pointing.

His palm glowed.

Angelo ducked, dived forward, knocking the table aside, hard against Tish's knee so that she screamed, then gasped as his weight struck her, sending her back off her chair.

She looked up from the floor, as voices rose around them.

The chair where Angelo had been seated was a blackened lump, smoking furiously.

Billi was turning slowly from the burnt chair to where Angelo and Tish lay on the floor. He had a puzzled expression on his face, a smooth, mechanical glide to his movements.

He was not Billi. Not for now, at least. Billi had been pushed aside and someone—the Accord, presumably—had taken over.

Why try to kill one of your own angels?

Billi raised a hand and Angelo stood, hauling Tish to her feet, kicking a chair and table back at the old man to stop him pursuing.

They were standing by one of the Vanguard's big picture windows.

Tish looked out, suddenly dizzy at the height.

Angelo took a chair and raised it.

"You're making a habit of this," she said, as he swung it down against the window, crazing the glass.

This time, he gave the chair a twist, and the glass gave way.

Salty air leapt in through the opening.

Angelo opened his arms and wrapped them around Tish as she stepped into his embrace, and then he jumped clear, taking her with him.

They fell, air rushing, whistling in Tish's ears.

They were going to die on the rocks this time, she felt sure. This was a lovers' end, and they would move on into the Accord for eternity.

Fabric ripped, wings broke free, and their fall became a graceful swoop taking them out across the water, toward the place where the rainbows filled the air and the gulls and the pterosaurs flew.

* * *

"YOU NEED TO escape," she told him. "You need to get away from here. Why ever did you stay here in the first place after they found you?"

He shrugged. "I don't think they expected me to still be here," he explained.

They were on an island, one of the many islands where the Grand River became the Grand Falls and tumbled over the cliffs to the sea far below.

"If you want to get away why can't you just... I don't know... snap your fingers? If you're of the Accord then you should be able to just slip away and reappear somewhere else."

"Like a god?" he laughed. He raised a hand and snapped his fingers. Nothing happened.

Tish stood and looked down at the seated Angelo. Time to confront things.

"If you're no god, then who are you? What are you? Who are these people chasing after you? If they're agents of the Accord, then why is this happening? What have you done?"

He let her finish. He smiled. He shrugged. "I don't know," he told her. "I don't know who or what I am. I don't know why these people are chasing me or who they are. I don't know what I have done, if I've done anything at all. I don't remember much before a few tens of days ago. I don't understand at all, but I can tell you one thing."

He waited. She asked, "What's that?"

"I love every moment of this existence. Every last detail. I'm soaking it up. I'm a sponge. I want more. I want ever and ever more."

Tish heard the buzz of a motor—a flyer, perhaps. "You have to get away from here," she said. "They'll destroy you."

"Will you come with me? Will you share it with me?"

She nodded. She remembered that moment, walking back into the Falling Droplet and realizing that she was irrevocably changed. She felt that again, only more so. She hoped it would carry on happening, because she wasn't finished yet.

Er-jian-die

I HAVE NO past. I have no future. Only now.

I have many pasts and many futures, but as me, as *this*, there is only now. I am a composite. I have been cast for this occasion, for this task.

I am of the Accord.

I AM ASSEMBLED from the many, from the multitude. I will go back to the multitude.

I am of the Accord.

I am male, in this body. My skin is dark, my hair short, straight. I am slim and strong and fast, of course. Why would I be anything else?

I am enhanced. In many ways.

I am not alone. I will not be alone when I step out of this cabin. There are two others. Two like me, Ee and Sen. We are a team.

I step out through the cabin door, having opened it first. My others are here already. Their heads turn, we nod simultaneously. I join them at the rail.

We are high up, on the deck of a faux sailing ship that is really powered by twinned gravity-wave microgenerators below decks. Above us, sails bulge in a manner designed to appeal to the grand touristas.

We are only a few hours from port. I know this for a fact, like I know much for a fact.

I close my eyes. We close our eyes. Together.

Data flashes.

We open our eyes.

He is here, on the *Lady Cecilia*. The anomaly.

In a realm where everything is known to the Accord—where everything, by its nature, *must* be known to the Accord—he is different. He is unknown. He, by his very nature, does not conform with the rules that govern our existence, your existence, everyone's existence.

He must be found.

He must be stopped.

He must be reabsorbed before he becomes self-propagating.

I turn. We turn. Together.

We smell him.

He has been here, on this deck, recently. He must be nearby.

We will seek him out, find him, reabsorb him, before the *Lady Cecilia* docks. We know this for a fact.

THE LADY CECILIA docks at Penhellion, sliding smoothly into her space in the harbor.

We have not found him, the anomaly.

We have found places where he has been, places where he has spent long hours alone, no doubt doing battle with his perverse nature. They do that. They don't understand, but they try. They are you and me, us; it is their nature.

It is their nature to hide, and to run. This one has been here, in this world called Laverne, for longer than initial data indicated. Re-run analyses give him perhaps twenty more days' existence in which to accumulate knowledge, experience, before he was first detected.

His development is not linear. Those twenty days are days in which every aspect of his self has become exponentially more complex and data-rich.

This one is no babe in arms, then. He is a whirl-wind, a destroyer of worlds.

He does not know it, of course.

Our task is to stop him from finding out.

PENHELLION IS A city built into a cliff. They could have built it on top of the cliff. They could have built it a few kilometers along the coast where the cliffs are not anything up to 1,200 meters high. Human nature is not such, and they built it in the cliff. We built it in the cliff. We are of the Accord.

Data flashes.

There are agents in this city. Many agents. They will look out for him and their reports will be relayed to us whenever they hold anything of relevance.

They do not know they are agents. They do not know they have been selected. Sanji Roseway does not know that she is watching, as she happily stocks her fabric stall on Fandango Way. Neither do the street musician, Mo Yous, or the bar-owner,

Milton Goldenhawk, or the dreamcaster, Serendip Jones. They will not know when they are reporting, or when they have reported. That is not their place.

We did not see him leaving the *Lady Cecilia*, but he has done so. Those extra days, that logarithmic escalation of his survival instinct and wiles, have made a difference.

We must not underrate him.

But first, we must find him.

HE HAS BEEN quiet, which has not helped us in our task. He should be like a whirlpool, drawing in the human debris of this society, feeding on it. Such activity sends out signals, leaves traces, a pebble dropped in our collective pool.

But with experience comes guile and with guile, restraint. Perhaps he has stabilized. That would be unusual, but not a first.

We remain in Penhellion, studying and using our agents to study. He will break cover. He will reveal himself by his actions. They always do.

WE PROXY INTO a bar—a bar through the eyes of another.

There has been a ripple—only the slightest of ripples, but detectable nonetheless. He has emerged.

We look across the bar. We are behind the bar, its surface finely polished flutewood. The barroom is crowded, which is good. Picture windows show sunlight splitting into separate colors through water droplets. I like rainbows. I am not an artist, but once I think a part of me was a part of an artist. Alizarin crimson. Venetian red. Monastral blue. Yellow ocher. I could paint that view a million times and in every instance it would be different.

My team, my others, are also proxying this bartender, and our gaze is drawn away from the picture windows, and we look along the bar.

Another bartender is serving, or rather, not serving, but leaning on the flutewood bar-top, chatting. She is of indeterminate age, as are most adult humans. She has long auburn hair with natural wave, wide eyes with burnt umber irises.

She is talking to him. The anomaly. He has the shape of a man, but we find it hard to focus our eyes—this proxy's eyes—on that shape and determine any detail. He swirls and flows. He is drawing her in.

"Tish?" we say, addressing the bartender. She looks, we nod toward the crowded room. This proxy is not communicative, but his meaning gets across even so.

Tish moves off to serve other customers.

We withdraw, as data flashes.

The Falling Droplet. We are several levels away, in this cliff-face city. We open a channel through the consensus, arriving in seconds.

We enter the bar. It looks different from this perspective, from the crowd rather than from behind the bar. I look around, orientating myself. We each look around. We scan faces, locating Milton the bartender and then Tish the other bartender.

I see him. I point.

He is intense. I feel dizzy, sick, as if I am being sucked in even though I know that cannot be so, due to the heavy levels of security built into my being.

I am aware of the others, Ee-jian-die and Sen-jian-die, turning to look. I sense their turmoil.

I open my hand and spotlight him. That should stun him, lock him into a pool of slowed time so that he will be swimming through perceptual treacle.

He is unaffected.

He drops a glass, ducks, moves, is gone.

We channel, and are standing where he was.

We know of the other exit. We look, and he is there, reaching for the door.

We close our eyes, lock minds, shift consensus. There is no door there. There never has been a door there.

He ducks, vanishes again. He is channeling too, although he does not know it. Short, desperate hops. He reappears by the windows, snatching a chair.

He does not understand what is happening. He is resorting to violence, the chair his only weapon against us.

I smile. He is making it easy.

He swings the chair—but not at us, at the window. It shatters, he turns, he throws himself after the chair.

We look out of the smashed window at the sea and rocks below.

He is not dead.

He cannot be dead.

He can only be reabsorbed.

* * *

WE REMAIN IN Penhellion, even though our anomaly has probably moved on now. He would be foolish to remain, after our first contact. We do not think he is a fool.

HE IS STILL here. Or rather, he has not gone far—only as far as the cliff-top community.

We tackle him immediately when contact is made, through our proxy Billi Narwhal.

He pulls the same trick and evades us.

He is fast, but he appears to be a creature of habit.

He has another weakness, too—the woman, Tish Goldenhawk. She is with him. She appears to have retained her integrity too, which is a bonus.

He is an anomaly. He can be detected by his disruption patterns, but equally, he can lie low. That is the nature of an anomaly. Or *one* of its natures.

But Tish Goldenhawk… If we find her, there is a high probability that we find him.

Tish Goldenhawk

"WHO ARE YOU? What are you?"

Tish Goldenhawk has traveled the length of Laverne's main continent with the man she calls Angelo, and finally she realizes that her invented name for him, "Angelo," is a more appropriate label than "man."

She has traveled the length of the continent with him, but today is the first time she has seen him kill, although she suspects it is not the first time he has killed. She has dispensed bread and feathers for his victim before confronting Angelo.

She has traveled the length of the continent with him and she is ill, drained both physically and mentally, like a scag addict.

He smiles. He shrugs. He says, "I don't know. I did not know the first time you asked me and I have not yet made that discovery. You are beautiful. Death is beautiful. I soak up beauty. That is as close as I have come to defining myself—I am a receptacle."

DEATH. TISH HAD never witnessed violent death until today. She hoped young Ferdinand would find peace in his absorption into the Accord.

They were walking, Tish and Angelo at the front, and his ragged band of followers, now numbering some twenty-four, doing as their role demanded, following.

Angelo accumulated followers. It was his nature. People he encountered, people with a sharp enough sense of perception, of distinction, were always able to detect his special nature, his divinity, the fact that he had been touched by the Accord.

They wanted to be with him.

They wanted to share with him.

They wanted to give to him.

And he, like a child with toys made of flesh and not even the slightest sense of responsibility, took.

The first time Tish had found him with another, she had ranted and raved, and he had smiled and looked puzzled, and she had seen that he had no concept of what she was feeling, and anyway, she could never be the first to cast stones in matters of infidelity.

Blind to herself, Tish had first seen the weakness in others. In Maggie and Li, who had joined the group late but had given so wholeheartedly, she had first seen the addict look in the eye, the transformation of devotion into something physical, something living. They each of them carried a cancer, and that cancer was Angelo.

Ferdinand had been one of the first to join. Tish and Angelo and three or four others had stayed the night in a grand ranch-house somewhere a few days to the northwest of Daguerre. The welcome was warm—as welcomes for Angelo tended to be—and the seventeen year-old son of the owner had been cute and, instantly, devoted.

Ferdinand had come with them. Told his parents he was guiding them to the river-crossing and just carried on with them, and then they'd had to speed up a bit, hitching a ride on a goods wagon, because their welcome at that ranch would never be as warm again.

Ferdinand supplanted Tish as Angelo's favorite, if he could be said to have such a thing. To be honest, she was not too put out by this development, as already she was starting to feel that psychic leeching that would only get worse.

Ferdinand went from fresh-faced disciple to hollowed devotee to shuffling, skeletal wreck in only twenty or so days.

It happened among them—it was happening to all of them, only at a slower rate—and yet it had taken far too long for Tish to notice. In the worlds of the Diaspora suffering had long since been banished. It was not even something readily recognized, like a language newly encountered. There was a whole new syntax of suffering for them to learn.

"WHAT AM I? I don't know. But I can tell you that it is like flying. I wish to fly and I fly, but once I am up there it is only the air and a few feathers that prevent me from plummeting. So tenuous the thread of existence!

"You are strong, Tish. So much stronger than the others. You hold me together. You are my air, my feathers. Without you... well, I don't know what I would be without you to support me, to contain me."

SHE WAS GROWING weak. Had been growing weak.

But not as rapidly as Ferdinand.

She came close-up on them early that morning, when the sun was still heavy over the mountains, painting them gold and pink.

Angelo was holding him, his arms easily enfolding the wasted frame.

Tish almost turned away. She had seen this kind of encounter often enough by now. She closed her eyes and thought back to those few precious nights when it had just been the two of them, sleeping rough, both enfolded by his wings.

She had been strong then.

She opened her eyes just as Ferdinand started to vanish.

She watched. She could see through him. See the stones, the thorn bush, the tussock grass, the inside of Angelo's embracing left arm, previously obscured by Ferdinand's bony torso.

Things blurred. Things dissolved, melted, slipped away from this existence.

He was gone.

Angelo turned to her, his expression startled as if he did not know what had happened, had not expected it to happen; but beneath the surprise there was satisfaction, a thrill of pleasure, of strength, and the first hint of that crooked-toothed smile.

Er-jian-die

"YOUR AIR, YOUR feathers... so poetic. If you weren't such an innocent I'd say you had the crassest line in smooth-talk, but you don't have a clue, do you?"

We have her. We have him. I see him through the eyes of Tish Goldenhawk and it is as if a distorting lens has been removed. He is male, of indeterminate age, of mid-brown skin tone and dark hair. He is beautiful and engaging.

He draws you in.

Even at this remove—proxied and many hundred kilometers distant—he draws you in.

We debate, as he moves out of view. Act now, via proxy, or attend in body, allowing a short interval in which he might detect our approach and take evasive action? We do not know how much his powers have grown.

Data flashes.

Ee-jian-die takes the proxy, turns her head so that he is back in our field of view. Sen-jian-die and I withdraw, lock, open a channel through the consensus, step through.

There is momentary disorientation and then we are standing on a plain, surrounded by cacti and thorn bushes and oddly balanced round boulders.

The two of them are there, locked in conflict. A short distance away there is an encampment of bubble tents and track trikes. The people there look on, too damaged to stir.

She has him in the beam. She stands, knees slightly bent, body tipped forward, one arm stretched out, palm first, fingers straight, and a beam of white light lances from her hand to him, the anomaly.

He stands there smiling.

He looks at us as we materialize, although he should not be able to turn his head at all.

He raises a hand so that he mirror's Tish Goldenhawk's stance and his palm cuts out the beam, reflects it.

It shines on her face and she crumples, sobbing, more damaged than she had been before.

Ee-jian-die appears at my side, his proxying of Tish abandoned.

He looks ashen, damaged by the encounter, even at a proxy.

I allow myself to be identified as leader, even though we three are equal; we three are far greater than we three alone. "Your time is up," I tell the anomaly. "Let these people go. Come back with us. Allow yourself to be reabsorbed."

He smiles in a way that indicated he is both amused and puzzled. "Reabsorbed?" he said. "*Re... ?*"

I nod. "You are a glitch," I tell him. "A chaotic anomaly. The Accord contains all the individuals who have lived and then died since its inception. You are a bug in that process, a self-resonant fluctuation in the billions upon billions of human elements within the Accord. A remix error. You're a strange attractor and you need to be smoothed over. Come with us, you will not be lost, you will simply be reabsorbed."

"But how... ? How can I be reabsorbed if I am not yet dead?"

He doesn't know. He has grown, but he does not know.

"*This* is the Accord," I tell him. "We are living the afterlife. The afterlives."

"What happens if I say 'no?'"

"We will force you."

"And if you fail?"

"You will carry on growing. Like a leak in a pool, you will continue to drag in those about you, soaking them up until they are husks. They are drawn to you. We are drawn to you. You are like a black hole in human form. You will suck us all in and the Accord will fail to be. It will crash on a galaxy-wide scale."

He—this thing, this entity, this *it*—is smiling. "So, if I believe you, then I—" it thumped its chest in apelike display "—am an alternative to the Accord? An alternative reality?"

It laughs. "I like this," it says. "It is all so beautiful. So, so beautiful."

We strike, synchronized.

Ee locks him in the immobilizing beam, far more powerful than we have used so far. I lock him in a second, our combined beams more than doubling their intensity in combination. Sen moves in to interface, a physical connection with the Accord.

The anomaly is still smiling.

It turns and lashes out a beam of light and Sen flies through the air in several pieces.

It turns again, and lashes at Ee, and I sense our hold—if ever we had had a hold—weakening.

And then... light, dark, an absence that is where the pain would have been if my body had not immediately shut down those pathways. A lot of absence.

Mental silence. Ee-jian-die and Sen-jian-die have been returned to the Accord. They will reappear, but not here, not now.

I am still here, though. I have not been returned.

I open the eye that I am able to control.

I see sky, a thorn bush.

I see her. Tish Goldenhawk. Looking down at me.

"What can I do?" she says.

"Nothing," I tell her. The body that carries me is too fundamentally damaged. It could be repaired, of course, but what is the point? My task is over, I have failed. I will be reabsorbed. Someone else will be sent, and they will try again. The anomaly will have grown, but it will be fought, only not by me next time, or at least, not by the combination of traits that is this me.

"What happens to us when he has sucked us dry?"

She is strong, this one.

"If this is the Accord, then where does the data go when he has absorbed it? You said he's some kind of black hole—what's inside him?"

"Who knows?" I say. "The physically dead enter the Accord and we live on, again and again, for eternity. But attractant anomalies like this remove us from the afterlife. It's like asking where the dead went before there was an Accord. They died. They stopped being. They ended. If he takes us from the Accord, we end."

"What can I do?" she repeats, and I realize that she does not mean to ask what she can do to help my mortally damaged body, but rather what can she do to stop the anomaly, the attractor, her lover.

"He said I was his air, his feathers, that I held him together," she said. "I want that to stop."

In that instant I want to paint her. Like the rainbows, I could paint her a million times and each would be different, but always her strength, her purity, would come through.

"You have to get close to him," I tell her.

Tish Goldenhawk

"YOU HAVE TO get close to him," this wreck of a human construct tells her. "Hold him."

Tish Goldenhawk nods. In her mind she can see Angelo holding Ferdinand, absorbing him. She knows exactly what this agent of the Accord means. "What then?"

"That's all," he tells her. "I will do the rest."

* * *

ANGELO WAITS FOR her in the encampment, smiling. She should have known he would not go on without her.

"I'm sorry," he says. His words have no meaning. They are just vibrations in the air. "They tried to kill me."

She nods. "They're dead now," she says, wondering then at the lie—whether she has made a fatal mistake already.

He shakes his head. "One lives," he says, "but only tenuously. He does not have long, I think."

He turns. "We must move on," he says. "There will be more of them. Another day and we will reach a city, I think. A city would be good."

She looks at him, tries to see him as she had once seen him, a charming, exciting escape. That had only ever been one of her fantasies. She tries to see him as her lover, but cannot. Tries to see him even as human, but no.

"I can't," she says in a quiet voice.

He turns, raises an eyebrow.

"I can't go on." Getting stronger. "I'm leaving. Going home. You don't need me anymore."

"But..."

"No buts," she says. "I can't do this. I'm exhausted. Drained. I'm leaving."

He is not human, but there is so much in him that *is*.

"You can't," he says. "I... You're my support. My feathers, the air that holds me up. The air that I breathe!"

"I'm tired," she says. "You can't lean on me anymore. I'm none of those things... I'm not strong enough. Can't you see? It's *me* who needs supporting!"

"I will always support you," he says.

He opens his arms, just as he had for Ferdinand, who had been too weak to continue.

He steps forward.

She waits for him to come to her, to hold her.

Scent of cinnamon, of dry, dusty feathers. She holds him.

She senses the flow, the seething mass of energies. They came from... beyond.

He gasps, straightens.

She holds on.

He is looking down at her. He knows. He dips his head and kisses her on the brow.

She holds nothing, holds air, hugs herself. She drops to her knees.

There are feathers, nothing else. She gathers some. She will cast them for him, with bread, when she gets back to Penhellion.

She does not doubt that she will go there, go home.

Poor Milton. Poor Druce. She has changed. She does not know what can be salvaged, but she will go home now and she will see.

She stands.

Even if nothing can be repaired, she has no regrets. She would do it all again.

She is of the Accord.

They all are of the Accord.

The Wedding Party

Simon Ings

THE RISK IS in standing still.

It can come at you quickly. A gas lamp sets a tent alight and six Somalian refugees die in the flames—Ta-da!

Or it can be subtle. Last year, a great many Somalian refugees gave up their flight altogether, boarded boats in Aden, and headed home—and why? Maybe because the Yemeni authorities let on how many Palestinian refugees had already died in the camp they were bound for—the camp at Al Ghanaian.

The point, either way, is this—the risk is in standing still.

I've said to my wife: "Aiden's dead. Mocha's closed out."

I said to her: "Lebanon to Syria to Cyprus. Come on."

I said, "He hasn't any choice."

This is her brother we are talking about. My lover—which is a joke. Rather, he is the other side of that coin I once coveted—Redson and Hope, that long-wished-for alchemical wedding.

Slip through Europe, that's the ticket. If you can call it slipping. Slump through Europe. Slouch through Europe. Squat, squeeze, shimmy through Europe, to the Red Cross camp at Sangatte, just a short walk away from the Channel Tunnel.

Kurdish gangs patrol the camp, which isn't even a real camp—just a converted railway warehouse. The Kurds organize the escapees; they arrange transit attempts through the Tunnel; they know what's what. Whether you're a single man from Iraq or Iran, or a family from Afghanistan, Kosovo, or Albania—it's all the same to them. You don't get through without you paying the fee.

And you pay the fee. Of course you do. The risk is in standing still. The risk is in standing up—standing up, I mean, to them. There are riots in Sangatte, as you would expect from eight hundred and fifty refugees crammed into quarters meant for two hundred. All of them trying somehow, anyhow, to scrape together that fee.

I've said to Hope—that's my wife's name, Hope—"Get Redson to Cyprus and I'll do the rest." And I'm already promising more than I should. The Snakeheads have much of this route I'm suggesting sewn up—from the Balkans to Sangatte, some say.

She says nothing. She looks out the window at the poisoned Devonshire countryside. No sound impinges from outside. The foot-and-mouth crisis has occasioned a wholesale slaughter of livestock in this region. Nothing moves. It is as though the holocaust has been extended even to the insects and the birds.

"He hasn't a choice!"

She looks out the window at the rain. If you can call it rain, drizzle scrubbing the land and the sky into one.

Drizzle subsumes everything, the yellowish particulate—faint traces of a bruise—that must, I suppose, mark a nearby pyre. It subsumes too, and utterly, the fine spray from the hose, which runs above the five-bar gate. The hose spans the farm track on thin scaffolding. And there's the bucket where I dutifully scrubbed my boots an hour—Jesus, no, two hours ago. Impatient, I turn her chair; I force her to look away from the window, away from the near-bankrupt ruin that was a Devon dairy farm (it's not even ours, we just rent the house).

She hates it when I pull her chair about, when I take advantage of her condition. I stroke her head. "Stop it," she says.

"He really has no choice," I insist. "If it was anyone else he'd have got away with it. But Beneson was the only left-footed striker on the team. The national team. They won't let it go."

Redson—my lover, ho ho; anyway, my brother-in-law—he was working the qat caravans out of Somalia when he surprised a burglar, coming in through his kitchen window. Got terrified. Shot him—and thought that he was within his rights so to do. And he would have been—had the burglar not turned out to be a national hero.

Hope can do this. She can get him out. Overland from Mogadishu to Nairobi. Round the lake to Kampala and from there by air freight to Libya. By boat to Lebanon, then Syria, Cyprus, "Come on!"

Hope can do this—because she has done it herself. After we split she went back home to Malawi, as safe a country as you're going to get in central Africa, working at the Dzaleka refugee camp in Dowa. Only she got caught up with the Congolese mafia that run the bus concessions out of Lilongwe and Blantyre, and had to run in the end. If you can call it running. They drove her and drove her, nowhere was safe. And when she had had enough of running—if you can call it running—she bit the bullet. She slipped through, slunk through, squeezed herself painfully through Europe's ever-tightening net—did a good job of it, too—but in the end it was too much. She had to call me, make some sort of peace with me, beg me to help her cross the Channel into Britain. Which I naturally did.

The snakeheads have Europe sewn up. From the Balkans right through to Sangatte, so they say. And that was enough for me. I got out of all that, and quick. For several years now, the nearest I've come to that line of work is to sort out the illegals who haunt Cricklewood. I'm a sort of fly-by-night foreman-cum-bus driver. You know what it's like—two navvies this way, and three navvies that and jump quick in the back of the van before we all get nicked. Seeing to the casual labor market of Cricklewood is more than enough to fill my day, and this morning I found myself seriously wondering if I'm up to this fresh obligation.

But Redson is my lover, the other side of that coin I put such store by. And call me sentimental but I cannot bear to think of them parted like this. These two people. These two half-people, I should say, because it seems even now that they are only the halves of a single person, a person I might once have drawn together. A person I loved. Hope/Redson. Redson/Hope.

I've said to her: "Calais's as tight as a bitch. So I'll take him through Ouistreham. They've just axed the frontier post and there's boats sailing to Portsmouth all day."

"You mustn't," she says. "No. Stop it." Her torso flexes uselessly. Her head bobs and tosses.

I am stroking her neck. "Please." I am shucking her shirt free and stroking her breast. "Please."

"It's safer," I tell her, "it's really come on. It's so much safer now."

My hand does its business. The tears come and I wipe them away for her. I settle her back in her chair and I know I have won.

Hope has done her business and I have done mine. Redson has landed up in Sangatte, because it's safer for us to follow the migrant flow, because the Snakeheads have their nostrils raised and aquiver for the innovations of a competitor.

Anyway, I got him out of there last night and paid the Kurd his bloody fee. Then, soon as we were out of sight, I legged it with Redson back over the fence, away from the Tunnel, and back onto the highway system. It took a while to find the van—when I go shopping I'm always losing the damn thing in the multi-storey. It's not big—people movers are taller.

We reached Ouistreham by first light. Redson sat there blinking up at the buildings like an inner-city kid on an excursion trip—he's a natural tourist, a camera on legs.

I've rented us an old villa on the Riva Bella—the white sand beach near to town. Redson needs to sleep if we're to make a start tomorrow, but the end is in sight, the biggest hurdle yet to cross, and the door had swung open on the room holding all my gear—he saw everything. It took an age to calm him down. "It's so much safer now." Though surely the size of the van is clue enough, what I have planned for him.

Redson is younger than Hope by two years. They have a Malawian mother, dead of AIDS. They have a Scottish father, a lapsed minister who vanished as soon as they got of an age to start asking about passports and paternity. There is another brother, a half-brother, through whom I first met them—Olaf, a surgeon at the hospital where I did my placement. It was him who taught me how to fillet skin flaps for the scores of amputees we were dealing with then. Malawian roads, for all that they are practically empty, are some of the most dangerous in the world.

Hope's skin is as dark as Olaf's—she's as dark as any pure-bred African. Dad's pallid genes kept out of sight, dwelling instead, deep in the bone, narrowing and tightening her features as she grew, lengthening her neck and her back. Dad's seed made her magically beautiful—people imagine she's desert stock, from Namibia or even further north. A regal Saharan beauty. They'd never guess the wet and windy truth.

Redson, though, he's the other side of the coin. Dad's seed floats on Redson's surface like a rash. It has gingered his hair and freckled his hands. Rough, blotched skin hangs off his heavy features like an old dog blanket. Stocky, hairy, unpleasure-giving. Until you understand the nature of my desire, my choice of lover seems ludicrous. You see, I was only half in love with him, just as I was only half in love with Hope. I loved the person they might be. But love's all done with now. Unsatiated, love gnarls itself into something else, something nameless.

He is saying things to me like, "Leave me alone." "I want to stay in France." "I can speak French." Only he is a murderer—in the law's eyes, if not his own. And where might he procure a faster, more reliable change of identity than from me, with all my contacts—and all of them on the other side of that maddeningly narrow strip of water, that Channel?

And I am sitting here holding his hands, reassuring him for what seems like hours, is hours—2pm now, and you can see the panic and the exhaustion battling it out through that mottled, gingerish skin of his as he slides down in his seat. I stir him, lift him, urge him to the room I have laid out for him—dark, cool, looking landward, in an upper storey overlooked by no one.

It is hard to let go of his hand, hard not to bring it to my face. It is hard to face tomorrow.

So after a catnap I walk into town and have an early dinner at a seafood restaurant done out like a Thirties Parisian metro. I order smoked cod and cider and though the food is excellent I realize I have made a very bad choice. I must not drink because of tomorrow, and without a drink, and surrounded by this décor, how can I not fill my head with thoughts of metros and train tunnels, nets closing in, of narrowing doorways and lids coming down—?

I am back before Redson wakes. Carefully, I let myself into his room. He sleeps nude, as usual. It is a warm night, so he has pushed the blankets back and made do with a sheet. I ease it down, past his shoulders, his flank, his knees. I resist the temptation to touch, to map his body with my hands, to relent. He has no choice; nor have I.

You can deaden nerves by acupuncture—that's the principle behind the blanket I'm laying over him. It's faster than gas anesthetics and safer too. Except that it sounds unnervingly like a fire as it crackles and crinkles, tucking itself around his sleeping flesh.

Ta-da!

Dawn breaks and I'm detaching the muscles from his right shoulder blade, rolling the shoulder girdle opposite to the direction of the cut to get the angle. It's still not light enough that I can douse the lamps I brought along, though the heat they give off is wicked, and I need still more light to safely free and divide the neurovascular bundle, where it emerges just beneath the serratus. Once the clavicle's free it's just a matter—or it should be—of closing the skin flaps over suction drains. Only it's the same problem with this arm as the last; in my hurry I've made the flaps too short. So I do what I did last time and saw off the acromion process parallel to the scapula, to make the wound more flat.

By now I'm exhausted and it's light outside, so I take another catnap, then I go back in and turn the lights out and open the curtains. There's a table under the window and I stand there, luxuriating in the cool coming in through the top of the sash, while I work on his arms, first one, then the other—disarticulating the elbows.

The bags I'm using are the cleverest, the scylliated insides sucking round and close over each body part. Pink goo runs across the seam like a cartoon smile.

In the afternoon I start on his legs and it's back-breaking work—I forgot how back-breaking. He's tall for the tank, and after careful measurement, I've plumped for pelvectomy. Work this radical is not without its sublime moments. Once the iliac vessels are out the way you can see the sacral nerve roots deep within the pelvis. But for the most part it's pure butchery, hacking the muscles of his back from the wing of the ilium.

And on with his blanket again. And a catnap for me.

It's dark again by the time the pelvis starts to open.

For two days, the drains do their work. For two days, Redson looks up at me, wide-eyed, his expression no different to the one he wore when we drove through Ouistreham. Mouthing. Trying to speak.

For two days, I hunt out things to distract him. Music for him to listen to. Things to read to him. But sound does not touch his spirit, and never has. He was born all eyes.

Even with all this equipment I cannot for the life of me jerry-rig the mirror he asks me for, so that he might look out of the window at the sky—"The sky, at least!"

Of course he cannot be moved.

"It was a long time ago." I am back to my reassurances. I really should have made a tape. A recorded lecture in an authoritative voice—Tom Baker or Leonard Nimoy. I've done this so many times now I'm starting to whinge. "We didn't know as much, then." "Hope had really bad luck." As soon as I opened the bags I knew it was hopeless, though I tried, God knows I tried. In that Calais motel room, the seams had closed so tight and pink around Hope's limbs, there was no hint of trouble. But when we got to England and I opened the bags to reassemble her—the seams had gone the brown of a pineapple cut through and left to the air. Some seams had parted altogether and dark little puckers had formed round each breach.

There was no smell. It all looked fresh enough. But there's fresh and then there's fresh. As Hope and I discovered.

"It's so much safer now."

At last, he begs me to put him to sleep. So we sleep. Our last night in Ouistreham, our last night in France. I haven't the energy to leave his side, so I shuck off my shoes and my shirt and my shorts and I curl up beside him, under the sheet.

Lay your hand on a man's chest, on his belly. There is so much bone and muscle in the way of the true treasures—the miracles of liver, kidneys, spleen, and heart. But touch his back, below the rib cage—and they are tantalizingly close.

Like this, Redson is a chest indeed, a box of clever treasures. Sea creatures dream away their incarceration inside him. Wrapped up in each other, joined together mouth-to-anus by slick bonds only Crohn's disease can reveal and eventually break, they are utterly dependent upon each other. And yet they are so different, each organ so utterly unlike its neighbor—how could they dream that they are One? Where does this dream of Oneness come from? When must we let it go?

In June of the millennium year, 2000—a Dutch lorry driver called Perry Wacker entered Britain in a rapid transit TIR lorry crammed with fifty-eight Chinese immigrants. He remembered to shut the lorry's sole ventilation flap, so as not to arouse the suspicions of customs officers. But he forgot to open it again.

All but two of his cargo asphyxiated to death.

But it's the fine levied on the lorry firms—£2,000 per head—that's done most to curb human trafficking by lorry. That and the technology, as even a well-insulated TIR rig is no defense against infrared and ultrasound.

The trend now is to shift fewer people in smaller vehicles. As the technology improves and the political climate hardens, it's a trend that can only continue.

I just have time for a quick breakfast at a brasserie outside the ferry port. Its Seventies décor reminds me of Portsmouth, which is at once my home town and our destination today. Even the name of this restaurant—the Britannia—points toward closure.

Then up the ramp onto the ferry.

The checks on this side of the Channel are cursory, much less stringent since the French decided to pull out their specialist unit. Portsmouth, on the other hand, bristles with every piece of tech going.

So this is how it's done—

Natural gas hasn't caught on as a fuel in this country as yet, and no one knows what an engine that runs on both gas and diesel actually looks like. The engine is largely fake, but all the parts are genuine and professionally assembled, and who in their right mind is going to take an engine apart? So the bags sit in metal casings, many of them in plain view, and never get spotted. And because the bags are cold-blooded, relying for their primitive metabolism on heat from the actual engine (it's in there somewhere under all the Meccano) nothing very remarkable ever shows up on infrared.

So we arrive—if not intact, then at least undiscovered.

Even Hayling Island is becoming gentrified now, though the softest of the creek beds have so far resisted development. I'm out the van, tinkering with the engine; taking the bags from their hiding places, stowing them in carriers. "Carrefour." "Lafayette."

There are old moorings among the reed beds, the wood all rotted away so only the holes are left—holes with a petrolish sheen over them where nothing grows. But who would notice them among all these reeds? What fills these holes is an essence of rotted wood and the microscopic carcasses of whatever fed on it, all mingled with the deliquescent remains of whatever fed on them. And so on—who knows how long a food chain? Though water covers the holes for much of the day, what fills the holes has very little to do with water.

The holes are something like the consistency of porridge and dogs have been known to disappear into them. One or two children.

So I am careful, and I resist the temptation to carry too much at one go, and within about fifteen muddy minutes I have found what I am looking for.

Two more trips and I'm done. In they go, one after another, and the colors released, as the oily sheen closes over each bag, are the same as you find on those maps, which pick out countries in different pastel colors.

Is the hole deep enough?

The risk is in running, if you can call it running.

The risk is in moving, and in being moved.

Each moonless night, hulks registered in Cambodia ply the seaways from Lebanon to Syria to Cyprus. Fishing boats from Somalia run aground on the beaches of Mocha; they run aground, or they sink.

Snakeheads throw women into the sea after their children, a mile from the Spanish shore. Then they torch their own ship.

Dozens of would-be migrants drown off the coasts of Italy and Spain each year as they attempt the crossing from the Balkans or North Africa.

So much horror, so much desire—sooner or later it stalls, bottlenecked at the Red Cross camp at Sangatte.

One hundred and fifty people a night are caught trying to travel illegally through the Channel Tunnel. Some hide inside goods wagons, breathing through hosepipes in a hopeless attempt to evade the carbon dioxide detectors. Others ride on the outside of the trains, wrapped in foil to keep them warm. Still others cram themselves into tiny compartments beneath the floors of passenger coaches, barely inches above the live rails.

February this year. An Iraqi Kurd dies after leaping twenty feet from a bridge onto the roof of a goods train—only to slip and fall across an electrified rail.

19th June 2001. Six Russians steal a speedboat in Calais, discover that the engine's missing, and elect to set out anyway, paddling it across one of the world's busiest shipping lanes.

31st July 2001. Two Lithuanian refugees cross the Channel on children's air mattresses. More than ten hours pass before they're picked up. They even have luggage.

The gates are swinging shut around Europe. The nets are tightening—meshes of infrared and ultrasound. Dogs. Carbon dioxide wands.

The traffic through Portsmouth was lighter than I expected, which means I've made it home before sunset.

"Home." Not Devon; that can wait till tonight. I mean the house I rent in Ferring, a little seaside town in West Sussex, a stone's throw from Brighton. I get in and already, within minutes, I'm picking up the ends of my life, I'm washing up dirty dishes, changing the sheets. Putting CDs back into boxes.

It's a big house.

I enter the garage and dig out the valves and gauges that will free Redson from his high-pressure prison.

The van—like I said, it runs on both petrol and natural gas. The gas tank is mounted in the back of the van. I've had customs officers want me to pull up the hardboard housing to reveal the tank—but beyond that they do not go. Maybe a few raps on the outside with a torch. But it's not a good idea to go peeking inside a pressurized container.

This is how it's done, you see: where the carbon dioxide detectors cannot go; where infra-red and ultrasound are blind—this is where the truly, irreducibly living part of Redson, head and torso, lives and breathes.

In the footwell of the passenger seat, I lay out freshly laundered blankets to make a nest for him.

It's important to have hold of all the parts during the crossing, in case you get caught. With all accounted for, you have some shred of defense, as you can argue that you meant no lasting harm to your charge.

But what would be the point in reassembling him? Hope and Redson reflect each other.

Redson/Hope—I cannot allow one half to mock the other.

The acid slew in the old post-hole must surely have eaten through the bags by now; must already be stripping Redson's arms and legs down to the bone, chewing through the bone, I don't doubt, given time.

In the back of the van, I check on my charge. He mustn't depressurize too fast, or the bends will take him. But the math you need in order to do this safely—it's easy enough; and I have done this before, many times.

I look at my watch, calculating the air he's got left.

Plenty, enough that I could leave him in there, unconscious, until we are all three met again, a wedding party, in that house among the pyres and the rain. Already in my mind's eye I am drawing the blinds on that bankrupt, poisoned countryside. I am rolling them together, torso to torso. Inevitable, irresistible, a contact more intimate than any embrace. I am blessing them, telling them, "Kiss!"

But no. It has been a long day. I am exhausted. It's over two hundred miles to Devon, and that union I have for so long desired to bring about.

I shall tilt the rearview mirror so Redson can look out. And he will help me stay awake.

Third Person

Tony Ballantyne

THE STEAM BOMB was a perforated metal shell the size of a tennis ball, filled with water and loaded with an F-Charge. On detonation it squirted needles of pressurized steam that drilled through anything within a radius of half a meter and left anything at a radius of one meter slightly damp. The bomb that landed in the hot street tore apart Bundy's upper thighs, punctured his stomach, and left his forehead covered in a refreshing pink mist.

"It came from up there, sergeant," murmured Chapelhow into his headset, pointing to the roof of a nearby house. Mitchell fired his rifle with a muffled crack and an overweight woman slumped forward and fell from the roof. No contest. Mitchell was a regular, she was just a conscript, flushed and confused by the hot Spanish sun. Mitchell lowered his black rifle and resumed his patient scanning of the surrounding area, black gloved hands ready on his gun, black booted feet planted wide.

Bundy was screaming without seeming to notice it. He was fumbling at his rifle with blood-slicked hands, trying to reload. Sergeant Clausen shook his head.

"He's done," he said. "Chapelhow, finish him."

Chapelhow felt his stomach churning; nonetheless he raised his cheap conscript's rifle to his shoulder and shot Bundy through the head, silencing his screams. The brass-bound round the wounded man had been trying to load slipped from his fingers and rolled across the road. Chapelhow was rubbing his shoulder through his thin silk shirt, the kick of the rifle too much for his thin frame.

"Take his gun," chided Sergeant Clausen impatiently, "we're going to need it."

Despite his thick black uniform, Mitchell looked cool. Just like the sergeant. They weren't sweating like the conscripts. They didn't have dark patches beneath their armpits from their exertions, nor did they have beads of moisture on their upper lips. They moved like lazy cats, turning this way and that to scan the dusty street.

"There'll be more, sarge," said Mitchell. "SEA always try for the pincher."

"I know. Chapelhow, Hamblion, go back toward the seafront. Singh, Reed, up toward the town. See if you can spot anyone else."

Chapelhow knew what it meant, to be paired with Hamblion. Hamblion was grossly overweight. He was expendable. If Hamblion was going back to the seafront, then that was were the sergeant was expecting the attack to come from.

Most of the buildings were shut up for the mid-day siesta. The only sign of activity came from a man in a white shirt, carrying little round-topped tables and setting them out in the shade just in front of his bar. The expendable Hamblion wad-dled past him, staying in the shade where he could, his arms burnt bright red from the sun, like sore corned beef, his podgy hand making his rifle look like a stick of liquorice. Chapelhow limped along on the opposite side of the street. The thin soles on his expensive leather slip-on shoes were coming loose, more suitable for a night out clubbing than for a conscripted soldier on a sortie. The sound of the sea and the shouts of the few children left play-ing on the beach could be heard up ahead. There was a scraping noise as a door opened in a house on the shady side of the street. Chapelhow jumped, he and Hamblion turning their guns toward it. Two middle-aged women walked out, chattering in Spanish. They wore floral print skirts, their hair permed in short curls. Both car-ried smart leather handbags.

Chapelhow relaxed, turning his rifle back toward the sea. The two women pulled pistols from their handbags and pointed them up the street at the sergeant. Chapelhow shot the one on the left, grunting as the recoil slammed the rifle into his shoulder again. Hamblion's fat finger caught in the trigger guard and he clumsily fired his rifle up into the air. A third person, a man dressed in the dark green uniform of the Southern European Alliance stepped out from the dark doorway and aimed calmly at the sergeant.

Hamblion paused in the act of loading his rifle, realizing there wasn't time. He dropped the gun to the floor and stepped forward in front of the man in green, his body giving a great hiccup as the enemy fired.

Chapelhow shot the second of the Spanish ladies and calmly reloaded. He could see Hamblion hanging onto the soldier as the enemy emptied his rifle into his fat body, wobbling waves spasming up and down his length with each shot.

Now Chapelhow shot the soldier. Sergeant Clausen's voice sounded in his headset.

"Chapelhow. Get Hamblion's rifle and fall back to me."

"Okay, sarge." Chapelhow scooped up the rifle and limped back up the road.

"What now, sarge?" Mitchell queried through the headset.

"We're going into the town."

"Won't that make us easier to pinpoint?"

"Yes. But there are too many of them around. We'll use the civilians as cover."

"We need a drink, sarge," said Reed from the other end of the street.

"And something to eat," added Singh.

"We do," agreed the sergeant. "There'll be cafés and bars in the town. Shops. We can get something there."

Chapelhow came limping up to the sergeant and Mitchell, a rifle slung over each shoulder.

"Got any money, Chapelhow?" asked the sergeant. Chapelhow reached awkwardly into the breast pocket of his paisley shirt.

"I've got about twenty euros, sarge," he said, sorting through the bills. There was a yellow piece of notepaper there with the words "You are Andy Chapelhow" scrawled hurriedly across the top.

"I've got money," said Singh.

Chapelhow was unfolding the yellow notepaper, looking to see what else was written there.

"There'll be time for that later," said the sergeant, batting at Chapelhow's hand. "Come on. We'll go into town."

The sergeant touched the pale-green pouch that hung from his belt and looked at Mitchell. "We can round up some more recruits when we get there."

"We'll need them," said Mitchell.

Chapelhow nodded in silent agreement as he looked back at the mound of flesh that had been Hamblion, his hot blood spreading in a pool in the middle of the road, reflecting the scorching sun.

THE CENTER OF the town was a maze of shady twisting alleys built on a hill. Alleys filled with the hot spicy smells of lunch, with the chatter of conversation that echoed from the tiled and crowded tapas bars, alleys filled with little tables at which couples drank wine and families of tourists ordered sausages and chips and spread out pictures for their children to color.

Chapelhow and the rest walked past all of this, alert and exhausted.

"Where are we going?" asked Reed brightly.

"Right through the town and out the other side," said Mitchell.

"Why can't they just send a helicopter or a flier to pick us up?" complained Reed, only just eighteen, and consequently an expert at everything. Chapelhow envied her for her certainty. More than that though, he envied her for her walking boots, for her light jacket, and shorts. Reed had been out hiking when the sergeant had conscripted her.

"They will send us something," said Mitchell patiently. "But if we're too obvious about it, the Europeans will just wait until we are on board and then shoot us down. That's what an exit strategy is all about. Both us and the helicopter have to rendezvous unnoticed by the enemy."

"So where are we going?"

"That's a secret. What if you got captured?"

"Hmm. Is that why you won't tell us what's in that package you are carrying?" She pointed to the cylinder the Sergeant had strapped to his belt. "Did you steal it from the SEA? Is that why they are chasing us?"

"You don't need to know that, Reed," smiled Mitchell.

There was a crack and Singh span round, raising his rifle and pointing it at a nearby table. The sergeant knocked the gun up into the air.

"Hey, hey, hey," said the diners at a nearby table. There was some angry shouting in Spanish. Chapelhow's headset translated the words of a patrician-looking older man for him. "You watch where you're pointing that thing. We'll sue you and your army." The man jabbed a finger angrily in their direction.

"It was just a champagne cork," said the sergeant.

A mustached waiter smiled as he filled the glasses of the diners. Chapelhow thought it was funny, how quickly people adapted to technology. Only halfway through the Twenty-first century and already people believed in surgical strikes and targeted weapons. They felt safe, even with a war going on around them. Chapelhow grinned to himself. They wouldn't be so complacent if they knew how old the guns were that he and the other conscripts carried.

"We should hide the rifles," said Reed. "We stand out carrying them. What if they inform on us?" She pointed to the diners.

"Then they enter the field of combat and we can shoot them," replied Mitchell in a loud voice. He wanted the smiling waiter to hear.

Sergeant Clausen was getting impatient.

"This is no good. We need to eat and we need more conscripts." He tapped a finger against his teeth, thinking.

"We're going to have to split up," he said suddenly. "Mitchell. You and Singh take the rifles and the package. Get up high where you can watch us. Reed, Chapelhow and I will go eat and get talking with the locals. See if we can press some recruits."

"What about your uniform, sarge?" asked Reed.

"Good point." he replied. "You can help me buy some civvies, Reed."

SERGEANT CLAUSEN LOOKED different in civilian clothes. Dressed in a white open-necked shirt, a gold chain around his neck, he looked younger and more handsome. But with a dangerous edge to him. Chapelhow could see that Reed had picked up on it. She was only just eighteen and she hadn't yet learned about men like Clausen, he guessed. "You look good, sarge," she said, obviously coming on to him.

"It took too long," complained the sergeant. "Bloody shops shut for lunch."

"Let's go here," said Reed, pointing to a restaurant that backed onto the sea. Behind it they could just see a terrace poking out, white-jacketed waiters moving about in the cool breeze.

"No," said the sergeant. "We need to get inland. We could be seen from a ship kilometers out on that terrace. Picked off by laser. They could see us back in Africa."

"Is that where the package comes from, sarge?" asked Reed cheekily.

"Shut up about the package. That's an order."

There was a café on a corner that gave a good view down the three streets that led to it. The sergeant chose a table and positioned his team so they could watch every approach. He ordered a carafe of red wine and a large bottle of water.

"Don't drink the wine," he said. "Don't get drunk."

He glanced up at the second-storey window of a nearby building. Chapelhow saw a shadowy movement within and guessed that Mitchell and Singh were up there.

The sergeant was listening to the voices from the tables around him. For the first time since his conscription, Chapelhow missed his headset, he missed being able to understand what the Spanish were saying. And then, in the midst of the hubbub, he heard English voices. A little girl squabbling with her sister. And over there, a young couple, sharing their meals with each other, the woman holding out a forkful of fish to her boyfriend to taste.

Sergeant Clausen smiled.

"I'm just going to the toilet," he said, clapping his hands on his knees. He stood up and walked off, taking something from his pocket as he did so.

The waiter arrived with their water and their wine.

"Are you ready to order?" he asked in heavily accented English.

"Steak, chips, and salad for all three of us," said Reed. She shrugged at Chapelhow. That had been Sergeant Clausen's orders. Plenty of protein and carbohydrate.

"What's that?" she asked. Chapelhow had taken the yellow piece of paper from his pocket.

"I don't know," said Chapelhow. "It says 'You are Andy Chapelhow. This paper is kept in Andy Chapelhow's pocket…'"

"What does it mean?"

"I'm not sure."

Reed was already bored. "What do you suppose is in the package? The one that the sergeant gave to Mitchell?"

"I don't know. Africa is in the news a lot lately. There's a lot of technological development going on there and the West doesn't like it. It doesn't like being left behind. I think the sergeant's team was sent there…"

"What team?"

"I'm not sure. There's only the sarge and Mitchell left now. Look, forget the questions. All that's important is that we get that package delivered." And then maybe we can get back to normal, he thought.

Sergeant Clausen reappeared. Chapelhow quickly folded the paper back into his pocket. The sergeant sat down, took a drink of water and leant back in his chair.

"Hey!" he said, turning to the young couple at the next table. "Is that a north eastern accent?"

"Yes," said the young man delightedly. "We're from Darlington."

"What a coincidence! My grandparents were from Darlington. I used to go there as a child. Is that shop still there on the High Street? The one that sold all those nice sweets?"

"I don't know which one you mean," said the young woman suspiciously.

"Hey, it's probably gone by now. My name's David by the way. This is Pippa and Andy."

"I'm Tom and this is Katie," said the young man. He wore a new yellow shirt with white buttons, new shorts, and new sandals. Chapelhow guessed he had been dressed for his holiday by his girlfriend.

The waiter approached the couple's table with an ice bucket.

"We didn't order this," said Katie.

"Compliments of the house," said the waiter. "Enjoy your holiday." He took a white linen-wrapped bottle from the bucket and poured them both a glass of white wine.

"He probably thinks it's your honeymoon or something," said the sergeant. "You are an attractive couple."

He held up his own wine glass. "Cheers."

They all drank to each others' health.

"That's very nice," said Tom.

"So, David, what are you doing here?" asked Katie, suspiciously.

"Oh. Enjoying the sun and the local food. Relaxing and forgetting my troubles. The war's not going so well, is it?"

"I thought as much," said Katie. "You're a soldier. I could tell by the way you were sitting to attention."

David Clausen laughed. "Bright girl. We could do with someone like you in the forces."

"It's not going to happen." She sipped at her wine primly. "I won't join up."

"Why not? Don't you believe Britain has the right to defend its interests?"

"Of course. It's when Britain starts interfering in other countries' interests I get uncomfortable. Particularly those who are not as well off as we are. Because your sort of fighting isn't about defense, is it David? It's just about money. Which corporation is bankrolling your regiment?"

"I hear it's not going well in Africa," said Tom, frowning at Katie as he changed the subject.

"It's not as bad as you'd think," said David, still smiling at Katie. "The Orange States have split from the Southern European Alliance. The SEA is fighting a war on two fronts now."

"Don't the SEA have some sort of way of controlling the animals?" asked Tom. "That's what I heard. That must be nasty."

David Clausen laughed.

"I'd rather be attacked by an elephant than another soldier. At least elephants don't shoot back at you." He lowered his voice and spoke in confidential tones. "Actually, Tom, it's the mosquitoes that are the worst. You don't get any peace at night."

"I think it's cruel to the animals," said Katie.

"So do I," agreed David. "But it's crueller to the soldiers. It's weird, isn't it, Katie? People are more concerned about animals than humans. They all agree that the war is a just cause, but they are not willing to fight it themselves."

"Just cause? I heard the Orange States have perfected cold fusion. I wonder how much that would be worth?" She paused, making her point. "Anyway, the soldiers choose to fight. The animals don't."

"Not true anymore," said David. "They've got this drug, you see. They call it Third Person. It sort of detaches you from the scene. Once you've taken it, you lose all sense of identity. It's like you're reading about someone's life, rather than taking part in it. They give it to civilians to press them. Conscripts don't really have a choice whether they fight or not. Look at Pippa and Andy here."

Chapelhow looked across to Reed to see how she was taking it, being spoken about like that. She didn't seem to mind.

"I don't believe it," said Katie. "They'd never allow it. They'd ban it."

Clausen laughed. "You'd think so, wouldn't you? But the government knows which side its bread is buttered on. The big corporations bring in too much money." He gave a brilliant white smile. "And," he tapped his nose at this point, "little secret. Anyone who kicks up too much of a fuss gets put under the influence themselves."

He yawned and stretched, leant back in his chair, soaking up some rays. "Oh, they'll outlaw it eventually, I'm sure, but I reckon we've got a year or two left yet."

"I don't believe you."

Tom was looking at his glass of wine in horror.

"Katie," he said.

"No way," Katie's eyes widened with horror as she stared at the glass in front of her.

"You don't get complimentary bottles of wine for being an attractive couple," said Clausen, suddenly businesslike.

"But why us?"

"Because you're young, fit, and healthy. And besides, you're British, unlike just about everyone else here. I do this to the locals, and I get sued from here to dishonorable discharge."

"What about that family over there?" asked Katie desperately.

"You can't expect me to take the parents and leave the children to fend for themselves, can you?" said Clausen. "What sort of a monster do you think I am?"

He pulled out two sheets of electro paper from his pocket and spread them on the table before them.

"Just sign these contracts and you've enlisted."

Katie and Tom looked at each other, and then they signed them, as they weren't "I" anymore but someone else. Just observers.

The waiter turned up again carrying five plates of steak and chips and salad. He placed two before the young couple.

"Eat up your meal," said the sergeant to Katie and Tom. "You'll need all the energy you can get."

THE PLATOON REGROUPED under the awning of a modern hotel, set on the edge of a wide road that led inland.

"This is Katie Prentice and Tom Fern." Sergeant Clausen was introducing the new conscripts to Mitchell.

"They look fit," said Mitchell, hungrily tearing away at a sandwich the sergeant had brought him. Behind him came the roar of a diesel engine. A blue and white bus pulled away along the road, black smoke spilling over the hot tarmac. Mitchell pinched Fern's arm with mayonnaise-smeared fingers.

"Nice muscle tone. Do you work out?" he asked.

"Yes," the couple answered in unison.

"We go to the gym three times a week," added Prentice.

Mitchell nodded. He hefted the package in his hand. A cylinder, about thirty centimeters long. Chapelhow always thought it looked very heavy. Mitchell passed it to the sergeant.

"Well, Prentice," he said, "with any luck, you'll be back there within the week. Not long now, I hope."

Singh handed them their conscripts' rifles and showed them how to work the action that loaded and ejected bullets.

"These are ancient," said Fern.

"They're good enough," said the sergeant. "Mitchell. Save these two; they're the healthiest. Put Reed, Chapelhow, and Singh on point."

"Got it sarge. What now?"

The sergeant gave a smile.

"We're headed inland. I thought we'd take the bus. They're never going to dare open fire with all those civilians around."

"Good idea."

"Come on."

They walked from under the hotel's awning into the hot sun, Chapelhow blinking as they went. He had never liked direct sunlight. The bus stop was just up the road a little, a small metal awning with several tourists sheltering beneath.

"Just relax on the bus," said the Sergeant. "Save your energy for later. Reed and Chapelhow at the front. Singh at the back. Prentice next to me. Fern next to Mitchell."

It wasn't too long before a bus pulled in. The sign on the front said *Adventureland*. Chapelhow had heard of the place, a big theme park built up in the hills.

"This is the one," said the sergeant. "Off we go."

They climbed on board. Chapelhow and Reed sat next to each other at the front.

"Have you any more ideas what this?" asked Reed, looking at the yellow sheet of paper that Chapelhow had taken from his pocket.

"I sort of remember," said Chapelhow. "I think Chapelhow wrote it when the sergeant pressed him. He was in a bar on the cruise ship; his boyfriend had gone to bed. Too much sun. He was just having a coffee when the sergeant joined him. I think Chapelhow sort of fancied him, as he was flirting with him. He shouldn't have accepted that brandy…"

Chapelhow frowned.

"I… Chapelhow," Chapelhow blinked, rubbed his forehead. "…Chapelhow started to write this before the drug could properly take effect…"

Reed took the piece of paper from him and began to read out loud.

"'You are Andy Chapelhow. This paper is kept in Andy Chapelhow's pocket. I am Andy Chapelhow. But already I feel like Andy Chapelhow is someone else. I must remember, you must remember who you are. It's like a story, Andy. You've got to see that all stories are told from one point of view. That point of view, the narrator, he's you. You've got to look out for the narrator. Find him and you find yourself. Don't lose your identity. You are Andy Chapelhow. Say it now. I am Andy Chapelhow.'"

"'I am Andy Chapelhow'," repeated Reed. "I don't think that's right. What does it mean when it says 'find the narrator'?"

"I think its talking about point of view," said Chapelhow. "Like a story written in the third person. One of the characters will have the point of view, the reader will see what they see, they will empathize with them, but they won't really believe that they are there."

Reed looked puzzled. She shook her head.

"Nah. I don't get it."

The bus halted. Four well-dressed women got on. Permed hair and smart leather handbags. They dropped a handful of euros in the tray and made their way to the back of the bus.

The driver gunned the engine and they set off. They had left the town behind, driving into the full glare of the Spanish afternoon, riding along a smooth gray road that was climbing into the distant hills.

Chapelhow felt a tap on his shoulder.

"Hey, how did you pay for the meal, Chapelhow?"

"With my card, Sarge, how else?"

The sergeant's face flushed red and he swore. The well-dressed ladies in the seat opposite pursed their lips. Now that Chapelhow came to think about it, they looked just like the four women who had just boarded the bus.

The sergeant interrupted his thoughts.

"I thought you said you had money!"

"That was Singh. I only had twenty euros!"

"Damn. Look at this!"

He held up Chapelhow's mobile, confiscated from him when Chapelhow had been pressed. There was a text message displayed.

Hello there, Sergeant Clausen. Chapelhow's bank is part-owned by the SEA, didn't you know? Nice of you to pinpoint yourself like that.

We have a proposition for you. Just leave the package on the bus, get off at the next stop, and we'll let you go unharmed. We won't even track you to your rendezvous point.

Do we have a deal?

"It sounds like a good deal to me, sarge," said Reed.

"Like you have a say in things. I've punched for an emergency extraction. It will cost a fortune, it will risk the lives of the extraction team, but we need to do it. Get ready to move. Shit."

Chapelhow turned to follow his gaze.

Four more well-dressed ladies stood by the side of the road. There was a bus stop there, right in the middle of nowhere. Nothing but scrubby land could be seen, baking in the hot sun. The driver was already decelerating.

"All that permed hair," muttered the sergeant in disbelief. "Did they conscript a Spanish townswomen's guild or something?" He pulled a grenade from his pocket.

"There are greenhouses over there, sarge," said Reed. She pointed to the low, steamy plastic shapes that glinted oddly in the distance. "They could be workers from those?"

"Dressed like that?" said the sergeant. He clicked a thumb down on the button and called out to the driver.

"Hey, Pedro. You stop this bus and I let go of the button, got it?"

The bus driver let off a rapid stream of angry Spanish. Chapelhow's headset translated. "You threaten me, señor, and I'll sue your ass off."

"This isn't a threat," said the Sergeant easily. "It's a suicide attempt. I just can't bear the thought of you stopping here. You compendre?"

Reed giggled.

"Sarge, what's the use of speaking in Spanish when your headset's translating everything?"

The driver stamped down on the accelerator, causing the bus to jerk violently and the sergeant to nearly lose his balance. The women by the bus stop pulled pistols from their handbags and took aim. They didn't fire. There were too many civilians on the bus. Chapelhow held the gaze of one of them as they drove past. She smiled at him and shrugged.

"Who did that?" asked Reed. She was pointing across the aisle. The two well-dressed women opposite were slumped forward in their seats, their eyes closed.

"Mitchell and Prentice shot them while you were distracted," said the sergeant. "I tell you, that girl shows promise. It's a shame she didn't enlist voluntarily. Now, watch the road, you two. See if you can do as well as Prentice and spot any other spies before they pull their guns." He turned to the driver. "Pedro, open the bus door."

"Stop calling me Pedro."

The driver opened the door anyway. The sergeant took hold of the nearest of the dead women by the collar of her silk blouse. He rolled her out of her seat and through the door, then sat in her place. Chapelhow turned to watch the body tumbling along the road, limbs flailing like a rag doll. There was a shout of indignation from further up the bus.

"Do you mind? We have children with us!" Chapelhow's headset spoke with a German accent.

"Something behind us, sarge!" That was Singh's voice. "Long green thing. Coming up fast."

"Troop car," said Mitchell. "Get down fast, Singh. It will have a laser targeting turret…"

There was a tinkle of glass and sudden burst of static that was quickly killed.

"They got Singh," said Mitchell. "How much longer, sarge?"

"Pickup craft is coming in now," said the sergeant. "Approaching from the right-hand side of the bus, the side with the door."

Reed and Chapelhow were calm.

"Think we're going to make it, Chapelhow?"

"I don't know. Does it matter? The mission is the important thing. As long as we get the package on the pickup…"

A low rumble sounded, followed by a supersonic boom off to their right. Then another one, then another.

"Stop here, Pedro," shouted the sergeant.

A roar of diesel and they were all thrown backward as the driver accelerated again. There was a popping noise and the driver began to scream. Red blood was spurting from his right hand.

"I'll sue you, you and your fucking army, senor!"

"Sue us for a million. We'll pay. This is more important." He swung his gun to the driver's head. "Now, are you going to stop the bus?"

There was a squeal of brakes and they were all thrown forward. A child started to cry. There was a series of popping sounds as the sergeant fired his gun in the air. Lines of sunlight shafted down from the roof, one after the other. He spoke, his headset translating into Spanish.

"Okay, my name is Sergeant David Clausen. I am part of the Naghani Associates regiment of the UK army. Any claims for compensation should be made to Naghani Associates in the first instance. Listen up now. This is a grenade." He held a dark egg shape up in the air. "I have set a motion sensor on it. If you remove it from its place here on the luggage rack it will explode." Carefully he placed the grenade on the rack. "Further," he added, "I have set the timer for ten minutes. More than enough time for us to get safely off this bus."

His words were repeated in German and English.

There was a low rumble of indignation, but already the passengers were moving from their seats.

"Chapelhow, Reed. Wait for three people to get off, and then you follow them out. I'll send out Prentice in the middle of the crowd, then me. Fern and Mitchell can bring up the rear. The civilians should provide us with enough cover. Okay, go!"

Chapelhow and Reed waited for three young men in shorts to climb off the bus. They smelled of old aftershave and alcohol and seemed quite excited by their adventure. They were pointing to a rapidly growing dot on the horizon.

"That must be the pickup," said Reed. "It doesn't look that big. Do you think we can all get on board?"

"Probably not," said Chapelhow. "Probably just enough space for the sergeant and Mitchell."

"Maybe he'll try and squeeze Prentice on too," said Reed. Behind her the driver was whimpering as he stared at his hand. "Okay," said Reed. "Our turn."

They both got off the bus, rifles held at the ready. The afternoon sun beat down on their heads. Chapelhow felt the uneven ground through the thin soles of his shoes.

"Keep moving, Reed," he said. "Come away from the door."

A dusty wind blew up. The pickup ship was descending. Not much bigger than a large car, it was little more than a silver wing with a large transparent canopy on top. Chapelhow saw the pilot scanning the skies through a large pair of dark goggles as she descended.

More passengers were spilling out into the sun. Three wheels dropped down from the pickup just as it was about to hit the ground. It bounced once on its undercarriage. The pilot slid back the canopy with a whirr.

"Come on," she called. "Get on board."

The sergeant was pushing his way forward.

"Out of my way," he called. Mitchell and Prentice followed behind. "Prentice on first," shouted the sergeant, handing her the package.

"Told you," said Reed. "There's not enough seats for all of us. I wonder what will happen when that thing takes off? Who is carrying the point of view for this story?"

"What do you mean?" asked Chapelhow.

"Like it said on that sheet of paper in your pocket. Who has the point of view? You, or me, or the sergeant? Will the story follow the pickup, or stay here on the ground?"

But Chapelhow didn't answer. An olive-colored arrow had slid to a halt on the road behind the bus. A hatch opened in its side and soldiers came tumbling out. Real soldiers, dressed in the green of the SEA and carrying state-of-the-art, limited radius weapons. The sort that were safe to use when civilians were around. One swung a tube in the direction of the sergeant.

"You're closest," said Reed to Chapelhow.

Something was fired from the tube. Steam bomb. Lazily it flew through the air toward the sergeant, about to follow Prentice on board the pickup craft. Chapelhow flung himself forward into its path and

The Farewell Party

Eric Brown

GREGORY MERRALL HAD been part of our group
for just three months by the time of the Farewell
Party, though it seemed that we had never been
without his quiet, patriarchal presence. He was a
constant among the friendly faces who met at the
Fleece every Tuesday evening, our confidant and
king, some might even say our conscience.

I remember his arrival among us. It was a bitter cold night in early November and the village
had been cut off for two days due to a severe fall
of snow. When I saw him stride into the snug—
an anachronistic figure in Harris tweeds and
plus-fours—I assumed he was a stranded travel-
er.

He buttressed the bar and drank two or three
pints of Landlord.

There were nine of us gathered about the
inglenook that night, and as each of us in turn

went to the bar to buy our round, the stranger made a point of engaging us in conversation.

"There are worse places to be stranded in West Yorkshire," I said when it was my round. "The Fleece is the best pub for miles around."

He smiled. "I'm not stranded—well, not in that sense," he said, offering his hand. "Merrall, Gregory Merrall."

"Khalid Azzam," I told him. "You've moved to Oxenworth?"

"Bought the old Simpson farm on the hill."

I knew immediately—and I often look back and wonder quite how I knew—that Merrall would become part of our group. There was something about him that inspired trust. He was socially confident without being brash, and emanated an avuncular friendliness that was endearing and comforting.

I noticed that he was nearing the end of his pint. "It's my round," I said. "Would you like to join us?"

"Well, that's very kind. I don't mind if I do."

So I introduced him to the group and he slipped into the conversation as if the niche had been awaiting him—the niche, I mean, of the quiet wise man, the patriarchal figure whose experience, and whose contemplation of that experience, he brought to bear on our varied conversations that evening.

IT WAS A couple of weeks later, and I'd arrived early. Richard Lincoln and Andy Souter were at the bar, nursing their first pints. Richard was in his early sixties and for a second I mistook him for Gregory.

He frowned at my double-take as he bought me a pint.

"Thought for a second you were Merrall," I explained.

"The tweeds," he said. "Bit out of fashion." Richard was a ferryman and I'd always thought it paradoxical that someone who worked so closely with the Kéthani regime should adopt so conservative a mode of dress.

We commandeered our table by the fire and Andy stowed his trumpet case under his stool. Andy was a professional musician, a quiet man in his late thirties with a trumpeter's pinched top lip. He conducted the local brass band and taught various instruments at the college in Bradley. He was the newest recruit—discounting Merrall—to our Tuesday night sessions. He ran a hand through his ginger mop and said, "So, what do you think of our Gregory?"

"I like him a lot," I said. "He's one of us."

Richard said, "Strange, isn't it, how some people just fit in? Odd thing is, for all he's said a lot, I don't know that much about him."

That gave me pause. "Come to think of it, you're right." All I knew was that he was from London and that he'd bought the old farmhouse on the hill.

Andy nodded. "The mysterious stranger…"

"He's obviously well traveled," Richard said.

That was another thing I knew about him from his stories of India and the Far East. I said, "Isn't it odd that although he's said next to nothing about himself, I feel I know him better than I do some people who talk about themselves non-stop."

For the next hour, as our friends hurried in from the snow in ones and twos, conversation centered around the enigmatic Mr. Merrall. It turned out that no one knew much more than Richard, Andy, and me.

"Very well, then," said Doug Standish, our friendly police officer, "let's make it our objective tonight to find out a bit more about Gregory, shall we?"

Five minutes later, at nine o'clock on the dot—as was his habit—Gregory breezed in, shaking off the snow like a big Saint Bernard.

He joined us by the fire and seconds later was telling us about a conversation he'd had with his bank manager that morning. That provoked a round of similar stories, and soon our collective objective of learning more about our newfound friend was forgotten in the to and fro of bonhomie and good beer.

Only as I was wending my way home, with Richard by my side, did it occur to me that we had failed abjectly to learn anything more about Gregory than we knew already.

I said as much to the ferryman.

He was staring at the rearing crystal pinnacle of the Onward Station, perched miles away on the crest of the moors.

"Greg's so friendly, it seems rude to pry," he said.

A week later I accidentally found out more about Gregory Merrall and, I thought, the reason for his insularity.

I ARRIVED AT the Fleece just after nine, tired from a hard day on the implant ward, but eager to tell what I'd discovered. The group was ensconced before the blazing fire.

Ben and Elisabeth—in their fifties now and still holding hands—both looked at the book I was holding. Ben said, "Tired of our conversation, Khalid?"

Andy Souter laughed, "If we're all doing our own thing, then I'll get my bugle out and practise."

I smiled. Everyone turned my way as I held up the novel, my hand concealing the name of the author.

"*A Question of Trust*," Samantha Kingsley said. "I didn't know you were a great reader, Khalid."

"I'm not. I was in Bradley today, and this was in the window of the bookshop."

"So," Richard said. "Who's it by?"

"Three guesses," I said.

"You," Stuart Kingsley said. "You've retired from the implant ward and started writing?"

"Not me, Stuart. But you do know him."

Sam cheated. She was sitting next to me, and she tipped her stool and peeked at the author's photo on the back of the jacket.

"Aha!" she said. "Mystery solved."

I removed my hand from the byline.

Richard exclaimed, "Gregory!"

"This explains a few things," I said. "His experience, his reluctance to talk about himself—some writers don't like it known that they write." I opened the book and read the mini-biography inside the back flap. "'Gregory Merrall was born in 1965 in London. He has been a full-time freelance writer for more than thirty years, with novels, collections, and volumes of poetry to his name.'"

Five minutes later Gregory hurried in, hugging himself against the bone-aching cold. He crossed to the fire and roasted his outstretched hands before the flames.

He saw the book, which I'd placed on the table before me, and laughed. "So... my secret's out."

"Why didn't you tell us?" Richard said, returning from the bar with a pint for our resident writer.

Gregory took a long draft. "It's something I don't much like talking about," he said. "People assume a number of things when you mention you're a scribbler. They either think you're bragging, that you're incredibly well off—would that that were so—that you're some kind of intellectual heavyweight, or that you'll immediately start regaling them with fabulous stories."

"Well," Sam said, "you have told us some fascinating tales."

Gregory inclined his head in gracious assent. "It's just not something I feel the need to talk about," he went on. "What matters is not so much talking about it, but getting it done."

The evening unfolded, and at one point some-one asked Gregory (it was Stuart, a lecturer at Leeds and something of an egghead himself), "How do you think the coming of the Kéthani has affected how we write about the human experience?"

Gregory frowned into his pint. "Where to begin? Well, it's certainly polarized writers around the world. Some have turned even further inward, minutely chronicling the human condition in the light of our newfound immortality. Others have ignored it and written about the past, and there's a vast market for nostalgia these days! A few speculate about what life might be like post-death, when we take the leap into the vast inhabited universe."

Richard looked at him. "And where would you put yourself, Gregory?"

Merrall picked up his novel and leafed through it, pausing occasionally to read a line or two. "I'm firmly in the speculative camp," he said, "trying to come to some understanding of what life out there might be like, why the Kéthani came to Earth—what their motives might be."

That set the subject for the rest of the evening—the Kéthani and their *modus operandi*. Of the nine regulars around the table that night, only three of us had died, been resurrected on the home planet of the Kéthani, and returned to Earth: Stuart and Samantha Kingsley, and myself.

I looked back to my resurrection, and what I had learned. I had become a better human being, thanks to the aliens, but in common with everyone else who had been resurrected and returned to Earth, I found it difficult to recall precisely what it was I had learned in the Kéthani dome, quite how I had become a better person.

At one point Andy Souter said, "I read a novel, a couple of years ago, about a guy who was really a Kéthani disguised as a human, come among us to change our ways."

Gregory nodded. "I know it. *The Effectuator* by Duchamp."

"I've heard rumors that that happens," I said. I shrugged. "Who knows?"

Sam lowered her pint of lager and asked Gregory, "Do you think that happens? Do you think the Kéthani are amongst us?"

Gregory considered. "It's entirely possible," he said. "No one has ever seen a Kéthani, and as they obviously possess technology far in advance of anything we know, then passing themselves off as human wouldn't pose that much of a problem."

Andy said, "But the morality of it... I mean, surely if they're working for our good, then they could at least be open about it."

"The Kéthani work in mysterious ways..." Sam said.

Andy went on, "We take them for granted... we assume they're working for our good. But we don't really know, for sure."

Six pints the worse, I turned to Gregory and said, "Well, you write about the... the whole thing, the Kéthani, death, and revival... what do you think?"

He was some seconds before replying. He stared into the fire. "I think," he said, "that the Kéthani are the saviors of our race, and that whatever they have planned for us when we venture out there—though I don't presume to know what that might be—will be wholly for our good."

After that, talk turned to how things had changed due to the coming of the Kéthani. I said, "The change has been gradual, very gradual. I mean, so slow it's been hardly noticeable." I looked around the table. "You've all felt it; it's as if we're treading water, biding our time. It's as if a vast sense of complacency has descended over the human race." I'd never put these feelings into words before—they'd been a kind of background niggle in my consciousness. "I don't know... Sometimes I feel as if I'm only really alive among you lot on Tuesday nights!"

Richard laughed. "I know what you mean. Things that once were seen as important—everything from politics to sport—no longer have that... vitality."

"And," Stuart put in, "England is emptying. Come to that, the world is. I don't know what the figures are, but more and more people are staying out there when they die."

And with that thought we called it a night, departed the cozy confines of the snug, and stepped out into the freezing winter night.

The Onward Station was like an inverted icicle in the light of the full moon, and as I made my way home a brilliant bolt of magnesium light illuminated the night as another batch of the dead were beamed up to the waiting Kéthani starship.

A COUPLE OF weeks later the conversation returned to the perennial subject of the Kéthani, and what awaited us when we died.

Richard Lincoln posed the question: would we return to Earth after our resurrections, or would we travel among the stars as the ambassadors of our alien benefactors?

Gregory looked across at me. "You returned to Earth, didn't you, Khalid? Why, when all the universe awaited you?"

I shrugged, smiled. "I must admit... I was tempted to remain out there. The universe... the lure of new experience... it was almost too much to refuse. But—I don't know. I was torn. Part of me wanted to travel among the stars, but another, stronger part of me wanted to return." I looked across at Richard Lincoln, who was the only person I had told about the reasons for my suicide, and my return to Earth. "Perhaps I feared the new," I finished. "Perhaps I fled back to what was familiar, safe..." I shrugged again, a little embarrassed at my inarticulacy under the penetrating scrutiny of Gregory Merrall.

He turned to Stuart and Sam. "And you?"

The couple exchanged a glance. Stuart was in his mid-forties, Sam ten years younger, and they were inseparable—as if what they'd experienced, separately, in the resurrection domes on that far-off alien world, had brought them closer together.

Stuart said, "I hadn't really given much thought to my death, or resurrection. I naturally assumed I'd come back to Earth, continue life with Sam—we'd been married just over a year when I had the accident—go back to my lectureship at the university. But while I was in the dome, I... I learned that there was far more to life than what I'd experienced, and would experience, back on Earth."

"And yet you returned," Gregory said.

Stuart looked across at his wife. "I loved Sam," he said. "I was tempted... tempted to remain out there. But I reasoned that I could always return to the stars, later."

Sam said, looking at Gregory almost with defiance, "Two days after Stu died, I killed myself. I wanted to be with him. I couldn't live without him, not even for six months." She stopped abruptly and stared down into her drink.

"And?" Gregory prompted gently.

"And when I got up there, when I was resurrected... I mean, I still loved Stu, but something... I don't know—something was different." She smiled. "The stars called, and nothing would be the same again. Anyway, I decided to come back, see how it went with Stu, and take it from there."

I said, "And look what happened. 'Happily ever after,' or what?"

"We both felt the same," Stuart said. "It was as if our love had been tested by what we learnt out there. We considered going back, but... well, we fell into the old routine, work and the pub..."

He laughed and raised his pint in ironic salutation.

"That's very interesting," Gregory said. "I've done some research. In the early days, only two in ten who died and were resurrected chose to remain out there. The majority opted for what they knew. Now, out of every ten, seven remain. And the average is rising."

"Why do you think that is?" Ben asked.

Gregory pursed his lips, as if by a drawstring, and contemplated the question. "Perhaps we've come to trust the Kéthani. We've heard the stories of those who've been to the stars and returned, and we know there's nothing to fear."

"But," Elisabeth said, with a down-to-earth practicality, "surely the draw of the familiar should be too much for most of us, those of us who want to return and do all the things on Earth that we never got round to doing."

But Gregory was shaking his head. "You'd think so, but once you've experienced resurrection and instruction by the Kéthani, and gone among the stars—"

Stuart interrupted, "You sound as if you've experienced it first-hand?"

Gregory smiled. "I haven't. But I have interviewed hundreds, maybe even thousands, of returnees from life among the stars, for a series of novels I wrote about the Kéthani."

"And?" I said.

"And I found that the idea of a renewed life on Earth, for many, palls alongside the promise of the stars. And when these people experience life out there, they find life on Earth well-nigh impossible." He smiled. "'Provincial' was the word that came up again and again."

We contemplated our beers in silence.

At last I said, "And you, Gregory. What would you do?"

He stared at us, one by one. "When I die, which I think won't be long in happening, then I'll remain out there among the stars, doing whatever the Kéthani want me to do."

A FEW DAYS later I received a package of books through the post. They were the *Returnee* trilogy, by Gregory Merrall, sent courtesy of his publisher in London.

That week at the pub, I found that every one of us in the group had received the trilogy.

"I don't know what I was expecting," Stuart said, "but they're good."

"More than good," said Elisabeth, who was the literary pundit amongst us. "I'd say they were excellent, profoundly moving."

Gregory was away that Tuesday—visiting his publisher—so we didn't have the opportunity to thank him. That week I devoured the books and, like Stuart and Elisabeth, found them a heady experience.

He had the ability to write about ideas and the human experience in such a way that the one complemented the other. His characters were real, fully fleshed human beings, about whom the reader cared with a passion. At the same time, he wrote about their experiences in a series of philosophical debates that were at once—for a literary dunce like myself—understandable and page-turning.

I canvassed Stuart's opinion on the following Tuesday. I wondered if he, as an intellectual, had been as impressed by Gregory's books as I had. He had, and for an hour that evening before the man himself turned up, all of us discussed the Returnee trilogy with passion and something like awe that we knew its author.

At one point, Stuart said, "But what did you all think about the finale, and what did it mean? Gregory seemed to be saying that life on Earth was over, that only humankind's journey among the stars was what mattered."

Ben nodded. "As if Earth were a rock pool, which we had to leave in order to evolve."

At that point Gregory came in with a fanfare of wind and a swirl of snowflakes. We fought to buy him a drink and heaped praise on his novels.

I think he found all the fuss embarrassing. "I hope you didn't think it a tad arrogant, my having the books sent."

We assured him otherwise.

"It was just," he said, "that I wanted you to know my position." He smiled. "And it saved me giving a lecture."

Elisabeth asked, "What are you working on now, Gregory?"

He hesitated, pint in hand. "Ah… well, I make it a rule never to talk about work in progress. Superstition. Perhaps I fear that gabbing about the book will expend the energy I'd use writing it."

She gave a winning smile. "But on this occasion…"

Gregory laughed. "On this occasion, seeing as I'm among friends, and I've almost finished the book anyway…"

And he proceeded to tell us about his next novel, entitled *The Suicide Club*.

It was about a group of friends who, dissatisfied with their routine existence on Earth, stage a farewell party at which they take their own lives, are resurrected, and then go among the stars as ambassadors of the Kéthani.

OVER THE COURSE of the next few weeks we became a reading group devoted to the work of one writer, Gregory Merrall.

We read every novel he'd written, some fifteen in all. We were enthralled, captivated. We must have presented a strange picture to outsiders—a group of middle-class professionals continually carrying around the same books and discussing them passionately amongst themselves. We even arranged another night to meet and discuss the books, to spare Gregory the embarrassment, though we didn't forego our usual Tuesday outings.

Only Andy Souter absented himself from the reading group. He was busy most nights with his brass band, and he'd admitted to me on the phone that he'd found the novels impenetrable.

One Saturday evening I arrived early and Stuart was already propping up the bar. "Khalid. Just the man. I've been thinking…" He hesitated, as if unsure as to how to proceed.

"Should think that's expected of you, in your profession," I quipped.

"You'd never make a stand-up comedian, Azzam," he said. "No, it struck me... Look, have you noticed something about the group?"

"Only that we've become a devoted Gregory Merrall fan club—oh, and as a result we drink a hell of a lot more." I raised my pint in cheers. "Which I'm not complaining about."

He looked at me. "Haven't you noticed how we're looking ahead more? I mean, at one point we seemed content, as a group, to look no further than the village, our jobs. It was as if the Kéthani didn't exist."

"And now we're considering the wider picture?" I shrugged. "Isn't that to be expected? We've just read fifteen books about them, and the consequences of their arrival. Dammit, I've never read so much in my life before now!"

He was staring into his pint, miles away.

"What?" I asked.

He shrugged. "Reading Gregory's books, thinking about the Kéthani, what it all might mean... It brings back to me how I felt immediately after my resurrection. The lure of the stars. The dissatisfaction with life on Earth. I think, ever since my return, I've been trying to push to the back of my mind that... that niggling annoyance, the thought that I was treading water before the next stage of existence." He looked up at me. "You said as much the other week."

I nodded. After Zara left me, and I killed myself and returned to Earth, I withdrew into

myself—or rather into my safe circle of friends—
and paid little heed to the world, or for that
matter to the universe outside.

The door opened, admitting a blast of icy air
and the rest of the group.

For the next hour we discussed an early Gregory Merrall novel, *The Coming of the Kéthani*.

Around ten o'clock the door opened and a
familiar figure strode in. We looked up, a little
shocked and, I think, not a little embarrassed,
like schoolkids caught smoking behind the bike
shed.

A couple of us tried to hide our copies of Gregory's novel, but too late. He smiled as he joined
us.

"So this is what you get up to when my back's
turned?" he laughed.

Elisabeth said, "You knew?"

"How could you keep it a secret in a village the
size of Oxenworth?" he asked.

Only then did I notice the bundle under his
arm.

Gregory saw the direction of my gaze. He
deposited the package on the table and went to
the bar.

We exchanged glances. Sam even tried to peek
into the brown paper parcel, but hastily withdrew her hand, as if burned, as Gregory returned
with his pint.

Maddeningly, for the rest of the evening he
made no reference to the package, stowing it
beneath the table and stoking the flagging conversation.

At one point, Stuart asked, "We were discussing your novel—" he indicated *The Coming of the Kéthani*, "—and we wondered how you could be so confident of the, ah... altruism of the Kéthani, back then? You never doubted their motives?"

Gregory considered his words, then said, "Perhaps it was less good prophecy than a need to hope. I took them on trust, because I saw no other hope for humankind. They were our salvation. I thought it then, and I think so still."

We talked all night of our alien benefactors, and how life on Earth had changed since their arrival and the bestowal of immortality on the undeserving human race.

Well after last orders, Gregory at last lifted the package from beneath the table and opened it.

"I hope you don't mind my presumption," he said, "but I would very much like you opinion of my latest book."

He passed us each a closely printed typescript of *The Suicide Club*.

TWO DAYS LATER, just as I got in from work, Richard Lincoln phoned.

"The Fleece at eight," he said without preamble. "An extraordinary meeting of the Gregory Merrall reading group. Can you make it?"

"Try keeping me away," I said.

On the stroke of eight o'clock that evening all nine of us were seated at our usual fireside table.

Stuart said, "I take it you've all read the book?"

As one, we nodded. I'd finished it on the Sunday, profoundly moved by the experience.

"So… what do you all think?"

We all spoke at once, echoing the usual platitudes—a work of genius, a brilliant insight, a humane and moving story…

Only Andy was silent. He looked uncomfortable. "Andy?" I said. He had not been part of the reading group, but Gregory had posted him a copy of the manuscript.

"I don't know. It made me feel… well, uncomfortable."

A silence ensued. It was Sam who spoke for the rest of us, who voiced the thought, insidious in my mind, that I had been too craven to say out loud.

"So," she said, "when do we do it?"

Andy just stared around the group, horrified.

I tried to ignore him. I wondered at what point I had become dissatisfied with my life on Earth. Had the ennui set in years ago, but I had been too comfortable with the easy routine to acknowledge it? Had it taken Gregory Merrall's presence among us to make me see what a circumscribed life I was leading now?

Sam and Stuart Kingsley were gripping each other's hands on the table-top. Sam leaned forward and spoke vehemently, "Reading Greg's books brought it all back to me. I… I don't think I can take much more of life on Earth. I'm ready for the next step."

Beside her, Stuart said, "We discussed it last night. We're ready to… go."

They turned to look at Doug Standish, seated to their left.

He nodded. "I've been treading water for ten, fifteen years. Unlike you two—" he smiled at Sam and Stuart "—I haven't been resurrected, so I've never experienced that lure... until now, that is. I'm ready for... for whatever lies ahead."

He turned to Jeffrey Morrow, on his left. "Jeff?"

The schoolteacher was staring into his drink. He looked up and smiled. "I must admit I've never much thought about my own leaving. I've had all the universe, and all the time in the universe, ahead of me—so why rush things? But... yes, it seems right, doesn't it?"

Beside him, Richard Lincoln said in a quiet voice, "Earth holds very little for me now. I suppose the only thing that's been keeping me here is—" he smiled and looked around the group "—the friendship of you people, and perhaps a fear of what might lie ahead, out there. But I feel that the right time has arrived."

Ben and Elisabeth were next. They glanced at each other, their hands locked tight beneath the table. Elisabeth said, "We're attracted to the idea. I mean, you could say that it's the next evolutionary stage of humankind—the step to the stars."

Ben took up where his wife had left off. "And we've noticed things on Earth... the apathy, the sense of limbo, of waiting for something to happen. I think by now it's entered our subconscious as a race—the fact that life on Earth is almost over. It's time to leave the sea."

A silence ensued. I was next to give my view.

"Like Sam and Stuart," I said, "I experienced the lure while on Kéthan. And like Ben, I've noticed something about the mood on Earth recently, as I said a while back." I paused, then went on, "And it isn't only that more and more resurrectees are electing to remain out there— increasing numbers of people are actually ending their lives and embarking on the next phase."

Sam said, smiling at me, "You haven't actually said, Khalid, if you want to be part of this."

I laughed. "I've been your friend for twenty years now. You're a massive part of my life. How could I remain on Earth when you're living among the stars?"

I paused, and turned to Andy. "Well... what do you think?"

He was rock still, silent, staring down at his pint. He shook his head. "I'm sorry. It's not for me. I... there's a lot I still need to do, here. I couldn't possibly contemplate..." He stopped there, looking around the group. "You're serious, aren't you?"

Stuart spoke for all of us. "We are, Andy. Of course we are."

Sam nodded. "There... that's it, then. I suppose the next thing to do is discuss how we go about it?"

Andy retreated into his pint.

Richard said, "Perhaps we should ask the man who initiated all this, Gregory himself?"

"I don't know about that," I said. "Don't you think he might be horrified by what he's started?"

Stuart was shaking his head. "Khalid, remember what he said a couple of weeks ago—that he was ready to go? And he wrote the book that endorses the group's decision, after all."

I nodded. Richard said, "So... tomorrow we'll buttonhole Greg and see what he says."

We fell silent, and stared into our drinks. We were strangely subdued for the rest of the evening. Andy said goodbye and left before last orders.

THE FOLLOWING DAY on the ward I could not concentrate fully on my work; it was as if I were at one remove from the real world, lost in contemplation of the future, and at the same time remembering the past.

It was almost ten by the time I arrived at the Fleece. The others were ensconced at our usual table, illuminated by the flames of the fire. It was a scene I had beheld hundreds of times before, but perhaps it was the realization that our Tuesday nights were drawing to a close that invested the tableau with such poignancy.

Significantly, Andy Souter was conspicuous by his absence. No one commented on the fact.

The contemplative atmosphere had carried over from the previous evening. We sat in silence for a while, before Richard said, "Odd, but I was thinking today how insubstantial everything feels."

Jeffrey laughed. "I was thinking the very same. There I was trying to drum the meaning of metaphor in Bogdanovich's *The Last Picture*

Show into a group of bored fifth years... and I couldn't help but think that there's more to existence."

"I feel," Sam said, "that we'll soon find out exactly how much more."

I voiced something that had been preying on my mind. "Okay, I know you're going to call me a hopeless romantic, but it'd be nice... I mean, once we're out there, if we could remain together."

Smiles and nods around the table reassured me.

Before anyone could comment on the likelihood of that, Gregory Merrall strode in. "Drink up. I seem to recall that it's my round." He stared at us. "What's wrong? Been to a funeral?"

Sam looked up at him. "Gregory, we need to talk."

He looked around the group, then nodded. He pointed to the bar.

While he was away, we looked at each other as if for reassurance that we did indeed agree to go ahead with this. Silent accord passed between us, and Sam blessed us with her radiant smile.

"So," Gregory said two minutes later, easing the tray onto the table-top, "how can I help?"

We looked across at Sam, tacitly electing her as spokesperson.

"Gregory," she began, "we were all very affected by your novel, *The Suicide Club*. It made us think."

Gregory smiled. "That's always nice to hear. And?"

"And," Sam said, and hesitated.

Gregory laughed. "Come on—out with it!"

"Well... we've come to the conclusion, each of us, independently, that there was something lacking in our lives of late..." She went on, neatly synopsizing what each of us had expressed the night before.

She finished, "So... we've decided that we need to move on, to make the next step, to go out there."

Gregory heard her out in silence, a judicial forefinger placed across his lips.

A hush fell across the table. It was as if we were holding our breath in anticipation of his response.

At last he nodded and smiled. "I understand," he said, "and to be honest I've been thinking along the same lines myself of late." He looked around the group, at each of us in turn, and continued, "I wonder if you'd mind if I joined you?"

THE PARTY WAS set for the first Saturday in February, which gave us less than a fortnight to settle our affairs on Earth and say our goodbyes. I resigned my internship at Bradley General and told my colleagues that I was taking a year's break to travel—which was not that far removed from the truth. I had no real friends outside the Tuesday evening group, so the farewells I did make were in no way emotionally fraught.

I considered contacting Zara, my ex-wife, and telling her the truth of my going, but on reflection I came to realize that she was part of a past life that was long gone, and almost forgotten.

I put my affairs in order, left instructions with my solicitor for the sale of my house, and bequeathed all I possessed to Zara.

Gregory Merrall insisted that he host the farewell party, and it seemed fitting that this should be so.

I would attend the party along with Sam and Stuart but, as we had died once and been resurrected, we would not take part in the ritual suicide. I wondered what I might feel as I watched my friends take their final drink on Earth.

On the evening before the party, the doorbell chimed. It was Andy Souter. He stood on the doorstep, shuffling his feet, his ginger hair aflame in the light of the porch. "Andy. Get in here. It's freezing!"

He stepped inside, snow-covered, silent, and a little cowed. "Coffee?" I asked, uneasy myself.

He shook his head. "I won't stay long. I just…" He met my gaze for the first time. "Is it true? You're all planning to… to go, tomorrow night?"

I showed him into the lounge. "That's right. We've thought long and hard about what we're planning. It seems the right thing to do."

Andy shook his head. "I don't know. I have a bad feeling about it."

I smiled, pointed to the raised square of the implant at his temple. "But you're implanted, Andy. You'll go when you die…"

He smiled bleakly. "I know, but that's different. I'll die of natural causes, or accidentally. I won't take my life at the behest of some stranger."

I said, "Gregory's no stranger, now."

He stared at me. "Isn't he?"

"You don't like him, do you?"

"I don't know. Put it this way, I'm not wholly convinced."

I laughed. "About what, exactly?"

He looked bleak. "That's just it. I don't know. I just have this... feeling."

I said, "Look, we're going to the Fleece at nine for a last drink. Why don't you come along, say goodbye."

He shook his head, "I've said goodbye to everyone individually." He held out his hand. "Take care, Khalid."

THE FOLLOWING EVENING Richard Lincoln knocked on my door, and I left the house for the very last time. We walked in silence past the Fleece, through the village and up the hillside toward the beckoning lights of Merrall's converted farmhouse.

Our friends were already there, armed with drinks.

There was, unlike our last few nights in the Fleece, a party atmosphere in the air, a *fin-de-siècle* sense of closure, of new beginnings.

We drank and chatted about the past. We regaled Gregory with incidents of village life over the past twenty years, the emotional highs and lows: the break-up of my marriage, the resurrection of Ben's father; the going of Father

Renbourn... It was as if, with this incantatory summoning of the past, we were putting off the inevitability of the future.

Then we ate, seated around a long pine table, a lavish meal of roast beef and baked potatoes. Conversation turned to the Kéthani, and our mission as ambassadors among the stars.

A little drunk, I laughed. "It seems impossible to reconcile my life so far, the insignificance of my existence until now, with what might happen out there." And I swung my wine glass in an abandoned gesture at the stars.

Gregory said, "We will be taken, and trained, and we will behold wonders we cannot even guess at."

Beside me, Sam said, "I wish Andy was coming with us."

A silence settled around the table as we pondered our absent, skeptical friend.

We finished the meal and Gregory poured the wine. He went around the table, clockwise, and tipped an exact measure of French claret, laced with cyanide, into each glass.

Sam, Stuart, and I sat together at the end of the table. I felt a subtle sense of exclusion from the act about to take place. Later tonight we three would report to the Onward Station, would be beamed up in the same transmission as our friends, and begin our journey to the stars.

I was aware of my heart thudding as I watched my friends raise their glasses and Richard Lincoln pronounce a toast. "To friends," he said, "and to the future!"

"To friends, and to the future!" they echoed, and drank.

I watched Richard Lincoln relax, smiling, and slump into his seat, as if asleep, and I reached across the table and gripped his hand as if to ease his passing. I looked around, taking in the enormity of the fact that my friends of so many years were dead, or dying... Jeffrey leaned forward, resting his head on his arms; Doug Standish sat upright, a smile on his stilled face; Ben and Elisabeth leaned toward each other, embracing, and died together. At the head of the table, Gregory Merrall slumped in his seat, his head flung back in death.

A silence filled the room and I felt like weeping.

Someone was clutching my hand. I looked up. Sam was staring at me through her tears.

We stood and moved toward the door. Already, our friends' implants would be registering the fact of their death. In minutes, the ferrymen from Onward Station would arrive to collect their bodies.

I took one last glance at the tableau of stilled and lifeless remains, then joined Sam and Stuart and stepped into the freezing night.

Stuart indicated his car. "We might as well go straight to the Station."

I said, "Do you mind if I walk?"

I sketched a wave and set off along the footpath that climbed across the snow-covered moorland to the soaring tower of the Onward Station in the distance.

Their car started and drove away, and soon the sound of its engine died and left a profound silence in its wake.

I strode across the brow of the hill, my boots compacting snow, my head too full of recent events to look ahead with any clarity.

At one point I stopped, turned and looked down at the farmhouse, dark against the snow. The lights glowed in the windows, and it reminded me of a nativity scene.

I was about to resume my march when, from the corner of my eye, I saw movement at the back door. At first I thought it was a ferryman, arrived early—then realized that I had heard no car.

I stared, and caught my breath in shock.

A figure stepped through the kitchen door and strode out into the graveled driveway, and in the light of the gibbous moon I recognized the tweed-clad shape of Gregory Merrall.

At that moment I felt very alone. I wanted Sam and Stuart beside me, to affirm that I was not losing my senses.

As I watched, he stopped in the middle of the drive and stared up at the stars, and my mind was in chaos.

Why? I asked myself... Why had he—

And then the explanation came, falling from the heavens.

Gregory raised his arms above his head, as if in greeting or supplication, and from on high there descended, across the dark night sky like the scoring of a diamond point across a sheet of obsidian, what at first I thought was a shooting star. The vector it took, however, was vertical. It fell like a lance, heading for the farmhouse below, and I could only gasp in wonder, breathless, as it struck Gregory Merrall.

He vanished, and the light leapt up and retraced its course through the night sky, heading toward the waiting Kéthani starship.

My face stinging with tears, I set off toward the rearing obelisk of Onward Station. I thought of Andy Souter, and his suspicion of Gregory Merrall, and his decision not to join us... and I wondered if Andy had been right to turn his back, this time, on the new life that awaited us.

I was sobbing by the time I reached the Station. I paused before its cut-glass perfection, this thing of supernal alien beauty on the harsh Yorkshire landscape.

I wondered whether to tell Sam and Stuart that we had been lured to the stars by an... an impostor. Did it matter, after all? I tried to marshal my emotions, decide whether what Merrall had done could be considered an act of betrayal, or of salvation. I wondered if I should go ahead with what we had planned.

I turned and stared out over the land that had been my home since birth, a land slowly emptying due to the ministrations of a mysterious alien race. Then I looked up at the stars, the million pulsating beacons of light, and I knew that there was only one course of action to take.

I hurried into the Station, to join my friends and to begin the new life that awaited me out there among the beckoning stars.

About the Authors

Jeffrey Thomas is the author of the critically acclaimed short story collection *Punktown* and the forthcoming Solaris novel *Deadstock* (2007), which continues the investigations of Jeremy Stake ('In His Sights'). His novel *Monstrocity* was nominated for the Bram Stoker Award and his stories have been reprinted in various *Year's Best* anthologies. His previous titles include *Everybody Scream!*, *Punktown: Shades of Grey*, *Punktown: Third Eye* (as editor), *Terror Incognita*, *Letters From Hades*, *AAAII-IEEE!!!* and *Thirteen Specimens*. He lives in Massachusetts.

Neal Asher's *Polity* universe is one of the most dark, dangerous and downright *fun* settings in modern science fiction, and includes the novels

Gridlinked, *The Skinner*, *The Line of Polity*, *Brass Man*, *The Voyage of the Sable Keech*, *Prador Moon* and the recent *Polity Agent*. His short fiction has been published in a wide variety of locations, from *Asimov's* to the British small press and most places in-between. He lives in Essex, England.

Jay Lake lives in Portland, Oregon with his books and two inept cats, where he works on numerous writing and editing projects, including the World Fantasy Award-nominated *Polyphony* anthology series from Wheatland Press. His current projects are *Trial of Flowers* from Night Shade Books and *Mainspring* from Tor Books. Jay is the winner of the 2004 John W. Campbell Award for Best New Writer, and a multiple nominee for the Hugo and World Fantasy Awards. Jay can be reached through his blog at *jaylake.livejournal.com*.

Greg van Eekhout's short fiction has appeared in a number of magazines and anthologies, including *Asimov's*, *Fantasy and Science Fiction*, *Realms of Fantasy*, *Starlight 3*, and *Year's Best Fantasy and Horror*. His story "In the Late December" was a Nebula Award nominee. He lives in Tempe, Arizona, where he works as a freelance instructional designer, studies martial arts, and loiters in coffee houses and brewpubs. His website is *www.writingandsnacks.com*.

James Lovegrove is the author of several highly acclaimed novels in the SF genre. His first book, *The Hope*, was published in 1990 and he has since gone on to produce a diverse and eclectic body of work including the novels *Escardy Gap* (with Peter Crowther), *Days*, *Untied Kingdom*, *Worldstorm*, *Gig* and *Provender Gleed*. He lives in the south-west of England with his wife and son.

Paul Di Filippo is one of the most prolific – and unclassifiable – authors working in the genre today. His short stories have won him much critical acclaim and he has been a finalist for the Hugo, Nebula, BSFA, Philip K. Dick and World Fantasy awards. His short story collections include *The Steampunk Trilogy*, *Ribofunk*, *Little Doors*, *Lost Pages* and *Strange Trades*, to name but a few, and his novels include *Ciphers*, *Joe's Liver*, *Fuzzy Dice*, *A Mouthful of Tongues* and *Spondulix*. He lives in Providence, Rhode Island.

Peter F. Hamilton is often credited with having spearheaded a movement to revitalise the space opera genre, with his epic, grandiose *Night's Dawn Trilogy*, comprising *The Reality Dysfunction*, *The Neutronium Alchemist* and *The Naked God*. Certainly known for his mammoth-sized volumes, he writes short fiction only infrequently. His most recent novels are the two acclaimed volumes in the Commonwealth Saga, *Pandora's Star* and *Judas*

Unchained. Peter lives near Rutland Water, England, with his wife Kate, daughter Sophie and son Felix.

One of the most literary authors working in the science fiction field today, **Adam Roberts** is also a doctor in nineteenth century literature. He has published an array of studies and literary criticism, including *The Palgrave History of Science Fiction*, and his novels include *Salt, On, Stone, Polystom, The Snow, Gradsil* and the forthcoming *Splinter* (Solaris 2007). He lives in London with his wife and daughter.

Stephen Baxter is one of the pre-eminent writers of modern hard SF. His epic *Xeelee* sequence is vast in scope and encompasses the entire history of the universe, in a gritty, awe-inspiring tale of war amongst the stars. The most recent instalment is the short story collection, *Resplendent*. Other novels, as well as Baxter's vertiginous output of short stories, tackle everything from the US space program to anthropomorphic mammoths, to HG Wells's *The Time Machine*. His most recent novel, *Conqueror*, is part of an ongoing alternate history sequence that began with *Emperor*. He lives in Northumberland, England.

Ian Watson is the multi-award winning author of nearly fifty books, including the *The Embedding, Hard Questions, The Jonah Kit, Mockymen, The Flies of Memory* and *The*

Butterflies of Memory. He wrote the Screen Story for the Stephen Spielberg movie *A.I. Artificial Intelligence* and is now recognised as one of the established masters of the field. He lives in a village in Northamptonshire, England.

Mike Resnick is the author of more then fifty science fiction novels, 175 stories, twelve collections, and two screenplays, as well as the editor of more than forty anthologies. He is the winner of five Hugos, and according to *Locus* is the leading short fiction award winner in science fiction history.

David Gerrold is a Hugo and Nebula winner, and while still in college wrote "The Trouble With Tribbles", which was voted the most popular *Star Trek* episode of all time. His award-winning novelette, "The Martian Child", has been turned into a movie starring John Cusack, and will be released in 2007.

Mary A. Turzillo's "Mars is no Place for Children" won the 1999 Nebula, and her "Eat or Be Eaten" was finalist for the British Science Fiction Association award. Her first novel, *An Old-Fashioned Martian Girl* was serialized in Analog magazine. Her work has appeared in *Asimov's, Fantasy & Science Fiction, Interzone, Science Fiction Age, Weird Tales, Oceans of the Mind, Lady Churchill's Rosebud Wristlet* and elsewhere in the US, Germany, Italy, Czechoslovakia, China, and Japan. Founder of the Cajun Sushi Hamsters from Hell, she taught creative writing by teleconference for NASA's Science through the Arts. Her web page is *www.dm.net/~turzillo.*

Brian Aldiss is one of the grand masters of the science fiction genre, a pioneer in the development of SF as literature and a champion of the New Wave movement. His vast treatise on the genre, *Trillion Year Spree* (with David Wingrove), remains one of the most important studies of the field, and many of his novels, including *Non-Stop, Hothouse, Greybeard* and *The Helliconia Trilogy* are now considered classics. His most recent novels are *Sanity and the Lady* and the forthcoming *Harm* (2007).

Keith Brooke is an author with a split personality. His science fiction and fantasy novels – *Keepers of the Peace, Expatria, Expatria Incorporated* and *Lord of Stone* – have appeared at regular intervals throughout his career (amongst a plethora of short stories), whilst he's kept himself busy running the acclaimed *Infinity Plus* website (*www.infinityplus.co.uk*), running the University of Essex website and writing popular children's novels under the pseudonym Nick Gifford. His latest novel, *Genetopia*, was published to great acclaim in 2006, and with Nick Gevers he is currently working on editing a mass-market collection of their *Infinity Plus* anthologies, to be published by Solaris in 2007.

Simon Ings has lived a colourful life and his SF novels – *Hot Head*, *City of the Iron Fish* and *Hotwire* – are brooding, literary attempts to put that life into fiction. His most recent novel, *The Weight of Numbers*, marks a move away from genre fiction but nevertheless continues to explore the same themes. *The Eye: a Natural History* is his recent, non-fiction, exploration of the eccentricities of vision. He lives in London, England.

Tony Ballantyne has been steadfastly working to establish himself as one of the foremost writers of modern British science fiction. His stories are published widely and his novels, *Recursion* and *Capacity* have received a great deal of acclaim. He lives in Oldham, England, with his wife and two children.

Eric Brown has written over twenty-five books and eighty short stories. He is twice winner of the BSFA award for short fiction and his recent books include the collection *Threshold Shift*, the fix-up *The Fall of Tartarus* and the forthcoming Solaris novel *Helix* (2007). He remains one of the most important British writers working in the field today and his humane, character-driven fiction continues to receive critical acclaim. He lives in Cambridge, England, with his wife and daughter. His website is *ericbrownsf.port5.com*.